FLOCKS OF WINGS FILLED THE SKY—

They were all colors and shapes, so beautiful and graceful that Lady Celia laughed with pleasure to see them. "Catch some for me, Andrew!" she teased.

She turned to look for Sir Andrew, but found the Baron beside her instead. "Why, you should have sent me word of your coming, Philip," she said politely.

"It is no matter," he assured her. "I shan't be staying."

"Then you have come in good time to see this charming spectacle," Celia said, gesturing at the fluttering, swooping wings.

He looked where she pointed, but as he did, the wings began to cluster into a great cloud, more and more of them, coming from all directions and massing together till they covered the sky as far as she could see. They merged into one great creature, then broke apart again, combining and separating, shifting and melding, finally forming a horde of monsters whose vast wings cast the countryside in shadow.

But the darkness gave no relief from the sudden, overpowering heat. Blinded by shadows, scorched by the fiery breath of dragons, she did not know where to run for shelter, where to seek for protection. . . .

SEASON OF SHADOWS

Volume One Of The Summerlands

ELLEN FOXXE

Enjoy!

Ellen Foxxe

DAW BOOKS, INC.
DONALD A. WOLLHEIM, FOUNDER
375 Hudson Street, New York, NY 10014

ELIZABETH R. WOLLHEIM
SHEILA E. GILBERT
PUBLISHERS

Cover art by John Howe.

DAW Book Collectors No. 989.

First Printing, June 1995

1 2 3 4 5 6 7 8 9

DAW TRADEMARK REGISTERED
U.S. PAT. OFF. AND FOREIGN COUNTRIES
—MARCA REGISTRADA.
HECHO EN U.S.A.

PRINTED IN THE U.S.A.

SEASON OF SHADOWS

Volume One Of The Summerlands

ELLEN FOXXE

Enjoy!

Ellen Foxxe

D A W B O O K S , I N C .
DONALD A. WOLLHEIM, FOUNDER
375 Hudson Street, New York, NY 10014
ELIZABETH R. WOLLHEIM
SHEILA E. GILBERT
PUBLISHERS

Cover art by John Howe.

DAW Book Collectors No. 989.

First Printing, June 1995

1 2 3 4 5 6 7 8 9

DAW TRADEMARK REGISTERED
U.S. PAT. OFF. AND FOREIGN COUNTRIES
—MARCA REGISTRADA.
HECHO EN U.S.A.

PRINTED IN THE U.S.A.

SEASON OF SHADOWS

Chapter 1

Smoke hung so thick over the field that it was impossible to see beyond a foot or so. It stung the defenders' eyes and made their lungs ache. Worse yet, it provided damnably good cover for their winged assailants, who dove again and again into the clouds of ash, attacked, and flew off to the safety of the trees beyond the blaze. Muskets roared, voices shouted, and the creatures screeched with an eerie, high-pitched wailing sound.

Damned vicious animals, Sir Andrew thought, guiding his horse onto the half-cleared land. Battle-trained, the mare was too well-schooled to shy at the fire that sparked here and there from the smoldering timber, but she advanced reluctantly with her ears laid back. On Sir Andrew's order, the mounted soldiers behind him galloped into the fray with an enthusiasm bordering on frenzy, risking injury to the very people they had come to defend.

Until the attack, the colonists had been peacefully engaged in clearing the forestland, but now they were frantically firing their muskets skyward, apparently in a random attempt to hit anything in the vicinity. Sir Andrew shook his head in disgust at this waste of effort and ammunition, and a frown of concentration creased his strongly defined features as he surveyed the chaos on every side. He was not accustomed to having untrained civilians under his command, nor to fighting an enemy that attacked from the sky—but he had not become Lord Marshal of the King's armies without first learning to adapt his strategy to the ever-changing fortunes of war.

Above all else, Sir Andrew was an experienced officer. Many believed that only his command of the royal army had allowed King Thorin to remain on the throne of Albin for the last three years, though ultimately even Sir Andrew's skill could only postpone, not prevent, the inevitable outcome of the civil war. The populace, incited by the religious rhetoric of the Deprivants, had risen against the monarchy and the nobility, and overthrown their rule in every corner of the country. Conscripted by the King's own forces to defend the land against invasion from Acquitania, they had risen up in prodigious numbers and defeated the royal army, using the very skills and weapons that had been forced upon them. The war with Acquitania had left too few experienced soldiers in the ranks of the royalists, and too many suspicious accidents had plagued the army, always at the most critical times. Sir Andrew suspected that the peasants had received as much help from Acquitanian spies as from the Deprivant seditionists.

Even here in the Colonies, relations were far from easy between the exiled royalists and their Deprivant neighbors. The Scrutinors, the most fanatical Deprivant sect, had found the mother church too tainted with worldliness to suit them, and had come to the new land to create a society in their own ideal image. Sir Andrew had little patience for these self-styled warders of souls, and they in turn tolerated him, he knew, only because his military prowess was needed to defend the colony of Thornfeld from the increasingly savage attacks of the monstrous winged beasts that inhabited the deep forest. Which were the greater threat to the survival of his followers, he wondered, the Deprivant Scrutinors or those cursed flying creatures?

Turning to address an order to Captain Jamison, he saw, through a thin patch in the smoke, that one of the things was swooping toward a man who knelt against a fallen log, head bent, reloading his musket. The creature's iridescent indigo feathers gleamed in a sudden shaft of sunlight, and the black stone blades in its grip flashed like glass. Sir Andrew pulled his own matchlock from the saddle and fired without hesitation. Knocked backward by the force of the shot, the creature crashed to the ground at the edge of the clearing, but its fall went unnoticed in the general tumult.

The confusion spread as the colonists, increasingly frustrated, continued to aim in vain at the swiftly diving enemy. Sir Andrew understood their fury. Clearing the trees would be the first step in claiming the land, land that was needed to feed the ever-growing number of settlers who were arriving at the colony. But beyond that, land represented security, the establishment of a permanent home that no one could confiscate, he thought bitterly. His own estates back in Albin had been seized by the revolutionary government, the Chamber of Statesmen, along with those of others who had supported the King's cause. The Chamber's aim was to reduce the remaining aristocracy to abject poverty by forbidding them to own property or engage in trade. They could thus be destroyed without the necessity of further bloodshed, and the new rulers of the land could pride themselves on their clemency.

Sir Andrew had organized those of the nobility he could persuade to join him, using the remains of their wealth to purchase the ships and stores needed to reach the New World and begin again. An ignorant rabble now reigned in his homeland, opportunists and manipulators who'd seduced the hearts of the people with their empty promises of a future paradise. The settlers' rage at the wild flying beasts was of a piece with their wrath at those who had forced them into exile.

Sir Andrew felt it as keenly as any of them, but he knew that anger gave no advantage in battle. It only made one reckless and vulnerable to the strategy of a more disciplined adversary. Studying the field, he realized that the enemies' advantage could be used against them. Turning to his captain again, he ordered Jamison to deploy their units in formation along the four sides of the partially cleared field, then he sent others to gather the scattered colonists into the ragged lines thus formed.

Against ordinary forces, such placement would have resulted in the soldiers shooting one another, but with the adversary restricted to the air, the cross fire created an impassable space above the span of the whole open field. Every shot served to attack the enemy and to defend the soldiers on the opposite line. Now, their winged assailants could only reach the colonists by flying through a hail of musketballs to certain death, and the creatures very soon gave up the attempt. They retreated into the trees at the edge of the forest, where they could be heard for some time making plaintive keening wails, almost like a lament. Gradually the sound died away, to be replaced by a series of short, angry cries that echoed from tree to tree around the clearing as the defeated beasts watched the victors on the field below.

Sir Andrew dismounted and inspected the field of battle, ordering his troops to hold their position and guard against further attack. The farmers and laborers who had been caught up in the conflict obeyed his orders as readily as the militiamen, for his tall, imposing stature and his air of decisive assurance inspired confidence in time of crisis, even in those who distrusted the aristocracy and despised his high rank and title. He still wore the uniform of a King's officer, and it, too, enhanced his authority, with its gold epaulets and scarlet sash, its polished sword with finely wrought silver mountings. His brass-buttoned coat and white breeches were smeared with soot now, and his dark hair had come unbound and hung in dank, unruly tangles about his face, yet he cut a commanding figure nonetheless as he strode through the smoke, taking stock of the casualties.

Several colonists had suffered wounds and were being tended by their fellows, but mercifully, no one had been killed. The thick smoke must have made them difficult targets. Still, he was surprised to find only a few carcasses of the winged creatures on the field. Despite the smoke and the notorious inaccuracy of the muskets, he had expected more of the animals to be brought down. After all, many of the colonists were experienced hunters, and their prey were mere beasts who could not have—could they?—their human opponents' ability to take evasive action. More of the musket shot must have found its mark than could be accounted for by these dead creatures. Where were the injured ones?

Then, as he stepped over a smoldering tree trunk, he saw a gleam of vivid blue among the tall weeds where the mud of the field melted into the uncut forest. Approaching cautiously, he found that it was indeed one of the creatures, its feathers now spattered on one side with dark red where a musket ball had pierced its wing. Its head rested against a fallen log, and he could hear its harsh, rasping breath, though it gave no other sign of life. He had never been so near to one of the beasts before, and he now saw that its dark blue-black feathers were intermixed with others of a deep glossy green, the color of summer leaves.

Sir Andrew caught the attention of Captain Jamison and beckoned to him. "This one's still alive. It must have been stunned when it fell."

The captain raised his weapon, pointing it at the creature's head. "I'll put the monstrosity out of its misery."

"No." Sir Andrew pushed the muzzle of the musket away from the creature's face. He could not have said, at that moment, why he did so. They couldn't leave it there to suffer, after all. Perhaps it was the oddly man-like shape beneath the great wings that gave him pause. "See that it's secured, and take it to the stockade," he ordered. "The town Warders must decide what to do with it."

The captain glanced at him curiously, but obeyed the command without question. He had fought at Sir Andrew's side for years in Albin and trusted that if his commander wanted this done, it was for a good reason.

While the soldiers carried off the still stunned creature, its companions in the trees set up an uproarious noise, and Sir Andrew, fearing another attack, ordered the militia to fire toward the forest. As the first volley exploded, the air was filled with the flapping of wings, and the creatures fled deeper into the woods, leaving behind them a sudden silence that seemed unnatural after the constant cacophony of the last hours.

Sir Andrew watched as they disappeared into the trees, and he thought, not for the first time, how little they really knew about these strange animals. Perhaps he should take one of the dead ones back to Carl. The naturalist would no doubt be delighted at the opportunity to study one of them at close hand. Carl had said that they were completely unknown to Albinate scholarship, but if anything could be learned from their carcasses, he would be the one to discover it. Sir Andrew instructed the soldiers to put a dead creature into the wagon with the live one, and take it to Silverbourne Manor, his own estate. He saw the looks and shrugs they exchanged, but he offered no explanation. They thought he was wasting their time on a ridiculous whim, and they might be right, at that. But Sir Andrew was disturbed by doubts about the creatures, and he was not one to let a riddle go unresolved.

By the time Sir Andrew and his entourage reached the town center, news of the battle—and of the captured monster—had already spread. Townspeople stopped and stared as the wagon went by with its bizarre burden, and as it neared the stockade the number of curious onlookers increased. Shopkeepers, artisans, trappers, farmers, members of the militia, all began to close in until the press of people in the road made further progress impossible.

"Whoa up, easy there." The wagoner halted the cart horses and looked helplessly to Sir Andrew for instructions.

Troubled by the unrest in the crowd, Sir Andrew turned back to the cart. Folk made room for him to pass, but he had barely reined in his horse when a rock was sent flying into the side of the wagon. "It's nothing but the Devil's spawn—'twill curse the town to harbor it!" a fierce, piercing voice declared. Sir Andrew knew the voice all too well. He searched the crowd and soon spotted the tall, narrow-faced Ministra, dressed in the gray homespun of the Deprivant Church.

"Their very plumage betrays their origin, bright and shining as Lucifer's, but reeking of corruption," the man beside her proclaimed.

The Scrutinor Ministers were performing for the

crowd, as usual, Sir Andrew observed. Scattered throughout the mass of people were several of their followers, easily identifiable in their gray garb, urging their neighbors to heed the Ministers' warning. Like most sects that practice righteous self-abasement, the Scrutinors were quick to condemn to eternal torment all those who disagreed with them. Where that left him, Sir Andrew didn't bother to speculate. His only concern at the moment was to deliver his charge to the stockade without further harm being done.

The curiousity seekers jostled each other as they strove to gain ground and catch sight of the strange monster. "If we spare this demon from Hell, we shall offend the Good God!" Ministra Cirana admonished.

"This land is accursed, and we are sent to cleanse it of such unholy filth," Minister Arhan seconded.

The mob, already eager for revenge, would be easy to incite to violence against the captive creature, Sir Andrew realized, and he would be powerless to prevent it without injuring some of the townsfolk. He ordered his soldiers to surround the cart, but this only frustrated the people's efforts to see the beast, and reinforced their belief that it was somehow a threat. Impatience rippled through the crowd, making itself felt as folk started to push forward with more determination, muttering ominously among themselves. Accustomed to dealing with the King's enemies, Sir Andrew was at a loss to resist an adversary he was bound to defend. He would have no choice but to let them do their will.

But just then the conspicuous figure of Rolande Vendeley shouldered through the throng, drawing all eyes, as usual. In her gold damask shirt and doeskin leggings, beneath an embroidered green tunic and fox-fur cape, she made an unmistakable contrast to the Scrutinor leaders as she took her stand beside them.

"Free ale for all at my place of business, in honor of this day's victory!" she announced.

A ragged cheer went up, and the air of menace palpably diminished. The bulk of the townspeople drifted away, determined to reach Rolande's shop before the supply of stout was drained dry. Rolande cast a self-satisfied smile at the Deprivant Ministers, receiving stern looks of disapproval in return. Wrath against the ungodly was not accounted a sin amongst the Scrutinor sect, and the Ministers would willingly have turned that wrath upon the merchant then and there, preferably with a bullwhip, had circumstances permitted. Rolande made them a mocking bow.

Sir Andrew nodded to the wagoner to continue along the rapidly clearing street. Ministra Cirana stood firmly rooted to her chosen spot, but she made no attempt to interfere as the cart passed her. When it was safely on its way, Sir Andrew dismounted and offered his hand to Rolande. "Your assistance was most welcome, Mistress Vendeley."

She turned to him with a honeyed smile, belied by the coldly appraising look in her eyes. "It is my duty, sir, as well as your own, to maintain order in the colony."

Rolande owed her place among the town Warders solely to her wealth, which had persuaded prominent members of the community that she might be useful to their plans for the future of the settlement. Sir Andrew had opposed her admission to the Wardership, a fact that had no doubt been reported to her. "No one," he had argued, "could say for sure who she was, or where her sympathies lay." When pressed, she claimed to have been forced into exile for mysterious crimes committed on the King's behalf, but she was resolutely silent as to particulars. Her faction among the Warders, however—folk who were in debt to her, Sir Andrew suspected—had overruled his objections, and he had bowed to the will of the majority with what grace he could. Now, though he resented her assumption of authority, he did his best to hide the fact.

"But I suppose that, as a soldier, you must find it difficult to control your fellow citizens," Rolande added, provokingly.

This deliberate challenge did anger him, but he refused to give her the gratification of a sharp retort. A man of his station did not lower himself to quarrel with a common tradesman—but that fact failed to afford him much satisfaction. "If you will excuse me," he said stiffly, "I must see that the creature is properly secured."

"By all means, we mustn't allow it to die prematurely. It would be most unfortunate to lose such an opportunity."

Something in her tone held Sir Andrew back. "How do you mean—an opportunity?"

"To set an example, of course! Those wretched things have harried our progress long enough. I say it's time we put an end to it! We'll take our winged insurrectionist and hang him up at the forest's edge, so the rest may see what becomes of those who dare attack our farmers. Perhaps then we'll be left in peace to clear the land for our crops."

Her voice shook with anger, but Sir Andrew knew that it was not selfless concern for the welfare of her fellow settlers that moved her. She had provided many of them with the wherewithal to establish their farmsteads—tools, seed stock, oxen, even weaponry—and in return she would own a share of all that they produced. Most of the colonists had not enjoyed his advantages, Sir Andrew reminded himself. They had lost everything they owned in Albin, or had never owned anything to lose. If they prospered here on

Vendeley's bounty, she was entitled to an honest profit. Very likely it was just this lust for gain that had lured her to these shores.

It was, he supposed, the way of all business. Without such commerce there would be no progress, but as a member of the nobility he was not accustomed to considering the mercantile point of view. Dealing in goods or gold, he had been raised to believe, was a sordid enterprise unworthy of a gentleman. But this was the New World, and he would have to learn new ways.

"I trust you agree," Rolande was saying, "that *something* must be done about these creatures of yours. If not by force of arms, then by force of example."

Mine? thought Sir Andrew, but aloud he said only, "What you suggest would serve no purpose. They are not rational beings, they cannot be expected to draw conclusions from example."

"Their actions show intention," Rolande protested. "Wherever we attempt to clear ground the flock appears and attacks—in no random manner, moreover, according to the reports I have received, but rather in an orderly formation."

"Any flocks of crows may do as much," Sir Andrew said patiently. "Mere ants and bees wage war in armies as organized as our own—" Carl's words. His lessons on the martial behavior of brute creation were among the few that the young lord had taken to heart. "—but we need not conclude therefore that they are possessed of intelligence, or that they reason as we do."

"Then what do you propose to do with the beast?" Rolande demanded. "Make a pet of it, perhaps?"

Sir Andrew had been asking himself much the same thing, all during the ride back to town. Why had he insisted that the creature be taken alive? What *did* he propose to do with it? He was determined, however, not to admit to Rolande that he had no answer. Smiling, as if he found her arrogance amusing, he said, "A pretty notion! My thought was simply that, as the brute is of no use to us dead, we might do as well to let it live. By observing it, we may learn something to our advantage, after all—a better means to defend ourselves against its kind, perhaps. But suppose we wait till the Warders meet, to decide upon its fate, shall we?" With a nod of dismissal that was barely civil, he turned to his mare and prepared to mount.

Rolande gave a perfunctory bow, then spun on her heel and stalked off without another word. She would present her proposition before the entire Wardership if necessary, she decided, but she'd not waste her time arguing with His High-and-Mighty Lordship. She had more important business to attend to.

Her shop was a prominent feature of the town's main street. While most of the buildings lining the dirt road were constructed of rough logs or wattle and daub, Rolande's establishment was one of the few multistoried, wood-framed buildings yet erected in the colony. Its lower windows held real glass, a luxury imported at great expense from Acquitania. Though not perfectly transparent, they let in light enough to make the amber necklaces glow, and the bolts of silk and satin shine more brightly, it seemed, than ordinary wares. The shop offered an amazing array of merchandise: glass and ceramic bottles and jugs, brass candlesticks, jars of rare spices and unguents, combs of jet and coral, hand mirrors in silver frames inlaid with mother-of-pearl. In the room beyond was a stock of more practical goods, from copper pots and iron nails to sturdy muskets and knives.

It was in this room that many of the colonists had gathered to drink the dark ale that Simeon Pryce was still pouring out, with a free hand, when Rolande arrived. Simeon had been her agent and principal man of business since they had come together from Albin, and his history was as clouded as her own. He was a black-haired, dark-eyed man with a haughty air and an insolent smile. Too insolent, some thought him, but no one had yet lodged a complaint against him with the Warders.

He set the jug down on the counter as Rolande entered. "Have you shown the new weapons," she snapped, "or have you just been sharing 'round the libations?"

"Warming up the crowd, Mistress, so they'd be inclined to spend." There was an edge to his voice, but his manner was respectful as he made way for Rolande behind the counter. An array of flintlock muskets, recently sent from Albin, was laid out on the board.

Holding one up, Rolande declared, "If not for the timely arrival of the cavalry this morning, many of you good folk might be moldering in the burial ground by now!"

Those who had been in the forest that day knew that she spoke the truth. They stopped talking among themselves and turned toward her, and the rest soon fell silent and listened. They all knew that the merchant would have more to say. She didn't speak just to hear her own voice.

Rolande ran her hand lovingly down the polished stock of a new musket. "I have been fortunate to receive a rare shipment of arms, far superior to anything yet devised for the slaughter of game—or of enemies! This, my friends, is a flintlock. When you've tried one of these, you'll think your trusty musket of no more use than a hollow twig."

"Fine talk," said one landowner, "but talk won't blast those feathered demons out of the sky. What can this newfangled gun of yours do that a matchlock can't? Tell us that and be done with it."

"Why, only one small thing, not worth your while to hear, perhaps," Rolande replied, taking her time. She was clearly enjoying herself. "A flintlock can be loaded and fired twice or even thrice in the time it takes to make a single shot with your musket, that is all."

"Impossible!"

Rolande merely leaned back against the wall, cradling the weapon and smiling to herself, as her customers argued excitedly about her outrageous claim.

" 'Twould explode, I tell you—"

"Nay, but I heard talk of such a thing, in Averwell, not six months past."

"Talk!"

"How can it fire so fast, that's all I ask to know?"

"You ask how?" said Rolande, barely raising her voice. "It sparks by means of a flint and a spring, in place of a slow wick. Does that satisfy you?"

The room had grown quiet as she spoke, but now the clamor rose again.

"'Tis some trickery."

"It can't be done, woman!"

"No?" said Rolande.

"Prove it, then—"

"When I've seen this marvel for myself, I'll believe it, and not before."

"As you wish," said Rolande, "of course." She led her audience into the stableyard, and told Simeon to stand a bag of grain up against a fence post across the way. From a hundred feet back she cocked the musket and fired, then handed it to Simeon to be reloaded, as a thin stream of oats poured onto the ground. In an impossibly short time, she had grabbed the weapon back from him and fired again, and a second hole appeared in the sack, spilling out oats, while Simeon reloaded the gun once more. The townsfolk could only stare, astonished at the speed and ease with which he readied the musket and returned it to Rolande.

"No more talk," she said, and fired again. As the third ball ripped into the sack of oats, Rolande laughed aloud, picturing Sir Andrew standing there before the fence post.

* * *

It was late afternoon before Sir Andrew arrived back at his manor house, exhausted, angry, and with a throbbing headache. He went directly to the salon, poured himself a generous measure of brandy, and dropped into a slat-backed armchair at the long walnut table. His houseman had left him a cold supper of roast fowl, cheese, and bread, but he had little appetite for it, though it occurred to him that he'd eaten nothing since dawn. Beside the platter, a rolled document from the clerk of the Wardership awaited his attention.

Resignedly he broke the seal, rose wearily, and took the parchment to the slant-front secretary by the tall mullioned window, where the light was brightest. Spreading out the document on the open writing flap, he found it to be a proposal to limit grazing rights on the Common until such time as more land could be cleared. No doubt those who supported the measure hoped that it would encourage farmers to expand their holdings away from the town, but was this the way to go about it? How could they justify the restriction of free access to the public lands? Pushing the document aside, he took some more brandy and turned his attention to the food. The thought of further administrative drudgery only made his headache worse.

Could he really make a success of governing this godforsaken settlement? Between the Deprivant lunatics and the Vendeley bitch, would it be possible to maintain any semblance of reason and moderation in the community? His encounter with Rolande still rankled. Her word carried considerable weight in the colony—more in some ways than his own, for the common folk were always readier to follow wealth than honor.

For the thousandth time, he cursed the King's mad decision to run for the coast on the day of the fateful battle of Breicenshire. Had His Majesty only had the sense to stay safe behind the walls of Avenford, Sir Andrew's troops might have arrived in time to— Hell! What was the use? At least he'd known whom he was fighting in those days, and what was expected of him. Now he was embarking upon a new career in this blasted wilderness, and he knew himself ill-suited to it. He had never been a diplomat. He had no honeyed words to make others cleave to his cause, and no patience for negotiating with fools.

More than ever, he felt the pain of his losses, for more than his lands had been taken from him. His King, his country, and the very order of his existence had been snatched away in a moment's decree, and though he knew that he'd been lucky to escape with his life, he was hard-pressed to feel thankful for his luck in this barbarous exile.

He removed a tiny golden box from his pocket and looked at the miniature portrait of a chestnut-haired lady set inside its lid. If only Lady Celia were here with him, she'd soon put the sanctimonious Ministers and the upstart merchant in their place. But without her, all his endeavors here were meaningless.

Lady Celia had come as a bride to Wildmoore, an estate in Werrick, which neighbored Stoneridge, Sir Andrew's father's estate. From the first, Sir Andrew had been captivated by her bright, bold eyes and lively wit. She was the one woman he had ever wanted to marry, and she was already another man's wife. The fortunes of war had, perhaps to the good, kept him away from her for months at a time, but whenever he was at home he contrived to visit the Baron and his charming wife—preferably at hours when he might hope to be received by Her Ladyship alone. She had soon made it clear that his company was not displeasing to her.

When his father, Viscount Edenbyrne, died, and Sir Andrew returned to claim his inheritance, the war was already going against the loyalists. He snatched what time he could to be with Celia, but as the King's fortunes took a desperate turn, he was forced to abandon his own concerns to return to the field. It was then that she had given him the locket-box as a token, for luck.

Perhaps it had brought him luck, for he had survived that disastrous campaign, but there had been no luck to spare for the cause of the monarchy. The rain had fallen in sheets for two days, turning the low-lying ground into a marsh that bogged down the cavalry, the major advantage the royal forces possessed. One flank had been tricked into chasing a troop of revolutionaries into a swamp where their confederates waited, perched in trees, to annihilate the horsemen with a hail of arrows. Prince Erich had been killed through mischance when a cannon exploded, and Sir Andrew had scarcely heard word of this catastrophe when a messenger reported that the reinforcements to the Palace guard had been delayed by the washing out of a bridge.

Mustering the remains of his forces, Sir Andrew had galloped toward Avenford to defend the palace, but to no avail. Halfway to the capital, he was intercepted by the news that the King, fearing that all was lost, was trying to reach the coast to escape by sea. Too late, Sir Andrew had turned about and ridden for Asheport, arriving only to find that the revolutionaries had already succeeded in capturing the royal galleon.

When he made his way back to Werrick at last, in defeat, Celia was gone. His steward gave him her message that the Baron had been killed at Breicenshire, and she had fled to Acquitania along with others from Albin's highborn families, to seek refuge until their own land should be safe for the nobility. She had left no other clue to her destination, for no doubt she herself had not known where she would be received. It would be folly to try to search all the realm of Acquitania for her. Nevertheless, he had determined to do just that, if need be, but events had moved too quickly for him.

The Chamber of Statesmen, having publicly executed the royal family and installed themselves in the palace, declared the property of all the nobility forfeit, leaving him with no home to offer Celia even if he should be able to find her. She would be sheltered in luxury by foreign nobles sympathetic to her plight; he could hardly take her from such a safe haven to share with him an existence of penury and humiliation. He must find the means to provide for her, despite the Chamber and its despicable prohibitions.

In a desperate attempt to salvage what he could, he had mounted his expedition to the New World, with as much fanfare as possible, so that word of the venture would spread, even to the exiles in Acquitania. Celia would know where he had gone. She would send word to him, and then he could let her know his plans to establish a home for them both, a home no one could take from them. . . .

He had sent trusted agents to seek her out, as well, and implore her to wait in safety until he had rebuilt his estate in the new land and made it fit to receive her. And surely she had sent spies into Albin to learn what had become of him. He had left word for her there with those of his people who had chosen to remain, in case she failed to hear of the great expedition. One way or another, he had been certain, they would find each other again.

But there had been no sign of her in the months that followed, and he had no way of knowing whether she had received any of his messages, or indeed whether she was still among the living. He met every ship that anchored at the harbor, always in hopes that this one would bring word from her—but that hope was beginning to grow weaker, even as his doubts of his fitness to be a colonial squire grew ever stronger.

It did not relieve his worries when the door behind him was suddenly thrust open and a young girl in buckskin bounded into the room. Sir Andrew rose hastily. "Your—Katin—" he began.

"I heard that you drove off another flock today," she cried, shaking a leaf out of her sun-bleached hair. "Is it true that they fight with bows and arrows?"

"Of course not." Sir Andrew walked over and shut the door firmly. "Who told you such nonsense?"

"Jerl Smit. He says the hermit told him that, but I suppose he was only baiting me."

Sir Andrew smiled. "Or the hermit was baiting him."

"Like enough." She perched on the arm of the settle and looked up at Sir Andrew. "Please sit down, sir. You look sore battle-weary."

Sir Andrew hesitated, then dropped back into his chair and leaned his head on his hands, with his fingers pressed to his temples. "I am tired," he admitted, "but it's the Dep ranters and Trader Vendeley who harry me, more than the bird-creatures."

Katin studied him for a moment with the eager solicitousness of a physician. "Have you the headache again? I've something here that will help you." She took a hide bag from her belt, and pulled out a handful of woodruff to show him. "I'll steep this in water. Wait here." Without waiting for a response, she dashed from the room, and was back all too soon with a steaming cup of a decidedly unappealing tisane. "This will cure your pains," she said confidently.

Perhaps forever, Sir Andrew thought. The girl had no doubt acquired some interesting flora in her woodland wanderings, but had she any actual knowledge of their properties? He did not reach for the proffered cup. "My dear child, I know you must pretend to be studying such things, but there's no need to carry the masquerade to such extremes."

"Oh, but it's not pretense! Carl has lent me books on the medicinal properties of herbs and bark—useful plants grow wild here in great abundance. Besides," she added, half-sullenly, "I must occupy myself with something. I wasn't raised to be idle, you know." She placed the cup before him. "Pray oblige me by taking this, My Lord."

Well, he thought, as he drank, it probably couldn't make him feel much worse than he already did.

Satisfied, Katin returned to the other topic that absorbed her interest. "Jerl also said you'd brought back bodies of some of the flying beasts. Is *that* true?"

"One," Sir Andrew said cautiously. "I mean to give it to Carl to study." He paused, then told her what she was bound to hear in any case. "We captured a live one as well."

"Alive!" She leaped up again in her excitement. "Where is it? In the stables?"

"More or less alive. It was wounded in the fighting and stunned senseless when we brought it back. It may have died by now."

But she was not so easily put off. "But where is it?" she demanded again.

"I had it taken to the stockade. Should it survive, it will be secure there until the Warders decide what to do with it."

"I must see it at once! Only think, perhaps I can heal its wounds—" She seized her bag of herbs from the table and ran to the door.

"Katin!" Sir Andrew called after her—too late—for she was gone in a clatter of footsteps down the hall. Once again she had left him feeling at a loss. He was a soldier, and a bachelor, in God's name. Who was *he* to have the girl in charge—and she halfway to woman's estate? A lady ought to take her in hand, of course, but there was no woman of his household to whom he could entrust her, and it was out of the question to send her to the Ministra. More than ever, he wished that Celia were with him.

But at least it seemed that Katin's potion was not about to have any drastic ill effects—indeed, his head was feeling rather better. He decided that it was time he had a talk with Carl. He ought to find out what he'd been teaching the girl. Besides, there was the matter of those feathered creatures to consider. . . .

Sir Andrew's father had been the patron of Carl Schellring's studies of Natural Philosophy for many years, and Sir Andrew had inherited the responsibility as a matter of course. Of all his people, Carl had been the most enthusiastic about the proposed voyage to the New World. What had been a tragic necessity to most was to him a heaven-sent opportunity to study and record forms of life hitherto unknown to scholars of the civilized world. He had not been disappointed.

The sound of horses brought Carl to the door as the wagon drew up before his thatched cottage. "M'lord," he greeted Sir Andrew, "I trust the morning's skirmish was successful?"

He would be the one person in the settlement who hadn't heard, Sir Andrew reflected. It seemed to him that his old tutor had been exactly the same for as long as he could remember—spare and wiry, with a shock of unkempt white hair and skin burned leathery through exposure to the elements, as he pursued the secrets of the natural order. His air of absent indifference to everything else had not changed with the years either. Indeed, he seemed to have less attention than ever to spare for human affairs.

"We drove them off again," Sir Andrew told him, "but it becomes more difficult to do so with each encounter. They've begun to attack in greater numbers, and they no longer flee at the sound of musket fire. I've brought you the carcass of one of them. Perhaps you can—"

But before Sir Andrew had finished speaking, Carl was already at the rear of the cart, gazing down at the feathered creature lying stiffly in the straw. "Astounding, fabulous, the stuff of myth! *Could* these be warm-blooded . . . ?" He seemed to have completely forgotten Sir Andrew, who still stood at the head of the wagon, a half smile on his face. He ordered the wagoner to help Carl carry the creature inside.

The cottage consisted of one large room with a small loft above it. The floor was crowded with trunks of books that spilled into heaps, making walking hazardous. A long pine table in the center of the room held more open volumes, candles, dried plants, bones, and anatomical drawings of various sorts of beasts. On a bench in the corner stood a row of cylindrical glass bottles with broad stoppers, a magnifying lens on a brass tripod, and an array of calipers, lancets, and other instruments whose purpose was not immediately clear to Sir Andrew. Another bench was completely covered by a very long, presumably dead, snake. There was nowhere to sit.

Carl quickly cleared a space on the table for the nearly man-sized creature, and at once began a series of painstaking measurements. "Facts first, my boy," he muttered, though it would have been difficult to say whether he was addressing the creature, himself, or Sir Andrew. "Facts first and then hypotheses."

Only when the wagoner had departed did Sir Andrew broach the subject on his mind. "I would like your views on a matter pertaining to these beasts," he said uneasily.

Carl started. "Of course, of course, M'lord. I have been remiss. Will you have a seat?" He looked around vaguely, then took up the snake and draped it over a rung of the ladder leading to the loft. "How may I serve you?"

"I don't understand how it is that we haven't killed more of the things."

"Surely that is a military affair?"

Sir Andrew waved a hand, dismissing this. "No, the fault's not with our tactics. If it were only a matter of shooting birds—" He hesitated. "The fact is . . . it's as if they perceive our intentions and take action to evade the brunt of our attack."

"I see."

"Do you deem it possible—" Even as he spoke, Sir Andrew felt that the idea was preposterous. "Could it be that they are intelligent, as we are?"

Carl shook his head knowingly. "Your question is understandable, M'lord, but ill-founded. Many creatures are quite adept at their own defense, so much so that they may give a superficial appearance of intelligence, but behind their inborn actions there is nothing that we would be justified in calling *reason*."

The very argument he had offered to Rolande. But from her he had been careful to conceal his doubts. "Yet they carry weapons of stone and use them to good purpose, as our own wounded can attest."

"Most interesting," said Carl, "but hardly a unique phenomenon. It may be mere imitation, or an example of such primitive recourse to tools as is exhibited by the common otter which uses a stone to break open shellfish." He removed a great leatherbound book from a stack by the door and opened it to an engraving labeled "THE TZIMPANZEE."

"These beasts, found only in the jungles of Xanistee have, as you see, a form remarkably similar to that of humankind, and they have been observed to exercise a rudimentary use of objects at hand, such as sticks and stones. One might conclude from this that they are more than wild animals, yet they live altogether in a state of nature; they display no true thought, nor any moral knowledge that would raise them above the bestial condition." Carl turned over the page and ran his finger down the text. "Here Kenneran tells us, 'In such a case, one may with difficulty distinguish between a debased form of humanity and an advanced race of animals.' "

Sir Andrew took the book and regarded the illustration with satisfaction. He'd heard of these Xanisteen monsters, but had not imagined that they were quite so manlike in appearance. Give the beasts feathers instead of fur, and they'd be the very creatures he had to deal with. Carl's information was reassuring, and Sir Andrew returned the book to him with thanks. "Very enlightening indeed. If I know *what* I'm fighting, I can decide *how* to fight it. Pray let me hear any further conclusions you may draw from your study of this specimen."

For the first time that day, he felt a sense of relief—

and his headache was quite gone, too. "You have much eased my mind in this matter," he added thoughtfully. "Regarding Katin, however. . . ."

* * *

The night was quiet, but from where he stood watch by the stockade, Jerl Smit could hear them massing in the forest, just beyond the edge of town. There was a steady, soft swish of wings as they gathered in the trees ringing the settlement. He paced nervously, unable to stay still. Was there a purpose in their actions, were they mustering their forces to attack? Ought he to sound the alarm? Deciding to turn the question over to a higher authority, he reported to the officer on duty, who mobilized the militia to stand on alert, then sent the boy back to his post.

Jerl was nineteen, tall, strong, and weathered from working out of doors. An itinerant farmworker, he'd come to the colonies in search of an opportunity he could never expect in Albin—the chance to work his own land, at his own will. The Deps had been full of high-flown talk about handing over estate land to the peasants who farmed it, but once the Church took power it proved a worse master than the nobility had been. Jerl often thought of his brothers and sisters, who'd spent their youth tending other folks' crops—folks no better, in Jerl's opinion, than his own kin—and who were now forced to give over the better part of their harvests to the Church coffers. He was sometimes homesick for familiar surroundings, but he did not regret his decision to leave.

Still, at times like these, he could not but be aware of the isolation of the colony, which was, after all, no more than a tiny enclave of civilization carved out of the vast wilderness of the New World. Sometimes Jerl, like many another colonist, felt hemmed in and helpless between the formidable barriers of the ocean and the endless forest. Threatening in their very massiveness, in their eternity, the woods seemed to wait for the passing of Thornfeld with its merely mortal denizens. Denser, darker than the woodlands Jerl had known in Albin, the forbidding forest loomed over the young colony, mysterious and impenetrable, harboring all manner of unknown dangers.

He circled the stockade again, listening, half-wishing that the creatures would make some move and give him a chance to take action. It was maddening, knowing that they were out there, invisible in the dark trees. Could they see in the dark, like owls?

Then the silence of the night was pierced by a series of fluting calls. Jerl moved closer to the trees, resting his musket in the crook of his arm. He could just make out the silhouette of a great winged form crouched on the thick branch of an oak. It looked larger than the others, but perhaps it merely seemed so because its wings were spread wide, held rigidly aloft. It sounded the call again. Wings stirred restlessly in the trees, and Jerl shuddered in response. The other creatures gave a deep series of trills.

Suddenly the first creature broke into a fierce volley of song that howled through the trees and sent chills down Jerl's back. As each passage came to an end, the surrounding creatures responded with the same eerie, warbling call. Jerl crept closer, drawn to the sound, mesmerized. Then the moon cleared the clouds, and he saw that a round cage or basket of woven twigs had been hung from a branch of the great oak. The other creatures fell silent as their leader called out a long, repetitive song, then held up something too small for Jerl to see, and placed it in the cage. The majestic wings thrashed, and the beast burst into a fury of cries that was answered by a crescendo of shrills from the others. The hair prickled at the back of Jerl's neck. Their sounds were like nothing he had ever heard, yet he felt, in his feverish trance, that he understood their meaning.

The bizarre chorus continued until the first light of dawn, when it ceased with an uncanny abruptness, and Jerl started and shook himself like a man awakened from a dream. With a great thrusting of wings, the creatures rose into the dawn and flew off to the forest, leaving him crouched at the foot of a tree, drenched in dew, his every muscle cramped and aching. He stood stiffly and made his way to the oak where the twig sphere still hung, swinging a little now, in the rush of the beasts' passing. He climbed up and seized it in shaking fingers, then shimmied down with the cage under his shirt, and ran with it to the safety of the stockade wall. Panting as if he had come a great distance, he leaned against the sheltering logs and examined his find, trying to reach between the closely-woven twigs without damaging the delicate structure. He could feel something hard and smooth within, slightly sticky to the touch. At last he succeeded in shaking it free, through the hole in the side of the cage, and found that he was holding the skull of some small, sharp-toothed animal he could not identify. It had been stripped clean of all flesh and fur, and bleached white in the sun, but its jaws and fangs were streaked with drying blood.

* * *

Some prayers were answered with the arrival of the galleon a few weeks later, and some nightmares began. Word soon spread that a ship had been sighted, and the entire colony turned out at the waterfront, drawn by the rare chance of news, supplies, and travelers from home. From his vantage point on a platform set up for the benefit of the town Warders, Sir Andrew spotted Rolande's billowing green cloak as she stood apart at the landing, no doubt awaiting the delivery of some new rarities. He thought of the flintlocks he'd acquired from her for the militia, and wondered about her source of supply for such goods. He knew little of the ways of trade, but Vendeley seemed to prosper beyond the means of most merchants.

His attention was drawn back to the passengers from the vessel, who had begun to arrive at the shore in the ship's boats. It was the usual mixed lot—gentlemen and ladies with their retinues of servants, Deprivant Scrutinors in their gray garb, craftsmen, traders, farmers, and others who were probably criminals transported to the colonies to save the new government the trouble of hanging them. But all the colonists were criminals in the eyes of the Chamber of Statesmen, transported for the crime of loyalty to the Crown, or heresy against the Deprivant Church. And any one of these new arrivals could bear a message from Celia.

Sir Andrew, attired in his blue uniform, white waistcoat, black stock and collar, made himself conspicuous, standing well to the fore, in hopes that someone would be asked to point him out, and one of the travelers would approach him with news of her, or a letter. It was, therefore, easy for Lady Celia to notice him, though it was some time before he caught sight of her at the center of the throng of gentry who had come ashore before the others. She was waving her fan to attract his attention, and laughing at his astonished start of recognition.

Despite the welter of preparations for journey's end, she had taken some care with her appearance that morning. Her hair had been carefully arranged in flowing curls, beneath a broad-brimmed hat with a gay satin ribbon. Smaller bows of the same emerald hue adorned the bodice and skirt of her green silk frock. But Sir Andrew noticed none of the finery intended for his benefit. He had eyes only for the inviting smile, the fair flawless skin and graceful, willowy form that had haunted his dreams for over a year. Within moments he stood before her, with no memory of having leaped from the platform and pushed his way through the indignant crowd. He could not embrace her before the entire colony, of course. He could only bow to her and stare like a fool, stammering, "Celia—how—how is it possible?"

She took his hand. "My dear, everyone has heard of your famous expedition. I knew I should find you here—though not perhaps so readily! Now do you mean to keep me standing about in the spray all morning, or may we repair to some place a bit less *open?* This is Castilian silk!" Lowering her voice, she added simply, "I bring news."

He knew that she meant news of Albin. Offering her his arm, he said with perfect correctness, "My carriage is just behind that stand of trees, Baroness. You will come back to Silverbourne with me?"

"Of course."

Lady Celia made a sign to her steward, and Sir Andrew was forced to wait for what seemed an eternity, while arrangements were made for her people to follow. When at last he was handing her into the carriage, Katin jumped down from a nearby tree, from which she had been watching the new arrivals, and looked questioningly at Sir Andrew. "One moment," he murmured to Celia, then crossed to Katin and said quietly, "The Baroness Lindley has come from Acquitania with news—perhaps it may concern you. Will you return to the house with us?" He gestured toward the carriage.

"Thank you, I shall ride," said Katin. Without waiting for a reply, she ran to her horse, mounted in a leap, and galloped off toward Silverbourne.

Sir Andrew looked after her for a moment, frowning to himself, but then he joined Lady Celia in the carriage and was able for a time to forget his worries.

The departure of the carriage was observed with considerable interest by Rolande, who was supervising the loading of a number of chests consigned to her. Turning to Simeon, she drew him aside and said, "Take Sir Andrew's bill to his houseman yourself, and while you're there, find out from the lady's servants who she is and what business she has with His Lordship." She gave the title an ironic sneer.

Simeon smiled. "Their business seems clear enough to me."

"There's more mischief afoot than lust, these days, and well you know it," Rolande hissed. "Just do as you're told!"

Not by so much as the flicker of an eye did Simeon's face betray his unease. Was she hinting that she guessed at his own plans? But Rolande had already turned away to give orders about the new kegs of brandy, and she seemed to have forgotten him.

When Sir Andrew and Lady Celia came into the main hall, they found Katin waiting for them, still disheveled from her ride and half-dancing with impatience. "What a time you've been," she cried. "I've been here for an age! What news of home?"

Sir Andrew glanced around anxiously, then opened the door to the salon and stepped back to let Katin and Lady Celia precede him. But Lady Celia hesitated, looking uncertainly from the girl to Sir Andrew.

"These are matters better discussed in private," she demurred.

"I assure you—" Sir Andrew began, but Katin interrupted, saying with a gracious air, "I've no wish to intrude. I'll go out to the kitchen until I'm sent for. I'm perishing for something to eat in any case." She met Sir Andrew's eye for a moment, then bowed and raced away down the corridor.

Lady Celia led the way into the salon and sank onto the settle, arranging her skirts about her gracefully. "My dear Andrew," she said, "who *is* that extraordinary child?"

* * *

Simeon had done his best work, flirting with Lady Celia's young maidservant over a drink of strong cider in the kitchen. He'd soon learned that Baroness Lindley was one of the Albinate nobility who'd sought refuge in Acquitania after the civil war, and that was enough to put her in the wrong, for Simeon's purposes. His masters had little love for those who'd evaded their grasp and reached foreign shores with the bulk of their fortunes intact. Of her business, though, he had been able to discover little save that she and Sir Andrew had long been lovers, and he looked forward to informing Mistress Vendeley—respectfully, of course—that she'd been wrong, and he right. Still, he knew he'd be ill-advised to dismiss out of hand the possibility that the mistress knew more than the maid.

The girl having departed to see to Her Ladyship's belongings, Simeon was about to take his leave, when Katin burst into the kitchen, stopping just long enough to hack a piece of cheese from the block, as if executing it, and shove it into her mouth.

"You've no manners at all, my lass," the cook remonstrated. "You can ask for what you want, like anyone else."

"I had a lot of fine manners once," Katin said cheerfully, through a mouthful of cheese, "and much good they did me." She impetuously kissed the cook, who swatted halfheartedly at her. Noticing Simeon, Katin frowned, swallowed, and demanded, "What's he want here?"

Simeon grinned at her. "Maybe I was waiting for you."

"Don't you be believing that," the cook said sharply. "That one was making up to a little chit of a lady's maid in here, not a minute ago."

"She can have him, and welcome," said Katin.

Simeon slipped up to her. "You could do worse than me, I'll have you know. Maybe I'm going to be an important man one day." It was not like him to give himself away, but something in the girl's absolute self-assurance made him reckless. Suddenly he wanted to impress her.

"Aye, maybe," she said. "And maybe fish will fly."

Simeon laughed. "Stranger things than that could happen in this country of demons." He moved closer.

Katin edged away from him, not in fear but in disgust, until the brick fireplace was at her back. "That will do," she said softly. She still held the cheese knife, and her stance and look dared him to take another step. "Trifle with me, and my master will have you flogged from one end of town to the other."

"Here, none of your devilry in my kitchen," the cook ordered. But Simeon had already stopped in his pursuit. He stood staring at Katin, her head framed against a great gray cooking pot that hung above the hearth. There was something uncannily familiar about the sight that held him in check.

Who *was* the little bitch-whelp, anyway? he asked

himself. What was her place in Sir Andrew's household? She was supposed to be a 'prentice forester, or something of that sort, but she behaved with too much freedom for one in such a lowly position. He'd never heard so much as a suggestion that His Lordship was bedding the girl—and that sort of thing couldn't well be kept secret in a close community like this. Could she be his bastard brat, or was she too old for that? And what was it about her face, silhouetted against the gray disk of the pan, that reminded him of something . . . ?

Sir Andrew secured the door to the salon before he answered Lady Celia's question. "I'm afraid she may very likely be our sovereign," he said. "As far as I know, she's the only member of the House of Obelen to escape the insurrection."

"The royal family—? Do you mean to tell me that that acrobatic hoyden is the Princess Oriana?"

"I've not dared tell anyone but you." He poured two glasses of brandy and handed her one, then drew up a chair beside her. "She's known as Katin Ander here, supposedly a student of pharmacognosy, living under my patronage."

"Then she *wasn't* on board the *Golden Dove* when it was taken! There were rumors, but of course the Chamber denied them."

Sir Andrew shook his head. "She was there, but she had the sense to leap overboard in her shift and swim to shore. When I arrived—too late to be of use—" he added with bitterness, "I found her pretending to scavenge in the muck for spoils, along with all the village mudlarks, as filthy and bedraggled as the rest. It was a clever ruse, I grant you. If they'd recognized her, they'd have sold her to the rebels in a trice, and she knew it."

"How in the world did *you* recognize her, then?"

"Most easily. When we rode up, the rest scattered, but the Princess stood her ground and cursed us roundly for coming so late to her aid. 'Small thanks to you that I wasn't drowned or hacked to collops by a pack of verminous louts!' Her Highness said in greeting—and a great deal more beside. The difficulty was not in recognizing her, but in preventing her from revealing herself to all the countryside, once we'd found her."

At that moment, Lady Celia's laughter seemed recompense enough for all that he'd been through. "That is the royal temper, to be sure!" she chuckled. Armies of the King's enemies might hold no terrors for Viscount Edenbyrne, Lord Marshal, but Lady Celia could easily imagine him nonplussed by a helpless girl shrieking like a fishwife. "But why has she remained in disguise here?" she asked. "Are not your colonists loyal to the Crown?"

"Most perhaps, but even here I don't believe she's safe. Oh, I know the Chamber hanged some other poor girl in her place, but as long as there are those who know that she lives, they'll not rest easy. They'd pay anything for her head. I don't doubt that they have their spies in the Colonies." He drew from his pocket the box Lady Celia had given him, catching her smile as he opened it. From within it he took a small silver coin bearing the likeness of Katin's head. "Everyone has seen these cursed coins His Majesty minted, with the images of the royal family. I keep her as distant from the townspeople as I can, lest she be recognized."

Lady Celia shook her head. "You forget, my love, I saw Oriana often at court, yet I should never have known her in this guise. She's brown as a peasant girl, I believe she's grown taller, and her hair—! What hasn't been hacked off, evidently with an ax, is far lighter than I remember it. You may find it harder to persuade folk that she is the Princess, than to keep it a secret."

"Perhaps you're right," Sir Andrew said thoughtfully. "That would suit Her Highness very well. She finds this new life of hers much to her taste, you see. She has more freedom as a commoner that she ever enjoyed as Princess of the Realm. If I wished to declare her rightful Queen of Albin and its territories tomorrow, I don't know that she'd agree to claim the title. In truth, it's more than I can do just to keep her in order. But perhaps now that you're here, you'll have more influence over her than I."

He had thought to make her laugh again, but though she smiled at him still, her eyes were grave now. She had spared him as long as she could. "The danger is greater than you know," she said with a sigh, "not to the Princess alone, but to all of New Albin."

Sir Andrew clenched the coin in his fist, and for a moment she saw in his features the commander of the cavalry, who dealt only in death or defeat. He rose abruptly and turned away from her, as if unwilling to show her that visage. "And so," he said harshly, "even here at world's end we are not to be left in peace? What more can they do?" With an effort, he turned back to her, forced himself to speak more calmly. "Tell me."

"These colonies are declared subversive to the welfare of the government and people of Albin, because, the Chamber claims, they have united in sedition against the State."

"United! We barely have news of the nearest settlement—there are not even *roads*—"

"Oh, no one believes it, my dear, but they must at least make a show of justifying the declaration of hostilities. They cannot very well declare that their aim is to turn the fabled resources of the New World to their own profit."

"Is anything known of their plans?"

"We too have our spies. If their reports are to be believed—and I have no reason to doubt them—the Chamber means to muster a vast fleet and several thousand soldiers, to occupy and subdue each colony in turn."

Now they had taken even his hopes for the future—all that he had left. "How soon?" he asked flatly, as if the subject did not interest him greatly, and he inquired only to be polite.

"Our information was that they'll not attempt the crossing before summer, if the ships can be readied by then. But preparations are already underway."

How to keep Oriana out of their hands? The colony would not survive an attack of such magnitude. Surrender might save the commonalty, perhaps even some of the nobility, but it would doom the Princess. "We can put up some defense, but we shall not stand for long against forces of that strength, and the settlements are too widely scattered to attempt a common resistance," he said slowly. Each word pained him, but he went on, "You must return to Acquitania, with the girl. You will still be safe there."

"I did not come here to be safe!" Lady Celia snapped shut her fan and gestured forcefully with it as she spoke. "Send Her Highness, by all means, but for my part, I have spent nigh unto three months in a ghastly ocean crossing, sick unto death and tossed by gales such as you cannot imagine, and now that I am here I have no intention of going back."

Even in his despair, Sir Andrew had to smile at her determination. "Celia, we've no choice."

"Very well, I shall return to Acquitania, providing that you come as well."

"Impossible. The defense of the colony is my responsibility. It will be for the town Warders to decide whether to fight or surrender, but if the vote is for resistance, I shall be needed here."

"And you will need me here."

This was true, but changed nothing. "I tell you, we shall lose."

But Celia was unmoved. "We've already lost, have you forgotten? If this battle too is lost, we shall be no worse off than we were. They've taken everything else from us already—all we have left is each other. They shall not take that as well. If you stay, I shall stay." As if the matter were now settled and done with, she set down her glass, rose, smoothed her skirts, then held out her arms to Sir Andrew with a radiant smile.

He caught her to him hungrily, breathing deeply of the familiar, delicious scent of her hair. He must persuade her to go, of course, but not yet, not now. "I could never best you in an argument," he whispered.

"You never will, my dear," murmured Lady Celia, "so don't waste your breath—for Heaven's sake, just kiss me."

Chapter 2

". . . Thus we now face an evil more powerful than any we have encountered since the inception of this colony," the Reverend Hrabanus said portentously from his place at the front of the assembly hall. The hall was a large open room with a huge hearth occupying the wall at one end. Facing the rows of high backed wooden benches occupied by the Warders was a broad oak table where Marcus Farnham, the Headman, sat flanked by the Wardership's two secretaries, one of whom was recording the minutes of the meeting while the other sharpened worn quills.

"We have found in this land natural disasters and vicious monstrosities, but never yet have we encountered a foe so determined to bring us to our knees as this one will be . . ." the Reverend droned on.

Ministra Cirana rose, scowling. "Enough! Let us face the truth!" she said shrilly. "God has visited this invasion upon us because we have been unrighteous." She cast a glance at the nobles and merchants, her gaze coming to rest on the two Reverends, representatives of the old Church of Albin, which had been overthrown along with the monarchy but remained a force to be reckoned with, here in the Colonies. Most of the aristocracy still adhered to its tenets. It was a deliberate insult, the Ministra thought, that Sir Andrew and Lady Celia had chosen to ask the blessing of the Reverends upon their marriage covenant, and had neglected to extend a similar courtesy to the representatives of the Scrutinor Deprivants. The Scrutinors considered the Reverends even more reprehensible than the lay folk, since their influence led others astray from the ways of righteousness. The old Church might preach vigilance in the battle between good and evil, but it was far too moderate in its tolerance of human frailty. Such a faith was a mockery of religion, in the view of the Ministra—little better than outright devil worship. "We cannot withstand the force of divine wrath," she continued. "Our sole hope is to flee, before the avenging powers land upon this shore to smite us."

Minister Arhan rose to second this. "We must secure a safe haven, where we can wait until the danger is past."

The danger will never be past, Sir Andrew thought. *We will have to fight them or they will sweep across the land like locusts.* He wondered how the Scrutinor Ministers could reconcile their conviction that the invading army represented the wrath of the Good God with their desire to flee from the confrontation. If war were God's will, was it not their duty to accept it . . . ? But as usual, he gave up the attempt to make sense of their views. Did they expect the colonists to spend the rest of their lives living off the fruits of the wild land, like the forest bandits? If the settlers abandoned this town and later raised another, it would only meet with the same fate. Surely, even the Scrutinors had enough foresight to see that. But no, it seemed that they, and many others, were quite capable of blinding themselves to the obvious.

Before he could voice his own objections, however, Rolande Vendeley rose to speak. "If we flee, we must by necessity abandon all ties—not only with the other colonies, but with the Old World, which has been the sole source of those few comforts afforded us in this wilderness."

There was a faint stirring at this, for the Wardership was composed of the most powerful of the colony's inhabitants—those who benefited most from contact with Albin and Acquitania.

"There'll be no more comforts in the grave," a voice behind Sir Andrew objected.

"But how are we to know that our destruction is truly what the Chamber intends?" Rolande argued. "This threat may be no more than mere rumor."

Sir Andrew was on his feet at once. "You question the Lady Celia's word?" he demanded.

"By no means," Rolande replied with a veneer of civility. "But she was not in Albin herself. She could have received a false report, perhaps one originated by the Chamber, for their own purposes. I say that we must investigate the truth of this ourselves before we abandon our businesses, our farms, and our homes."

"And how are we to manage that?" the Ministra questioned.

"To send our own messengers to Albin would be the surest way." Rolande turned to her with the self-satisfied look of one who has gained a point, for her own mission was to hinder for as long as possible the implementation of the colony's defenses, and it seemed to be going well, but as usual Sir Andrew opposed her.

"That would take far too long," he protested, cutting off a further retort from the Ministra. "By the time such messengers went and returned—even if the Albinate fleet hadn't already sailed—it would be too late for the colony to prepare an adequate defense."

Rolande sighed as if much put upon. "Very well, then we shall simply have to do the next best thing. We must question all of the recent arrivals from Albin to see if there is word to substantiate these claims."

"Delay and more delay. Unready as we are, we barely have time to prepare our forces if we begin at once!"

"What is the point of preparing for a battle that may never—" Rolande began, only to be cut off by the Ministra's cry, "We cannot cross swords with Sovereign God, by any means, however long the time allotted!"

Headman Farnham rose. "Order! We must have order here—we must—"

More voices joined the sides already in protest, and the Headman banged his gavel so hard that it left crescent-shaped marks in the oak table, but all factions ignored him.

Sir Andrew rubbed his temples, waiting for a chance to be heard. There was no doubt in his own mind that the colony was in danger. Celia's information fitted all he knew to be true of the Deprivants' ways. Having succeeded in seizing all the resources of Albin, they had every reason to try the trick again against the sparsely populated and ill-defended colonies. But how, Sir Andrew wondered, could he convince these popinjays to stop defending their own nests and face the unpleasant necessity of preparing for war—yet again.

He was bred and trained for war—never so sure of himself as in the field, yet he could not help but recall with loathing the devastation he had seen at Breicenshire and elsewhere—the bodies of men and women lying bloated in the mud, the crazed half-human cries of the rabble as they ransacked the fine houses left unattended. *This time they will not spare us,* he thought with grim certainty. In Albin, too much bloodshed might have sullied their cause in the eyes of the people, but what was to restrain them here, in all this great empty land?

And even should a massacre somehow be averted, the Princess would still be in the gravest danger. His first duty, he reminded himself, was to defend her—in spite of herself, if necessary.

Abruptly, he was brought back to the business at hand as the words, "So it is decided" rang through the hall. He looked up to see Marcus Farnham reseating himself, and for a moment Sir Andrew feared that he would be forced to ask one of his neighbors what had been decided. Then the Headman continued, "The council shall consist of the Ministra Cirana, Mistress Vendeley, Elliott Cavendish and, of course, since the military point of view is indispensable, Lord Edenbyrne. They shall examine all matters pertaining to the defense of the colony in the event that such an invasion as is rumored should indeed occur. One month from now, they shall report their observations to the next sitting of the Wardership." Headman Farnham leaned back with the air of a man who has rid himself of a troublesome burden.

A month? It was too absurd, Sir Andrew decided, even to merit an argument. Let the rest argue—he would take action himself. He wanted to get away from the airless hall at once, to speak with Celia and tell her what had transpired. Perhaps she could see a way to make the council's enterprise less than totally useless. But his hopes for an early adjournment were dashed as the Ministra rose yet again.

He forced himself to attend to her, as she said, "We have a more pressing problem than an attack still months away. We face immediate and mortal danger from the flying demonspawn who harry our efforts to clear the land. Already three of our people have died—one of them Mistress Broaquin's son." She pointed to the woman in question, who nodded stonily. "How many more must perish before we take strong measures to eradicate this threat to our livelihood and our children?

"Aye, our children! You know that three other colonies have failed in the last year—three out of ten! Caldenport in the far north may have succumbed to natural causes, but the other two were destroyed by the winged fiends, mark my word! If you doubt it, those few who survived the massacres, by God's grace, can tell the truth of it. Hannah Franesh of Holistowe is away trapping, but here is Paeter Cellric of Oxwold—listen to him—listen to the fate of the children of Oxwold!"

A tall, gaunt man rose reluctantly to address the assembly, and everyone turned to him, including Sir Andrew. Cellric's story might have some bearing on the defense of Thornfeld, if not from the coming invasion, at least from the menace of the winged ones.

"As I have told the Ministra," Cellric began, "the events leading to the final dissolution of Oxwold, these six months past, began with a most brutal slaughter. It was a day not unlike any other, most of the able-bodied men and women were engaged in clearing land, fishing along the shore, or planting in the fields which lay about a mile or so from the main village. A number of children were left in the care of our Ministra, who gathered them for lessons in the church. Somehow a flock of the flying beasts managed to insinuate themselves between the farms and the village. . . . It must be true that the beasts have demonic powers, for how else could they have done this unobserved? None of the farmers saw signs of them flying overhead, or they would have given the alarm. But there were feathers scattered throughout the yards.

"When we arrived back at the town in early evening,

we found several adults dead, among their number the Ministra and four others who had tried to guard the youngsters. Some had tried to reach nearby houses, and lay dead upon the steps. There were scattered around the floor of the church and the road outside blue and green feathers shed by the beasts who had committed this atrocity." There was a profound silence as Cellric paused then said, "Of the children there was no sign. Although we searched the forest for them, nary a trace was found. There was, needless to say, great fury in the colony, and we ceased working the land to devote ourselves to a campaign to seek out the nesting place of the beasts and eradicate their threat. Thus we mounted armed expeditions and combed the woods, killing as many as we could hunt down." He hesitated, as if uncertain that his listeners would accept what was to come. "Deep in the woods, we came upon a—a community of sorts. In the trees the beasts appeared to have constructed hutches—they had doors and windows and such like—and they varied in size and, as far as our brief surveillance revealed, in usage—"

Sir Andrew was now all attention. Nothing in his experience had revealed the creatures capable of building such complex structures—or of such sophisticated social organization. But he did not doubt Cellric's testimony. It fit all too well with his own growing doubts about the enemy he'd been fighting—an enemy he'd grown to respect. Now, he could no longer rule out the possibility that they were capable of such things. And if they were, this would make them much more dangerous—or . . .

". . . having discovered the nesting place of the enemy, we brought as large a force as we could muster and drove off the beasts with muskets, then searched the compound for any sign of the children, but we found no trace of them," Cellric was saying. "One thing above all was clear, though—that we must eradicate the vile beasts who had wrought such villainy in our lives. So we burnt the structures and all the surrounding trees to rid ourselves of their infestation. From that time on, there was war between us and the beasts, who repeatedly attacked our farmers in the fields, our fishermen when they approached the shore—they even made nighttime attacks against the houses on the outskirts of town.

"We chose the largest houses of the village and garrisoned them with provisions and stout fences, and nets running between the fences and the roofs to provide protection from the attacks of the beasts. Here, by night, the townsfolk gathered for protection while by day we mounted raiding parties to seek the vermin in the woods and destroy them.

"There is no telling how long this state of affairs might have continued, but for the vilest treachery. One evening in early winter when the night was damp and raw, travelers dressed in the manner of ordinary folk presented themselves at each of the garrisoned houses. They requested hospitality for the night and were invited in to stay. Later, when all the members of the households were asleep, the 'travelers' cut down the nets, and the beasts attacked in force, viciously. The townsfolk fought back as best they could, but the attack caught them unaware and most were slain before they could raise an effective defense. Those who could, fled, hiding in the woods until the slaughter was over. I myself survived only because I was hit on the head with a stone and, falling senseless, was mistaken for dead.

"When I recovered, all were either dead or in hiding." He paused, recalling the horror of the scene, then took a deep breath and said, "In time, those who had secreted themselves in the woods crept back. We buried the dead and tended the wounded, but there was no doubt that too few were left for the colony to survive, and the Church declared that the settlement was accursed. We could not stay after what had occurred, so we separated and went to colonies where we had family or acquaintances—or at least no reminders of the past."

"What of the travelers?" someone asked. "What became of them?"

Cellric shook his head, looking perturbed. "Of that I have never been certain. Their bodies were not among the dead, so it was supposed that they escaped before the carnage began, but as to who they were or what their motives could have been, I cannot conceive."

"Fiends in human form—sent to do the Devil's work, and vanished with the dawning of God's day!" the Ministra declared triumphantly. "The question before us is, how are we to ensure that no such atrocity is repeated here?"

Surprisingly, Rolande rose to support the point. "The Ministra is correct," she said, impressing everyone with the weight of this matter by the sheer act of agreeing with one known to be her enemy. "What does it profit us to protect ourselves from phantom armies from afar, if we succumb to real marauders here at hand? I move that we form small parties to comb the woods systematically and kill any of the beasts we find." This was seconded by a voice from the back of the hall, followed by several others.

One by one, other voices joined angrily in support of the need to take action against the enemy within their reach. Rolande smiled silkily at her supporters, pleased, for as long as the colonists were distracted by their efforts to chase down the flying pests, they would not be readying the colony's defenses against the Albinate forces that she—even more surely than Lady

Celia—knew were preparing for invasion. And if new land were cleared in the process, that would be more profit to her as well. When the Chamber's forces won, she would gain control.

Shouting to be heard over the rest, Sir Andrew began, "We have no way to eradicate them." The voices faded away and died to quiet as he spoke. "We have beaten them off in small skirmishes, but if we plan to seek them out and challenge them in large numbers, the toll will be heavy. Our militia are farmers, hunters, tradespeople—not trained soldiers. The enemy are a race of winged warriors!"

Rolande snorted in derision. "Warriors, say you? Why it was you, Your Lordship, who told me they were mere unthinking brutes."

Galling as it was to admit it to Vendeley—and before the Wardership—Sir Andrew answered, "I may have been mistaken. The longer we fight them, the less certain I become as to their true nature. They are no demons—we have seen them die—but we must at least allow for the possibility that we are dealing with intelligent beings. Goodman Cellric's tale suggests as much, and those who guard the captured one swear that it tries to speak to them like a man."

"The more reason to destroy them!" Rolande cried. "If they attack with deliberation, and not in all innocence, as wild beasts might, they are the more formidable an enemy, and the more blameworthy! How say you all?" she appealed to the assembly. "Do we take the offensive and hunt them down, or wait for them to slaughter us where we stand?"

Headman Farnham called for a vote, and her motion was carried overwhelmingly. Riding on her success, Rolande, with a glance that was a direct challenge to Sir Andrew, asked, "And why should we coddle one of the enemy here in our midst? We humored His Lordship at our last meeting and voted to keep his pet in captivity—but I say there's been time enough to study it, and now we should stop wasting bread on it and destroy it."

"Let it be so," Minister Arhan decreed, as if the matter lay within his authority to decide. "Whether they be beasts or feathered devils, they are evil—and have brought us nothing but ill luck. We have said so all along, and now time is proving it so."

"What will we gain from killing the creature?" Sir Andrew asked. "Even should they be capable of understanding example, it will make no difference. We've killed others in our battles with them, and it has not deterred them."

In truth, Rolande cared little for the creature's fate, but she knew that Sir Andrew wanted to preserve it alive, and it suited her purposes to challenge his authority, perhaps undermine his influence. "It will put heart into our people, assure them of our resolve to eradicate the menace," she declared. "It will allow them a measure of vengeance for their losses! They need such a sign in this dark time—and it is our duty to see that they have it. If the prisoner is indeed some manner of human foe, then let him be executed like one, in a public ceremony on the Common, before the assembled community!"

Sir Andrew could sense the futility of protesting further. The colonists wanted blood, and only a ritual sacrifice would satisfy them. Rolande's motion was carried easily, and a date for the execution was set for four days hence, when the last hunting party should have returned to the settlement.

When the session adjourned, Sir Andrew left the hall furious and frustrated, as usual, and with another blinding headache.

* * *

"What news?" Katin almost pounced upon him as he entered the salon, where Celia sat calmly at her embroidery frame. He winced and asked Katin, "First, would you do me the kindness to brew another cup of your herb-remedy for me? My head's pounding fit to crack."

"I'll fetch it at once!" Katin bounded away eagerly, delighted at the chance to practice her newfound skills.

"My dear, you look as if you've just come from the ramparts," Lady Celia observed, sticking her needle into the tapestry work and rising to greet him. "And not as victor, I'm afraid."

Sir Andrew dropped wearily into his customary chair. "That is very much how I feel. I'd forswear these cursed meetings if there were anyone I could trust to represent the real interests of the colony's defense."

Celia laid a soothing hand on his forehead. "I shall stand for the Wardership myself, next polling time," she promised. "Then I shall be able to fight with words, and leave you to fight with powder and shot."

He grasped her hand gratefully. "Should Thornfeld still exist by then, that would be ideal," he said. "No one could withstand you in debate. How have your powers of persuasion fared with our young Queen?"

"No power on earth, I fear, will move her to flee to Acquitania. She declares that she will sooner join the bandits in the wilderness than beg an old enemy to protect her from a new one. The life of a colonial commoner suits her, it seems, better than that of an exiled monarch. She says—and with some reason—that the Dep army isn't coming to look for her, that they have no reason to suspect her presence here, and that she has no more to lose from the invasion than anyone else, if the colony is made subject to the Chamber."

"You sound as if you agree with her," Sir Andrew reproached her.

"Well, as her loyal subject, naturally I should like to see her out of harm's way, but equally I am bound to acknowledge the royal prerogative to make mistakes."

"But she's only a child—"

"Nonsense, my dear, she's an Obelen—she never was a child. But suppose her so, who has appointed *you* Regent, to govern her?"

"I am appointed by default," Sir Andrew said dryly. "As are you, now. Can we permit her to risk her life—and that of the House of Obelen—by staying here?"

"Ah, can we *prevent* her? That is the question, Andrew. You know as well as I that Oriana's of an age to know her mind. Had it been some plague, instead of this insurrection, that left her as sole heir of the royal family, she would now be directing the affairs of Albin. Her advisers would attempt to influence her, no doubt, but her will would be law, in the end, despite her youth."

Sir Andrew knew better than to argue the point. She was right, but still he felt responsible for the Princess's welfare. He'd brought her to the New World in the belief that she'd be safer here than elsewhere, but what if, instead, he'd led her into a trap? If her enemies found her here, he would be to blame for her downfall, the end of the royal line. . . .

Katin's return prevented further discussion of her position and her character. Sir Andrew accepted the steaming cup with relief, thinking that the girl's presence in his household had at least some compensations. She'd been making herself genuinely useful with her simples and salves.

"What did the assembly decide?" she demanded, when he'd downed the tisane.

He briefly explained what had transpired at the meeting, then said, "Vendeley will be dragging the townspeople over hill and dale in search of the winged ones. The defense council will spend all their time arguing with each other over meaningless details, and I'll have no part of it. No one will address the matter of the colony's defense from the real threat—the Albinate army that will indeed invade, regardless of the Warders' petty concerns. One way or the other, *all* the citizens must be taught the proper use of arms—even if I have to pay them out of my own pocket to come to the stockade and learn."

"It is by just such actions," Katin objected, "that the royalists in Albin doomed themselves. If we hadn't schooled the common folk in weaponry, they'd never have been able to defeat us."

"I am aware of that." Sir Andrew clutched the empty cup so hard that Lady Celia was sure he would break it. She gently took it from him, but he hardly seemed to notice. "But what other choice have we?" he continued. "Even with all of the colonists armed, we will have but a small force. We cannot afford to be masters now. We have built a community—such as it is—it is ours, and if we have to fight side by side with peasants and tradespeople to defend it, then we shall."

Katin was silent for a moment, then she nodded assent and said, "What do you mean to do, then?"

"If no one else will look to the immediate preparations for war, I shall do it myself—before it is too late. I plan to exercise my authority as senior military officer in the colony to review the state of readiness of our citizenry and fortifications—and take any steps I must, to make them battle worthy." He rose and paced the room uneasily, but at last turned to Katin, his expression grave and stern. "I shall do all that I can, Your Highness, but it will be a long, bloody undertaking, and very likely futile. To ensure your safety, I must insist that you travel to Acquitania on the next available vessel."

Katin sighed. "We have been over this time and again. There is nothing to be gained by discussing it further."

"Nonetheless," Sir Andrew persisted, "I would be remiss in my duty to protect Your Highness if I—"

"You forget yourself, Lord Marshal," Katin said coldly. "Your duty is to protect and *serve.* You know my will in this matter. It is not your place to question it!"

She had not availed herself of her royal dignity in quite some time, and the effect was all the more striking, in contrast to her usual offhand demeanor. She somewhat compromised her majesty, however, by slamming the door on her way out.

From the window, they soon saw her dappled horse disappearing in the direction of the woods. "I wonder," Lady Celia mused, "how *I'd* look in buckskin breeches . . . ?"

Sir Andrew had to smile. "Enchanting, of course. Celia, what am I to do about her?"

"My dear, if you'll take my advice, you'll concentrate on matters you *can* control."

"No doubt you're right," Sir Andrew admitted, not sounding convinced. "But I think I'd better go after her, all the same."

* * *

Simeon was trotting briskly along the edge of the farmland near the forest, bound for a farmstead not far from Silverbourne Manor to deliver a demand for payment. He could have sent someone else on such an errand, but chose to attend to it himself, and he had deliberately contrived to come this way rather than take a shorter route bypassing Sir Andrew's estate. In the weeks since his suspicions regarding Katin had been aroused, he had devoted as much time as he could spare to keeping her under observation, searching for some definite answer to the mystery. Now, as he saw her thunder into the woods, he turned his horse to follow her, avid to know what she was about.

The hermit, Frend Pierson, had lived in the woods as long as anyone remembered. He claimed to have been a sailor from the first ship to discover this land, who had been washed overboard and survived on his own for years before more of his own kind had returned. His reasons for choosing to isolate himself from the comradeship of the colonists gave rise to much speculation, however. He was rarely seen in town except for a monthly visit to trade furs and collect supplies. Jerl had heard it said that he was a little mad or that he secretly practiced the black arts and held concourse with spirits to no good purpose—but this last came mostly from the Scrutinor Ministers, and Jerl distrusted it. Jerl didn't know how much of Pierson's tales to believe, but he did credit what the hermit told him of the forest and its strange creatures. Everyone said that Pierson possessed superior knowledge of the ways of all the forest animals, and Jerl had therefore come to him for guidance about the bird folk, as he thought of them. The creatures had compelled his interest from the first, but had become an obsession since the night he had witnessed their fierce ritual. The hermit claimed the ability to communicate with them, and he agreed to teach Jerl, after hearing his confused account of that night. "Your people will need someone to parley for them, if it's come to this," he said, examining the object Jerl had taken down from the great oak. He never referred to himself as a member of the colony.

"I don't understand," Jerl answered uneasily. "What does it mean?"

Pierson shook his head. "I'll teach you what I can of their tongue, then they can tell you as much as they want you to know of their secrets."

Jerl still found it hard to accept that the bird folk could speak like human beings, but some instinct made him believe it. He tried to imagine what it would be like to talk with one of them, and the thought made him dizzy.

"They dwell deep," the hermit said, and Jerl looked at him, puzzled. "Very deep in places of great nests and fallen oaks. They too suffer under great shadows—great shadows hang over us all."

That's true enough, Jerl thought. Something was in the air. Rumors flew around the colony regarding a coming invasion, but no official announcement had yet been made. Nonetheless, he had been doubling the time he spent practicing with his musket, in anticipation of the need. But before he could question the hermit further, the old man rose, staring at the clouds as if he were listening for something. Shaking his head, he muttered, "We are all running short of time . . ." and walked into his shack, seeming to have forgotten Jerl's presence. Jerl knew it would be useless to try to recapture his attention now. He picked up his musket and started back through the woods.

* * *

" 'Then let them come!' the Queen replied,
'We shall again to field,
An hundred score of times, and more,
But never once shall yield!' "

Katin sang lustily as she rode the short distance into the woods from the track along the outer fields. She tethered her horse to a hickory tree and made her way through a dense barrier of old oaks and cypress to a small clearing she'd marked as her private refuge.

"And shall a child of Albin's Rose
Now hide her head in shame
Behind the walls of foreign foes,
A traitor to her name?"

She sang furiously, adding her own verse to the traditional ballad. Queen Albarosa, The Warrior Queen, was her own grandmother, Katin's favorite of all her myriad distinguished ancestors. *She* wouldn't have allowed herself to be exiled twice, without a fight, whatever her advisers might say! Who was Sir Andrew to dictate the actions of his betters? How dare he?

But here Katin's breeding—the endless lessons in court etiquette and the courtesy befitting a Princess of the Blood—made her reproach herself for her summary treatment of her host and defender. No one knew his loyalty to the House of Obelen better than she did. If he'd been caught smuggling her out of Albin, he'd have been hanged—and he could have recouped all his fortunes by betraying her. He had put her welfare before his own without question, and in times like these such devotion to duty was not to be taken for granted.

Katin knew she owed her life to Sir Andrew, and aside from that, she owed him an apology. She had been taught that it was not beneath the royal dignity to sue for pardon when one was in the wrong, and she resolved that she would properly express her regrets—not for her decision to stay, which was unshakable—but for her unworthy behavior.

Suddenly she heard a rustling, almost at her feet, in

a pile of leaves left from winter at the foot of one of the great oaks. She froze, staring at a movement in the dead twigs and leaves, her personal and political concerns forgotten, at the thought of venomous snakes. She raised her ash stick silently and waited, motionless. Again the leaves rustled and shook, but now she thought she heard another sound—a low, plaintive whimpering. Katin held her breath and listened till the noise came again. It was hardly threatening, it sounded like an animal frightened or in pain. That decided her. If it was hurt, perhaps she could treat it.

Wounded animals can be most dangerous, however, as she knew well enough from the hunt. She moved forward slowly, and cautiously pushed aside the twigs and leaves with her stick, uncovering a small soarhound lying half-buried in the foliage. Its pointed ears were too big for the tiny body covered with gold fur. As it tried to scramble to its feet in the unstable debris, its broad paws slipped out from under it, and it collapsed with a soft thud on its stomach, whining piteously.

Katin laughed aloud and stretched out a hand warily toward it, not wanting to startle the pup—or to be bitten. The webs that extended along its sides from its front to rear legs were intact, but it was clear that it was too young to use its feet steadily, much less to glide gracefully from tree to tree, as the adult soarhounds did. The nest must be nearby, then, in the oak above them. She soon spotted the hole, some fifteen feet up.

"Come on, little one, back to your nest with you." As she reached for the scruff of its neck, it looked at her with big terrified eyes and scrabbled backward.

Katin sighed, made soothing sounds, and offered the pup her finger to sniff. Deciding it liked her salty scent, it licked her finger, then pressed closer to her hand, nosing her palm with its pointed little muzzle. Katin gently stroked the soft fur behind its ears, then, bringing her other hand around, she scooped up the pup. It started to whimper again, but as she rubbed its head, talking to it softly, it stopped squirming and settled down. Tucking the pup into her vest, she climbed the tree, finally reaching the nest with its complement of three yapping baby soarhounds, but no sign of the mother, which must be off searching out food for her brood. She removed the whelp and set it down so that it rested against its littermates. It looked at her for a moment then stuck out a paw and jabbed the nearest pup in the nose.

Katin shimmied back down the moss-covered tree, and, finding her spirits much improved, she determined to return to Silverbourne at once and ask Sir Andrew's pardon for her unseemly behavior. She started back toward her horse, singing as she went,

> " *'T'will be a fine day for the hunt,'*
> *Quoth she, 'To seek the sleek young buck.*
> *Then let us ride to Wyldendale,*
> *And bend the bow to try our luck.'*
>
> *'We shall not hie to Wyldendale*
> *However fine the day will be.*
> *Who rides to hunt that shadowed vale*
> *Not huntsman, soon, but prey will be.'* "

She had reached her favorite part—when the wounded stag turns into the forest warlock and defeats the craven bridegroom—when Jerl strode out of the woods into her path.

"Good day, Goodman Smit," Katin said, cordially enough.

"I heard you singing," he said gravely. "It's not safe

for you to wander around in the forest alone. There are wild animals—and the bandits—"

"*You're* wandering around alone," Katin pointed out. "I know these woods as well as you do. Besides, I am not far from home, and I am armed." She drew a slender dagger from her belt.

Jerl laughed. "That might do for trimming your nails, girl, but it's hardly a weapon."

"It is!" Katin shoved the knife back into its sheath. "People have been killed with such, many a time." This was true, but as far as Katin knew this had happened at court, when the victim had been set upon unawares. How much of a defense would it provide against a well-armed bandit, or a hungry bear? But to Jerl she said only, "Anyway, I've nothing bandits would want to steal. Have you, that you need a great gun to defend yourself?"

Jerl flushed. She knew very well he owned little but the clothes on his back—much-patched brown homespun breeches and a faded yellow shirt—and the powder horn and scuffed leather cartridge case that hung by leather thongs from his belt. She was mocking him—but what had she to give herself airs about? Being a member of Sir Andrew's household didn't make her—curse the girl anyway! What did he care what she thought? "I was visiting the hermit, if you've no objection, and I've guard duty soon."

"Why then I'll not keep you from it," she said with a bow.

"Well, what business have *you* out alone in the woods?" he demanded.

"I've herbs and roots and bark to gather—leaves and mushrooms and spore balls—all of considerable use!" Why was she explaining herself to this lout? It was absurd. "I've work to do, I can't stand about nattering—and haven't you your guard duty to think of?"

Abashed, Jerl muttered, "Yes," and turned away, but he suddenly looked back at her and added, "I think you sing awfully well," before he disappeared among the trees.

For a moment, Katin stared after him, startled, and felt unaccountably sorry that she'd driven him away. Then she reminded herself that she had more important matters to resolve and started again to where she had tethered her horse. But she had barely taken two steps when she heard a familiar sound, and she backtracked to the great oak and searched the ground again. There among the leaves was the soarhound pup, mewling its pathetic whimper. When she knelt down, it waddled over to her and pressed its head against her hand.

"Idiot!" She picked it up. "If you jump out again, I shan't put you back." The pup gazed at her trustingly, as if it knew this was a lie. Katin looked up and saw that a full-grown soarhound was looking out of the nest, which might complicate the matter of returning the pup. Not much was known about these "New World gliding canids," as Carl called them, but the adults had formidable fangs, and Katin had no doubt that they'd use them to defend their nests. This one showed no sign of attacking, but climbing the tree did not seem the wisest course at the moment. As Katin considered the problem, the pup nestled into the crook of her arm, stuck out its long pink tongue and licked her wrist.

Simeon, from his watch post in a stand of hemlocks, wondered whether to offer his assistance—but what did the girl want to do? If the soarhound would only attack her, he could shoot it, and so maybe gain her gratitude—and, more importantly, her confidence. But the creature withdrew its snout into the hole, and before he could make any move, Sir Andrew strode into the clearing, apparently in search of his young retainer. This was promising. With rekindled interest, Simeon drew as close as he dared, without leaving the shadow of the trees.

As Sir Andrew came to a halt before her, Katin said, "My Lord, I'm glad you came."

Sir Andrew hesitated, taken aback at this unexpected welcome. But like the soldier he was, he charged onward. "We must talk about the matter of your safety. It may not be my place to tell you your duty, but those who should do so are dead," he said with deliberate bluntness. "If you join them, the House of Obelen dies with you. I cannot believe that you have fully considered that fact. It is not a matter to be decided by royal whim."

"I know, I apologize—ouch—stop that." She yanked the soarhound pup's claws from her sleeve. Sensing her displeasure, the pup tried to crawl under her arm and hide.

"What have you there?" Sir Andrew asked.

Katin held it out to show him. "It fell out of its nest. I was about to put it back, but the mother's in there." She gestured toward the tree.

Sir Andrew shook his head, recalling something Carl had taught him. "You shouldn't have picked it up. Now it has your scent on it, the others will probably reject it."

"But what am I to do with it, then? It's too young to survive on its own."

"You'll just have to abandon it or take it home, I suppose." The real question was where her home was going to be. "It would cause a sensation at the court—they'll never have seen the like in Acquitania."

He didn't get the reaction he expected. Katin neither flew into a rage nor dismissed his words with cold contempt. Instead, she put the pup down on the ground by her feet, then stood up straight and said in a calmly regal voice, "Allow me to explain my decision to remain, My Lord, as I ought, in common courtesy, to have done before. It is possible that I might save my life by throwing myself upon the mercy of the Acquitanian court—although revolutionary agents are as likely to seek me there as here, you know. My safety would be by no means certain in such a conspicuous position. But even supposing the throne of Acquitania could protect me—do you suppose that such protection would be without its *price?*"

Without waiting for his reply, she went on, "I'd be forced to marry into the royal family—all very comfortable for *me,* to be sure, but just what *they* need to justify their claim to the throne of Albin! In God's name, sir, have generations of my kin and countrymen died defending our land from foreign pretenders, only to surrender to them at last? For that is what you ask of me, make no mistake—to surrender my country to save my skin—to betray the House of Obelen to preserve it! Better to let my line perish honorably with me than turn to treachery by breeding a generation of Obelens whose loyalty is to Acquitania!"

A soldier knows when he is beaten. Sir Andrew regarded his sovereign in silence for a moment, his usual deference touched with a new respect. From her disheveled hair and sun-browned face to her worn work boots—one of which was presently being chewed by the restless soarhound puppy—she looked every inch a queen. He bowed. "Your Highness is presently right," he said at last. "I have allowed my concern for your person to blind me to the best interests of your House. Forgive me."

Katin shook her head. "And I have allowed the license of my position here to blind me to the debt I owe Your Lordship. But if my behavior has not always become a monarch, I pray you will not think me insensible to that obligation. Had I the honors at my disposal that by rights should be mine to bestow, the world should know of your faithful service on my behalf—stop that, stupid," she said to the soarhound, who seemed determined to gnaw through the toe of her boot. She picked it up by the scruff of the neck and resignedly tucked it into her jacket. "Perhaps I'll call it Lucifer, since it fell from above," she said archly. "That would infuriate our Scrutinor friends.

"And as to my safety," she added, "since it troubles you so greatly, I suggest that you teach me to shoot a musket, to defend myself—and the colony. Jerl Smit says my dagger's no more use than for paring my nails."

As soon as the pair left the clearing, Simeon ran toward his mount. At last his suspicions were confirmed, his questions answered—and the answer was worth more than gold. The reward the Chamber of Statesmen would pay for this information would make him rich and powerful. Such a coup deserved something more than mere money—perhaps the governorship of the newly secured colony once the Chamber won the upcoming battle. Simeon pictured himself ensconced in pomp and glory, wielding absolute power over the colonists. . . .

He did not even for a moment contemplate telling Rolande of his discovery. No doubt if he told her what he knew, she would simply turn the situation to her advantage. She was the Chamber's agent, and he was there merely to assist her. As long as this was so, there was no guarantee that the Chamber wouldn't simply give her the credit for the success of the mission. She would certainly do her best to paint it that way. No, there was no reason to trust Vendeley with something of this magnitude. After all, it was he who had had the persistence to ferret out the truth about the girl—he who had the intelligence to track her down. He would send his report directly to the chamber of Statesmen, bypassing Vendeley completely . . . but how to prevent her from finding out?

No matter what he reported, the Chamber would contact *her* at once—if only to demand why she hadn't been aware of her subordinate's activities. No doubt she'd claim that his information had been premature, or that he'd intercepted her report and substituted his own, to attempt to take credit for himself. They might well believe her. Her word would weigh more with them than her lackey's.

No, he must not merely reveal his secret to the Chamber, or hand the Princess over to their agents, when the army arrived. He must also see to it that Vendeley was utterly discredited in their eyes. As he trotted through the woods, evolving his scheme, he sang to himself in satisfaction, echoing Katin's song without thinking what he sang.

"Who rides to hunt that shadowed vale,
Not huntsman, soon, but prey will be."

Chapter 3

In the cell, Katin removed the poultice of goldenseal and comfrey and gently swabbed the creature's wound. It slightly retracted its wing, but made no move to avoid her ministrations. It lay in the straw seeming nearly lifeless, hardly stirring when Katin approached, or even when she stretched out its wing to tend to its injury. Carefully she pulled the feathers apart and examined the site where the musket ball had penetrated. The wound had almost mended, and Katin would have been pleased and proud about the effectiveness of her healing skills, except that the creature only seemed to grow weaker and weaker, for all her efforts. As far as she could see, it was sound and whole, aside from this one wound, and the guards told her it had eaten what it was offered, yet it was apparently dying, despite her. Carl had told her that some wild creatures simply could not survive in captivity, but she could not help feeling that her attempts at healing were somehow at fault.

"They're going to kill him, you know. Why bother to heal him?"

Katin looked up to see that Jerl Smit had come to relieve the guard on duty outside the cell. On Sir Andrew's orders, she was never to be left alone with the creature. The prohibition was irksome, but she knew that his caution was justified. Most of the guards paid no attention to her in any case, but Jerl was staring into the cell, resting the muzzle of his musket on the crossbar. "You might as well spare yourself the trouble," he said bitterly.

Katin shrugged. "It's good practice for me. Besides, Sir Andrew means to prevent the execution, if he can. But it's dying anyway," she added in frustration. "And I don't understand why!"

"Don't you? I do," Jerl said darkly. "But you'd not believe me."

Curious, Katin took up his challenge. "Why shouldn't I? Tell me, if you know so much."

"If he's dying, he's dying of despair," Jerl said defiantly. "Despair can kill." He could sense the creature's desperation, though it gave no sign of life, and the feeling drove him to distraction. He felt feverish, lightheaded—not just the way Katin usually made him feel, but almost dizzy.

Katin watched him pace restlessly back and forth before the cell. "I suppose despair's as good a name as any other," she said, after a moment's silence. "Unless it has hidden wounds, I can't account for its weakness."

"Don't call him 'it,' he's a—a—person."

"Oh? I see. No one else can be sure what they are, but of course, *you* know everything. How do you even know this one's a male?"

Jerl didn't know how he knew. He was as certain of the creature's gender as of his own, but he couldn't prove that he was right. "I don't know for sure, but he probably is. He's a soldier—"

"There are women soldiers!" Katin was quick to point out.

"Well, but not many. Anyway, all the bird folk

we've seen look the same. Maybe their women and children are together somewhere, and only the men come to fight us."

"I expect we all look the same to them, too," Katin said, dismissing the idea.

Jerl didn't want to argue. He felt that he'd go mad if he couldn't confide in someone. "Maybe he's not male," he conceded, "but he's not an animal, anyway. It's better to call him 'he' than 'it.' "

"What makes you so sure of that?" Katin demanded.

"Didn't you hear about Paeter Cellric's testimony to the Wardership? He said they live in cities—deep in the forest—and Frend Pierson says the same—"

Katin shook her head. "Sir Andrew told me about Cellric's story. He only said they build structures of some kind, like huts, but that's no proof that they're human. There are great birds in Xanistee that weave hutches for their nests, and beavers can build dams and dens with several chambers. Carl showed me a book—you can read it yourself, if you like." She saw his expression, and at once realized her mistake, but it was too late to recall her words. Of course he couldn't read, and he thought she had intended an insult. "I mean, there are drawings—" she began, blushing.

But Jerl wasn't listening. Stung, he snapped at her, "Your friend Schellring doesn't know everything! I suppose those birds and beasts can talk, too, can they? The bird folk have a language of their own—does he know that? Pierson can speak to them, and he's teaching me their tongue!"

Katin sighed. "No doubt he believes it," she said patiently, "but that doesn't make it so. Everyone knows he's crazy."

"He's not! He knows more about the forest than any of us. The bird folk have told him things. . . ." It *did* sound crazy, but he pressed on, determined to convince her somehow. "They're people like us. He told me they call themselves the Yerren—"

At that, for the first time, the creature stirred and slowly raised its head. It opened its large, bright eyes and gazed at Jerl, as if waiting for something.

"Yerren . . . ?" Katin said softly, and it turned to face her, then trilled a few low, musical sounds at her before weakly lying back in the straw.

"What did it—he—say?" Katin gasped.

"I don't know, I couldn't hear." Jerl unlocked the cell and came to kneel beside the Yerren. Hesitantly, he half-whistled and half-chanted a phrase the hermit had tried to teach him. The pitch of the voice, he'd said, was as important as the sound itself. The Yerren made no response. Jerl tried again.

"What are you saying?" Katin asked.

"That we're friends, that we mean him no harm."

"Let me try." To Jerl's surprise, she sang from memory the phrases he had mastered only after considerable time and effort. They sounded more natural to him in her high-pitched voice, and the Yerren seemed to think so, too. It stared at her for a moment, then uttered a rapid series of notes, in an angry, rising tone, and turned away.

Katin looked expectantly at Jerl, but he shook his head. "I didn't recognize any of those words. I only know a few. Maybe if he said it again." But the Yerren only lay still, seeming exhausted by its efforts, and nothing they said could rouse it again.

"Never mind," said Katin. "He's too weak, we should let him rest. Whatever it was he said, it was quite clear that he doesn't believe we're friends. You have to bring the hermit here to talk to him—this could be most important."

"I don't know if he'll come, but I'll ask him."

"Why haven't you told anyone about this before?"

"Who'd have believed me? You said yourself, everyone thinks he's crazy. What do you think now?"

Katin hesitated. "I don't know what to think," she admitted. "It might have been meaningless sounds, I suppose, but he certainly seemed to be speaking to us. We can't ignore the possibility. If he can answer questions. . . ." Excited, she stood up and began to gather her medical supplies together. "I'm going to tell Sir Andrew! And you must fetch the hermit here as soon as you can."

"I'll try. Maybe he is crazy," Jerl said slowly. "But if he's crazy, then I am too—and maybe I am. I can't explain about the bird folk, I don't understand it myself. It's so strange, I think I must be crazy sometimes. They make me feel . . . I don't *know*—I just believe they're people." He shrugged helplessly and turned to go.

"I think Sir Andrew does, too," Katin was saying, when suddenly, without warning, the Yerren leaped up and pushed past her, knocking her aside. "Jerl! Stop him!" she shouted, scrambling to her feet.

Jerl should have been able to stop the Yerren. He was far larger and stronger than it was, but the moment it had leaped up, he'd been stricken by a wave of confusion so overwhelming it had the force of a physical blow. For a moment he couldn't tell where he was. He seemed to be running toward himself, looking at himself through the Yerren's eyes, and seeing a monstrous, deformed enemy. Then it was bolting past him, and he could only lunge at it clumsily, too late. Its talons slashed across his shoulder, and it easily broke away from him, leaving him staggering and giddy as it darted through the door of the cell. By the time he and Katin raced into the corridor after it, the Yerren had disappeared around a corner.

The Yerren's lightness made it impossible for them

to catch up to it as it ran wildly. It found the passageway to the drill yard, and they turned the corner in time to see it barrel by one of the watchmen coming on duty. The man drew himself into position and raised his musket, but the Yerren threw open its wings and vaulted over him through the open door into the yard as the shot went wild. The watchman raced out the door after him, shouting for assistance as several soldiers in the yard came running, and Katin and Jerl pounded through the door in pursuit.

They might as well have tried to run down a deer. Before anyone could come close enough to seize it, it had reached a ladder leading to the top of the stockade wall. A soldier farther along the wall braced his musket against one of the stockade posts and took aim at the escaping prisoner as it perched on one of the watch platforms, but it was not still for two moments together. As he fired, the Yerren had already swooped from the platform, its wings spread against the sunlit sky. They could do nothing but watch it disappear over the distant trees.

The soldier on the wall lowered his weapon. Those on the ground looked at one another uncertainly, and then looked at Katin and Jerl. At the moment when the Yerren had launched itself into the air, Jerl had cried out as if in pain, and fallen to his knees, shaking, hiding his face in his hands. Now he rose slowly, supporting himself against the stockade wall. His shirt was soaked with blood where the Yerren's powerful talons had raked his shoulder. He tried to stand to attention when Captain Jamison approached them, but he had to lean back against the wall again, lest he fall.

"Smit, consider yourself under arrest," said the captain. "We'll have the whole damned Wardership on our necks now, because we couldn't keep one miserable, half-grown prisoner in custody! How the hell could you let it escape?"

"Don't be absurd. Can't you see this man's wounded?" Katin cried. She turned to the watching soldiers and ordered, "Take him inside, to a cot, and fetch me some water, and the salve and clean bandages from the creature's cell, at once!"

Startled, some of the soldiers moved to obey, then looked to Captain Jamison for instructions. He hesitated, then resignedly gestured for them to do as she said. The boy did look pretty bad, at that, he thought. There'd be time enough to deal with him later.

Katin faced him again and said imperiously, "If anyone was to blame for the creature's escape, it was I, and I shall answer to the Wardership for it, if necessary. Your guard was only doing his duty. I told him that the creature was dying, and he had no cause to doubt my word. It was only shamming, but I was fooled and thought there was no danger. I carelessly turned my back on the thing." Inventing wildly, she went on, "He only opened the cell to let me out, and then the creature suddenly attacked me. I'd likely have been killed if he hadn't come to my assistance. He fought it off most bravely, but no one could have stopped it. With your leave, sir, I must go and attend to his wounds now." She bowed and marched off after the soldiers who were supporting Jerl between them, as they half-dragged, half-carried him into the stockade.

Captain Jamison watched her depart with some interest. She did not look in the least as if she had been attacked by a fierce wild beast, but if she stuck to her story—true or not, he didn't care—it could make matters easier for all of them. There was bound to be trouble, of course, if not from the town Warders, then from the Dep Church. These days there was nothing but trouble—and folk were expecting an execution.

But if the boy was, in fact, seriously wounded—and in the defense of a fellow-colonist—his actions might be represented as heroic rather than irresponsible, in a well-worded report. Blame might be laid to the creature's inhuman ferocity. That would sit well with the mood of the town. Well, his immediate duty was clear, in any case. He sent a courier to apprise Sir Andrew of the situation.

Katin was puzzled by Jerl's condition. When she washed his wounds, she found that they were not really very deep or ragged. The bleeding had nearly stopped already. Yet he seemed as dazed and weak as if he had lost a great quantity of blood, or suffered some stunning blow. Perhaps he was shamming, too, she thought, and with good reason. She contrived to treat the long scratches and bandage his shoulder without allowing the others to see that he was not badly hurt. The soldiers who had escorted them stayed near the door, unsure of their orders and ill at ease. Was Jerl under arrest, or not? Should he be under lock and key, should he be in shackles? They knew him well enough to doubt that he'd try to escape, and besides, he didn't look as if he could. And what of the girl? They didn't much want to cross her. Though neither would have admitted it, they were rather intimidated by Katin. Finally, they took up their post outside the door.

"Jerl?" Katin whispered. "What ails you? Look at me." She bathed his face with a wet cloth, wishing she had some smelling salts or southernwood.

With an effort, Jerl said, "It will pass, now he's gone."

This didn't make much sense to Katin, but at least Jerl looked somewhat better. "The Yerren, do you mean? What will pass?"

"He—he hit me."

Keeping her voice low, Katin assured him, "Don't worry, it looked like a lot of blood, but the wounds aren't deep at all."

Jerl looked at her blankly. "What blood? What wounds?"

Katin couldn't find any bump or cut on Jerl's head, but she decided that he must have hit his head against the wall in the cell, while he was struggling with the Yerren. He was talking nonsense. He claimed that the Yerren had hit him without touching him—twice—once in the cell, and again in the yard, when it had thrown itself from the wall and unfurled its wings. Not patient by nature, Katin did her best to hide her disbelief. "Where did it hurt?" she asked reasonably. "Was it your head?"

"My head, my heart—I don't know—it didn't hurt, not exactly. It was more like grief, or fear, but so keen I couldn't bear it, I couldn't breathe. . . ." His look begged her to understand, but how could he expect it of her, when he didn't understand himself? "What's the use—maybe I'm just crazy. But it's only when they're near, I tell you. That's why I left the door of the cell open— I know better than that! But he had me all confused—"

"Hush," Katin said hastily. "You didn't leave it open." If anyone had heard him confess to his carelessness, she decided, she would say that he was delirious and raving. He *was* raving, anyway. "Never mind," she said soothingly. "You should rest yourself now, don't talk. You're in a fever." Quite at random, she started to tell him about the soarhound whelp, Lucifer, and how he'd dragged a discarded wig up into the rafters of the salon and tried to make himself a nest. By the time Sir Andrew arrived to fetch Katin, both were laughing, and Jerl felt almost himself again.

But even Katin seemed daunted by the tongue-lashing Sir Andrew gave them both, in front of half the regiment. Jerl said nothing to defend himself. He couldn't imagine trying to explain to someone like Sir Andrew about the Yerren, and the way they affected him. Besides, he felt that he deserved the commander's censure. He'd known that he wasn't fit to guard the Yerren, and he should have made some excuse, or claimed to be ill, and let someone else stand watch over the creature. The fact was, he'd wanted to see Katin again. And now he'd only gotten her into trouble. It was his fault the Yerren had escaped. He'd been on duty, it was his responsibility—not hers—to guard the prisoner, but she was taking all the blame, and he couldn't contradict her story without branding her a liar before everyone! What would he do if Sir Andrew had her flogged? He rather hoped that the Wardership would order him to be executed in the Yerren's place.

Katin was experienced enough at court diplomacy to guess that much of Sir Andrew's rage was intended for the benefit of his audience. Every witness to his tirade would soon be embellishing the tale in the alehouse and the cookshop. The whole town would know that Sir Andrew had been incensed at the creature's escape. She only repeated, humbly enough, that her own carelessness was to blame, that she was sorry, and that Jerl was badly injured to be kept standing about. His wounds ought to be sewn with cobblers' thread, but she had not dared attempt it—might she take him to Carl?

Sir Andrew assented to this, as she expected, and ordered Jerl to be taken to his carriage. Then he more or less threw Katin in after him. "Every idiot in the Wardership and every gossip in the village will think *I* put you up to this!" he shouted. "Did you ever think of that?"

"Not after that performance they won't, My Lord," Katin said with a chuckle, as the carriage pulled away from the stockade. "Upon my word, I thought you'd strike me."

"I may yet," Sir Andrew said gloomily. "It's as well the creature won't be executed, but this was *not* the way to go about it!"

Jerl could only stare at the two of them in astonishment. Katin didn't seem in the least concerned about Sir Andrew's displeasure now. "Oh, but you don't understand—we didn't let him go. I was telling the truth," she was saying. "Well, that is, some of it was the truth. The creature—they're called the Yerren—actually *deceived* us. That must prove they have intelligence! And it seems they can speak, too, in their own language—" She excitedly told Sir Andrew about their attempts to communicate with the captive Yerren. He listened attentively, and interrupted her only once—to tell the coachman to take them directly to Carl Schellring's cottage.

But Carl was not convinced by their new evidence. "It is not uncommon for some birds and animals to sham wounds, or even death, to deceive a predator," he pointed out. "And any raven can be taught to repeat sounds and words, without understanding their meaning. However . . . I am forced to admit that there are characteristics about these creatures that I am hard-pressed to explain by analogy." He fetched a wide-mouthed jar and set it on the table before them. "There is, for instance, the matter of the creature's brain. I've preserved the organ in spirits for future study, but I have already made several observations which may bear upon the question." He drew an imaginary line around the glass, outlining the brain. "The creature's brain is much larger in proportion to its body than one would anticipate, and its forebrain is extremely well-developed, which could be a sign of intelligence—"

"Could it talk?" Sir Andrew interrupted.

Carl cast an uneasy sidelong glance at the brain in the jar. "I take it you refer to true speech. We simply have not enough facts to lead us to a definite conclusion, M'lord."

"Perhaps not," Sir Andrew said impatiently, "but neither can we ignore the facts we do have. Any one of them, taken by itself, might be explained as you suggest, but taken together they carry conviction. They form a pattern which suggests a certain conclusion. You yourself taught me to examine evidence in this wise."

"True, M'lord, but the suggested conclusion is only that—a suggestion—a possibility. I taught you that such possibilities are not to be hastily accepted. It takes time to investigate all alternative explanations thoroughly."

"We don't have time," Sir Andrew said simply. His mind was racing ahead, recalculating the strategies for defending the colony based on this new possibility. "Supposing that we could communicate with the creatures . . . that they could understand the danger of invasion. They'd be an obstacle to the Chamber's plan to exploit the land's bounty. The Deps wouldn't hesitate to eradicate them."

"You think they could be frightened away?"

"By no means," Sir Andrew said thoughtfully. "They fight like the devil's own. . . ." He spoke as if to himself, and fell silent, lost in thought, for some moments. Then abruptly recalling himself to the present, he said to Carl, "You told me that the creatures couldn't be very strong, given the relative size of their muscles and the lightness of their bones, but young Smit grappled with the one that escaped today, and it got the better of him. You'd better have a look at his wounds. Katin thinks they should be sewn shut—"

"Er, well, that part wasn't exactly true," Katin admitted. "They're no more than nasty scratches, really, but I was afraid if Jerl stayed in the barracks someone would discover that he wasn't much hurt. . . ." At Sir Andrew's look of disapproval, she said defiantly, "Well, what's the good of it, if he's found out? It was my fault, really—"

"No, it wasn't," Jerl said miserably. "I was on watch—"

"Quiet, both of you!" Sir Andrew frowned at Jerl. "If you weren't truly wounded, how did you come to let the creature get away? I want the truth this time."

Jerl knew that Sir Andrew wasn't going to like the truth any better than Katin's lies, but he had no choice. "It was the Yerren's doing—he cast a spell on me!" he blurted out. With no expectation of being believed, he haltingly explained the stupefying madness that had come over him in the Yerren's presence.

At least Sir Andrew didn't accuse him of lying. "A fit of some kind?" he asked Carl doubtfully.

Carl was intrigued. "Are you quite sure the creature didn't bite you?" he asked Jerl, and went on without waiting for an answer. "The venom of certain reptiles can produce a delirium such as you describe . . . or perhaps, in this case, it is introduced into the blood of the prey by means of the talons. . . . Spiders, now. . . ." He began to search through a pile of books, muttering to himself about scorpions.

Sir Andrew sighed. "You'll stay here until you're healed," he told Jerl. "That is, until those fictitious wounds of yours would be healed, if you had them." Katin was right—no purpose would be served by throwing the boy to the wolves. And Captain Jamison, too, had suggested that the garrison might be spared some of the townsfolks' indignation if Smit were believed to be suffering from grievous injuries. "But there's to be no talk of spells—that's an order. I won't have the colonists encouraged to believe that these—Yerren—are some sort of demons! I don't care what you think it did to you, you'll keep it to yourself, or I'll have you horsewhipped—is that understood?"

"Yes, sir," Jerl said gratefully. "Thank you, M'lord. I've no mind to tell anyone, I swear to you, in God's name. They'd think me mad."

Could Master Schellring's idea explain what had happened to him, he wondered. It seemed to him that he'd been stricken with that hideous giddiness *before* the Yerren had touched him, but it was hard to remember just what had taken place. And what of the time he'd witnessed the Yerren at their gathering, and experienced something of the same sort—none of them had bitten or clawed at him then. . . . He was as bewildered as ever, and his shoulder throbbed cruelly, but after the day's disasters, he was so relieved to be alive and at liberty that he hardly cared. And the most remarkable event of the day, in Jerl's view, was one that eclipsed all else and gave him hope—for the first time, Katin had called him by name.

Chapter 4

"This is not Albin, sir," Marcus Farnham said, when the delegation of Warders had crossed the hard ground of the drill yard at the stockade to confront Sir Andrew. "We are all affected by this threat, and all have a say in how we shall face it."

It was with difficulty that Sir Andrew held his temper in check. He was not accustomed to justifying his actions to others, nor did he have time for these interruptions. As Farnham went on, castigating him for having taken measures on his own authority that should by rights be referred to the council, Sir Andrew continued observing the practicing of those who had shown up that day in response to his offer of two pence a day to any who would drill with muskets. He was far from satisfied with the recruits. Different folk showed up daily, and none would be truly experienced in case of battle, but with some training they could at least swell the ranks of able defenders instead of being a burden on them.

Katin, delighted at the prospect of action, had been his most enthusiastic volunteer from the first. And he was bound to admit that she had been of help, encouraging many of the townswomen to join in the training, instead of leaving the defense of the colony to their menfolk. Sir Andrew smiled, watching her struggle with a musket as tall as herself, but once she had it braced, she hit her target squarely.

As the last words of Headman Farnham's diatribe died away, Sir Andrew gave his attention to the assembled company—Franham himself, portly and pompous, wearing a plain brown dress coat and breeches with a ribbed silk waistcoat that strained over his girth; Mistress Vendeley, flamboyant as always in a suit of crimson velvet and a short red silk cloak, satin slashed and embroidered with floss and twisted silk thread, and lined with taffeta; Ministra Cirana, a reproach to the rest in her severe, unadorned Deprivant gray; Elliott Cavendish, a gentleman with a large estate, dressed, as suited his station, in a fine suit of dark blue wool and a lace-trimmed shirt; and a large, prosperous farmer in worsted, whose name Sir Andrew didn't remember.

None of you has much love for me, he thought. Despite the losses he himself had suffered, he knew they still saw him as a representative of the privileged aristocracy, whom resentment and envy painted as an adversary. But he would make them respect his will.

Standing straight as the oak posts of the stockade, he said, "To be sure, this is not Albin—in Albin I was not hampered at every step in the performance of my duty by those in whose interests I was attempting to act! We are engaged in war, not in a political exercise. Unless we take *immediate* action to improve the state of our defenses, we are almost certain to be defeated. We have no time for the petty tyranny of officials. As the military commander of this colony I am charged with the grave responsibility of protecting your lives." There was in his tone both an irony which he could not completely suppress and a deliberate challenge. "If my behavior does not meet with the approval of the Wardership, I shall tender my resignation, and allow you to choose a successor whose actions you can approve."

"You can't do that," Cavendish objected.

Rolande watched narrow-eyed from a pace or two behind the others, observing all their reactions. She would have welcomed Sir Andrew's proposal, but she held her tongue for fear of appearing to favor an action so obviously against the best interests of the colony. No one else in the community had Sir Andrew's expertise in military matters, and the Wardership was well aware of the fact.

Headman Farnham slapped his hand against the stockade wall. "We did not come here to—"

The Ministra's voice rose shrilly. "I have long held that you are anathema to those who would practice in all piety and humility the dictates of the Good God, but I have never thought to find you such a bald traitor to our citizens."

"Traitor, am I?" Sir Andrew demanded. "I will fight to the death to defend the colony, but I will not stand by and allow you to set yourselves tamely out for slaughter!" Now certain of their attention, he said, "A war cannot be waged—much less won—unless a single cohesive will drives the people fighting it. We cannot afford to act at cross-purposes. If I am trusted to represent this body in its military endeavors, I shall do whatever I deem necessary to provide us with the means to withstand the coming assault. If you cannot trust me, then you must find someone you can all agree to follow."

At first, the members of the delegation remained silent, surprised by this tirade, but a moment later they renewed their objections. Ignoring them, Sir Andrew turned, strode into the central building of the compound, and slammed the door behind him. *Curse the girl, now she's got me slamming doors,* he thought.

Few, even among those who despised Sir Andrew, truly believed there was anyone else as capable of leading the militia—and a time of crisis was not a good moment to be floundering in search of leadership. The Headman drew the others aside, engaging them in a hasty consultation.

Sir Andrew took his seat behind the table that served him for a desk. It seemed unlikely that they would accept his resignation, but if they did so, he could return with Celia to Acquitania, where she would be safe. Surely the Princess would accompany them, on the understanding that she need not reveal her identity. If Celia was right, it was unlikely that any of the aristocracy in exile there would recognize Oriana now, grown and changed as she was.

He had worked hard to establish his household here, but if all was to be lost to a foundering, ill-considered defense, it would be best to abandon Silverbourne now, while they could still take what they owned away with them, and live in some independence . . . somewhere . . . maybe to the west, where there was said to be rich farmland fed by a great river. . . .

There came a knock on the door, and the Warders entered, Headman Farnham in the lead, nervously smoothing his waistcoat down over his paunch. He peered at Sir Andrew with the expression of one who has swallowed something distasteful. "I think I speak for the entire Wardership when I say that we wish you to remain in command."

Sir Andrew accepted this decision with something of regret as his plans faded away. He said, wanting to be certain that they understood each other in full, "Then I will decide the manner in which we address this threat. I will not have interference, demagoguery, or any restrictions imposed on my conduct of our defense."

"As you wish." Farnham made the concession with ill grace, but gave no sign of trying to dictate any of his own conditions.

The matter settled, Sir Andrew drew their attention to a crudely-drawn parchment map spread out on the table. It showed the town buildings, the stockade, the harbor, and the forest along the Destiny River. Beyond the fringes of the forest on the map was the blankness of the unknown. "I have spent days visiting the docks, farms, and garrisoned houses at the edge of the settlement, and sent small companies of soldiers up and down the coast, to judge the spots where the Chamber's forces will be most likely to land. We must fortify the harbor—although there are miles of coastline where they can come ashore. We must also install outposts at strategic points along the shore, with watchers to alert the colony once the enemy is sighted. That means construction, requiring laborers and materials. The Wardership must approve the necessary expenses without delay—without taking counsel for a month or remanding the matter for further consideration!"

He looked at each of the Warders in turn, and meeting with no objections, he went on, "We have but a few months to prepare. Look here." He ran his finger across the map, over the open area between the town and the forest. "This is all the land we've cleared to date. If we are attacked, we will need supplies to sustain us, and a plan to get them where they're needed. The farmers must be persuaded—or commanded—to hold back from selling everything they can against future need. May I count on the Wardership to use its influence to accomplish this?"

The delegation looked at one another uneasily, then the Headman cleared his throat. "It will be seen to," he said decisively.

Satisfied, Sir Andrew turned to the matter which had been occupying his thoughts ever since the escape of the Yerren. "Very well, then I have something further to say. We are all agreed that we cannot combat two enemies—the flying creatures and the Chamber's armies."

"We've been over that," Ministra Cirana objected. "Neither, in your view, can we do away with the beasts."

"That may not be necessary," Sir Andrew said, "or even desirable."

There was a sudden silence in the room.

Sir Andrew reviewed his reasons for believing that the Yerren, as Jerl called them, possessed intelligence. The Warders remained unconvinced, but he persisted, "As you know, we have heard testimony that they have cities—even as we do—in the forest. If we can locate the city of the Yerren, we may be able to forge an alliance. If they were to join with us, it would swell our forces considerably."

" 'Tis a fantasy!" Rolande said with outright derision. "An alliance? Why not with the bears and wolves as well?"

Ignoring her, Sir Andrew continued, "If the creatures cannot be persuaded to join us, at least a truce might be struck—and this in itself would relieve us of one threat. I propose, therefore, to seek the leaders of the Yerren."

He wished there were someone else he could appoint to this task, so that he might oversee the military preparations of the colony himself. But he could trust Captain Jamison with the fortification of the town, while the establishment of a military alliance could not be left to a subordinate.

Support for his position came from an unexpected source. Ministra Cirana, seeing an opportunity to remove Sir Andrew from the center of influence, said, "If the creatures can be made to desist from their ravages, then I for one must assent to this proposal."

Rolande was torn. On the one hand, like the Ministra, she saw certain advantages in having Sir Andrew out of the way. On the other hand, suppose he were to *succeed* in this mad venture . . . ? It could put all her plans and prospects in jeopardy. Rolande was not one to underestimate an adversary. She knew that Sir Andrew was no fool, and if he was convinced the thing was possible, she could not afford to assume that he was wrong. She listened as her fellow Warders voiced their approval of the idea. Headman Farnham nodded placidly, now ready to follow Sir Andrew's lead completely. It was for her to speak. "If the Wardership supports this expedition of Sir Andrew's, then it is not for me to place obstacles in its way," she said with every appearance of humility. "However, it seems fitting that an official delegate of this body should accompany him. Surely in meeting with these creatures for the first time, the *civil* powers should be represented as well as the military. I am accustomed to travel and trade with peoples of many sorts. I feel it my duty to place my experience at the service of the community in this matter, if it pleases my fellow Warders."

Sir Andrew was aghast. The last person he needed underfoot was the troublemaker Vendeley, and there was no doubt in his mind that her interests did not lie in diplomacy. "This mission may well be dangerous," he protested. "I cannot guarantee the safety of a—"

"I am quite capable of looking after my own safety, sir," Rolande said sharply, then, for the benefit of the Wardership, she added in more moderate tones, "Naturally, I should not expect His Lordship's protection. I shall travel on my own account."

The others, pleased at the prospect of having one of their own included without having to sacrifice their own concerns to go themselves, wholeheartedly approved Rolande's offer, and Sir Andrew was overruled. Having gained a good deal of ground already, he thought better of pressing his advantage too far. He could think of no reason to refuse—no reason, that is, that they would find acceptable. "Then that is settled," he said curtly. "As to the other members of my party," he gave a slight emphasis to the word "my," "Frend Pierson, the hermit, has agreed to serve as guide and interpreter. His knowledge of the Yerren and the forest will be invaluable. I shall also take Jerl Smit, one of the militiamen."

"The one," Rolande said angrily, "who allowed that creature to escape us. He should be in the pillory!"

"Allowed . . . ?" said the farmer, looking at her in surprise. "I'd heard that the lad was half-killed in trying to prevent its escape."

"If he'd attended to his guard duties, instead of flirting with Sir Andrew's saucy little herbalist, the thing would have had no chance to escape!"

Flirting? Sir Andrew thought, startled. The Princess and a common laborer? Impossible, surely. But he suddenly wanted to hear Celia's views on the matter. Jerl had not returned to the barracks after his supposed recuperation. He'd made himself useful enough around the estate that Sir Andrew's steward had kept him on. When not on duty at the stockade, he could see a good deal of Katin, if she allowed it. Unlikely as that seemed, Sir Andrew thought it was as well that he'd be taking Jerl away from Thornfeld for now. . . . Aloud, he said only, "I was more to blame for the Yerren's escape than the boy—I ought not to have allowed young Ander access to the prisoner. But it is too late to redress that matter now. Smit can be of more use on this mission than in the stocks. He is the only person aside from the hermit who possesses any ability to communicate with the Yerren, he is trained in arms, and has no attachments to prevent him from leaving the colony for as long as necessary.

"And one more thing—until we reach an agreement with the Yerren, there is to be a hiatus on the burning of the forest."

"But if no more land can be cleared, how will we provide farms for those who require them?" Cavendish objected.

"If we can come to terms with the Yerren, it will be possible to clear land without having to fight for every inch of it. But we cannot hope to negotiate in good will while continuing to antagonize them."

"Well, then, we'll do what we can to stop the burning until your return, but when does Your Lordship propose to mount this expedition?" Headman Farnham asked, without, Sir Andrew noted, suggesting that the matter be put to a vote in the Wardership.

"As our circumstances do not admit of delay, I mean to set out at once—if that should meet with Mistress Vendeley's convenience."

His sarcasm was not lost on Rolande. A trek into the uncharted wilderness, with a lunatic for a guide and Sir Andrew in charge, was not in the least convenient, now or later, but she had no choice. "Of course," she said. "I shall order the necessary supplies." Still, there might be something to be gained from this fool venture, she reflected. The Yerren were attractive and exotic, and she knew there were those in the courts of the Old World who would pay dearly to add one to their private menageries. Once the Chamber had gained control in New Albin, a profitable trade could be established, and the more she knew about these Yerren the better. . . .

* * *

The forest rose around them, dark and forbidding, the great trees which had grown here for hundreds of years undisturbed hindered their progress with branches so thickly interlaced that passage had to be hacked through them. Damp earth scented the air. They could hear small animals taking flight through the underbrush at their approach and the anxious calls of the birds in the trees. *Birds?* Sir Andrew wondered. *Or do the Yerren have watchers in these trees as well?* He peered upward, but the thick foliage made it impossible to see into the treetops.

As they plodded on, the heavy growth closed in around them like a great net. Somewhere in the lush depths lurked dangerous beasts—perhaps some that the colonists had not yet encountered—and wild men and women who lived as bandits, having been driven from the settlements for various offenses. Sir Andrew looked over the rest of his party, and thought that they were as well prepared as any group could be, for an expedition into unknown territory. Rolande strode forward confidently, armed with a flintlock pistol and dagger at her belt, and another knife hidden in a sheath in her boot. Jerl forced his way through the dense underbrush, clearing the clinging branches with a hand ax. He was eager for adventure, ready to prove himself. The hermit was an old man, but one who had survived in these woods longer than anyone else. He was probably better prepared than any of them for the forest's dangers.

He had imparted what he knew of the rumored city of the Yerren, but this had proved sparse enough. *"A city untold leagues north, hidden within the treetops, protected by ferocious guardian spirits. A forest of heads beyond the falling water. A place where ageless demon birds invade the portals of protection."* It sounded like mere legend to Sir Andrew. Had Pierson not provided him with more practical advice, he would have given up the idea as the pursuit of a mere phantasm. They must follow the path of the streams that ran down from the mountain pools, the hermit said. The Yerren could find food in a wide-ranging area, but they had to dwell in proximity to water. As the party moved deeper into the forest, Pierson pointed out the places where the foliage of the trees had been cut away, to allow the Yerren hunters to use the upper branches as observation posts. He was confident that they could find one of the Yerren cities, and he held out hope as well that they would be able to reason with the Yerren. "They are a peaceable people by nature," he told Sir Andrew, "but fearless in fight when threatened."

It was a slender hope, perhaps, that Sir Andrew could convince the Yerren to join in a defense against the coming invasion, but without reinforcements, the colonists had little chance of defeating the Chamber's forces. There was nothing to lose in appealing to the Yerren, and everything to gain, as he had told the Warders. Or was it that he simply couldn't bear to stand and watch as the days drifted by, waiting helplessly for the enemy to arrive?

They made camp in the shelter of a ring of beech trees. Within the clearing, the noises of the surrounding forest seemed muffled and distant. Jerl and the hermit had gone to hunt for game in the woods around their camp. Rolande sat on a fallen log, brushing the mud off her boots with a handful of leaves. The forest, which was barely twilit during the day with what sunlight filtered through the dense foliage, was rapidly darkening as the sun set. Sir Andrew built a fire in a circle of stones, and lit one of the lanterns they had brought, but the small pool of warm light did not reach far into the gloom.

"I'm soaked halfway to my knees," Rolande complained. "Must we wade through every patch of swamp we come across?"

"It's spring—the winter runoff makes everything damp. And Pierson says we must follow the water."

Rolande pulled off her boots, wincing. "We're following a madman, if you ask me."

"You," Sir Andrew said pointedly, "didn't have to come."

"No doubt you would have preferred that. Without a representative of the *civil* authorities, there'd be no one to stop you from making your own arrangement with the Yerren—and returning with your own private army, to take control of the colony. Is that your plan?"

Sir Andrew was too astonished to answer, at first—and then too contemptuous. He turned away from her without a word, and began to build up the fire.

His silent disdain, his *dismissal* of her, infuriated Rolande more keenly than any insult he could have voiced. "You may think you're too good to answer me, My *Lord,* but you'll answer to others before long!" she snarled. If he survived the coming battle, she'd see him denounced to the Chamber for treason. She hoped they'd hang him here, where she could see it, not take him back to Albin for execution.

For a moment longer, Sir Andrew ignored her, then, with his back to her, he said with deliberation, "I don't know why you came on this journey, but it wasn't in order to protect the colony from me. Now I give you warning—this once only. I have the lives of the entire community on my hands. If you try to endanger this enterprise in any way, I shall do whatever I must to stop you."

"You will regret taking that tone with me," Rolande

said evenly, giving no sign that she was raging inwardly. Damn him, she'd said too much! He was suspicious. But he knew nothing, she told herself. Her words could have meant only that the Wardership would call him to account for his actions.

She must not allow his lordly airs to goad her into betraying herself. She knew better. But Sir Andrew stood for everything she'd hated for as long as she could remember. The carriage trade, who could beat her from their doorways, drive her from the road, lock her up and starve her with one word to the magistrates. . . . Every bitter memory of her life seemed at that moment to be Sir Andrew's fault.

She'd started life as a wharf-brat on the docks of the capital. She'd never seen her father, and her mother hadn't lasted much past Rolande's tenth birthday, succumbing to one of the recurring waves of wasting sickness that periodically swept through the slums. Rolande—who was then Jen Quick—had proved well able to take care of herself from the start. From pickpocket and cutpurse, she graduated to runner for the smugglers along the coast, before she was thirteen. By the time she was sixteen, she had a name for being smart, dangerous, and willing to dare anything, for a price.

The Dep seditionists had drawn her in with their talk of overthrowing the monarchy, the nobility, and establishing God's natural order upon the earth—rule by those whom God had graced with strength and wits and courage, not those who inherited power and wealth through no merit or sweat of their own. In such an order, Rolande thought, she would command others, and never again run from anyone. Whenever Dep preachers came to the wharves to stir up discontent among the poor, Rolande had listened eagerly. She had been discontented with her lot for her entire life, but never before had anyone suggested that she could change it. Indeed, there had never before been any way for her to do so.

To the Dep cant of self-denial and virtue she paid less heed. If their revolution succeeded, they'd no doubt enjoy the trappings of power and wealth like any other victors—and Rolande meant to be on the winning side, for once. Her fervent conversion to Dep principles, and her reputation for cunning and daring, brought her to the notice of Church leaders in the early days of planning the revolt. It was they who had taken the trouble to educate her in the ways of the world and set her up in a variety of guises, to infiltrate quarters where treason behind the scenes would be most effective.

And now, when she was so close to achieving everything she'd struggled and schemed and risked her life for, time and again, no sneering, superior *gentleman* like Sir Andrew was going to stand in her way. Let him wander the wilderness as long as he liked. He'd find some surprises waiting for him when he returned to the colony. His decision to embark on this foray had only given her the opportunity she needed, to undermine the measures he had ordered for the colony's defense, while he was out of the way. It was a pity she couldn't be there to carry out her plans herself, but Simeon was capable of attending to the tasks she'd set him.

Rolande frowned, thinking of Simeon, and wondering how soon she could rid herself of the ferret. If he were spending his time drinking and gambling while she was gone, she'd have his hide on her return. He was good at what he did, but he was too sleek by far, and too full of himself. Sooner or later, it would make him careless, and Rolande didn't mean to pay the price for his mistakes. No one, lord or lackey, was going to stop her now.

* * *

Jerl returned to the campsite with a brace of pheasants and a hare, which he spitted and set to cook over the fire. "Smit, what's become of Pierson?" Sir Andrew asked him.

Jerl looked startled. "Hasn't he been here? He said he was going to look for signs of the Yerren along the creekbed. I thought he'd be back by now."

Sir Andrew frowned. "But there's no open water here. We won't reach the stream again until we cut back around to the north."

"No, sir," Jerl said, unexpectedly. "There's some kind of brook across to the west. We heard the sound when we first set out, and he went off to find it. Shall I go look for him?"

Sir Andrew considered. "He's not likely to be lost. We'll wait a bit—" He broke off as a rustling in the trees nearby brought him to the edge of the encampment. "Frend Pierson?" he called out. There was no response except for a snapping of twigs as something large came nearer.

Jerl dropped the stick with which he was poking the fire and grabbed his musket, and Rolande's hand went to the pistol at her belt. As Jerl started toward the trees where he could see the leaves moving, the bushes shook and Katin's soarhound pup suddenly came bounding into the clearing, followed after a moment by an exasperated and muddy Katin. Her bow and quiver were slung over her shoulder, and she carried a dead squirrel, skinned and gutted. "A good even to all," she said, with an awkward bow.

Princess or no, Sir Andrew thought, *this time I'll—* "What, in the name of God, are you doing here?" he shouted. "What must I do, keep you under lock and key? Did you come all this way alone?"

"I was never far behind you, My Lord," Katin said

shamefacedly. "I'd not have made myself known, but Lucifer smelled your dinner and got away from me." At the sound of his name, the pup, who was sniffing around the campfire, looked up and yipped proudly. "Bad dog!" said Katin. He trotted to her and bounded up at her knees, wagging his tail wildly.

"How dared you follow us, when I had forbidden it?" Sir Andrew demanded. "We'll lose two days in taking you back and—"

"But you can't do that!" cried Katin. "That is—you needn't! I'll be no hindrance to you. I know the woods, and I'm trained in the hunt. I could be of use."

"But we're going into dangerous ground," Jerl said uneasily. "We don't know how the Yerren will receive us." He gazed at Katin with much the same uncritical adoration as the soarhound exhibited, Sir Andrew thought grimly.

"Everyone in New Albin is in danger!" Katin argued. "If we can't come to terms with the Yerren, we've none of us long to live, isn't that so?" she appealed to Sir Andrew. "And I can help—I know I can. I *have* to go to them." For a moment she looked as if she might cry, but then she drew herself up and looked straight at Sir Andrew. "You know you mustn't lose time, sir, and it would be of no use to take me back, besides. I'd only follow you again."

Her words were spoken matter-of-factly, not disrespectfully, but they were not the words of a dependent to her master. Sir Andrew could see Rolande listening with quickened interest to the exchange, wondering why he allowed the girl to disobey him with impunity. Though Katin played her part well, as a rule, he knew that others in Thornfeld must also be wondering about the nature of her position in his household. *I might as well have the town crier announce her true station and be done with it!* He was angry with himself for revealing before the others that she'd disregarded his wishes, but he was angrier with her.

Fixing her with a look of grave disapproval, he said sternly, "You know I promised your father that I'd look after you. You do not make it easy."

Katin flushed crimson. She understood that his rebuke was intended as an explanation that would satisfy gossipmongers, but it was directed at her as well. He had reminded her that his oath of allegiance to his King bound him to protect her now. "I'm sorry, My Lord," she said contritely. "I'll go back if you wish, but please let me stay. I didn't come just for a lark, truly." *Jerl understands,* she thought. "I felt I'd no choice."

"No more have I," sighed Sir Andrew. "I can't send you back by yourself, and we can't spare the time to escort you." And she was right that the invasion was the greater threat, and outweighed the danger of the Yerren. "You'll have to come with us. But you'll do as you're told and give no trouble, or you'll wish you'd stayed behind, before I've done with you!"

"Yes, sir," Katin said meekly. But she soon recovered her spirits. "You'll not regret it," she promised. "I'm a fine archer, I'll help feed us all." She held out the squirrel, and Jerl took it from her and spitted it along with the hare. "Where's Frend Pierson?" she asked him.

They had all forgotten the hermit. "I knew it!" Rolande exclaimed. "That old lunatic's wandered off and forgotten us. We'll never find our way home now, we'll be lost in these verminous woods forever!" She slapped furiously at a gnat. "I *told* you—"

"Nonsense!" Sir Andrew said sharply. "He'll be back when he pleases, I daresay, and we are not lost."

"*I* could find my way back without him," Katin said pertly to Rolande.

Rolande turned on her, glad of a target for her rising panic. "If you and your beau there hadn't let that cursed creature get away, we wouldn't have to roam around the woods till we lose our way. We could have questioned it and found out where their city lies, instead of hunting through the trees and being devoured by blackflies!"

For a moment, the Princess only stared in regal disbelief that a mere merchant should address her in such a manner, but then Katin, the commoner, snapped, "A fine thought, that! Did you plan to question him before or after you'd butchered him?"

"That will do," said Sir Andrew, wondering which of them he'd most like to see eaten by wolves. Possibly Jerl. "I'll go have a look for the hermit myself. Stay here, and attempt to behave with some civility. We have a long journey before us. Together."

Katin felt rather put upon. She knew that Sir Andrew expected more of her than of Rolande, but she was trying to behave as she supposed people of the lower classes did. Surely royal forbearance would be out of place in one of her assumed position. But she said, "Just as you say, My Lord." From her vest pocket she took a handful of half-crushed pennyroyal leaves and offered them to Rolande. "Here, rub some of this on your skin. It will keep most of the insects away."

Rolande looked doubtful, but accepted the herb and tried some of it on her neck. Satisfied, Katin dropped down beside Jerl, who was cutting up the cooked meat, and helped herself to a haunch of hare. Jerl looked up at Sir Andrew. "Shall I go, too, sir?"

"No, keep watch here," Sir Andrew said curtly. Picking up the lantern, he strode into the woods, glad of a reason to leave the lot of them behind and walk off his anger—and his doubts. Though he denied it, even to himself, Rolande had rekindled his own fears that he'd misjudged Pierson, that he'd committed them all to a dangerous and—worse—fruitless pursuit of the will-o'-the-wisp. Had he persuaded himself that the hermit's mind was sound, that his word was reliable, only because he so desperately wanted to believe it? It was not like him to make rash or hasty decisions, but the colony's situation did not allow for due deliberation. Had he let the need for haste cloud his judgment too far?

He forced his way through the thick growth, making a circuit roughly around the perimeter of the camp, pushing as far as he dared into the surrounding darkness. If he ventured too deep into the woods, he might lose the pale glow of the fire, and be unable to find his way back, for attempting to mark the trees to make a path was pointless in the gloom. Altogether he was gone the better part of an hour. He neither saw nor heard the brook Jerl had spoken of, and he wondered if that had indeed been the hermit's destination. No doubt it was farther afield, and they would have to wait until the light of morning to find it, if Pierson hadn't returned by then.

Jerl kept the last watch of the night, sometimes tending the fire, sometimes prowling the edge of the campsite to listen for bandits or animals. He knew, though he could not have explained how he knew, that there were no Yerren nearby.

"There's been no sign of him," he reported to Sir Andrew, as the party rose with the first dim light filtering through the overhanging branches.

"So I see. We'll search out the water you heard yesterday. We may as well start looking for him there."

Rolande brushed some of the tangles out of her hair with her hand. "I suppose we've no idea at all of where we should be going, without his advice?"

Little enough, Sir Andrew thought, but he said only, "He may be injured, or lost. We can hardly leave him behind. Lead the way, Smit." His tone made it clear that he didn't want to hear any more from Rolande on the subject of the hermit's sanity. Wisely, she held her tongue.

The ground grew spongier as they followed Jerl toward the sound of water until they finally broke through the trees to a rocky outcropping. Sir Andrew looked down over the tumbled boulders, rubbed smooth by the passage of a shallow stream. On the bare rocks, there was nothing to betray whether the hermit had come this way.

Sir Andrew divided the party into two groups, taking Katin with him, and sending Jerl and Rolande to search the terrain along the brook running upstream. "Don't go far," he told them. "If you cover half a league without seeing anything, then return here."

Sir Andrew turned downstream, with Katin at his side. They trudged through the mud, scanning the trees for the hermit's telltale crosshatches to mark the path back, but they found no sign of his passing. The sun, unshaded along the stream, beat down relentlessly, and they stopped often to drink, clinging to the great rocks that littered the bed and the banks. Sir Andrew was kneeling on a granite boulder, splashing his face with the cold water, when a gun shot sounded from upstream, and he leaped to his feet, grabbing his musket. Racing up the bank, with Katin following, he envisioned every sort of catastrophe that could have befallen the others.

When they reached the point where the stream took a sharp turn to the west, he stopped to let Katin catch up to him, and tried to decide whether it would be more risky to leave her there alone, or to let her follow into the unknown danger around the bend.

"What is it?" she panted, drawing up beside him with the pup in her arms.

"I don't know. Wait here, and stay on your guard. Don't move from this spot till I send for you, unless you must escape some danger."

Katin dutifully repressed a desire to argue, and said resignedly, "Very well. Don't worry, I'll be safe enough up there." She pointed up at the nearest tree, then dropped her pet and grabbed a low branch to pull herself up. Sir Andrew leaned his musket against the trunk and gave her a boost from below, while the pup scrambled up the tree after her. Watching for a moment as she disappeared into the dense foliage, Sir Andrew thought, *A damned good idea—I should have thought of it.* As long as she stayed still, no one could possibly find her.

He retrieved his musket and cautiously started to follow the bend in the stream, but he had not gone far before he heard Katin shouting his name. Without hesitation, he turned back. If she were in danger, his first duty was to shield her. And if she wasn't, he'd drown her in the stream like an unwanted kitten!

"It's only Jerl," Katin called, as she ran to meet him. "I saw from up there—he's looking for us. He must have fired that shot to summon us back."

A little farther on, they could both see Jerl standing atop a high boulder, apparently quite safe. When he caught sight of them, he waved his musket to urge them on, then clambered down and started toward them. There was no sign of Rolande.

"Vendeley?" Sir Andrew asked, as soon as Jerl was within earshot.

"I left her to watch—we found him—he's fallen down a hole," Jerl said anxiously. "I think he's alive still, but she said we shouldn't move him."

"A hole?" Sir Andrew demanded, as they made their

way north along the stream, with Jerl in the lead. "How—"

"Take care!" Jerl grabbed Katin as she started to push past him to see what lay ahead. "It's not solid here, there are great hollows underground. He must have fallen right through a thin patch of earth."

The stream gave way to marshland and disappeared. "It runs underground here, though the caves ahead," Jerl said. He led them by a circuitous route toward the spot where Rolande waited, leaning against a tree and staring down at something they couldn't see.

As they approached, she looked up. "He's not moved."

Sir Andrew knelt at the edge of a jagged opening in the earth, and Jerl handed him a lantern. Peering over the rim, he swung the lantern in an arc, and made out the prone form of a man at the bottom of the pit. "Give me some rope," he ordered.

"You mean to go down there?" Rolande said, surprised.

"How else do you propose to get him up here?" Sir Andrew said impatiently, as he secured one end of the rope to the nearest tree.

"The rest of the cave could fall in on you."

"It seems solid enough. It will probably hold, if you stay off it. All of you, stay back from the edge." He tossed the free end of the rope into the hole and began to climb down. Bits of dried vegetation, loose stones, and sand trickled from the rim as the rope rubbed against it.

The descent brought Sir Andrew within inches of Frend Pierson. Jerl lowered a lantern, and Sir Andrew saw that the hermit lay sprawled facedown amid a pile of debris that had broken off from the roof of the cave when he fell through. His head was resting against a cracked piece of shale, but Sir Andrew could see that he was still breathing. Examining the gash across the hermit's forehead, he was relieved to find that the bone did not appear to be broken. He'd seen wounds enough in battle to know that this one was not mortal. From the waterskin at his belt, he poured water over the wound and wiped away the dirt.

The hermit stirred and groaned. Sir Andrew pulled him up so that he leaned against the mound of fallen rock, and made him drink some of the water. He coughed a little but gradually came to his senses and looked vaguely around the cave, not seeming to notice Sir Andrew at all. At last, he asked, "Where is this place, do you know?"

"The bank collapsed, and you fell into this cavern."

The hermit glanced up at the opening above them. "Fell . . ." he said, more to himself than to Sir Andrew. "I? No, I think not. I was pushed."

"Pushed! Who pushed you?"

The hermit sounded almost amused. "The ground opened and swallowed me. When such a thing happens, the question is not 'who?' but 'why?' "

He raves, Sir Andrew thought. *The wound.* "You've been down here all night," he said gently, taking the man's arm. "Come, we must get you up out of this pit."

The hermit impatiently shook him off. "First, I must find it. You may go, you are in my way." He began searching through the loose stones which had fallen from the mound when Sir Andrew had moved him.

"Find what?" Sir Andrew demanded. "There's nothing here but rock and earth."

"And feathers," the hermit observed, picking up a long stiff plume and handing it to Sir Andrew. "No bird lost that. Yerren have been here."

"Not for some time," said Sir Andrew. "This is old." Unlike the feathers of their recent captive, and the other Yerren the colonists had slain, this one was a matted, dusty brown.

"Very old," the hermit agreed absently. He stood gazing down at the ground, seeming lost in thought.

"Well, is this what you wanted to find? You cannot stay down here longer."

"Perhaps," Pierson murmured, "but—no, I think this is it." Suddenly he seized hold of a white knob sticking out from a loose pile of rubble, and tugged at it. Dirt and leaves flew everywhere as he unearthed a thick white bone some three feet long.

Sir Andrew stared at it in astonishment. "What in God's name is that?"

"This is the reason," said the hermit. "As I told you."

Chapter 5

The way became steeper as they climbed through a series of switchbacks curving up the hill. The ground was covered with springy moss, and mushrooms sprouted from dead branches. The hermit used the long bone as a walking stick to make his passage easier, while Jerl hacked with the small ax at the foliage in their way.

They were almost ready to stop for the night when they stepped from the dense trees onto a clear patch of stony ground to find themselves looking up at a wall of water rushing over an outcropping of granite, to pool in a basin below.

Katin stared in wonder and stretched out her hand to capture some of the water. It flowed from a cavern a third of the way up the rock, and above the opening the granite continued to rise into the crest of the hill. She was well-traveled despite her youth, but never had she beheld such a marvel. "We must never let anyone take this land from us!" she said fiercely.

"Is it yours, then?" said the hermit, in a tone of polite inquiry.

Rolande laughed. "We could claim it in the name of King and Country, if we had a king, or a country."

Jerl, too, felt the exaltation that the glorious sight

stirred in Katin. "This is our country now," he said suddenly. "And we don't need a king. We've claimed it in God's name, and our own!" He spoke up so rarely that the others were startled to silence. Sir Andrew, about to rebuke him for his treasonous sentiments, instead decided to let it pass. Let him have his say—talk like that wouldn't endear him to the Princess.

Indeed, Katin turned on him angrily. "You sound like a Dep! Why didn't you stay in Albin, to butcher your betters and call it God's will?"

"I don't hold with them!" Jerl protested.

"You don't hold with the Crown either, it would seem!"

"So it is the Crown that owns the land?" the hermit asked Katin.

"Yes, by right! Who else?"

The hermit shrugged. "Does it matter? We can but borrow a place on the earth for a time. Who can own a country save the dead, who are one with the land for eternity?"

"While we live, it matters," Katin said, but she looked at Jerl as she spoke, not at the hermit.

Afraid that she would say too much, Sir Andrew drew her back from the brink of the cascade. "Come away from the edge. The stone's wet here, you could have a dangerous fall."

Perhaps she took his meaning, for she said only, "I was thinking we should give this place a name."

Sir Andrew studied the rocky hill beyond the waterfall. "It may have one already," he said, turning to Frend Pierson. "It is mentioned in the account you gave me, is it not?"

The hermit didn't seem to hear him. He gazed off into the woods, as if listening for some distant sound, but at length he answered, "It could be so. Their legends tell of a wall of water that divides the realm of flight from that of the crawling creatures below. We've come up a steep slope, and it rises more sharply ahead."

"Do you wish to rest?" Sir Andrew asked, concerned. It was easy to forget that Pierson was much older than the rest of them.

"No, no, walking does not tire me," he said absently, and fell silent again, looking into the distance with a frown.

Rolande looked up from refilling her waterskin. "Well, *I* wish to rest, if my wishes are to be consulted."

"We'll make camp soon. Let's get beyond the falls first. It may be drier there."

"Something is there, on the other side," the hermit said.

They all turned to him. "What's he blathering about now?" Rolande demanded.

"The calls of the birds have changed. Something has entered their territory and frightened them."

"*We* have," Rolande said impatiently.

The hermit shook his head. "No. Here they are quiet, waiting for us to pass by, but yonder—something threatening has come among them."

"Some animal?" Sir Andrew suggested.

"Likely enough—a wildcat, perhaps. But it could well be some of the Yerren. I had thought we would encounter them before now."

"They aren't near us," said Jerl.

Now the others turned to stare at him. "I'd know if they were—" he began, and stopped abruptly, remembering Sir Andrew's orders. Here in the forest, it hadn't seemed to matter, but Sir Andrew's look silenced him.

"On my word, they're both mad!" said Rolande.

"How the devil would *you* know what's over that hill, boy?"

Jerl vowed never to open his mouth again. It seemed every time he said anything, he was in more trouble. But the others had already heard him speak of the Yerren's powers—all except Vendeley, and if they found the city they were seeking, she'd see for herself the way the Yerren affected him. He wouldn't be able to hide it. "I can just tell when they're nearby, that's all," he mumbled.

To his relief, the hermit nodded. "Some folks have a sense for them, just as some can tell when it will rain, or when danger is nigh. It may be rare among us, but all the Yerren have some such sympathy with one another. They think us little more than animals, because we lack it."

Sir Andrew looked at him thoughtfully. "Why did you not tell me this before?"

"What does it matter? I have told you now."

"Intuition," Katin said suddenly.

The hermit shrugged again. "If you like to give it a name, that is as good a name as any other."

Insanity would be a better one, Rolande thought. "This is all most enlightening, no doubt," she said, "but we'll not get anywhere if we stand here and discuss it much longer. Are we going over there or aren't we?"

"We must," said Sir Andrew. "The city of the Yerren, if it exists at all, lies beyond that wall. We can deal with wildcats, if we must." He studied the terrain around them, plotting the best course. "We can't cross the spill here. We'll have to ford the stream at a shallower point, then cross back again just beyond the basin." He pointed to a ridge a short way to the left of the waterfall.

"I knew it, wet boots again," Rolande said glumly.

The others followed Sir Andrew onto the bare rock running along the edge of the stream as it continued for a way north from the basin. From there it rose over the surrounding land to form a ledge, leaving them a narrow passage between the side of the hill and emptiness.

They made their way onto the ridge passing just beyond the waterfall on a track about six feet wide. The land on their left dropped away sharply. Katin looked back at the cave from which the falling water rushed, but could see nothing within. A chill shiver went through her, and she told herself that it was colder here, where less sunlight could penetrate the narrow passage. It was silly to feel that something sinister was lying in wait for a chance to sneak out and attack them. But the forest itself was growing darker as the beeches and hawthorns of the lower slopes gave way to rock pines and mountain mulberry.

Sir Andrew, Rolande, and Jerl all carried their weapons at the ready, aware of how vulnerable they could be if anything should come at them on the narrow ridge climbing upward. No one spoke.

But at last they emerged from the pass onto the green clearing beyond the hill, without encountering any threat. The stream flowed rapidly down from the highlands and crossed the glade to form a small crystal pool that spilled into a cavern in the hill behind them. The pool drew the tired and dusty travelers like a lodestone.

As soon as they had dropped their packs in the shelter of the trees at the edge of the clearing, Katin ran across the grass and clover to the edge of the water. Sir Andrew called to her not to stray far, but it was already too late.

Before he'd done more than call her name, a pack of men and women dressed in half-tanned skins came swarming down from the top of the hill above the pool, lowering themselves on ropes. They made straight for Katin, with practiced speed.

"Bandits!" Jerl yelled, scrambling for his musket.

Sir Andrew was already bracing his flintlock against a boulder, aiming for the man nearest to Katin.

She started to run back toward the campsite, but she had little hope of reaching it before the first of the bandits caught her. If she could stay ahead of them long enough, she thought desperately, the others might be able to pick them off. The odds did not look favorable. There seemed to be a dozen of the bandits, armed with pistols, and her party had only three guns among them. They were far outnumbered, but they had the cover of the trees, and the bandits had to run through an open field to reach them. . . .

The sound of musket fire was deafening, and plumes of black smoke drifted past her as she raced toward the woods. One of the bandits was knocked backward by a musket ball, and another cried out in pain and scrambled back toward the dangling ropes, clutching his bloodied shoulder. Then, just as Katin thought she might make it, a tall man rose from the weeds at the edge of the stream, long hair and beard dripping. Leaping from the water, he ran with long, loping strides, catching her from behind and throwing her to the ground. Furious, Katin rolled to a crouch, groping for her dagger. She hadn't escaped the revolutionaries only to die at the hands of some mountain savage. But the man who seized her was simply too large and too strong. She succeeded only in slashing his sleeve before he clubbed the side of her head with one massive fist, so hard that she fell to the earth again, dazed and half-blinded by wavering lights and shadows. She could not even struggle as her captor pulled her to her feet, holding her up before him like a shield while he backed away toward the hillside. The soarhound flung itself at him, snarling, but he kicked it aside, into the swiftly-flowing stream. It thrashed about for a moment, then instinctively spread out its webbed legs and let the water carry it, whirling, toward the pool.

Some of the other bandits clustered around Katin and the bearded man, knowing that her companions wouldn't dare shoot in her direction, lest she be injured. The rest fled to the ropes hanging down from the ridge, out of range of musket fire from the woods.

Jerl, his musket braced in the fork of a tree, frantically fired once more at the retreating figures, but in his haste the shot went wide. By the time he'd reloaded, they were too far away, and he pulled the musket free and started after them, ignoring Sir Andrew's order to hold his place.

He was driven back by musket fire exploding around him, and before he could try again, Sir Andrew pulled him out of the clearing and threw him against the trunk of a tree, then stood barring his way, the unyielding commander. "When I order you to stand your ground, Smit, you will *not move.*"

Wild-eyed, Jerl tried to push past him, but Sir Andrew unhesitatingly knocked him back with a sharp blow of the stock of his musket to Jerl's chest. Fighting for breath, Jerl gasped, "We can't let them take her!"

"We can't stop them by getting killed! Look up there!" Furious, he pushed Jerl to the edge of the woods and pointed to the top of the hill. Silhouetted against the pale evening sky, a line of figures crouched, muskets at the ready. Anyone who crossed the open clearing would be an easy target, while the enemy could withdraw over the crest in a moment.

Jerl watched in an agony of helplessness as two of

the bandits dragged Katin between them to the foot of the hill. "What can we do?" he whispered.

Sir Andrew's voice rang with frustration. "We'll go after them and get her back, but we'll have to wait. And if you want to help, you'll follow orders, you damned fool!"

"Yes, sir," Jerl said, his voice shaking.

"Patience," said the hermit. "If they wished to kill her, they would have done so at once."

Jerl knew they were right, but he remembered that despair, too, can kill, as he watched the two bandits truss the limp Katin in a net and raise her, supported by her captors, up the sheer side of the hill.

"Can you swim?" Sir Andrew asked him suddenly.

Startled, Jerl shook his head.

"Then go back the way we came. I daresay they'll be gone before you reach the waterfall, but I'll leave a trail for you to follow."

The hermit looked toward the rocky hillside, where the bandits were clambering over the ridge, pulling the ropes up after them. "That is a sheer climb—without a rope it would be almost impossible. And even if you could make it, it would take longer than going around the hill."

"That's why I mean to go *through* the hill," Sir Andrew said, shouldering his musket. "It's the only chance of catching them." He turned to Rolande. "Can *you* swim?"

She stared at the mouth of the cavern, where the stream flowed into the darkness and disappeared. "You can't—you don't know if it goes all the way through!"

"We know water's coming out the other side."

"But you don't know how deep—or—" She took a step back. "You can't go out there *now*—they're probably still watching from the top of the hill, waiting for us to come out in the open. They'd shoot us down before we were halfway across the field!"

"Maybe. But they wanted to get away, I think, more than they wanted to kill us. I can't wait for them to get across the top with her. Are you coming?"

"If you think I'd get myself shot—or drowned—chasing after that little chit of yours, you're as crazy as they are!" She jerked her head at Jerl and the hermit.

Sir Andrew smiled. "No," he said, "I didn't think you would." He turned and started off across the clearing, at a run.

Rolande stared after him, hoping to see him struck down by a rain of musket balls, but Sir Andrew ran on, unchallenged. *The bastard's going to make it!* She ground her teeth in fury. How dare he call her a coward! She, who'd been known for her daring since she was ten! Her common sense was telling her, *Let him go—he'll be killed—you'll be rid of him!* But her pride would not allow her to let herself be outdone by Sir Andrew.

Watching her, the hermit offered her a lantern, and she took it without a word and raced across the field after Sir Andrew. Unhampered by a musket, she caught up before he reached the pool, and the two ran on until they could hug the hillside, safe from attack from above. The soarhound, having struggled from the pool, was gazing up the cliff wall, yelping and shivering, its tail between its legs.

Without speaking to one another, they stripped down to their shirts and breeches and waded into the icy water. Holding their weapons and powder over their heads to keep them dry, they struggled not to lose their balance in the chest-deep water, as the force of the current grew stronger, flowing down through the cavern.

It was dark, not quite black, with the light flickering from the opening behind them. But soon that was shut out from view, and cold gloom descended on them. Rolande's lantern only allowed them to see the dark, wet walls that closed them in. The cavern was smaller than she'd thought, the stone ceiling only a foot or so above their heads. The walls of the cave jutted out, leaving scant leeway on either side of the channel cut by the stream, too narrow for a person to negotiate. Now and again, a tiny unnaturally white fish floated by, making Rolande pull back with distaste. They looked like the ghosts of fish, just what she'd expect to find in this stream's grave.

Suddenly she cried out and lurched forward, nearly dropping her pistol and powder, as something sleek and wet gripped her leg and held on, with sharp, piercing claws, pulling her off balance. Sir Andrew grabbed her arm to steady her as she flailed at the creature with her pistol butt, the lantern swinging wildly from her arm. She didn't dare fire the weapon in here, where the ball could ricochet back at her from the walls, or the very sound could bring down a rockslide upon them. With a yelp of pain, the soarhound let go and fell with a splash into the stream, floundering and paddling frantically till it managed to crawl up on the slippery ledge at the side. It looked reproachfully at Rolande, shook water from its coat, and sneezed.

"I'll drown that filthy little vermin!" She started toward the pup, but it backed away from her along the ledge, showing its teeth.

"Let be!" Sir Andrew ordered. "We've no time to lose—keep going, and hold that lantern steady. If it goes out, keep one hand pressed against the wall and move forward. Don't stop."

She didn't want to keep following him, but she did want to get out of this stone tomb as soon as possible—there they agreed. "I must be out of my mind to be doing this. We're all crazy on this godforsaken journey."

"If we save her, I'll see that you're rewarded," Sir Andrew said tersely.

"I'll see that you keep your word," Rolande shot back. "And who is this she-brat, that you'd lose precious time, and risk your life to get her back? Isn't your great mission to the feather folk more important than one little malapert minx?"

Her mockery was coming uncomfortably close to the truth, and he put her off with an insult that was sure to make her forget Katin. "If you're afraid, Vendeley, you can go back. You're not one of my militiamen, you don't have to follow me."

If only she could shoot him and lay the blame on the bandits! But it was still unsafe to fire a weapon in the close confines of the cavern. Sensing that she'd touched a sore spot, though, she probed further, refusing to be turned aside by his goading. "There was something odd about those bandits, too," she persisted.

"You find degrees of oddness among such villains?" From his tone it was clear he thought her little better than the cutthroats they faced.

"Since you think me such a scoundrel, perhaps you should listen to my opinion on the subject. Why did they take the girl?"

"You know why—she's a prize, young and fair." Saying the words brought more anxiety to his heart, and he picked up his pace, almost losing his footing on the slippery, mud-covered rock, till he forced himself to slow down again.

"The rest of us aren't so decrepit and ill-favored that we'd not fetch a good price—except your friend Pierson, perhaps," Rolande argued. "Why not take the lot of us, then?"

"We were too well armed. They'd have had to risk losing too many, trying to take us all."

"If they already had the girl? They could have forced us to surrender by threatening to slit her throat. But suppose they didn't think they could keep us all secure, get us back to their camp and hold us there—why didn't they take our goods? For those living wild, they'd be valuable, and they had the girl as surety. Mark my words, they wanted her only. Why was that, My Lord?"

"I daresay they know I'd pay a—high—" he had almost said *royal,* "ransom for her. How they learned that I can't say. They must have their informants in the Colonies, and when I find them out, I'll see them flayed in the marketplace!"

"But if they knew that," said Rolande, "they'd know that I could send word to my people to pay a goodly ransom for me. Why not—"

Sir Andrew couldn't conceal his irritation any longer. "I don't know! *I* claim no special understanding of the reasoning of criminals!" Trust Vendeley to make his apprehensions worse than they were before. *Had* someone put them up to abducting Katin? If so, who, and why? Did someone know the truth?

Rolande smiled to herself in the darkness. Her shot had hit home. He was hiding something, and that meant he had a weakness she could use.

The water grew deeper, threatening to reach his shoulders. Time seemed suspended, and Sir Andrew felt as if he had been slogging through the cavern forever, that there would never be an end to it. His legs were numb from the cold, his arms nearly so, from carrying the heavy musket over his head, and he wondered whether he'd be in a state to do any good by the time he emerged.

But suddenly, as they waded around an outcropping, the glint of light reflected off the water somewhere ahead of them, beckoning like a beacon. The water level began to drop, as the stream ran down through the ragged border of rock, still reaching to their thighs, but making walking easier than it had been before. Sir Andrew increased his speed, splashing toward the opening, and Rolande struggled to keep up with him, relieved that they were finally about to escape from their stone prison.

Indeed, when he stopped abruptly at the end of the cavern, she almost bumped into him. As she stumbled to a halt, he pointed to the opening, bright with sunshine. Water rushing by their feet, poured through the gap and dropped below.

"We're over the waterfall," she said. "It did go all the way through."

Sir Andrew braced himself against the rough wall of the cavern and peered over the edge. "Now we have to get down there somehow."

"That shouldn't be difficult," Rolande said smugly, "we'll just jump down. It's not great distance, and the water's deep enough. That is, I shall jump, but if you're afraid, you needn't follow me." She'd leaped from many piers in her day, from the sides of ships, from the roofs of warehouses overhanging the harbor, when no other means of escape was at hand. The fact that she'd been much younger at the time, she didn't bother to consider now.

Sir Andrew raised an eyebrow, then, with a final look at the water streaming over the edge, he said, "Very well, give me your pistol. You jump, and I'll drop our weapons down to you." He pressed himself back against the wall so she had room to pass, not believing for a moment that she'd make good on her boast.

Looking at the water rushing over the edge, Rolande regretted her rashness, but she wasn't going to admit as much to Sir Andrew. Shouldering by him, she handed him the pistol, then poised for a moment on the edge of the precipice.

The force of the water swept her over the side before she had a chance to change her mind, and she found herself falling wildly. *Sir Andrew is going to pay for this,* she thought, as she landed, flailing, in the basin, and struck for shore. When she had climbed to the point on the path closest to the falls, where Katin had reached to touch the water, lost in wonder at the sight, Sir Andrew called to her from above. He lowered the musket, stock first, and when it dangled as far as he could get it, he swung it toward her and released it. She caught it easily, and he tossed her the pistol, then jumped down, telling himself, *If that baggage can do it, I can.*

He had barely scrambled onto the rocky path when ropes dropped from the top of the hill and two forms descended alongside the waterfall toward the very place where Rolande waited. Sir Andrew grabbed his musket back concealed himself behind the boulders at the basin's edge, while Rolande disappeared silently into the underbrush. As the bandits approached the ground, Rolande grabbed one, pulling him from the rope, and slid her knife between his shoulder blades with too practiced a skill, then let his lifeless body drop and helped herself to the pistol at his belt. Sir Andrew had run up behind the other and struck the back of his head with the stock of his musket. Then he snatched not only the pistol but the rawhide jacket from the fallen man and threw it on over his dripping shirt. Rolande, observing what he was about, did the same. As they dragged the bandits into the bushes and took their place at the base of the cliff, the bearded brigand and one of his companions appeared at the top of the hill, and began climbing down the ropes. Between them they supported the net that held Katin, which was being lowered from above.

Sir Andrew braced his musket against the rock face of the hill, but he didn't dare fire it yet. Its aim was too uncertain, and he couldn't risk hitting Katin. If they could dispose of these two as they had the others, without alerting their comrades, so much the better. A sidelong glance at Rolande, caressing the hilt of her dagger, assured him that he had no need to tell her what to do. How a merchant came by assassin's skills like hers was a question for another time.

But luck, or the sixth sense of those who live by their wits, made the bearded bandit look down when he was still a third of the way from the floor of the forest. As soon as he had a good look at Sir Andrew and Rolande, he shouted, "Jump!" to his companion, and dropped from the rope before Sir Andrew had the chance to aim and fire. A moment later the other brigand did the same, but this time Sir Andrew swung out with the musket and caught him across the shins as he launched himself away from the hill.

The bearded man crashed to the ground, disappearing into the foliage. Sir Andrew sighted on the waving leaves, but then lowered his musket, reluctant to warn the other bandits by the sound of musket fire. Let him run away, the important thing was to get Katin down before the rest of the pack could reach her. As the other bandit tumbled to the soft earth, Rolande threw herself on him, grabbing him by the hair and yanking him up, the knife to his throat. She was amazed to see that he was just a boy, twelve or thirteen perhaps. "Why, lad, you're too young to be carrying off pretty maids—you'd not know what to do with her if you got her."

The boy spat. Rolande laughed and jerked him around toward the path.

But their caution had been to no avail. Several more bandits appeared at the top of the hill, perhaps alerted by their leader's shout. Catching sight of Sir Andrew below, they fired down at him, but the distance was too great for them to aim with any accuracy. He backed up against the hillside, protected by a shelf of rock overhead, and Rolande and her prisoner retreated behind a stand of boulders. Seeing her with the boy, the bandits hadn't fired at her, but she was taking no chances.

Then the bearded bandit rushed from the underbrush, pistol drawn, aiming point-blank at Sir Andrew.

He couldn't ready his musket or draw his pistol in time to prevent the other man from shooting. "Don't try it," the bandit advised him. "I can't miss you at this range." To Rolande, he said, without looking around, "Let the boy go if you want this one alive."

Fleetingly, Rolande was tempted to refuse, and let him do his worst. It would suit her very well if the bandits rid her of His Lordship. But then she saw that the others had started to descend the cliff face. They were too many—the only way to control them was to control their leader, and for that she needed Sir Andrew. Besides, even bandits could bear witness against one, and she didn't intend to betray the colony before a horde of witnesses. Best to hold to her alliance with Sir Andrew—for now.

At the bandit's command, she thrust the boy away from her and threw down her weapons. He gestured for her to go stand beside Sir Andrew, and again she obeyed, pretending to stumble, on the way, on the loose rocks on the path. Bent over for only a moment, she whipped the knife from her boot and let it fly, to sink with some force into the bandit's shoulder. He gave a grunt of pain, and the pistol wavered in his hand. He recovered quickly, but Sir Andrew had just time enough to race to his side, pistol in hand, and hold the weapon to the man's head.

Rolande retrieved her weapons, surprised that the boy hadn't taken the chance to grab them. But he had only backed away, watching wide-eyed as Rolande and Sir Andrew seized control of the encounter. *Scared,* she thought with contempt. *By his age, I'd lost count of the ones I'd killed.* It was an exaggeration, but more of fact than of spirit.

The bandit had managed to pull Rolande's knife from his shoulder, but with both Sir Andrew and Rolande holding him at gunpoint, he had no chance to use it. Sir Andrew disarmed him and pointed to his comrades, frozen halfway between the ridge and the ground. "Tell them to throw down their weapons," he ordered. Did the man have that much control over his band? It was essential to Sir Andrew's plans that he find out.

To his satisfaction, on the brigand's command, muskets and pistols clattered onto the rocks and splashed into the basin. Then, as the others started to climb back toward the top of the hill, Sir Andrew said, "Tell them to stay in sight. I'm going to bring the girl down. When I reach her, they're to let her down—carefully!" Without someone to guide her descent, Katin would be dashed against the stone hillside, and Sir Andrew could not trust anyone else with the task.

Rolande first tied the boy, then lashed the man's hands together with pieces cut from one of the dangling ropes. No sooner were their captives secure than Sir Andrew grabbed the other rope and started to climb. "If any harm comes to her," he said to Rolande, in a matter-of-fact tone, "throw him into the basin."

Katin, slowly recovering her senses, had no idea what was happening below. Her head ached, she felt weak and sick and very confused. She seemed to be suspended in a giant web, waiting for some monstrous spider to return and devour her. She thought she could hear her puppy crying, somewhere above her . . . was he caught in the web, too?

Now that the bandits had deserted her, the rope from which she was hung swayed in the wind, increasing her giddiness. With an effort that exhausted her, she grasped a stone outcropping and anchored herself against the rock wall, and it was thus that Sir Andrew found her, clinging like a moth, when he finally came level with her. Finding a foothold in the rough stone, he balanced himself so that he was able to take hold of her. In God's name, why was she so still . . . ?

She had to warn him lest he, too, be ensnared in the deadly web. "Go back," she whispered. "Kill the spider. It's coming for us."

"Don't be afraid," he said, the fear in his own heart stilled by the sound of her voice. "I have you. Let go, and hold to me." Blinking in bewilderment, Katin reached for him through the holes in the netting, and weakly grasped his sleeve, then suddenly clutched his arm and said, almost steadily, "Carry on, then, Lord Marshal." Supporting her slight weight with one arm, and holding to the rope with the other, Sir Andrew began the precarious descent with Katin clinging tightly to him.

Upon reaching the ground, he found Rolande engaged in apparently amiable conversation with the brigand chief, who sat with his back against a boulder. Jerl and Frend Pierson had arrived as well, having made their way back along the ridge. The hermit had bandaged the bandit's shoulder, and was building a fire of brushwood and pinecones. Jerl stood guard, with his musket aimed at the prisoners.

Sir Andrew's first concern was Katin. He carried her

to the edge of the falls, and cut her free of the netting, then bathed her face and bruised temple, making her drink from his cupped hands.

Jerl tried to join them, but returned to his post at Sir Andrew's command. Clutching his musket, he glared at the bandit. "If you've hurt her—"

Ignoring him, the bandit addressed Sir Andrew. "Call off your mastiff," he snapped. "We didn't harm the girl. We had our agreement, and we acted strictly by it."

The icy water revived Katin quickly. She gained her feet, with Sir Andrew's help, and said courteously, "I'm quite all right now, thank you." *A true Obelen,* Sir Andrew thought. She had not shed a tear throughout the entire ordeal.

But only when she was away from the slippery brink of the falls, and seated safely at the fireside, did he turn his attention to the bandit leader. "What is this *agreement* you speak of?" he demanded.

"Oh, look, there he is!" Katin cried suddenly, pointing shakily to the mouth of the waterfall. Clinging to the narrow ledge of rock at the opening of the cave, the soarhound was gazing down at them and wriggling with indecision. Its cries could not be heard over the noise of the falls, but even in the deepening gloom they could see it yapping and throwing back its head to howl. While Katin had been perched on the cliffside, it had been content to wait, but now it felt abandoned, and it was determined to let the entire forest know of its distress. It looked over the edge, looked at Katin again, then shook itself a final time and hunched down to edge to the very lip of the precipice. Katin called, "Lucifer! No!" but in a moment it had launched itself into the air above the waterfall.

Its webbed legs caught the air like sails, and instead of plummeting to the earth it glided in a wide arc out over the water, curved about, descended, and landed—none too gracefully—in the middle of the deep basin.

Katin was on her feet at once, and nearly reached the waterside before Sir Andrew caught her. "Let me go—I can swim!" she insisted.

Sir Andrew kept a firm grip on her arm. "I know," he said, thinking of her escape from the *Golden Dove,* "but you're in no condition to do so now. I forbid it."

Katin stopped struggling, and immediately realized that her head was throbbing afresh, and that she was weak and giddy once again. "Yes, sir," she said sadly, watching the pup floundering in the water. It had drawn in its legs and was attempting to swim, but the webs only seemed to weigh it down. It didn't appear to be sinking, but it wasn't making much progress either. "Jerl . . . ?" Katin said.

"I can't swim," Jerl told her miserably. He hated himself. He couldn't do *anything* to win her regard. He hadn't helped to rescue her, he couldn't even fetch her pup out of a pond—she'd think he was bloody *useless.*

Sir Andrew sighed. The last thing he wanted to do was get soaked to the skin in freezing water again, to save Her Highness's damned dog. And he knew that she wouldn't dream of asking such a thing of him. But after what the girl had been through, he couldn't stand by and let her watch her pet drown. She looked white and shaken enough now—and heartbreakingly brave. "All right, don't fret," he said resignedly, and sat down on a rock to pull off his boots.

Jerl felt something tap his shoulder, and turned, startled, to see Frend Pierson poking him with the long white bone he carried. "Take it, lad," the hermit said, sounding amused.

Puzzled, Jerl accepted the bone, looked at it for a moment, then threw his musket to Rolande and dashed to the waterside. "May I, sir?" he asked Sir Andrew. "I think I can reach him."

Sir Andrew was more than willing to let him try. At worst, he'd have to drag both boy and dog out of the water. Jerl waded in as deep as he dared, and measured the distance to the soarhound, which was now resting on its outstretched webs and panting. The bone fell short. Jerl tried to edge closer, the water reaching to his collarbone.

"Take care!" said Katin.

"Don't drown yourself," Sir Andrew suggested laconically.

Suddenly, Jerl backed out of the basin, raced up the bank and returned to wade in again, feeling the bottom ahead of him with the bone. Satisfied that he could go no farther, he threw the bandit's net out over the pup, snagging it easily, then hooked the end of the net with the bone and triumphantly drew the tangle of cords and splashing limbs within his reach. Moments later, he laid the dripping soarhound in Katin's lap.

She clutched it to her, laughing. "Oh, thank you, Jerl—that *was* clever—" she began, then had to stop because the pup was licking her face so wildly. But Jerl was satisfied.

Sir Andrew herded them both back to the fireside.

Gesturing to the bandit leader, Rolande said, "Lorin here has a tale to tell you. I was right about your mysterious moppet. Someone wants that one, though God knows why."

"Is that true?" Sir Andrew demanded of the man, ignoring Rolande's gibe.

Lorin grunted, but made no attempt to deny it. He glanced narrowly at Rolande in a way that suggested he feared her more than Sir Andrew, and noting this,

Sir Andrew said suspiciously, "You two have met before, have you?"

Lorin shook his shaggy head. "This one's reputation is known in many quarters."

"How so?"

With another sidelong look at Rolande, the bandit said, "There's rumors that she's not one to trifle with. So, we don't."

Interesting, Sir Andrew thought. But this was not the time to pursue that subject. "Who made an agreement with you to abduct Katin Ander?"

"I don't know."

Sir Andrew grabbed him by the front of his greasy leather vest and said slowly, "I am not one to be trifled with either." To a man with a deep knife-wound, his grip must have been painful. He gave the bandit a shake, and let him drop. "Answer me!"

"I *don't* know, I tell you. It was a black-haired man hired us—he didn't give his name!"

Almost afraid to hear the answer, Sir Andrew asked, "Why did he want the—girl?"

Lorin laughed. "Why, he didn't say, but I think I could guess. Can't you?"

Suddenly Rolande stood over him, dagger in hand. "Stop wasting time," she hissed. "If you know my reputation, you know I'll slit your gullet and read the answer in your entrails, if need be. Who was it?"

Why does she want to know? Sir Andrew wondered uneasily, as the bandit looked from one of them to the other, then, seeing no help for it, muttered, "Devil Jack, we call him. He's known to others of us as Black Jack, in other places. But his true name I don't know."

"Then what does he look like?" Rolande pressed.

"How am I to tell? He comes always by night, swathed in a great cloak, and keeps his face hidden. I could only see his hair was dark."

Impatiently, Rolande slapped the dagger against her palm.

"Middling tall . . ." Lorin said nervously. "Spare-framed, I think. I might know his voice if I heard it again—he's an oily-tongued fellow. But if he stood before me now, I'd not know him from his face, so I tell you." The bandit shrugged painfully. "I only know he pays in gold. More than that I don't want to know of him."

Rolande sheathed her dagger and turned away from him. "You were right," she said to Sir Andrew, indifferently. "Some flesh-peddler who trades in green girls. You'll never find him."

That might be—indeed, it was the likeliest explanation—but Sir Andrew didn't mean to let the matter rest there. This man, whoever he was, could be a threat to the Princess. If he could be hunted down, Sir Andrew would do it. But there was no more he could do about that now. He doubted that Lorin knew any more than he'd told them—and even if he did, Sir Andrew decided, it might be as well if he said no more before the others. Vendeley was too curious about Katin already.

But there was another matter he *could* deal with now.

Rolande had, in fact, lost interest in Katin. It was the mysterious intriguer who concerned her now—and unlike Sir Andrew, she recognized him from the bandit's description, for he'd had dealings with folk like these many times, at her behest, to further the cause they were sent to undertake. But she hadn't put him up to this—what the hell was his purpose, then? She'd watched him well enough to see that he lusted after Katin, but she knew that he lusted after gold even more. Why would he part with a fortune merely to please himself with the girl, when there were other ways he could go about it?

And beyond that was the fact that the bandits, in the manner of their attack, had made no distinctions among the members of the party. Simeon had put her life at risk as well as the others', and that meant he'd been willing to risk her wrath to accomplish his ends, whatever they were. Had the bandits really been sent to kill *her,* and finding the task too dangerous, decided to help themselves to the girl instead? Lorin wouldn't have dared to tell her that. . . . But she couldn't question him further before Sir Andrew and the rest of them. She gave him a narrow-eyed look that said as clearly as words, *I've not done with you yet.*

The bandit shifted uncomfortably in his bonds. "Look here—I've told you what I know," he said to Sir Andrew. "And I could get my throat cut for it. Let us go. You've got the girl. You'll see no more of us, my word on it."

Sir Andrew looked down at him thoughtfully. "All in good time," he said. "We've another matter to settle first."

Lorin scowled. "You can't take us back and hang us. My people wouldn't let you get clear of the forest."

"No? I don't think they'll attack while we have you at gunpoint." Sir Andrew waved the threat aside, as if such arrant nonsense were beneath his attention. "I could hang you, make no mistake, but you'd be of no use to me dead. I intend to hire you."

Chapter 6

They followed the silver trail of the stream north, where it led them once again into deep woods. Katin was unusually quiet and subdued as she paced beside the hermit, listening with serious attention when he pointed out useful herbs and flowers to her. But she was quick enough, when her soarhound flushed a pheasant or a hare from the brush, to send an arrow after the creature, and more often than not her shot found its mark. They were soon laden with game enough to keep them for some days.

"I'll make us a stew with wild garlic and onion and carrot," Katin promised.

"Don't tell me that Carl taught you that?" asked Sir Andrew. He was pleased that they need not make camp in time to send out a hunting party before dark. They'd be able to travel farther, and even the soarhound was earning its keep.

"I'm not above learning a thing or two from your cook," said Katin, kneeling to pick some fat white mushrooms. But when she reached for a sprig of blue-purple flowers, sprouting from a hairy, dark green stalk, the hermit caught her arm before she could pluck it.

"Not that one, girl."

"But isn't it mendersleaf?" she asked, surprised.

"False mendersleaf—look at the yellow patch there. Look, but don't touch it. Those leaves hold a deadly poison. You'd have only to crush them in your hand to fall into fits and die in agony."

Katin hastily stood and walked on, but Rolande dropped back just long enough to have a look at the plant called false mendersleaf.

It was after another half day's traveling that Jerl, cutting through the underbrush with his hand ax, broke through into a clearing and suddenly drew up short, staring around him in disbelief. Then he shouted for the others, and when they crowded around him, he pointed wordlessly to the trunk of a nearby tree.

"What is it?" Katin breathed. "It's looking at us."

"It's only a carving of some sort," Rolande said brusquely. "Don't be a fool."

Katin stiffened. "I see that. But what does it mean?"

Pushing by them, Frend Pierson examined the two-foot-tall face that was incised into the bole of the tree, running his fingers carefully over the weathered image. The shape was oval, tapering from a broad brow to a fierce mouth, its teeth bared in a threatening snarl. The nose was slender, and the eyes a graceful almond shape. Strange whorls decorated the cheeks and spiraled out to form stylized wings on either side of the face.

"A steward of terror carved by stone in the living wood," said the hermit.

"There are more of them ahead." Sir Andrew pointed to another, several yards away, and immediately Jerl and Katin started toward it.

Beyond that they found still another.

"What do they mean?" Katin repeated, when all the party stood together before the third image.

Sir Andrew turned to the hermit. "Could these be the demon guardians the legends tell of?"

But it was Jerl who answered. "They are spirits of protection and vengeance," he said slowly, his voice strangely husky. He reached out to touch the brow of the stern, staring image.

"Frightening faces to scare away fools," Rolande scoffed, though she did find the carvings unsettling. It was because they proved Sir Andrew was right, she told herself. No mere creature had created these images—the Yerren were indeed people of some sort, and that could bode ill for her plans.

Jerl did not seem to hear. "They watch," he said. "They enfeeble the souls of the enemy, and turn their blood to water. They turn shadows to adversaries, and adversaries to shadows. They devour the heart from within and leave no wound. Let none dare to cross their gaze, save the defenders and the defended. For . . ." Then he starting babbling unintelligibly.

With a curse, Rolande pulled him away from the tree and shook him furiously. "Stop that raving, you half-witted loon! What's the matter with you!"

Since he had been about to do much the same thing, Sir Andrew saw no reason to interfere—but Katin did. "Leave him alone!" she cried, and flew at Rolande fiercely, trying to drag her away from Jerl. "Insolent, scurrilous upstart—"

Rolande pushed her away, only to find the soar-hound clawing and snapping at her shins. Enraged, she kicked the beast aside, shouting at Sir Andrew, "Devil take it, if you don't control that brat of yours, I will, I'm warning you!"

"Stop him!" yelled the hermit.

Katin screamed.

Jerl was coming at Rolande, his ax raised to strike.

She whirled about, in time to dive under the swinging blade, and pulled the pistol from her belt as she scrambled to her feet. But Sir Andrew had already seized Jerl from behind, pinioning his arms, as the hermit took the ax from his unresisting hands. He did not struggle with Sir Andrew, but fell limp, a dead weight in his grasp, and crumpled to the ground when Sir Andrew released him. He looked as white and lifeless as an empty shell.

Rolande stood over him, pistol cocked. "Is he dead?" she demanded. "I don't want to waste ammunition on a corpse."

The hermit knelt by Jerl, leaning over him protectively. "He is alive," he said. "And I suggest that you leave him alive, if you hope to have any dealings with the Yerren."

Katin felt faint. Her head throbbed where the bandit had struck her, and suddenly she was unbearably thirsty. She dropped to her knees beside the hermit and glared up at Rolande. "If you shoot him," she said thickly, "I'll kill you myself, you vicious bitch."

"Stand up and say that," Rolande suggested, smiling. "What's the good of hitting someone who's already on her knees?"

"Katin, keep still," Sir Andrew said tiredly. "No one's going to shoot Smit. Although," he added, with feeling, "I'm sorely tempted to, myself."

"It wasn't his fault," Katin protested. "He was possessed." She appealed to Frend Pierson. "Isn't that so?"

"Very likely," he agreed. "He was speaking in Yerren. He said, 'Beware, intruder. Beware the boundary, beware the power of the guardians. If their eyes behold you, terror will be your companion, waking and sleeping. Fear will follow you by day, and haunt your dreams by night. Begone, intruder.' I never taught him such words, and where else could he have learned them?"

Rolande shook her head, and Sir Andrew knew what she was thinking. They had only Pierson's word for it that Jerl had been speaking anything but gibberish. But at least those carved heads bore witness that they were in Yerren territory, he thought.

Rolande reluctantly put away her pistol, and said to Sir Andrew, "Very well, if you want to take the trouble to stand guard over this one, it's your affair. But I don't intend to be chopped into shreds by him." She took Jerl's weapons, then cut a length from a coil of rope and bound his hands behind him. He didn't stir, and no one else made a move to stop her. Even Katin could see the sense in such precautions.

Watching Rolande, it occurred to Sir Andrew that she was the one person on the expedition who *hadn't* caused trouble, so far. On the contrary, she'd been of considerable help. Could he have misjudged her? "You've not reminded me that you warned me the boy was mad," he said dryly. "I appreciate your forbearance."

Rolande shrugged, amused. "It hardly seemed necessary."

Sir Andrew turned on Katin. "As for you, I expect you to apologize to Mistress Vendeley."

Katin bristled. "She'd no call to—"

"Katin!" In a tone that had brought order to troops of soldiers half-crazed with battle frenzy, Sir Andrew repeated, "Apologize to Mistress Vendeley."

Unsteadily, Katin rose to her feet. She didn't feel in the wrong, but she would not openly defy Sir Andrew. "I beg your pardon," she said, as much to him as Rolande. "I didn't mean to give trouble."

"If not for Vendeley, I would most likely be dead now, and you would certainly still be in the hands of those forest vermin," Sir Andrew went on. "She was more responsible for your rescue than I, and risked her life with less reason. You will show her proper respect."

No one had told Katin of Rolande's part in her rescue, and once Sir Andrew had done so, she was both astonished and ashamed. "I—I'm most grateful to you," she said haltingly to Rolande. "Please forgive my behavior. I'm not myself. I think I'm in a fever." She touched her temple and winced. She was still badly bruised.

"No doubt you'd do the same for me," Rolande said contemptuously, and turned away from her, well pleased at the turn events were taking. Between the bandits and the crazed farmboy, she had no need to sabotage Sir Andrew's grand venture. It would fail of its own accord.

But the cream of the jest was that she had inadvertently redeemed herself in Sir Andrew's eyes, by delivering Lorin into his hands. Didn't the fool realize that she'd had no choice but to act as she did? Well, let him believe what he liked, let him believe he could trust in her—she was not going to undeceive him. If he was blinded by his own gentlemanly code of behavior, so much the better. It would give her another advantage over him.

"You should have told me you were ill," Sir Andrew was saying reproachfully to Katin. "Can't you brew that remedy of yours for yourself, if your head pains you?"

"It wasn't bad before. . . ." Would the tisane work for the pain caused by a blow? Katin had no idea. "I could try, I suppose. I've woodruff and willow bark. But I'd have to boil water."

Sir Andrew nodded. "We'll rest here, then. We can't

very well go on till we get Smit on his feet, in any case."

At this, the hermit rose and said, "I cannot agree. Even if we must carry the boy, we should take him away from these figures. It is their influence that seized him."

"But perhaps that was only because he touched it," Katin suggested.

"That may be, but it is as well to be sure. The farther off from these things, the better."

Sir Andrew sighed. He did not believe that faces of carved wood had the power to drive a man mad, he had no wish to try to drag Jerl through the woods, and he meant for Katin to have a rest before she walked any farther. "If we go on, we're as like as not to come across more of them," he pointed out.

The hermit considered this, looking around the clearing thoughtfully. "When I was a sailor. . . ." he murmured, then fell silent, seeming to forget the others entirely. He scratched a line in the earth, then took up the rest of the coil of rope that Rolande had used to bind Jerl, and tied one end to a branch of the tree bearing the sinister head.

"What in the devil's name is he doing now?" Rolande asked, as the hermit walked with the rope to the line he had made, then turned to Katin and said, "Come here and hold this."

Katin obeyed, and Sir Andrew, meeting Rolande's glance, said only, "He's measuring something, it would seem."

"I see no sense in it."

"Neither do I, but I see no harm in it. I'm going to make a fire." After a moment, Rolande joined him in gathering up kindling and deadwood.

The hermit took another rope and repeated his maneuver with the second carven tree, again bringing the rope back to the line he had drawn. This time he called to Rolande to take hold of it.

Curious, she dropped her armload of sticks and joined him, standing opposite the second tree. "Is there a purpose to this web you're weaving?" she asked with exaggerated patience.

"I believe that we may be inside a great circle, and if that is so, we must seek its center." He secured another rope to the third tree, and walked back to the line once more.

"Why?" Rolande demanded.

Holding his rope at the point where its length crossed the others, he went back to the tree and untied it. "Patience. I have nearly finished," he said, measuring his rope against hers, then against Katin's. Then he gathered up the ropes and said, "If the trees were in a line, then all the ropes would measure the same length when they crossed this mark. If the trees were chosen by chance, then the three ropes would have very different lengths. But the distance between the trees and the lengths of the ropes suggest a definite pattern. They are laid out in a circle—if there are enough of them. It may just be an arc."

Sir Andrew was now attending to his words carefully. When he had hung their cooking pot from a spit over the fire, he joined the others and asked, "Then if I were to walk over there," he pointed to his right, "I should find another of these heads?"

"That is so."

"Very well." Turning away from the direction they had been proceeding, Sir Andrew crossed the open ground and disappeared into the trees. Rolande pulled her gun from her belt and held it ready in her hand, as if expecting something to break from the woods and attack in response to his intrusion, but nothing stirred.

"It is there," Sir Andrew said, when he returned.

"What of it?" Rolande snapped. "Suppose we are surrounded by the damned things, what then?" Clearly, she didn't like the idea.

But Sir Andrew was much relieved by the hermit's calculations. They suggested a direction for their search, and—what was perhaps more reassuring—they suggested that Pierson knew what he was about. "If these are the ceremonial guardians of the Yerren, or a warning to their enemies," he said, "and if they lie in a ring, offering a circle of protection, then surely the Yerren must dwell at its center. Is that not your counsel?" he asked the hermit.

"You believe this babble of intruders and enemies?" Rolande interrupted. "What enemies could the Yerren have? These carvings are old, they've been here since long before *we* landed on these shores. What invaders were they meant to warn, then?"

"I have wondered, myself, how it is that we found them seasoned warriors from the first," Sir Andrew agreed. "But so they are. We are not the first to encounter them in battle."

"Like humankind, they war among themselves," the hermit explained. "The Yerren live in widespread clans, divided by the color of their plumage, and the different clans may fight over territorial claims in one generation, or form alliances in the next." He paused. "But they are capable of banding together to defend themselves against a common foe. For they have another enemy, some great enemy they refuse to speak of plainly. They say that it darkens the sky and casts shadows over the land, that its coming is foretold by the numbers of the years. They say," he concluded, "that its coming will be soon." He pulled a compass from a leather pouch at his belt, and walked from tree to tree, noting the exact facings of each carved visage.

"We must travel north to find the center," he told Sir Andrew.

"So we shall," Sir Andrew replied firmly, "when we've rested here and had a meal. See if you can rouse the boy." To Katin he said, "And you, set to brewing that concoction of yours. The water should be hot enough."

But Katin was feeling quite a bit better. "It hardly hurts now, My Lord." she said sheepishly. "I only needed to be quiet for a bit. I daresay I brought it on myself, with my foolish carrying-on and shouting." Then she brightened. "But if you've heated water, I could make some rabbit stew!"

* * *

Simeon was kept busy during Sir Andrew's absence, with the tasks Rolande had set him. First, in the small hours of the morning, when the moon was sunk low, he rode into the yard of the smithy with a cartful of barrels. The smithy was located at the edge of the fields just outside the town, and Simeon had timed his arrival according to his knowledge of the rounds of the town watchman. He knew that the smithy would be deserted at this hour except for a lone apprentice left on guard there, and this night the lad on duty was a devout Dep convert in Rolande's pay. He came out of the smithy as Simeon stopped beside the casks of musket balls which were being made on Sir Andrew's order, to be stockpiled against the invasion. Simeon motioned him to silence, then walked around to the back of the cart and laboriously, with the lad's help, rolled the barrels off one by one. These Rolande had received at the same time as the new muskets, with just such a necessity in mind.

They were sweating hard when they were done, for

lead shot is heavy, but Simeon hadn't dared enlist anyone else to assist him, lest a careless tongue let slip any word of this night's work. Having completed the first part of this task, he took a drink from the well in the yard, then walked back over to the barrels, where the youth was waiting. Picking up two of the long iron poles which leaned against the forge, waiting to be formed into some more useful implement, they pried the tops from two of the smith's barrels and scooped out enough shot to cover the top of the balls in the barrels Simeon had brought.

At last, laying the iron poles aside, they secured the tops of Rolande's barrels, then loaded the smith's barrels onto the cart. Simeon wiped the sweat from his brow and gave his helper a conspiratorial wink. "A good night's work. 'Twill bring confusion upon the heretics," he said quietly, offering the lad a small pouch of coins.

"Nay, to do the Good God's work is man's reward," the 'prentice said earnestly.

"Why, 'tis heaven's truth, and the most reverend servants of God who employ our unworthy selves will be pleased when your piety is reported to them," Simeon assured him. He pocketed the money again, checked the path to make certain that there was no one coming, and departed the way he had come.

As the sun lit the morning sky, he set about his next job. Many of those who had come to the colony had anticipated unlimited supplies of land in the New World, which would, in a short span of time, provide them with a reasonable livelihood. But the incessant skirmishes with the Yerren had delayed the clearing of sufficient arable land for everyone, and many of the new settlers were still scraping out a meager subsistence, barely able to survive.

Rolande, knowing full well the benefit of having folk in her debt, had extended credit to a number of settlers in such straits—and extensive credit to a select few of these, for not all of them had arrived on these shores of their own will. Many petty criminals were remanded involuntarily by the authorities in Albin. They customarily arrived in the summer when passage was easiest, thus accounting for the name by which this land was commonly known in Albin, the Summerlands.

Now that summer had just begun, Simeon was readily able to find among the men and women of Thornfeld a number of such recent arrivals, who, destined to suffer the hardships of colonial life under duress and penniless, harbored a particular resentment. They felt no kinship with the other colonists and had little trust even in each other—and that made them of particular value to Rolande.

Simeon spent the day visiting one after another of these debtors, explaining to them as carefully as Sir Andrew had explained to the Warders, the need to prepare for the invasion. He emphasized with equal fervor the importance of the watch points along the coast. Simeon's plan, however, called for his people to watch the watchers and make certain that when the Albinate fleet was sighted, word did not reach the colony—until it was too late. And he found, when he had explained the consequences of not cooperating, that his carefully selected henchmen were willing to comply. He combined threats of retribution with promises of pardons and rewards from the Chamber when they took power in the Colonies.

Simeon's final task was more complicated and required a visit to the hermit's hut. But for this he had to wait. . . .

* * *

Shortly after Sir Andrew's departure, Hannah Franesh returned from her trapping expedition, well-satisfied with her catch. Finding the message from Sir Andrew that he wished to speak to her of the dissolution of Holistowe, she paid a call to Silverbourne, only to find that he had departed.

Lady Celia welcomed her nevertheless, assuring her that she herself would gladly receive what information Hannah might be able to supply. Indeed, she knew that she was better suited to the task than Sir Andrew, being more patient and persuasive, and gifted, moreover, with a talent for inspiring confidence in others. That gift had served her well during the war, when obtaining information had meant staying a step ahead of the hangman. Now, seeing that her visitor would not be comfortable in the salon, she led her to a wooden bench beside the drying rack in the herb garden, and settled beside her as naturally as if it were her custom always to entertain her guests there.

The two women did not look as different as might have been expected, for Lady Celia had abandoned much of her finery of late, brushed the powder from her hair, and put away her ornate apparel and costly jewelry. They were simply too much bother.

She was accustomed to directing the affairs of an estate—for her husband had often been away on endless diplomatic missions—but it had rarely been necessary for her to leave her apartments to carry out her duties. Silverbourne was far smaller than Wildmoore, but also far less ordered, without the hundreds of tenants, farmers, and retainers whose families had worked the land and raised the livestock for generations.

Though Sir Andrew had brought a trustworthy steward from Stoneridge and hired reliable overseers, still Lady Celia found it necessary to deal directly with many household problems herself, and to ride the fields and visit the sheds to settle matters that she would once have left to others. She had taken to wearing riding dress much of the time—skirts without hoops and jackets of practical, almost military, cut. Her skin was not so fair, nor her hands so soft, as they had been. But her appetite had never been so good before.

Today she had put on a simple linen frock and a straw hat bound with ribbon while Hannah had, of course, dressed in her finest to call at Silverbourne Manor. She had not expected to be received by the Viscountess, but Lady Celia had soon put her at her ease.

"It was poison," Hannah said simply, trying to tug her unaccustomed skirts into place around her.

Lady Celia matched her blunt manner. "How can you be certain?" It seemed impossible that someone should poison an entire colony. But Lady Celia was a good judge of character, and looking at the strong, sensible face of the woman beside her, she could hardly believe that Hannah was given to idle fancies.

"Oh, I know there are those who would claim it was an act of God or nature, but I've never known wells to go bad so fast or so widely, have you? Why would good water suddenly turn foul? I say it was unnatural."

The idea was appalling. *But,* Lady Celia told herself, *if such is the nature of the enemy, we'd best know them as they are.* "Tell me everything, from the beginning," she said.

Hannah picked a handful of thyme from the patch by the scraped foot of the bench. "We were never a big community, mainly fisherfolk. But most of the first settlers were Deprivants, some of the most powerful leaders of the Scrutinors who turned their backs on Albin. When the first ships ran aground in the swampy bogs there, they declared that this was a sign from the Good God that they were to create a promised land out of the wilderness. I came much later, because my sister lived there. I stayed because the trapping was good, and it offered me a livelihood."

She began to peel off tiny flowers, watching them scatter on the light breeze. "But I can't say that living was ever easy at Holistowe. Folk used to say, among themselves, that it was the Devil who'd led the ship there. The land was poor for farming, although some tried, and they kept on until—the disaster struck." Hannah plucked another sprig from the ground. "It had been a terrible spring, raining ceaselessly, and that made fishing dangerous and destroyed much of the early planting.

"Then one day a stranger visited. He claimed to have had visions of a community so pure and righteous that it was in danger from the jealousy of the Evil One. He said he had the gift of second sight and would be able to tell more if he could scry in the town well. On market day, with the blessing of the town Elders, he leaned over the well for a long time until a fit seemed to come upon him. Then, he prophesied that a great plague threatened to overwhelm the Good God's righteous children, but that the sanctity of our prayers would protect us. And it wasn't long before a strange sickness did strike the town, but prayer didn't save the Elders. The Scrutinors claimed the stranger had been a demon in disguise, and they looked for him, but he was gone. This they interpreted as another sign . . . but some of us were not so sure.

"Then while everyone was laid low, bandits raided the town. They destroyed everything they couldn't carry away and burned down buildings as they went. In the end, most of the colonists survived the pestilence—but all of the leaders of the colony died."

"All?" Lady Celia repeated.

"Aye, that was the odd thing. There were few other

deaths, but all the most powerful Scrutinors died, as if it were a judgement on them."

"Or as if someone used the illness, if such it was, as a blind, so as to eliminate certain people?"

Hannah tossed the bare stem aside. "I have asked myself that. And I wondered if that stranger could have poured something into the well, when he did his scrying."

"But what would anyone have to gain by such an act?" Lady Celia mused, more to herself than to Hannah.

"I don't know, M'lady. Holistowe had nothing so valuable to offer, that someone would take such measures to gain mastery of the place. And none have come forward to try it, besides."

"The colony is still in existence?"

"In a manner. Of those who had land there, some chose to stay and try to rebuild. Others left for more fortunate settlements, once the Deprivant leaders were gone, and there was no one to insist that they must stay. For my part, I knew from my trading that there were more profitable places where we might dwell, and I brought my sister to live here, after the tragedy. I'm not one to stay where the land's unlucky."

"But if you are right in your suspicions, then what happened at Holistowe could happen here," Lady Celia said softly.

Hannah looked at her sharply. "It could, but why should it?"

"You have heard, have you not, of the coming invasion from Albin?"

Hannah nodded. "They say it was you, M'lady, who brought the news. But there's those that claim it's mere rumor."

"I wish it were so, but they are wrong. And I've no doubt the Chamber has its agents here in the Colonies, charged with undermining our defenses. Perhaps by eliminating those with the authority to order those defenses, if no other means offer." She felt a moment's relief that Sir Andrew was away from Thornfeld, though she knew that this was a fleeting respite at best. If the enemy were already in their midst, the only way to protect Sir Andrew would be to discover who they were.

"The Chamber, eh?" Hannah said thoughtfully. "I'd not put it past them. 'Twas their kind banished my sister here, and the Devil's own time I had finding her, too. Not but what I was glad of it, in the end." She gave Lady Celia an appraising glance, then said boldly, "We were poachers in Rivvenshire, the lot of us, and likely enough to hang one day. But here trapping's a respectable trade, and all this great woodland with its game free for the taking! Now if they think they can bring their laws and their sheriffs here—" She stared at the ground, her fists clenched at her sides. "Well," she said grimly, "let them try, that's all I say."

* * *

Jerl didn't remember saying anything about the carved heads, he didn't remember speaking in Yerren, and he certainly didn't remember attacking anyone with an ax. He would not have believed that he had done any of these things, had all the others not insisted—even Katin—that it was so.

He could only remember looking at the heads and wanting to draw nearer to them, to see them closer at hand. That much had surely happened. Katin had been next to him, she had said, "What do they mean?" and he had reached out to touch the image, as if to find the answer to her question.

He had asked it, "Who are you?" and then the lips

of the wooden face had parted, and it had answered him. For a long time, it had spoken to him, it had told him something of great importance—but what? The other heads had spoken, too. The three had surrounded him, and they were no longer visages of wood, but towering winged beings of immense power, who demanded something of him. But what was it?

He had understood at the time, he had known what he must do. But when they had revealed themselves in their true forms, he could no longer look at them, could not longer even stand. He'd covered his face with his hands, he'd fallen. . . .

And then he was lying on the ground, with Frend Pierson pouring water on his face and calling his name. When he tried to rise, he found that he couldn't move his arms. The hermit had helped him to sit up, and then explained to him what had happened, as the rest of them looked on, waiting to see what he would do.

But he could only stare at them, stammering protests and denials. Never easy with words, he had tried nonetheless to describe what he remembered, but, of course, they had seen nothing of the kind, and his own tale sounded to him like the delusions of a lunatic. With growing horror, Jerl realized that there could be only one explanation. He must be crazy. Dangerously crazy.

They had freed his hands to allow him to eat the meal Katin prepared, but before they moved on, Rolande insisted that he be tied again. The hermit and Katin argued that it was unnecessary, that they were traveling away from the rim of the circle with its carved guardians. Even Sir Andrew, reflecting that they would have to travel more slowly with a bound man among them, thought it sufficient that Jerl was unarmed, but Rolande had been the one attacked, and he yielded the decision to her.

And Jerl agreed with her.

He did not feel as though he might violently attack one of the party, but he had not felt so before, and yet they all said that he had done it. He had nothing against merchant Vendeley; he could imagine no reason to try to kill her. But he had tried. How could he be sure he wouldn't go berserk again—*and suppose it was Katin next time?* Miserable and humiliated, he allowed Rolande to tie his hands, without resistance or protest. As he stumbled along after the others, he prayed desperately to the Good God, either to cure him or to let him die. If only he'd been killed by the bandits, in a heroic rescue of Katin! It did not seem to him that his prayers could be heard from within the circle bounded by the guardians of the Yerren.

That night he lay awake, though he had rarely been so tired. It was not only that he couldn't find a comfortable position to lie in, with his hands tied, it was that he was afraid to sleep—afraid of his own dreams. At last he struggled into a sitting position, leaning against the tree behind him, and saw Sir Andrew watching him narrowly from where he sat by the fire, his musket beside him. The others were lying quiet, Katin and her pup curled together near the fire, Rolande stretched out beneath her cloak, farther off, her back to a fallen log, and the hermit lying amid the roots of a great tree, not far from Jerl.

Jerl met Sir Andrew's look and said quietly, "Do you think I'm crazy, sir?"

Sir Andrew had no ready answer. Before the business with the captured Yerren, he had always thought the boy sound and reliable. He had received good reports of him from Captain Jamison, and singled him out as one who would make a responsible sergeant, in time. He worked hard, and didn't squander his pay on gambling or drinking. He didn't get into fights in the barracks or cause trouble in town. He was ambitious, as the better sort often are, and had plans for land of his own, a farmstead. Even now, he was behaving as well as could be expected, to do him justice, giving as little trouble as he could. There was nothing of the madman about him.

"If you are, it's like no madness I've ever seen or heard of," Sir Andrew admitted.

The hermit rose and moved to Jerl's side, without a sound. "I'll loose him for now," he said. "He needs to sleep."

"Don't," Jerl said uneasily.

But Sir Andrew nodded. "We'll be on guard. Vendeley can do as she will, on her watch."

"It's Vendeley you should guard against, not this one," the hermit said softly. "If the forces that guard the Yerren possessed him, then they set him against the enemies of the Yerren. They know her for an enemy—"

"If such forces exist," Sir Andrew interrupted. "If such possession is possible." But he remembered his own doubts about Vendeley's reasons for joining the expedition. What did she hope to gain from this difficult, dangerous undertaking?

"No warning should be disregarded," said the hermit.

When another day and night had passed without any return of Jerl's frenzy, Rolande agreed that he should be left unbound. "Load him down with our supplies," she suggested. "That should keep him out of mischief. I'm tired of carrying more than my share." But she kept Jerl's musket, and the hermit now carried the ax.

The traveling had become easier as they followed the compass to the north. They came upon more areas of cleared ground, and found well-worn trails that led in the direction they were taking. But they saw no other trace of the Yerren until the following evening. They had eaten a hare that Katin had proudly prepared with savory herbs and aromatic grasses, and two large, pink-fleshed fish that Lucifer, to their surprise, had snagged from the shallow stream with his claws and dragged ashore. In the twilight, Katin was sitting with the pup in her lap and singing one of her favorite ballads, while Rolande and the hermit gathered firewood for the night. Jerl, who had slept little during the past night, was half asleep, listening to Katin's song, when he suddenly sat up and said confusedly, "They're all around us!"

Sir Andrew was on his feet at once, clutching his musket. "The Yerren? Where?" He did not need to ask how Jerl knew they were there. He found that he did not doubt it.

Katin laid down the soarhound pup and rose to her feet very slowly. "There!" she whispered, pointing. "And there, and there!"

Their plumage matched the green and black of the trees so exactly that it was hard to see them, even when staring directly at them. It was impossible to say how long they had been there, motionless, crouched on the branches overhead. But as Sir Andrew began to make out the shapes of folded wings and taloned limbs among the leaves, he saw that there were at least a score of the Yerren above them, armed with spears, clubs, stone knives, and bows with arrows ready-nocked upon the string.

"Smit!" he ordered. "Tell them we're not their enemies!" But Jerl was frozen, as still and silent as the waiting Yerren. It was Katin who came forward, moving with a curiously stately gait to the center of the small clearing, to call in a high, clear treble the words Jerl had taught her in the Yerren's cell at the stockade.

She sang them flawlessly, confidently, from memory, then drew a deep breath and repeated them.

"I *hope,*" she said to Sir Andrew, "that I've told them we're friends and mean no harm."

There was a stirring of leaves all around them, then, from high overhead, a Yerren they could not see called a deep, reedy series of sounds.

Sir Andrew turned to Jerl. "What did it say?"

Jerl shook his head. "I don't know. I'm sorry."

The hermit came walking slowly through the trees and joined them, gazing up into the dark leaves. "We're to throw down our weapons," he translated. "A reasonable request, if we claim to be friends."

"Not bloody likely!" said Rolande, from the edge of the clearing. She had Jerl's musket braced against a low branch, aimed upward. "If they want this, let them come take it!"

Sir Andrew hesitated only for a moment, then threw down his own musket and pistol at the foot of the nearest tree. "We've no choice," he said. "Surrender your weapons. Everything."

"You mean to let them slaughter us without a fight?" Rolande said, making no move to obey.

"We're surrounded and outnumbered. If they mean to kill us, they can, whether we're armed or not."

Katin gave him her dagger, and her bow and quiver, and he threw them after the rest. "They could have killed us before we even knew they were there," she said calmly. "But they only watched us. I don't see why they should attack now."

The hermit, unarmed save for a hunting knife and Jerl's ax, tossed them away and said to Katin, "You see, it is true that they use bows and arrows, but more for the hunt than for warfare. They fight most often on the wing, and they cannot draw a bow in flight. But they hunt from the treetops."

"Vendeley," said Sir Andrew.

Rolande gripped the stock of her musket and fought down her rising panic. She could see now that the damned things were everywhere, the trees were thick with them. She couldn't possibly hold them off long enough to make an escape, and even if she could, where would she escape to? She was city-bred, at home in the backstreets and the thoroughfares, not in the wilderness. She couldn't get back to the colony on her own.

Loyalty to the Chamber's cause demanded that she prevent Sir Andrew from reaching an agreement with the Yerren, and shooting a few of them now would probably accomplish that—but it would almost certainly get her killed as well. Rolande's loyalty to the Chamber did not extend to self-sacrifice. But the Yerren would probably kill them all anyway. . . .

Suddenly an arrow thudded into the branch that braced her musket, just inches from her arm, and Rolande let fire at once, without thought, into the trees ahead. A few leaves drifted down, and then the clearing was full of Yerren, seizing the weapons the others had abandoned, and quickly forming a ring around the disarmed party. Sir Andrew and Jerl both moved to flank Katin, the hermit spoke urgently in Yerren, and the pup, frightened by the musket fire, clambered up into Katin's arms, trying to hide under her vest.

Before Rolande could reload or draw her pistol, she was surrounded by four Yerren warriors, their black, glassy-tipped spears held ready.

Sir Andrew did not dare leave Katin, to attempt to defend Rolande—or to disarm her. "Tell them not to harm her!" he ordered Jerl and Pierson. Jerl looked at the hermit, who said something in Yerren to Rolande's captors. *But did he say what I told him, or something else?* Sir Andrew wondered, as one of the Yerren threatened Rolande with a spear and addressed a curt command to her in their own tongue.

Rolande did not need a translation. Making no sudden motions—indeed, barely breathing—she drew the knife and pistol from her belt and dropped them. Sabotaging Sir Andrew's mission to the Yerren seemed far less important at the moment than emerging alive from this encounter.

Nothing they had heard or imagined prepared them for their first sight of the city of the Yerren. The trees in these hills were larger than any they'd seen in the forests of Albin, with branches thick around as mill wheels and draped with thick woody vines of heliotrope and wild grape. In the treetops, some hundred feet overhead, were round hutches, their frames intricately woven of thin wooden slats, interlaced with small branches and vines. The roofs were pointed cones, neatly thatched. Between the buildings—for there was no denying that these were buildings—ran wooden walkways, bridges that connected the aeries in the trees, allowing the inhabitants to walk between them, for there was not space enough for them to fly among the structures. Scores of Yerren could be seen, flying above the city, entering or leaving buildings, stopping on the walkways to converse. Now and then the sound of their musical speech floated down on the wind.

Sir Andrew stared up into the branches, amazed at the intricacy of the structures. For the first time, he knew that he'd been right to undertake this pilgrimage, that there was at least a chance of success. Beings civilized enough to construct this lofty city could be reasoned with.

Rolande was thinking much the same thing, with far less satisfaction. She had never really believed in the city they were seeking, despite Paeter Cellric's testimony to the Wardership. She'd envisioned no more than a cluster of great nests, at most, and had not expected that the party would find even that, with the mad hermit as guide. It was against all reason that they should have reached this dream city, yet they had found it. And Sir Andrew would carry out his negotiations with its rulers, unless she could do something to prevent it.

Katin felt humbled by the sight of the great city above them, its graceful bridges and spires seeming to float in the clouds, wreathed with the radiance of sunset. "I see," she said to the hermit. "The land belongs to the Yerren, and we are the invaders. Small wonder they attack when we try to clear the trees."

"This is a vast land. There is room for the Yerren and for us."

It was, she thought, the first time she'd heard him speak as if he were one of them.

As they neared the city, Jerl was flooded with a profound sense of homecoming that he could not understand. He was hard put to keep himself from running forward, as if everything he cared about was to be found in the Yerren stronghold. When their captors had herded them to the foot of one of the great trees, Jerl said impatiently, "But how are we to get up there?"

As if to answer him, one of the Yerren warriors gave a long, piercing call, and at once long rope ladders were lowered from a sort of platform in the branches above. Jerl seized one at once and began to climb. The guards prodded the hermit and Rolande in the back and gestured to the nearest ladder, while Sir Andrew was forced up another. Katin, still carrying Lucifer, set him down and started up after Sir Andrew, knowing that the pup would follow her. Like a squirrel, it could climb anything. Above, more Yerren perched, black spears held threateningly in their taloned hands.

Under guard, the party was led along a series of walkways to a long hanging bridge, which they were made to cross one at a time, lest it break under their weight. It was built to hold the small, light Yerren, but it looked well constructed and sound to Sir Andrew. He went first, judging that if it would take his weight, it would hold the others, but he did not breathe easily till the last of his people had come safely across.

Yerren stopped to stare at them wherever they passed, and Sir Andrew heard the word *Ysnathi* repeated often, each time with the same falling cadence. For the first time, they saw the young Yerren, dashing along the walkways, tumbling in the air, the smallest clinging to their elders' chests as they flew. A flock of youngsters swooped close to see the prisoners, yelling "Ysnathi!" and were shooed away by the guards. They scattered and disappeared, their plumage glowing in the last rays of the sun. *Whatever they do with us, I'm glad I came here,* Katin thought.

Then they were urged forward again, to the entrance of a large round building, its sides constructed of interlaced vertical and horizontal wooden slats with spaces between them. The hermit had told their captors that they must speak with the leaders of the community, but when Sir Andrew saw this structure, he lost hope that they were being led to someone in power. It was all too clearly a cage.

Rolande recognized this, too, and said tensely to Sir Andrew, "You're not going to let them lock us up?"

"What do you expect me to do? We didn't come here to fight. If we comply, they may regard us as reasonable beings and listen to what we have to say."

"And they may just pen us up and butcher us!"

"Perhaps, but it will be safer to submit, for now. We're in no position to resist. I told you," he added, with a certain satisfaction, "that this journey would be dangerous."

Even Katin had to stoop to enter the low, narrow doorway to their prison, and Jerl and the hermit had to bend almost double to fit themselves through. But when their guards gestured for Rolande to follow, she balked and grabbed at a nearby branch. "I will not be caged in by a lot of feathered dwarves!"

"Vendeley, don't be a fool!"

The guards moved in to seize her, but she was taller and stronger than the largest of them, and, Sir Andrew saw, an experienced fighter as well. To subdue her, they would have to injure her with their spears, but this they seemed reluctant to do.

Then they won't stab me either, Sir Andrew thought. Hoping he was right in this conjecture, he pushed past the armed Yerren and grabbed Rolande by the shoulders, before she could break free of the Yerren and bolt. She was white, panting like a cornered animal, and Sir Andrew said urgently, "Listen to me! We can get out of that cage if we must—it's built to hold their own kind, not the likes of us! Look at it!"

Staring past him, Rolande saw that he was right. The wooden slats would not break easily, but they looked as if they could be disjoined far enough to force a way through the wall. Yerren prisoners might not be able to move them, but she and Sir Andrew, or Smit, could manage it. As she grew calmer, she regretted having let Sir Andrew see her terror of confinement. One didn't show one's weaknesses to an adversary. "All right—let go of me," she spat, and quickly turned to duck into the doorway, before she could change her mind.

When Sir Andrew had followed her, the door—a

solid slab of wood—was shut and barred behind them. Looking around the dim, bare chamber, Rolande demanded, "And what do we do now?"

"Rest," Sir Andrew suggested.

Chapter 7

Rolande shoved aside a basket containing nuts, grains, wild fruits, and bits of some small animals that weren't immediately identifiable. Evidently, the Yerren preferred their meat raw. Katin had fed most of the first lot to Lucifer, and their captors had then offered a quantity of dried meat, which was edible, if unpalatable.

"How long are we going to let them keep us here?" Rolande snarled. "And if you say 'patience' to me once more—" she added, shaking her fist at the hermit.

"You are forgetting our mission here," Sir Andrew said. "We must make them understand the danger of the invasion, and the advantage of forming an alliance with us. To do so, we must discover who holds authority here, and convince them to hear us out. All this will take time." *But do we have time?* he asked himself, remembering how long it had taken him to accept that the Yerren were intelligent beings. Would it take them as long to come to terms with their human enemies?

Echoing his doubts, Rolande said, "You've *tried* talking to them—it's useless! Pierson's yammered at them time and again, but pretty singsong words won't move them from their intent."

"They have no intent," Jerl said flatly. Exhausted

and distracted by the confusing clamor of feelings beating within him, he no longer cared whether the others believed him or thought him mad. “They're just watching us to see what might be learned, as we did with him.” He pointed to one of the Yerren who had gathered on the walkway nearest to the cage, to gaze curiously at the captives.

“Is that the same one?” Sir Andrew asked, turning to Katin.

“Well, he's the same color,” she said doubtfully, “but . . .”

“Of course he's the one,” said Jerl, surprised. “Didn't you know that?”

The Yerren Jerl claimed to recognize was talking with another one, and the two looked identical to Katin and Sir Andrew. But as they watched, the first one stretched out one wing to show the other, and Katin cried, “Yes—look—he has feathers missing just where the wound was. He must be the one.”

How had the boy known? Sir Andrew wondered.

It was Frend Pierson who had persuaded him to bring Jerl on the expedition, assuring him that the boy could communicate with the Yerren, but Sir Andrew had soon realized that Jerl understood very little of the Yerren language. “Why did you tell me he could speak to them?” he had demanded of the hermit.

“It was necessary for you to bring him,” Pierson had replied. “The real reason you would not have understood.”

Now, Sir Andrew looked thoughtfully at Jerl. “Can you tell the others apart?” he asked.

Jerl shook his head. “Not most of them. But that one talking to—ours—comes here often. I think he'd like to speak to us, but he can't . . . yet. But most of them don't find us important. We're just a vexation to them, compared to . . . something else that afflicts them. Something more threatening than we are."

"Take care, that one's raving again," said Rolande. "He'll probably try to strangle someone next."

But Sir Andrew, though watching Jerl narrowly, said only, "What sort of threat, Smit?"

"I don't *know!*" Jerl said in frustration. "They're waiting."

Rolande's patience was worn to a thread. "Let them wait! Are *we* to wait until they make up their minds to kill us? I say we've waited long enough. We should get out of here while we still can."

Sir Andrew wondered if she was right, but he was not ready to abandon the mission as a failure. "It may come to that," he said, "but we've come this far safely, and they don't seem disposed to harm us. If we bide our time, we may yet achieve our end."

Rolande paced the perimeter of the cage, testing the wooden slats with her fingers. She wanted to yell at the Yerren staring at them, to drive them away, but she didn't dare antagonize them when she was in their power like this. She couldn't bear their expressionless faces and piercing black eyes. How much longer could she stand to be locked up here? In the cage, she was haunted by old memories she had long tried to put behind her, memories that had given her no rest since the Yerren had taken them captive.

There were no guards posted over their prison, and Sir Andrew conjectured that the Yerren had not realized that their prisoners were much stronger than they were. That, at least, would be an advantage should they have to make an escape. But the Yerren did apparently regard them as dangerous, for none of them came within arm's length of the cage, except occasionally the youngsters—obviously daring one another to approach the captive monstrosities—and they were always ordered away at once by the adults.

But one evening, a tiny Yerren child did come close to peer in at them, when its elders had turned away for a moment. "Ysnathi," it whispered solemnly, and reached in toward Katin, who was sitting near to the wall.

The younger Yerren children, not yet fully fledged, looked strangely human, and Katin wondered whether she and her companions looked to the Yerren like giant children. *Perhaps that's why they can't bring themselves to harm us,* she thought. She moved closer to the child and saw that it was clutching a handful of small, blue bird's feathers, and offering them to her. Having learned the words from the hermit, she said, "Thank you," with great seriousness, in Yerren.

"Ysnathi," the child explained.

Lucifer bounded over to sniff their visitor, and the little Yerren wide-eyed, shouted, "Snimmer!" and stretched out its arms to embrace the pup.

But its cry alarmed the adults, who descended upon it and snatched it away, with exclamations of horror that required no translation. The child protested loudly as it was borne away, clearly preferring the company of the monsters and the puppy to that of its kin.

"What does *Ysnathi* mean?" Katin asked the hermit, looking at the little blue feathers.

He chuckled. "It is their name for us—it means 'the plucked ones.' "

Katin started to laugh, and even Jerl smiled, for the first time in days. "He must have thought we were cold!" Katin said.

"She," Jerl corrected her.

Katin was awakened in the early morning by Lucifer wriggling out of her arms and climbing over her to reach something behind her. She was nearly asleep again when she heard a low, warbled "Snimmer," and she rolled over to see that the Yerren-child had crawled into the cage with them, and was happily feeding the pup with bits of something from the basket of foodstuffs. Katin lay still, not wanting to frighten her away, but then Lucifer bounded over to lick her face, and the child followed, quite unafraid. She stared into Katin's face for a moment, then put out a tentative hand to touch her hair. With one finger, Katin lightly stroked her cheek and felt the soft down, so fine as to be almost invisible, that gave the child's face a faint aureole.

Sir Andrew woke suddenly, with a soldier's sense that something was amiss. *God's Name, it's not possible!* he thought, at the sight of Katin, the soarhound, and the young Yerren all curled together fast asleep, by the far wall of the chamber.

In a moment, he had picked up the child, hoping to thrust her out of the cage before she could be found there, but it was already too late. Yerren were converging on them from the sky and from all the paths of the city, it seemed, armed with spears and gleaming black stone knives. To make matters worse, the child, alarmed at this abrupt awakening, had begun to shriek and struggle as if Sir Andrew were murdering her, clawing and snapping at him frantically.

"What are you doing, My Lord?" Katin cried. "You've frightened her! Give her to me!"

But this Sir Andrew could not do, lest the Yerren blame Katin for the apparent child-theft. "Throw it out of here, man!" Rolande shouted, but before he could even set the child down, the door was thrown open, and the cage seemed to fill with shouting, murderous Yerren. Those in the lead faced Sir Andrew with weapons ready, but they could not attack while he still held the child.

The hermit, who had no idea what had happened, tried nonetheless to tell the Yerren what had *not* happened. The soarhound barked at Sir Andrew, in defense of its new friend, and the Yerren outside the cage clamored and wailed in a wild lament.

Very slowly, Sir Andrew knelt to lay down the child, intending to back away from her, but the Yerren started forward, spears raised, and he froze, knowing that they were only waiting for a clear shot at him.

Jerl could not even rise from where he lay. Gripped with a horror more intense and visceral than anything he'd felt before, he could only stare at the scene before him, without recognition or comprehension. Before his mind's eye was another scene, of a hideous giant clutching a tiny, helpless child—a child who cried to him for protection. *It was crushing the little one in its hands—in a heart's beat it would break her bones like twigs, it would tear her asunder—unless—* With a cry, Jerl leaped up and threw himself at Sir Andrew, tearing the terrified child from his grasp. He raced to the wall with her and stood looking around him blindly, seeming to have no idea what to do next.

But the child had quieted at once. She made no attempt to escape Jerl, but seemed rather to cling to him for safety. All the Yerren had suddenly grown still. Those who had threatened Sir Andrew did not turn on Jerl, but ranged themselves between the two, as if they were satisfied that the child was safe, so long as Sir Andrew could not reach her. The hermit spoke to them again, and now they seemed to heed his words, though they made no answer.

At last, Jerl turned and brought the child to one of the Yerren, who reached through a space in the wall to receive her. Jerl's eyes met the other's for a moment, and he felt again the sort of dizzying wave of emotion that had felled him when the Yerren prisoner had escaped from the stockade. But this time it was not wild desperation or crippling fear that seized him, but an overwhelming sense of thankfulness. Though he could not remember exactly what he'd done, he was sure that he had finally done something right.

"Are you satisfied?" Rolande asked Sir Andrew, once the Yerren had withdrawn, leaving them locked in alone. "Do you still think we should wait for them to decide what to do with us? You were nearly skewered!"

"The danger is less now, not greater," Jerl said calmly.

Katin seemed to accept this. "They trust Jerl, it would seem. That's sure to help our cause." She pulled Lucifer away from the basket of food, and he skittered up the wall and hung from the ceiling, ready to pounce. "This is no time to lose heart," Katin said confidently, "with success in sight."

"Success! Are the lot of you blind as well as crazy? These things are savages! There'll be no reasoning with them! Why should they listen to us, when they have us at their mercy? They know they can use us as they like! What's to stop them from coming in here and—" Rolande fought to regain control of her words, before they could betray her. But her memories had already given her away.

"Then this is not the first time you've been in prison," said the hermit.

Rolande turned on him with an oath, kicking the basket out of her way. "You prattling old bastard, if you think you can—"

But the food spilling from the basket had excited the pup, who launched himself from the top of the cage and landed, just then, on Rolande's neck. She swiped at him wildly, sending him tumbling across the floor and through a space in the wall, where there was nothing to break his fall.

"Lucifer!" Katin wailed, trying to peer down through the screen of leaves and branches below. "He's gone!"

"If I could fit you through there, I'd throw you after it!" Rolande shouted. "Imbecile! Our lives are at stake—can't any of you understand that!"

"Even if that were so," Katin said coldly, "it's hardly reason for you to kill my dog."

"Katin, that animal can fly," Sir Andrew responded impatiently. "We cannot." Their recent experience with the Yerren inclined him more to Rolande's view of them than Jerl's and Katin's.

"Exactly," said Rolande, thinking that just possibly she wouldn't have Sir Andrew hanged after all. "They're not about to let us go. We have to find a way out of here."

"If there's no change in our relations with the Yerren, we will return to Thornfeld at once," Sir Andrew decided. "If we've only wasted time by coming here, we must waste no more. Some understanding may yet come of today's happenstance," he said, with more doubt than hope, "but if not—we can get away from here, and we shall, this night."

Rolande had to be satisfied with that.

But something came of the day's events almost immediately. That afternoon, they were visited by a Yerren who entered the cage unarmed, although several armed guards were in attendance. About his neck, he wore a leather thong strung with claws of extraordinary length, and decorated with beads of the same black, glassy stone that formed their weapons. He carried a long bone similar to the one the hermit had been using as a walking stick, but it was clearly a symbol of authority in his hands.

"He's the one who's been watching us," Jerl said softly, and no one doubted him this time.

The Yerren addressed himself to the hermit, who told the others, "He is called Civornos. We are to accompany him to an assembly, where decisions will be made concerning us. More than that he cannot say, now, but should the decision of the priests be favorable, he will be able to tell us more."

"What if the decision isn't favorable?" Rolande demanded. "Will they free us or eat us?"

But before the hermit could ask any questions, Civornos had turned to the door, motioning to them to follow. The others looked to Sir Andrew, who said, "This is what we came here to do," and went after the Yerren at once. He was immensely relieved, almost exhilarated, to be doing something at last.

The guards fell into place around them, and they were escorted along more walkways and ladders, all leading upward. As they passed a small, windowless hutch, Sir Andrew saw that their muskets were being carried out the doorway, each one borne by two of the Yerren. Meeting Rolande's eyes, he knew that she, too, had noted where their weapons were kept.

They were taken to a platform high in the trees, and left there. When the ladders by which they had reached it were withdrawn, they had no way of climbing back down, since the flooring extended far beyond the supporting branches, on all sides. The Yerren who had brought them there simply leaped into the air and swooped down or rose with a thrashing of wings, for the smaller, interconnecting branches had been cleared away, leaving the area open to the sky. It formed a great amphitheater ringed by the massive tree trunks and the huge circling branches. Here and there, faces and patterns had been carved in the wood, and torches were wedged between forked branches at intervals around the circle.

They were in an indefensible position, Sir Andrew thought, exposed and vulnerable to attack from anywhere in the surrounding branches. He said nothing to alarm the others, but Rolande had no such scruples. "We're trapped," she muttered. "They can fill us with arrows as soon as they decide to sacrifice us to their demon gods!"

Yerren were drifting down from the sky to settle on the branches and platforms around them. Many wore leather necklaces or wristlets decorated with claws, small bones, and stone beads. "They're not armed," Sir Andrew pointed out, but he knew this was no proof that Rolande was wrong. For the first time, he turned to Jerl for information. "Do they plan to execute us here?"

"No . . ." Jerl said hesitantly. "Their plans have to do with something else. I don't think this is *about* us at all." His mind seemed to fill with conflicting emotions as the Yerren gathered—fear and curiosity and a matter of great moment that he should know about, but didn't. Something seemed to force upon him a picture of the eerie ritual he'd witnessed outside the fort, and the small blood-smeared skull. A powerful surge of dread swept through him, but now he understood that the fear was not his own. The Yerren expected an attack, great destruction, many deaths. It was not the war with the colonists that alarmed them; they regarded their earthbound foes with contempt. This was something far more dangerous, an unconquerable threat whose very existence hung upon the air like the first salt scent of an impending hurricane. "They're in danger, but . . . we're not the reason."

The hermit nodded. "Those I can hear are wondering why we've been brought here. They say that only Civornos knows."

"*He* doesn't want us killed," Jerl said confidently.

At no sign that they could see, a sudden silence fell upon all the assembled Yerren at once, and Civornos, standing with his wings outstretched, spoke out loudly in the stillness, seeming to address his words to the four Yerren grouped on the highest platform.

"He seeks the permission of the priests, to send an emissary to . . . the north," the hermit murmured. "The matter is of grave concern, not to this community alone, but to their entire clan."

Questions were posed or statements made, and answers given, then Civornos spoke at length, and the hermit told them, "He claims that we are not merely clever and dangerous animals, as many believe, but beings similar to themselves. That we must be dealt with as if we were a powerful new clan of Yerren, instead of a race of hairless bears."

There was protest and argument, much of which the hermit could not follow, but at last Civornos was allowed to continue, and he began to present the evidence for his outrageous claim. First he spoke of Jerl, who possessed that quality which distinguished Yerren from beasts. He called upon others to testify to the experiences of that morning, and drew the conclusion that all the Ysnathi must possess the same ability, that they had been thought to lack it simply because it was rare for those of different clans to commune in this way.

Katin, he maintained—referring to her as "the smallest of the lot"—had been heard singing by the patrol who captured them, and she was known to possess skills of healing. The wounded Yerren soldier came forward, at Civornos's bidding, to describe his treatment at Katin's hands—and the building where he had been held, that no animals could have constructed.

It seemed that Rolande's resistance to being caged had also impressed the Yerren favorably. To submit tamely to captivity suggested a base, brutish nature.

Further, there could be no question that the Ysnathi communicated with one another by means of a true language, and not with meaningless sounds and cries. Indeed, they were capable of learning the Yerren's own tongue, for many of them had heard "the gray one" speak in an intelligible manner.

As the hermit translated Civornos's speech for them, it became uncomfortably clear to Sir Andrew that he himself was the one member of the party who had done nothing to help their cause. On the contrary, it seemed to him that any success they might have now would come about in spite of his efforts, not because of them.

If he'd had his way, he'd have brought only the hermit and one or two of the more experienced militiamen with him on this venture. It was Pierson who'd persuaded him to bring Smit instead, and both the Princess and Vendeley had joined the party against his will. He had not even wished to allow Katin to treat the wounded Yerren, fearing that she would be hurt. Only her own persistence and the Yerren's seeming weakness had changed his mind. And he had tried to *prevent* Vendeley from showing resistance when they were captured and imprisoned. . . .

"The lot of you would have done better to come without me, it seems," he said grimly.

The hermit turned to him. "It is you who must speak for us now. They ask why the trees have been burned—what am I to tell them?"

Sir Andrew faced the priests and assumed his most authoritative manner. "We must clear land to grow the food our people need," he said loudly, and when the hermit had repeated his words in the Yerren tongue, he went on, "but it need not be land that the Yerren people inhabit. We five are come as messengers from our clan, to confer with you about a just division of the land, and in token of our good faith, we have ceased to burn any trees at all for the present."

There was a stirring and murmuring among the Yerren when the hermit had translated this, and Sir Andrew thought with elation, *At last!* Now, how to explain about the invasion? "A great danger threatens us all," he began, but no sooner had the hermit translated his words than another of the Yerren rose to address the priests, wings held wide in a menacing display.

When permission had been granted, the speaker delivered an impassioned tirade that provoked a marked response among the Yerren. Around the circle, wings were lifted and voices raised, though whether in accord or disagreement Sir Andrew could not tell.

The hermit frowned. "This one says that it is known to the priests why we have come. Their gods sent us to them as a sign that their enemies will be delivered into their hands. It is meet that we should satisfy the thirst of the people for vengeance, whether we be beasts or reasoning beings. At such a time as this, they dare not approach the . . . the High Lord about something so insignificant. They will earn his disfavor, the community will lose standing in the clan. They should not be wasting time over this matter, when the danger of—it sounds like 'shadow-season'—is nigh upon them."

Sir Andrew clenched his fists. "Tell them we bring them a warning—that all preparation will be in vain unless they heed us!"

"No, not yet," said Jerl. He looked rather dazed, but spoke clearly enough. "It's no use to answer a question that hasn't been asked. The priests won't hear."

Sir Andrew was not accustomed to being contradicted by an underling, but neither was he so obdurate as to ignore Jerl's advice. His own judgment had failed him from the first, where the Yerren were concerned, while the boy's *intuition* had proved most reliable. "Wait," he told the hermit resignedly.

But Civornos had not finished his oration. In answer to the other Yerren's challenge, he declared that this very danger constrained them to look to the mountains for guidance about the Ysnathi. "He says that we are not to be so easily dismissed," the hermit reported, "for among our number is a powerful warrior, a slayer of—" he paused, puzzled, "*shraik,* whatever that may be."

A warrior? Sir Andrew wondered. Was he, after all, of some interest to the Yerren? But the hermit, listening intently to Civornos, said suddenly, "Ah! He says that even an enemy who comes bearing the bone of the shraik is to be respected. They believe that *I* killed the creature—with a weapon more deadly than any they possess."

Civornos now gave an order to two of the Yerren who waited on another platform, and they raised up one of the muskets for the assembly to see, then carried it along a bridge of branches to lay it before the priests.

"If we—the 'wingless clan'—were to make common cause with them," the hermit translated, "our uncanny weapons might rout the bloodthirsty shraik at last, and therefore an emissary must be sent, for only the High Lord can decide upon such an alliance."

"Well, I like 'wingless clan' better than 'plucked ones' or 'hairless bears,' " Rolande muttered.

"We couldn't have a better advocate," Katin said with enthusiasm. Forgetting for once that she was not supposed to have been raised at court, she continued,

"He led his opponent on, to raise just the point he wanted raised, then he turned it to his own ends. He's a true statesman."

"Excellent strategy," Sir Andrew agreed. "We've come to the wrong place, it seems, but if he persuades them to send word to their leader, we may yet reach an accord."

They spoke in low tones, for the Yerren had fallen silent again, as if waiting for a sign. The sun had nearly set, and some of the Yerren lit the torches as the twilight deepened, but not until nightfall did any of the others stir.

Then one of the priests—the one, Jerl thought, who had led the ritual by the stockade—rose and uttered a long, haunting call that seemed to echo through the trees as it was taken up by others in the distance. More Yerren gathered, more than any of the party had seen at one time before, and Sir Andrew realized that they had no idea of how many of them there actually were. As they massed in the branches, many began to chant or sing a repetitive refrain that gradually grew in volume and intensity until it seemed to rise from the great well within the ring of trees and reach out to fill the night sky.

Suddenly every voice ceased as one, and the priest, his outstretched wings lit by torchlight, pointed upward with a long spear and gave a sharp, fierce call. From somewhere in the dark foliage a huge figure suddenly swooped into view above them. Its great leathern wings and long, pointed beak were outlined in glowing phosphor, and its head and neck were smeared with red dye. The throng of Yerren broke into savage cries and howls of rage, brandishing spears and shrieking defiance at the circling monster.

Jerl, too, cried out against the thing, though he could see that it was a construction of wooden shafts and leather, worn by one of the Yerren. A storm of hatred rampaged within him, a thousand images of death and destruction twisted in his thoughts like tendrils of smoke whipped by the wind. Bombarded from all sides, he struggled to rise to the surface of some great whirlpool determined to suck him down.

Then a ring of Yerren archers came forward, adorned with necklaces of amethyst and jet and bands of leather around their hands and wrists. One to each platform around the circle, they shot glowing, phosphor-tipped arrows above and below the figure, surrounding it with streaks of golden flame.

The flyer appeared to founder, and another group of Yerren warriors, bearing spears and knives, launched themselves into the air, diving about the effigy and brushing it with the tips of their wings. They drove it toward the trees, where, under cover of the dark foliage, the Yerren masked by the monster slipped out of the leather harness and left the beast hanging upon the branches. As the watching Yerren shrieked out in a chorus of rage and blood lust, the flyers closed in and fell upon the effigy, clawing and tearing with their black blades, rending the figure until it was torn to pieces, and the glowing shreds flew about them and drifted down into the night.

Chapter 8

They had been escorted back to their prison after the ceremony, but the next morning Civornos returned, still unarmed, but this time without a complement of guards. To their surprise, he opened the cage and invited them to emerge.

"It's some trick," said Rolande. "Archers hidden in the branches." She wanted desperately to leave the cage, but she could see no reason for the Yerren to allow it.

Sir Andrew, however, could see no reason for the Yerren to deceive them. "If they want to kill us, they can send a dozen soldiers in here to do it," he pointed out. "They've no need to trick us into coming out in the open." Still, he knew he had no gift for predicting the behavior of the Yerren. What seemed logical to him might well be unthinkable to them. "Smit?" he said.

"He means us well, sir."

Smit had been right so far, Sir Andrew considered, and surely the Yerren would think less of them if they refused to leave the cage. He was responsible for the safety of his people, but they were, in fact, no safer in the cage than out of it. He led the way to the platform where Civornos awaited them.

Shaded by a canopy of leaves and ringed by log

benches, it was decidedly a more pleasant place to hold a discussion than their prison. Addressing the hermit, Civornos explained that, as potential allies and slayers of shraik, they were entitled to more honorable treatment than they had received, though they would not be at liberty to leave the city until word had been received from the north.

"Then an emissary has been sent?" Sir Andrew asked eagerly.

Civornos's answer was strange. He was confident that this had been done, or soon would be, but he could not state with certainty that it was so. The decision of the priests had not been vouchsafed to the people, but he had been given permission to converse with them, and to grant them the status of *kairasi,* which led him to believe that his petition had been successful.

" 'Kairas' means 'with wings clipped,' " the hermit informed them, after putting several questions to Civornos. "During the day, we are free to travel about the city, though we will be prevented from descending the ladders to the ground. Were we prisoners of war, we would wait to be redeemed by our clan, or exchanged for prisoners belonging to this clan. As it is, we await a message from their overlord."

"We'll not be under guard?" asked Rolande.

When her question had been repeated to him, Civornos only said a few words and waved one arm, his folded wing trailing like a long feathered sleeve. "The whole community will be watching us," the hermit translated.

"But how could they keep prisoners of war in that way?" Katin asked. "Any of them can tell at a glance what *we* are, but if we were their own kind—"

"We would be a different color. We would still stand out."

"We're still prisoners," snarled Rolande, though her

suffocating sense of confinement was in fact much relieved.

"No," said Sir Andrew thoughtfully. "We're hostages, and as such we may have certain rights."

The hermit nodded. "He is our *renhith*—a word I've not heard before. Perhaps 'host' or 'guide.' "

"Keeper," muttered Rolande.

"We are invited to take meals with his household, and he wishes to ask us a number of questions, which, however, we are not obliged to answer."

"Tell him we accept with gratitude, and that we have come here to answer questions," said Sir Andrew. "I have much to tell him. Is he permitted to answer my questions?"

After a further exchange of words with Civornos, the hermit replied, "That will depend upon the questions you ask."

Civornos, they learned, was a leader of warriors, one who had killed shraik, and hence a person of high rank in his clan. Katin was enchanted with his dwelling, which was built around one of the great trees, in a ring of rooms two stories high, some enclosed and some open to the air along the outer wall. Several Yerren seemed to be in residence, whether kin or servants they couldn't tell, but it was clear that Civornos was master of the household.

His questions had mainly to do with the Ysnathi's capacity for warfare, and he soon realized that the others referred all such matters to Sir Andrew. "Why were so few of their people trained to defend the community?" he asked. When he had led attacks on them, they had seemed to him ill-prepared.

We held our own against you, Sir Andrew thought, but he replied only, "All of our people will take to arms when we deem the danger to be great enough."

To his surprise, Pierson translated the Yerren's answer as, "Let them do so, then."

He naturally wanted to know how their muskets worked, and naturally Sir Andrew did not intend to tell him. "When an alliance between our clans has been forged, as I hope it will, we shall reveal the secrets of our weaponry," he said.

Civornos evidently found this reasonable. "Would their weapons kill shraik?" he asked next.

"This is what he most wants to know," Jerl said softly.

"What are these shraik?" Sir Andrew asked, that being foremost among the questions he wanted answered.

The hermit hesitated. "If I ask that, they will know that we have never killed any. We may lose ground."

Sir Andrew sighed. "They'll find that out sooner or later. But tell him that a musket will kill anything that a spear can kill, far more easily, and at a greater distance—that one soldier with a musket can do the work of three spear-bearers."

When this had been said in Yerren, Civornos spoke directly to Sir Andrew, and the hermit translated, "He asks, why, if we are so well able to defend ourselves, do we seek an alliance with another clan?"

It was the question Sir Andrew had been waiting for. Between them, he and the hermit strove to describe the danger of the coming invasion in terms that would make sense to their host. It had apparently never occurred to the Yerren that other lands lay beyond the ocean, although, as Civornos remarked, he supposed that this strange new clan had to come from somewhere.

But when he heard that the enemy were not expected to arrive until the end of summer, he said only, "Then this war of yours will have to await its season. By then it may be too late."

Sir Andrew tried again to explain the threat the Chamber's armies would pose, not to the Colonies alone, but to the communities of the Yerren. But Civornos was apparently unmoved. "If the Season of Shadows takes a high toll," he told them, "we'll not have the means to engage another enemy, by then. All the more reason for your people to join forces with us now."

"Ask him," Sir Andrew said impatiently, "what this Season of Shadows is."

Civornos did not answer at once, and when he did speak, he told them little enough. "He says that the shraik come from the south during the Season of Shadows," the hermit said. "It is a time of great suffering for all the clan, and it is ill luck even to speak of it."

"We must speak of it, if we are to join forces against this evil," Sir Andrew insisted.

When this had been translated to him, however, Civornos abruptly rose and left them, with only a few hasty words of explanation. Sir Andrew turned to the hermit. "What did he say?"

"Only 'in the north.' "

Katin touched Sir Andrew's arm and nodded toward Jerl. He was staring after Civornos, glassy-eyed, his forehead beaded with sweat.

"What is it, Smit?"

Jerl started and turned back to them, pale but calm. "He's in pain," he said. "It's not that he refuses to tell us about these things—he just *can't*. None of them can . . . except maybe the priests."

"I might have known," Sir Andrew said in frustration. "If they could talk to us, we might make some *progress* at these negotiations! Of course they can't! Well, why can't they?"

Jerl shuddered visibly. "When they try . . . it's like flesh tearing, like hundreds of wounds. Not a memory of pain—the pain itself returns. The pain of *the whole clan.*"

The hermit nodded. "It is as I told you. They live in such sympathy with one another, that all the clan suffers when any one of them is harmed. That is why, if some of them are afraid, all behave as if they have been threatened."

Sir Andrew tried to imagine what it would be like to sense the feelings of all the other colonists, with all their varied viewpoints and emotions. It seemed impossibly confusing and distracting. How could he hope to reach an understanding with beings whose essential nature was so utterly alien from his own? As a strategist, he knew that it was vital—in war or in negotiation—to understand one's adversaries and one's allies. Would this be possible with the inhuman Yerren, who could not even answer his questions?

But perhaps this very enigma could work to his advantage. "If that is so, then there can be little subterfuge among them," he said thoughtfully.

"None, I should think, within their own clan. No matter what words a Yerren spoke, the others would know what it truly felt."

"And if we were to win the trust of some of them, the others would accept us as well?"

"I think so," said Jerl. "But it's to do with *warning* more than anything else. If one of them discovers some danger, the rest will know of it—that's what this power of theirs is for." He didn't know where this idea had come from, but it had to be so. It fit what he felt as no other explanation had done. "And if they decide we're *not* dangerous, maybe the . . . the *lack* of a warning will pass from one to another as well."

Sir Andrew knew that nothing in his experience was likely to help him in dealing with the Yerren. But could he really try to ground a plan on anything so nebulous as an absence of an imperceptible warning?

"Somehow, I thought you had a better plan than to lead us here to be caged like animals," Rolande said bitterly. Being free during the day made it all the harder to endure being locked up every night.

So did I, Sir Andrew thought. Too many days were passing, and for all he knew to the contrary, the matter of whether or not to send the emissary had been remanded to some Yerren council for a decision. If that were the case, it could be weeks before they received an answer, and then there was no guarantee that the answer would be favorable. With the threat of the invasion looming ever nearer, Sir Andrew remonstrated with himself for having done nothing but accept their fate, as if they had all the time in the world to resolve their difficulties. He had to act.

Now that he knew where the leader of the Yerren could be found, might it not be wiser to seek the mountains to the north, and try to find him? They could not afford to waste more time on intermediaries. It seemed possible, too, that the Yerren would respect them more for taking the chance than for waiting patiently. He might fail to persuade the High Lord of the value of an alliance, but he certainly wasn't accomplishing anything where he was. If the mission was to be a failure, the sooner he found it out, the better. He needed to know what was happening to Thornfeld. Had the Wardership kept their word? Had they obtained the cooperation of the farmers? And was the fortification of the coast proceeding according to plan? He did not doubt Captain Jamison's ability, but he wouldn't be satisfied until he'd examined the earthworks and watchtowers for himself.

* * *

Rolande was worried about much the same things. She didn't trust Simeon to be on his own for as long as this. Had he seen to the stocks of musket shot? Had he succeeded in inciting the farmers to defy the ban on clearing more forestland? Most importantly, had he posted the watchers along the coast? When Sir Andrew decided that it was time they made their escape, she seconded him fervently, against the objections of Katin, Jerl, and the hermit, who argued that they would thus sacrifice the gains they had made. Rolande was less enthusiastic when she found that Sir Andrew meant to continue northward, instead of returning to the colony at once, but she would even agree to that if it meant getting out of the bloody cage.

Sir Andrew peered out through a space between the cage slats, searching for any signs of Yerren still abroad, but there were none in sight. Only the buzzing of insects broke the silence. He pulled his head back, glanced at Rolande, and nodded, then, a moment later, Katin gave the same signal from the opposite wall.

"Press down on that side," Rolande ordered Jerl, who leaned forward, pushing with all his strength against the piece of wood in front of him. If they could force the slats far enough apart to allow Katin to crawl through, she could unbar the door for the rest of them. As Jerl tried to force the wood down, it gave slightly, but not enough to increase the size of the opening significantly. Rolande and Sir Andrew added their efforts, but the slats were simply interwoven too tightly.

"There's no help for it," Sir Andrew said, "we're going to have to break them, noise or no. At the center there, where there's less support from the cross slats."

They each chose one of the narrowest slats and braced it against one knee, trying to snap it across. Jerl drew a lungful of air and pulled back till the veins in his neck grew rigid, but the wood only bowed without breaking. "This isn't going to work either," he said finally.

"Yes it will," Rolande said grimly. "Stand aside." She withdrew the small bone-handled knife from her boot, and began to dig a groove around the slat, scoring the surface. "Now try," she said to Jerl. "Use both hands on that side, and I'll pull over here."

When the wood gave at last, and snapped along the cut, the sound was not loud, but it seemed to echo like a gunshot in the quiet air. All listened, waiting for the appearance of any Yerren alerted by the sound, but none came, and they swiftly broke more slats until they could force apart enough of the split pieces to allow Katin to squeeze through.

"Now for our weapons," Rolande said, returning the dulled knife to her boot. With a wary eye out for any Yerren who might be stirring, the party made their way onto the walkway. The blackness was not quite absolute; shafts of moonlight penetrated the darkness through spaces in the leaves above them, as they moved quietly along the paths and bridges.

Sir Andrew led the way toward the hutch where he'd seen their weapons secured, but Rolande stopped him as they approached it. "Stay out of sight," she whispered. "I'll take the girl and fetch our things. I can break in, and she's the smallest—the rest of you will just call attention to us."

So you're a skilled picklock as well as a trained assassin, Sir Andrew thought, watching as the two forms were swallowed up in darkness. "I don't suppose you can tell what Vendeley's thinking?" he asked Jerl, in an undertone.

"No, sir."

"Pity."

"Shall I go after them?" Jerl asked anxiously.

"No. She's right—the smaller the better, for that job."

"I don't know what the Yerren are thinking," Jerl said carefully, "only what they're feeling."

"More's the pity," said Sir Andrew.

Rolande studied the door of the storage hutch. "If there is a lock here, I'll take care of it. Then we'll gather our things as swiftly as we can." The face of the door was completely smooth, however, with no sign of a lock.

"Why would they bother with locks?" Katin asked. "If one of them stole something, the others would know, wouldn't they?" She pushed at the door, which swung back easily, and the two slipped inside.

Rolande chuckled. "You're not quite the dolt I took you for," she said, as they groped about the inside of the dark hutch in search of their weapons.

"No doubt that's high praise, from you." This was no time for a scrap with Mistress Vendeley, Katin told herself firmly.

"It is indeed. Here's one of the muskets."

Fortunately, their things were heaped together, and they soon gathered up everything they could carry and returned to the others, laden with muskets, pistols, knives, Katin's bow and quiver, and Jerl's ax.

The rope ladders were still at a distance, and as they moved slowly and quietly past the dark Yerren dwellings, Sir Andrew had all too much time to wonder about the wisdom of the course he had chosen. Now that they were free, should he avoid wasting even more time and just lead his weary party home, even if they had nothing to show for their efforts, and the Warders would delight in his failure?

When something struck him heavily on the back, he

staggered against Katin, and nearly fell from the walkway. Before he could even recover his balance, the soarhound pup scrabbled over his shoulder and leaped into Katin's arms, squealing in delight. "*Bad* dog," she whispered, hugging it to her, "where have you been?"

They found out soon enough, as a tiny feathered figure came running out from one of the nearby hutches, peering around in the moonlight until it spotted what it was looking for. It came to a stop in front of Katin and reached out its arms for Lucifer, crying, "Snimmer!"

"Oh, hush!" Katin breathed, and quickly dropped the pup into the little Yerren's outstretched hands. Satisfied, it turned back, and they hastened away toward the ladders, praying that the child had not yet been missed.

But Lucifer had other ideas. He gave his Yerren friend a farewell lick on the chin and wriggled from her arms to gallop after Katin. The child gave a piercing shriek and chased after her pet, wailing loudly.

With a muttered oath, Rolande turned back and dove for the young Yerren. She was going to be locked up again, or killed, because of this damned shrieking creature! She had her hands around the child's neck when Sir Andrew clubbed her from behind with the stock of his musket.

The Yerren-child fled without another sound or a backward look, and for a moment Sir Andrew thought of abandoning Rolande where she lay and trying to get the others safely away. There was no time to carry her down one of the immensely long rope ladders, and the Yerren would probably not harm her when they found her—would they? But it was already too late for such a decision. Doors flew open in the nearby buildings, torches appeared, and Yerren came swarming from all directions, blocking the pathways and bridges, cutting off their escape.

The throng was unarmed, and those who surrounded the escaped prisoners made no attempt to recapture them, or even to interfere with them. The Yerren were all staring to the north, Sir Andrew noted, and as he turned in that direction as well, several Yerren, larger than those he was used to, but still slight in comparison with the colonists, descended from the night sky and landed on a high platform in the center of the waiting crowd. There were half a dozen when they all assembled, and Sir Andrew could see in the torchlight that their feathers were a true sapphire, unlike the darker blue or gray-green of the Yerren he had seen before.

Rolande stirred and groaned, looking around vaguely. "Watchers . . ." she mumbled.

Sir Andrew glanced down at her. "They don't seem interested in catching us. Pierson, Smit, can either of you tell what this is about?"

Jerl shook his head. "I don't think they know either. They're all curious."

"It seems the newcomers can speak only to the priests," the hermit told him.

"They've come," said Jerl, "and Civornos, too." He pointed to a group of Yerren who looked to Sir Andrew exactly like all the others.

"Post watchers along the coast!" Rolande said urgently, her eyes closed again.

Sir Andrew turned to her in surprise. She was the last person he would have suspected of harboring secret fears about the invasion. She had always discounted the danger. But before he could question her, one of the priests stepped out from the crowd on the platform above, wings raised, and the Yerren suddenly fell silent. When he had spoken, they all turned to look at the group of human prisoners.

"They are messengers from the north, from the sacred mountain fastness," the hermit translated.

"They've been sent to escort us to the High Lord of the Tree-Green Clan."

* * *

Rolande need not have concerned herself over whether Simeon was neglecting the business at hand. His industry would have satisfied and, indeed, surprised her. Now that he had expectations of taking her place as Governor of the colony, when the Chamber had seized power, he felt that it was far more in his own interests to forward the success of the invasion. He had not only carried out Rolande's orders, but improved upon them betimes.

Having set in motion his preparations for the arrival of the Chamber's forces, Simeon turned to the task of blighting the chances for an alliance with the Yerren. He'd seen the havoc wrought by them, and he agreed with Sir Andrew that they might bring much-needed strength to the colonists' defenses. That wouldn't do at all. Not if he could prevent it.

To this end, he sat in the main room of the rough-hewn cottage that served as home to Feifer Tolen, one of the many aspiring farmers in the outlying lands of Thornfeld. That Tolen had a cottage at all, and farmed a small bit of cleared land, was proof of the fact that he owed a sizable debt to Rolande. There were others present, drinking raw ale around the unfinished oak slab table—men and women who had even less to show for their efforts than Tolen did. Most of those who had arrived in the New World within the last year had yet to see any land cleared for their use, and had been unable to establish farmsteads. The ban on burning forestland had left them at loose ends, without even certain prospects for the future.

It was ostensibly to discover a way to deal with their

plight that Simeon had organized this meeting, but he had been careful to summon only those he could most easily coerce to his cause. Since he was Rolande's agent, no one was surprised by this offer of help. After all, it was she who had outfitted many of them in the first place, and she stood to gain or lose with them. But the present state of affairs made loss far more likely than gain, and the faces ranged around the table were discouraged and bitter.

"We must clear more land," Tolen said defiantly. "Unless we do so, we will starve in short order."

"Perhaps the rest of the colony as well," Simeon suggested, pausing deliberately to sip his ale and let them ponder his words. He set his mug down with a thump. "How long can we sustain a growing community without producing more food?"

"Aye, there's no denying that," someone said.

"But the Wardership has declared that we must stop the burning," objected a thin, worn woman, "and they've the militia to enforce their will. What can we do, then?"

"True," Simeon said. "But it seems to me that we elect the Warders, and we should have a say in what happens to us. Or isn't that so?" he asked, too silkily. "Do the nobles call the tune here, too, for us to dance to? Is this prohibition what *you* wanted, or what Lord Edenbyrne and his toadies wanted?"

The farmers shuffled uneasily.

"That's as may be," one said, "but you don't say what will happen if we try to go against the Warders' orders. I can't afford to pay a fine, and I don't fancy spending time in the stocks, so I tell you."

There were murmurs of agreement from the others, and Simeon rose, spreading his hands in a placating gesture. "A most prudent concern," he said. "For if one of you violated the orders of the Wardership, it would be possible to punish you . . . but if all stand together, who is to cross you? It is as it has ever been, there is strength in numbers." He lifted the pitcher of ale and filled the earthenware mugs all around. "You know, of course, that Mistress Vendeley, leaving her own affairs unattended, has accompanied Sir Andrew to see that your interests are not abused." A hint of threat crept into his voice, as he continued, "But she will return, and when she does, there will still be debts to be paid. No one can survive by always paying out."

"And what of the feather folk?" a grave-looking man asked.

"Are you concerned for them now?" Simeon replied with contempt, deliberately twisting the man's question.

Undaunted, the farmer said, "I am not. I'm concerned for our welfare. They've been quiet since the burning stopped. If we burn more trees, we'll have to fight them off again. We're the ones who shall suffer."

"We've suffered before," said a woman with a bandage around her head. "One of the winged devils tore a furrow through my scalp you could plant a row of beans in. But I shot it out of the sky and stuffed a quilt with its feathers!"

"Well done!" said Simeon, laughing.

"Aye, everything that's ever been won was come by hard," another man put in. "We knew that well enough when we came to this place. I'm not afraid of a flock of half-grown featherlings."

"That's the way, my friends," Simeon said, exultant as he sensed the turn in the tide. "We shall claim that which is ours, standing side by side, to make a place in this world for all of us. And," he added enticingly, "I shall see that adequate weapons and shot for the defense of our work are supplied." It would be as good a way as any to use up the supply in the barrels he'd taken from the blacksmith's. . . .

Before many days had passed, Simeon found himself with a sizable contingent of farmers armed with axes, torches, and muskets. Once again billows of smoke filled the sky around the edges of the colony.

The Warders argued among themselves as to what should be done, but Rolande's faction supported the farmers, and many of the others had common interests with them as well. In the end, it was decided to hold off taking any action that would risk setting the citizens of the colony to fighting with each other. The final disposition of the land could be left until the return of Sir Andrew's party with news of the Yerren—*if* they returned, as many were already saying. It was widely believed that the Yerren had killed them, and that there was nothing to be gained by attempting to appease the beasts.

But Lady Celia worried that Sir Andrew's mission—perhaps his life—would be jeopardized by the renewed burning. And the Princess with him! Sir Andrew had resolutely refused to take her on such a dangerous expedition, and then the vixen had followed him anyway, leaving only a note that Lady Celia would not find till it was too late to stop her. She must have found Sir Andrew's party, surely. If not, she'd have come back by now . . . unless she'd lost her way, or met with wild animals, or worse. . . . Lady Celia was not one to waste time worrying about something she couldn't help, but she meant to give the girl a piece of her mind if she returned alive and well.

In the meantime, she turned to those matters she could try to mend. She visited farmhouse after farmhouse, to speak of the coming invasion and to ask, "How will we hold off the Chamber's army, with the Yerren on the attack again?"

But too often Simeon had reached them first, and they asked, "If we starve, how are we to fight anyone at all?"

When she argued that the proposed treaty with the Yerren was the way to resolve the problem, some said outright that it was moonshine and folly. Most were more polite, for the Viscountess was generally liked, but their views came to much the same thing. And others still, influenced by Simeon's talk of the aristocracy, were unwilling even to listen to her. There was no doubt where the canker at the root of this discord lay.

The fumes of rum and the smoke from long-handled pipes wafted from the door as Lady Celia entered the tavern. She still carried her riding crop as she strode across the dim chamber, seeking out her quarry. In the afternoon while the farmers and shopkeepers went about their business, the alehouse was filled mainly with idlers, off-duty soldiers, and those who had no other employment—a group that included not a few discouraged farmers.

Simeon had work aplenty, but it hadn't kept him from leaving Rolande's shop in the care of a youth in their employ and taking himself off to more amusing pursuits. The tavern offered not only drink and dicing, but the chance to talk to all manner of folk at one time.

When Lady Celia spotted him, he was deep in conversation with a skinny woman in patched buckskin. At first she thought he was engaged in a flirtation, but as she drew nearer she could hear that he was berating the wench for failing to perform some task he'd set her. So engrossed was he in this tirade, that it wasn't until Lady Celia's shadow fell across him that he looked up, and abruptly cut short his words. "Get you gone," he snapped at the woman, who glanced at Lady Celia and then scuttled away.

Simeon did not rise. Taking a draught from a mug of mulled rum, he said insolently, "I didn't think to find you patronizing this establishment, Your Ladyship."

Lady Celia, angry though she was at his machinations, was not about to be baited by such vermin. She had seen many like him at work in Albin, scurrying like rats about their masters' bidding, spreading unrest like the plague.

"And I would have thought to find you at your place of business at this hour," she said, "seeing to Mistress Vendeley's affairs."

But I am, Simeon thought. He grinned and said, "Why, if Your Ladyship has business with me, you might have sent for me. I'm most flattered that you should choose to seek me out yourself."

"I choose to speak to you in whatever den you dig! And if it be here, so much the better. The rabble that follow you can hear what I have to say as well." The room had grown quiet, and now that Lady Celia had the attention of the house, she said, "Is it not you who have encouraged the farmers to start burning the forests again?"

"I? What have I to do with farmers?"

"Do not trouble yourself to lie. When I paid a call of condolence on Mistress Broaquin, I found her in dread that her other children would fall to the Yerren, if they were forced to continue with the burning. Have you not threatened to withdraw the support that Vendeley provided the farmers, if they do not clear more land?"

Simeon looked up sharply. "Nothing is given without some return—not among those who must work for their bread. But what would Your Ladyship know of work, and the hardships of the common folk? The farmers have every right to band together to see to their interests—their interests, not mine."

"It is in no one's interest to bring down the wrath of

the Yerren upon us at this time—in no one's interest but the Chamber's! Those who seek to weaken our defenses are doing the Chamber's work, and doing it for a price, I daresay." She looked around the dim, smoky room as she spoke, staring down any who met her gaze. "It was just such infamy that brought down Holistowe and Oxwold, and I shall not stand by while the like happens here! Nor should any of you who value your life and liberty!" Turning back to Simeon, she said evenly, "I should take better care, if I were you, or soon the whole colony will know you for the Chamber's man."

Simeon rose to face her, his heart racing. Was she just making wild accusations, or did the jade know something? Covering his discomfiture with bravado, he said, "You threaten me? My friends are stronger than you and all your idle highborn lot. We will have what is ours by right."

Lady Celia could barely contain her fury, reminded as she was of the hardships she'd encountered on her hasty flight from Albin, and the indignities she'd suffered at the hands of ruffians like Simeon. She remembered well the carriage ride along roads rutted from the passage of armed men and artillery, muddy in the dismal rain, harried, fearful, and desperate to reach safety. More than once they'd been stopped by clutches of roustabouts drunk on ale and victory, who were relentless in their desire to pillage everything in a land they now perceived as theirs. Only unwavering courage and fortitude—and the cowardice of their attackers—had enabled them to fight off the rabble, and not without taking considerable losses of their own. How dare this feckless brute cant to her of honest toil and of rights?

When he came around the table and stepped toward her with a menacing air, she swung the riding crop, catching him a stinging blow across the cheek. A spot of blood appeared where the silver tip broke the skin. "As you behave like some rampaging animal, you may expect to be treated like one," she said with contempt.

Eyes blazing, Simeon pulled off the scarf around his neck and rubbed his cheek with it. "You should not have struck me. Perhaps in the past you were free to misuse people as you wished, but we are no longer in Albin. This, My Lady, is a new game, and the pawns will determine the order of the board."

Chapter 9

The journey through the steeply rising terrain was far from easy, and their escort, obviously frustrated at being restricted to the speed at which the colonists could travel by foot, forced the pace with an intensity that made Sir Andrew wonder what they feared. They kept mainly to the treetops or the air, only descending as far as the lower branches in order to urge the party along, or bring them fresh-killed game. Katin envied the ease with which they moved from tree to tree, stepping securely on branches that would have broken under human weight. Only Civornos, who accompanied them as their renhith, stayed near them, and talked of the proposed treaty. But when Sir Andrew asked precisely where they were bound, the answer was simply "Creshgahar," which the hermit could not translate. It was pointless, too, to ask how soon they would reach their destination, for the Yerren naturally had no idea how long it would take a group of Ysnathi to walk and climb to a place that they themselves would simply fly to. To describe a distance as "a day's flight" conveyed little to the human travelers.

But Sir Andrew had learned to read the signs, and as they approached journey's end, Jerl's increasing agitation told him that they were nearing a community of

Yerren. The boy thrashed and muttered in his sleep—words he didn't recognize when he was awake. Even during the day he often failed to hear when he was spoken to, but stared off to the north with a troubled, faraway look.

Katin was subdued also, exhausted by the hard pace and the steep rise of the land they had covered, but she made no complaint. Sir Andrew would have liked to call a halt more often, to let her rest, but time was too important now to allow for any unnecessary delay. And Katin did not expect it. She reminded herself that she had insisted on accompanying the expedition, and that it was up to her to keep pace with the rest.

Rolande did not hesitate to complain. After two days' traveling, her head still ached from Sir Andrew's blow, though the preparation Katin brewed for her did ease the worst of it. She knew they'd been right to stop her from throttling the Yerren-chick. In the madness of the moment, she'd have risked anything rather than return to captivity—but when she thought of the likely consequences had the Yerren caught her, she was appalled at her own rashness. Sir Andrew had probably saved her life as well as the child's.

If not for that cursed fledgling, though, the messengers might have dropped from the sky too late to find them. On their own, they could never have found the way to the exact place in the mountains where the Yerren High Lord kept court. She could have persuaded Sir Andrew that they were needed at Thornfeld, that it was simply not possible to reason with the Yerren. And now, instead, thanks to the featherbrat, they had *guides* to lead them to the very place! Sir Andrew's longed-for negotiations would take place after all—but at least she would be privy to them. There would be no secrets between him and the Yerren. And if she knew the exact terms of any treaty he managed to arrange, it would be much easier to see that they were violated.

It was Civornos who pointed out to them the first sight of their destination. There, near the crest of the black, craggy mountains, a series of large caves could just be seen, their dark openings barely blacker than the surrounding cliffs. As they drew closer, they could make out that the stone around the entrances was decorated with red, blue, and green plant dyes so that ominous representations of eyes and claws seemed to rise from the shelves of rock. The area was curiously devoid of life, except for a few heavily armed Yerren who appeared to be standing watch outside the entrances. But the constant activity of the Yerren city—the returning hunters bringing meat to be skinned on racks, the repairing of the hutches, the craftsmen carving bowls and tools with obsidian blades—all were absent here.

Nonetheless, Sir Andrew felt again the relief and sense of promise that the first sight of the treetop city had given him. Then, the certainty that the Yerren were civilized beings had held out hope, and now at last he would be able to lay his terms of alliance before someone with the authority to accept or refuse them. The journey had not, after all, been in vain. He would soon have an answer, and his talks with Civornos had led him to believe that the answer would be a favorable one. From the first, the Yerren commander had been plain about his approval of the plan, and Jerl assured them that he meant what he said. He wanted Ysnathi weaponry to use against the shraik, and he was willing to come to terms with the clan-from-beyond-the-sea to get it. "While our peoples war with one another, death waits on the horizon, to carry off victor and vanquished," he had told Sir Andrew. "It is folly to weaken ourselves in this wise."

He could not promise that the High Lord and his counselors would take the same view, but they would not have summoned the Ysnathi to Creshgahar if they saw no merit in the proposed alliance. A dismissal would have been sent by messenger. And he, Civornos, was not without influence in the north. Sir Andrew could tell nothing from the Yerren's manner, but Jerl claimed that Civornos wished to convey to them that he was confident of success, despite his cautious words.

Now, as the party climbed the last steep path to the caves above, Sir Andrew repeated to himself the Yerren terms of formal address and greeting that Civornos had taught him. He, too, felt that success was within his grasp. Their escort, who had been circling overhead as they toiled up the slope, descended as they approached the ridge before the caves, and followed them on foot.

Civornos was in the lead, but suddenly he stopped, gesturing for them to wait. The Yerren behind them also grew still, and Jerl seemed frozen in place, like one of the boulders strewing the way. "No!" he said, and then a throng of Yerren armed with spears and clubs boiled out of the cave entrances, swarming to intercept them, and shouting words that were clearly not meant in welcome.

Lucifer barked at them in defiance, then prudently disappeared through a hole in the rocks, but the rest of the party was blocked from retreating by their Yerren escort on the narrow cliff path behind them. Without warning, their escort had become their guards, and in a moment the other armed Yerren had swept forward and encircled them. As Sir Andrew moved to shield Katin, Civornos stepped forward as if to shield them all, his wings spread wide, his silence somehow more forceful than the clamor of their attackers. The foremost of them came to a halt before him, and the rest stood by as a loud and rapid exchange of words took place.

"What is the meaning of this?" Sir Andrew asked tensely. "I understood that they welcomed this conclave!"

"As did he," said the hermit, watching Civornos. "He is demanding an explanation."

But if he received one, it was lost in the stir caused by two Yerren who emerged from the largest cave and called out an order to the rest. At once the party of Ysnathi was pushed forward and ushered into the cavern, not as guests, but once again as prisoners.

The light that fell so brightly on the stony crags outside did not penetrate far within, and at first they could see nothing at all. The darkness was broken only by candles on tall wooden posts, and when their eyes had grown used to the dim light, they saw that these carved posts flanked a painted stone seat where a single Yerren rested. His feathers shone in jewellike tones of sapphire and emerald, and round his neck was hung a necklace of carved blue stones. Before the throne, the muskets and their other weapons had been laid in a heap, like an exotic offering.

Civornos had remained with the party, as the other Yerren merged with the crowd that stood in a ring around the chamber. When Civornos came forward to address the High Lord, Sir Andrew attempted to join him, but he was given no chance to use the solemn words of salutation he had mastered. He had no sooner taken a step than the surrounding Yerren flowed forward to drive him back. Civornos said something that reassured them, and they drew back again, but hovered close, waiting for an order to strike.

The High Lord spoke to Civornos, who answered at length, and the hermit told them, "He protests that their treatment of us is unwarranted, that we are messengers who have come to Creshgahar willingly, to speak for our people."

Jerl stood rigid, fists clenched. "He's telling them that he's angry with them. Very angry."

Civornos appeared composed and impassive to Sir Andrew, but the hermit said, "Perhaps. He says that he has brought us here under his protection, and that his own honor is at stake. Any who harm us will answer to him for it."

When the High Lord spoke again, Jerl relaxed, looking rather puzzled. No feelings came to him from the Yerren leader at all, though he could tell that Civornos was shaken by his words. "It is we who have betrayed Civornos, and shamed him," the hermit translated. "By false signs and lies we convinced him of our good faith. There is no merit in our words, our promises are hollow."

Sir Andrew felt an unpleasant sense of the ground shifting beneath his feet. He waited impatiently for the hermit to translate Civornos's reply.

"He argues that our interests are bound to theirs, and that there is, therefore, no reason to doubt our word."

At this, the High Lord rose and turned toward one of the many natural tunnels that branched off from the large chamber. In obedience to some summons not even Jerl could sense, a group of Yerren entered the chamber from a deeper part of the cave.

Many, Sir Andrew noticed, bore the signs of gunshot wounds, and he could see burn scars as well, too recent to have healed. At the sight of the Ysnathi captives, they broke into a furious outcry that Sir Andrew could well understand without translation. He had heard it from the crowd of colonists in the market square, when he'd brought the wounded Yerren to the stockade. They demanded blood.

Jerl suddenly shrieked. He fell to the ground and

rolled around frantically, whimpering, "Help me, I'm burning!" So real was the agony that twisted his features, that for a horrified moment Katin thought she could see the yellow flames licking along his jaw.

"Jerl!" she cried. "There's no fire—it's not you that's burning!" She dropped down beside him, trying to calm him, but she could neither hold him still nor make him hear her.

Sir Andrew managed to pull him to his feet, but he continued to struggle violently till Rolande said, "Just hold him there—" and struck him sharply across the face with the back of her hand, then with the palm. "What we don't need now," she said furiously, "is more nonsense from *you!*" His head jerked back with the force of each blow, and the real pain drove out the unreal, so that he twisted away to avoid being hit again. Satisfied, Rolande dropped her hand, and Sir Andrew released him, but he could only stare at them and gasp. "They're on fire!"

"But *you're* not," said Katin. She touched his hand and repeated urgently, "It's not you that's burning."

He looked down at her and nodded, swallowing hard, then turned to Sir Andrew. "The forest—and they—" He gestured at the wounded Yerren. "Again!"

The colonists must have started the burning again, Sir Andrew realized—after the Yerren priests had accepted his word that it had been stopped. The High Lord had consented to meet with them because of that promise, and now he believed that the clan had been deceived by these treacherous savages. It did not require Smit's intuition to see that. How could they recover their position now? *If I get back to Thornfeld alive, I'll find the thrice-damned fools responsible for this and wring their necks!* Sir Andrew vowed.

The responsible party was standing next to him, and cursing herself as heartily as Sir Andrew would have done it, had he known. She had not anticipated that the burning would begin again while she was still in Yerren territory. She hadn't meant to be away this long—and who would have expected the farmers to dare defy the Wardership so soon? Her plan to undo Sir Andrew's efforts at negotiation was working just as she'd hoped, but she hadn't intended to be surrounded by hostile, armed Yerren when it took effect.

Their captors did not seem surprised by Jerl's outburst, or even much interested. The High Lord had raised his wings and uttered a series of sharp staccato commands, and the Yerren warriors, who had been observing silently in the background, came forward and circled the group of prisoners again.

"What did he say?" Sir Andrew demanded.

"We are guilty of unpardonable crimes against his people, and we are to be executed at moonrise—thrown from the top of the cliff." The High Lord spoke again, and the hermit continued, "He says that as we are wingless, it will not be necessary to break our arms first. . . . "

"They think that's *funny,*" Jerl said in horror.

"Oh, they do, do they?" Rolande said grimly. "If these preening peacocks try to push me off a cliff, they won't be laughing long." She was almost glad it was to come to a fight at last. They were hopelessly outnumbered, but so far she had not found the Yerren formidable opponents. And if she could get to the pistols piled on the floor, not far from where she stood. . . . "We can fight our way out of here," she said to Sir Andrew.

But Sir Andrew had met the Yerren on the battlefield. "Are you mad? The others hadn't the authority to kill us—this lot won't hesitate. Don't do anything without my order!" To the hermit, he said, "Tell them that they will dishonor their clan by such an act. We are as angry as they about the burning, and we shall put a stop to it when we return."

The Yerren made no response. They seemed to be waiting.

"Tell them," Katin said suddenly, "that they must use unguent of aloe on those burns. If they don't know how to make it, I can show them."

The Yerren waited, apparently unimpressed.

"Tell them that if they mean to march us off a cliff, they're going to lose a lot of their people doing it!" said Rolande.

"It's no use," Jerl told them, when the hermit had delivered Rolande's warning. "They don't believe you. Not even Civornos."

The hermit laid one hand on Jerl's arm. "Then you must speak for us. Tell them that what we say is true. Say that we are not the enemy."

"But I can't! I don't know how to say all that in Yerren!"

"No matter. Speak, they are waiting."

"Yes, tell them, Jerl," said Katin. "They'll believe *you.*"

"Do as you're told, Smit," Sir Andrew ordered.

"And get on with it!" Rolande added.

Bewildered, Jerl turned to face Civornos, who now stood by the High Lord's throne. He couldn't remember a single word of Yerren. Not knowing what else to do, he said hesitantly, "They've told you the truth. You must believe us. It is against our will that the forest is being burnt. We came here to seek an alliance . . ." As he spoke, the now familiar feeling of dislocation began to steal over him. Without realizing it, he stopped talking, but the Yerren did not stop listening. Without words, he continued to speak to them, about everything the others had said, and about things that didn't concern them at all. He told them of the great war in his homeland, and the danger of the invasion that was coming from across the water. He told them about the hardships suffered by the colonists, and the journey he and his companions had made to find the Yerren city. He told them that he loved Katin, that she was a healer with compassion for every living being. He told them that he respected Sir Andrew, the defender of his people, and that he admired Rolande, who had the courage and cunning of a wolf. He told them of the learning and wisdom of the hermit, who had taught him about the forest and about the Yerren. He himself was nothing, he told them, a drudge, of no importance, who possessed nothing but hope for the future. He wanted what all his people wanted, a home in this fair new land, a family of his own, peace with his neighbors. . . .

Moonrise had long passed before they concluded their negotiations. Sir Andrew was exhausted, but jubilant, having finally accomplished what he had set out to do, at such a cost of time and effort. The land around the colony would be divided fairly between the two parties, leaving an adequate supply for the colonists' tilling, while the rest of the forest tract was to remain the Yerren's.

In return, the Yerren were to be supplied with muskets, powder, and shot to fight the shraik, and should the defense of the clan prove successful, their two peoples would join forces to repel the invasion from Albin.

The one thing that remained was to take word back to the colony and obtain the ratification of the Warders. But that, Sir Andrew suspected, might turn out to be a negotiation more difficult than the one he had just been party to.

* * *

"You want to do what?" Headman Farnham asked, as if he couldn't believe he was hearing right. "You have agreed to give weapons to our worst enemies?"

Sir Andrew sighed. It was hot in the assembly hall, and he wiped the sweat from his brow before continuing. There was something to be said, he thought, for the Yerren custom of holding assemblies in the open air. "Once we have come to an equitable arrangement with them, they will not be our enemies."

"And how can you be certain of that?" Elliot Cavendish demanded.

"They have no more to gain from continued hostilities than we do. Indeed, if we hadn't posed a threat to them to begin with they might never have attacked. They have their own concerns that outweigh any threat we pose—especially at this time. This is what they call 'the Season of Shadows,' a time of great danger for them."

"How so?" asked Farnham.

Sir Andrew had been dreading the task of explaining about the shraik, but it had to be done. The High Lord had attempted to describe the beasts, but Sir Andrew still had only the haziest idea of their nature. "The Yerren say that in the early summer of every fourth year a horde of great winged predators descends upon them, so many and so large that their passing blocks the light of the sun and casts the land in shadow. They devour every living thing in sight, and whole Yerren villages have been destroyed by them. The Yerren of the Tree-Green Clan flee to the mountain caves of the north, to escape the devastation, but even so, they suffer heavy losses. They are rarely able to kill many of the beasts, or drive them off, with their present weaponry. They believe that muskets might give them protection from these creatures, for the first time."

"And what is to prevent them from turning our own weapons upon us?" someone objected. "Our firepower is our greatest advantage against them."

"I believe that if we keep to the terms of our alliance with them, they will honor the peace. They set great store by their word—"

"You *believe!*" the Ministra scoffed. "And we are to chance our lives on this belief of yours? These are soulless creatures, cursed of the Good God and allied with the Evil One. Treating with such demonspawn will only damn us with them!"

"Aye, who has ever seen one of these shraik? Are we children to be frightened by tales of ogres and monsters?"

"If the featherfolk have muskets, we'll never be able to clear the forestland!" a farmer protested.

"This treaty will allow us land in plenty!" Sir Andrew replied, half-shouting.

"If the green devils honor it—"

"Without God there can be no honor!"

The Headman called for order, and asked Sir Andrew, "Did the Yerren offer you any proof of the existence of these shraik, M'lord?"

Impatient as he was with the delay, Sir Andrew could understand their caution. "I was inclined to doubt the reality of such monstrosities myself," he admitted, "but I have seen bones and claws belonging to them, that were too large to come from any other creature known to me. It may be that Goodman Schellring can cast some light upon the nature of the shraik for us." At his request, Carl had questioned the hermit at length about the Yerren's description of the fearsome shraik, and applied his vast knowledge of natural philosophy to this information. Sir Andrew was relieved to turn over to him the matter of defining the unknown beasts.

Carl rose unhurriedly, referring to his notes. He was not a whit in awe of the dignity of the Warders, whom he considered to be as ignorant and inconsequential as most other people. "As to the existence of these immense, winged raptors there can be little doubt," he began. "The bone which I have examined could only belong to an animal with a wingspan over thirty feet in length, which, though prodigious, is more readily to be accepted than the alternative solution—that it was the arm bone of a giant some twelve feet tall." He waited, tapping his sheaf of papers, until the exclamations and protestations of disbelief had died down, then continued, "I might have identified it as the fin bone of one of the great whales, save that it proved to be hollow, after the manner of birds' bones—and those of the Yerren. No, it appears unquestionable that we have to deal with a flying behemoth of a type hitherto unrecorded by students of the natural order.

"Now, the information I have received from Frend Pierson, gathered by him from Yerren who claim to have seen the beasts, is lamentably wanting in detail, but does suggest certain noteworthy features. It would seem that the shraik are not merely gigantic birds, in the accepted sense of the term, since they reportedly possess formidable teeth, in a long beaklike snout, and are, moreover, completely without feathers. Their hide is smooth and hairless, of a leathery texture, perhaps similar to—" he hesitated, but then concluded, "to that of certain eels, or the lizard *salamandre*."

The Headman frowned. "You seem to be describing something remarkably like a . . . dragon," he said carefully.

Carl looked uncomfortable. "The dragon is, of course, mythical, a mere creation of fancy," he said stiffly, "but . . . a creature with a certain superficial resemblance to the heraldic image, well—yes."

"But if such things exist, why has Pierson himself not seen them? He claims to have been here far longer than four summers, does he not?"

"Indeed he does, and I naturally put that very question to him. He replied that he had never ventured so far inland before, into the territory where the Yerren have their dwellings. His hut lies in the forest not far from here, and one can only conjecture that the shraik have not been wont to hunt near the coastline, in the past. But that, in my view, is a matter which we would do well to consider further."

"Why is that?" asked Farnham, not in the least sure what matter Carl was referring to.

The naturalist drew a long breath. "This pattern of return, by which the depredations follow a regular course of recurrence, is familiar to us from the habits of many flock-animals, particularly birds and fish. However, a period of one year in four naturally leads to the question, 'where do the creatures feed during the other three years?' That they come from somewhere in the south appears certain, for they have always been observed flying to the north—no doubt moving from a warmer to a cooler clime for summer—but varying their route of passage each year, so as not to deplete their supply of prey."

That they could kill on such a scale as to make a yearly change of course necessary was disconcerting enough, but Carl had not concluded his speculations. "In the past, the shraik have had no cause to seek other sustenance than what they found in the Yerren villages, for no host of large animals has ever before congregated near the coast, in the land where the colony now stands."

There was an uneasy silence in the meeting hall, as

the Warders weighed Carl's words. "You are suggesting," said Farnham, "that in addition to the supposed threat of invasion, we may have a plague of dragons to deal with?"

"It strikes me as a distinct possibility," Carl affirmed.

"The more reason to make common cause with the Yerren," Sir Andrew insisted, when the outcry about "dragons" had somewhat subsided, but few of his fellow Warders took this view of the matter.

"We'll need all our weaponry to defend ourselves—let the feather folk fend for themselves!"

"Fighting as one, we'll all have a better chance," Sir Andrew argued. "The meat of the matter is that the Yerren would be invaluable allies against the Chamber's forces. If we do not arm them against the dragons," damn them, now he was saying it! "they cannot fight alongside us. They need our weaponry, and we need their numbers."

"What says Mistress Vendeley?" Farnham asked finally. "You were party to this diplomacy, as representative of our civil authorities. In your view, ought we to deliver musketry into the hands of the Yerren?"

Rolande had been strangely quiet throughout the debate. She had allowed Sir Andrew to give a terse account of their experiences with the Yerren, and to present the terms of his proposed treaty, with scarcely an interruption. Now, she only said, temperately enough, that she had found the Yerren nearly unfathomable—hostile and threatening one moment, gracious and well-disposed the next. She felt unable to predict *what* they were likely to do at any time. They might well honor the terms of an accord—if such were their humor on that day, or the will of their mysterious gods—or they might decide that the colonists were again their enemies.

Accordingly, she said, it would be risky to deal with the Yerren, but then all negotiation involved risk, did it not? One could not expect to have certainty in such a case, and if Sir Andrew, who had undertaken their defense, believed that the Yerren could be trusted, then . . . perhaps the gamble would pay. . . .

Her tone was just doubtful enough to enflame the fears of those who already hated the Yerren, and those who mistrusted Sir Andrew. Her own supporters knew her true position, of course, and could be relied upon to oppose the terms of the treaty. Sir Andrew had no more chance of obtaining muskets for the Yerren than for the shraik.

Once again, he thought, he'd been guilty of underestimating the shortsightedness of the commonalty.

At last, Headman Farnham said wearily, "Let us leave the question of muskets for now." They were only going over the same ground they had covered time and again. "What of the matter of dividing the land between our peoples? It seems to me that upon that point we can agree in principle, for there is land enough in New Albin for all of us and more."

Sir Andrew was hoarse and worn with frustration. The important thing, he decided, was to achieve some measure of support for the alliance, of which he could send word back to the Yerren. He could try to win over the Warders individually—or perhaps find some way to arm the Yerren on his own, if it came to that—but if they could at least settle on fair boundaries, for now, they'd not have to prepare for war upon two fronts.

Argument upon this point was divided. There were those who thought that such an arrangement was of little import, those who felt that it was worth the effort if it secured peace, and those opposed to giving anything over to the Yerren. But Rolande could not openly resist a policy that would so clearly serve the colony's interests, for there was little enough to lose by adopting the measure. If the Yerren violated this agreement, it would be easy enough to take the land back. In the end it was decided to agree to the Yerren's conditions, on this point, and wait to see whether they left off their attacks, maintaining themselves in their own place and leaving the colonists to theirs. As a concession to Sir Andrew, it was further concluded that, if the Yerren proved trustworthy in this regard, the question of muskets could then be reconsidered.

It was the best he could expect, Sir Andrew realized, and considerably better than nothing, for he was convinced that the Yerren would let the colonists be, if they cleared only the land allotted to them. But he wasn't looking forward to bringing the news to Civornos, who waited at the hermit's hut to carry their decision back to the High Lord of the Tree-Green Clan. He had considered bringing Jerl along, but now he decided against it. He felt that he would be able to interpret the Yerren's reaction to his words well enough, without the benefit of Jerl's intuition.

The appointed meeting was as difficult as Sir Andrew had anticipated. Because the Yerren expressed feelings, though not facts, through their unspoken communion, they used few gestures, and showed no facial expressions that human beings could discern. But as Sir Andrew met Civornos's inhuman gaze, he thought he could read a cold, appraising look in the Yerren's eyes.

"He says that by the time your clan decides to trust them, it will be too late," the hermit translated. "The Season of Shadows will be upon them. Is it the intention of your people, he asks, to sacrifice the Yerren to the shraik?"

Yes, Sir Andrew thought, glad that Cirvornos could not sense his guilty feelings. He told himself that he was not personally responsible for the Warders' blindness, but he could not help feeling that he had failed both the colonists and the Yerren. After a long silence, he said, "You know as well as I that both our clans will be stronger if we cease to fight one another, and devote ourselves to our defense against more dangerous enemies. That is something gained." He listened to the steady beating of the rain on the thatched roof, as the hermit repeated his words in Yerren, then he continued, "I may yet persuade my people that our best chance of survival is to arm the Yerren and make them our allies. I am not alone in this belief. But if they will not heed my counsel, it may be that I can bring a troop of my warriors to Creshgahar, to fight the shraik. I can promise nothing, but it is too soon to lose hope." Suppose he were to ask for volunteers to go on a dragon-hunt, Sir Andrew thought. If he knew his men, not a few would find the notion irresistible.

Cirvornos didn't believe that they would see further concessions from the colonists. Yet he knew that the Yerren's best hopes lay in placating them, at least for now. Although his clan had made a fair defense of their lands so far, he feared that in time the Yerren's superior numbers would fall to the enemies' superior weaponry. And the Ysnathi were growing bolder all the time.

"I shall tell them that we will divide the land jointly, and that you will abide by that," he said. He and Sir Andrew agreed to send messengers to the hermit regularly, to allow them to exchange news. He was not satisfied, but the best he could do for his people was to counsel peace with the colonists—at least until the Season of Shadows was past.

* * *

Though damp from the rain, and uncomfortable in the unseasonably chilly air, Simeon waited patiently for Sir Andrew to depart from the hermit's hut. He was not disappointed in the result of his work. From what he'd overheard, it seemed that the colonists would receive no help from the feathered gadflies, and he felt that he deserved much of the credit for the failed alliance. The Chamber would have him to thank if their soldiers were spared attack from the air.

No sooner had Sir Andrew mounted his horse and ridden for Silverbourne than Simeon trod through the mud to the hermit's door. The poor weather gave him adequate excuse for his dress, consisting of a long surtout with a cape neckpiece that he had drawn up and buttoned to cover his face to his eyes. Above this he wore a broad-brimmed hat, shading the rest of his face. He knocked on the cottage door loudly enough to be heard above the storm.

"Ill night this, to be about," said the hermit, as he ushered his visitor to the hearth. He stirred the embers of the fire and asked, "What brings you here on a night such as this?"

"My need is great. My child is taken with breakbone fever, and I fear for her life." Simeon endeavored to charge his voice with desperate sadness, but he sounded more desperate than sad. He managed by surreptitiously rubbing a speck of ash from the hearth into the corner of his eye to produce a tear which slid down his cheek pathetically, but the hermit appeared not to notice. From the hard-packed earth beside the fire, he picked up a bowl and stirred it with a stick.

"Ah, petals fall so easily from tender plants." The

hermit set the bowl on a rough board. "Does the cough trouble her a great deal?"

"Dreadfully." Simeon eyed the rows of clay jars filling the wooden shelves that lined the walls, searching for the one that might suit his purpose.

"Indeed. Well, I have nothing to hand that will serve, for it needs a mixture of many herbs to treat the diverse ills attendant on this malady. You will have to wait while I prepare it."

That suited Simeon very well. He wanted the old man occupied while he looked around. "I will do whatever you bid," he said humbly, "only make haste, I beg you."

The hermit rose and set about gathering coltsfoot, pennyroyal, lungwort, and other simples from his bottles and jars, then started grinding them in a stone mortar.

Simeon paced about before the shelves, feigning a father's restless distress. "Does not hag's taper ease a fever?" he asked at random.

"Nay, that's useful for naught but coughs in cattle."

Burnt adder, was that the one? "The little one is in such pain," he said plaintively, fearing that the hermit would finish his preparations before he had found what he'd come for. "I have heard it said that burnt adder will lessen such pain."

The hermit shook his head. "I do not know who could have told you that. It is used only for making ink." He added a handful of heartsease to the mortar, and continued grinding the mixture together.

Then Simeon caught sight of a row of small jars, set on a shelf high above the table where the hermit was bent to his task. Scratched into the clay of the nearest was the name "madwort."

Simeon lapsed into silence. For a while he peered over the hermit's shoulder as he added a dollop of honey wine to the concoction, but as he bent over the fire to heat the mixture, Simeon reached for the jar of madwort and slipped it into the pocket of his greatcoat.

When the medicament was brewed to the hermit's satisfaction, he poured it into a bottle, corked it, and offered it to Simeon, who gave him a few pieces of silver in return, with expressions of deepest gratitude. It was an extravagant payment, but he supposed that a thankful parent wouldn't stint at such a time. *Fair enough,* he thought, *for what I've bought.*

Looking from the coins to Simeon's still obscured face, the hermit said, "Most generous, sir. For such a fee you should have something more. Pray wait but one moment." He turned and rummaged through the scraps in an old trunk, then pulled forth a small pouch, which he filled with some dried, pale purple flowers and handed to Simeon. "There may be more ills to come than the one of which you speak. Take this as well, for in good time, it will prove most useful."

Chapter 10

Sir Andrew woke at first light, as soldiers do, but he lay still, savoring the comfort of the down mattresses, the scent of fresh linen, and the softer luxury, the sweeter scent, of Celia's skin next to his. If he kept his eyes closed, he could imagine himself back in Albin, lying blissfully in her embrace, with no thought of imminent disaster. He had not known that peace since before the revolution, when his major duties had consisted of mounting skirmishes along the Acquitanian border. It had been so long that he was surprised he could remember the sensation at all.

Lady Celia stirred and murmured, "Andrew . . . come home. . . ."

He refused to open his eyes, yearning for more time to spend with her. He had meant to rise without waking her, but in a moment he felt her fingers lightly graze his neck, and he turned to gather her close again, kissing her hair, her mouth, her throat. Later she slept again, but Sir Andrew knew he had no more time to indulge himself in rest or pleasure.

Slipping from beneath the quilted coverlet, he rose silently and walked over to the washstand beside the window. He looked out at a peaceful field of wheat, golden in the morning sun, thinking, *It is hard to credit that all this can so easily come to ruin.* He pictured the field below trampled to mud by horses' hooves and strewn with bloody corpses, a sight all too familiar to him from the last battles he had fought—and lost—in Albin. He glanced toward the walnut four-poster bed where Celia lay. To lose everything a second time would be beyond bearing.

Lady Celia rose, drawing her dressing gown around her, and came to stand beside him. He put his arm around her and said, "I must go today to see to the fortifications along the coast."

Lady Celia sighed. "So soon?"

"I had far rather tarry here, but Captain Jamison tells me the construction has been hindered by accidents—and he believes that these problems are not the work of chance. I must see for myself what is taking place there." Lady Celia felt his muscles tense as he exclaimed, "For once I would have an honest battle where I can know my enemy's face! I've no patience for all this machination. Is it not enough that we have to deal with the Chamber's army—but now the Warders have all but destroyed our chance for an alliance with the Yerren by allowing the forest to be burned again! I tell you, there are factions among the Wardership who work against the common good. I wonder which of them stand to prosper from the victory of the Chamber."

"And now it seems we've a drove of dragons to contend with as well," Lady Celia said lightly. "To think that I used to complain that my life was dull! If ever I know tedium again, I shall savor it like a rare wine."

Sir Andrew had to smile, in spite of himself. Yet as he stared out the window, he saw not the pastoral scene outside, but a shadowy throng of faceless men and women working for the downfall of the colony, of his new life and newfound happiness. But among the illusive shadows of the Chamber's minions, one face stood out. "Still, from what you tell me, it is not so much the Warders, but Simeon Pryce who is to blame for the rekindling of the fires. It's no thanks to that wretch that we escaped with our lives."

Lady Celia nodded, her head against his shoulder. "That was my worst fear, that the creatures would blame you—and the Princess—for his actions. How I wanted to kill him!" Her voice grew harsh with anger. "I have sought out some of those who refused to take part in his scurrilous plan. They have suffered for their honesty."

Sir Andrew had been surprised at Celia's account of her confrontation with Simeon at the tavern. She so rarely lost her temper that he could hardly imagine her striking anyone. Now, remembering the deathly silence in the candlelit cavern, after the Yerren High Lord had pronounced sentence upon them, he said slowly, "Before I go, I believe I shall have a talk with Goodman Pryce."

When he arrived at Rolande's shop, Sir Andrew found Simeon hunched over a ledger at the far end of the counter. Simeon looked up when he heard someone enter, his expression turning insolent as he saw who it was.

The shop was still empty, and Sir Andrew closed and barred the door behind him. "I wish to have words with you—without interruption."

Simeon made a great show of pushing aside the ledger and walked with deliberate slowness to where Sir Andrew stood. "It is a privilege to wait upon Your Lordship's presence," he said with a smirk. "What business could Viscount Edenbyrne have with the likes of me?"

Sir Andrew had never before had occasion to deal

with Simeon directly, and now that he did, he perfectly understood Celia's fury. If ever a man needed thrashing. . . .

"Lady Celia tells me that you are behind the rekindling of fires in the forest."

At this, a dangerous light came into Simeon's eyes. He'd anticipated that there'd be trouble once Sir Andrew found out about his role in the burning of the trees, and he was prepared.

"I would not say she lies," Simeon said smoothly, in a tone that meant just that. "But in this Her Ladyship is mistaken."

Sir Andrew had no intention of bandying words with him. "If you are not the culprit, tell me who is."

"There is no culprit. It is the farmers who came to this decision, for their own sakes. Who will look to their interests, if they do not?" *Not,* his words implied, *the aristocracy.* He began to put away some tools lying on the counter, as if the conversation were of no import, and he had better things to be about.

The man's effrontery was intolerable. Sir Andrew leaned across the counter, barely resisting the desire to grab Simeon by the collar and shake him. "They did this of their own accord? Or at your instigation?"

"I merely explained to them where matters stood."

"By threatening to dispossess them of everything they own? That, I take it, was in the interests of their welfare?"

Simeon straightened like a snake uncoiling to strike. "Some of us have not the benefit of exalted birth and wealth bestowed upon us. We depend on our own toil for our bread. Perhaps if Your Lordship had experience of gainful labor he would better understand the necessities of commerce—and the plight of the poor." He spat the words contemptuously. "I've seen those being trained in arms at the stockade. It seems to suit you to have them killed in battle, yet when they seek to clear the land for which they are to fight, you forbid it."

Outraged, Sir Andrew exclaimed, "I have just secured a treaty—at risk of my life—that will allow land to be cleared in safety!" He stopped. What was he doing? He'd be damned if he'd justify himself to this viper, or let himself be turned from his purpose by Simeon's sly tongue. "What do you stand to gain from your treachery, Pryce?" he demanded.

At that, Simeon stopped sorting harness tack and grew still. Could Sir Andrew know about his dealings in the employ of the Chamber? His Lordship certainly suspected something. Simeon glanced toward the barred door. If he struck now, while there was no chance of disturbance, he could hide Sir Andrew's body in the cellar, and leave it in a ditch after nightfall. When the watch found it, they would lay the blame on the bandits. It seemed a foolproof plan. Deliberately, he laid the rest of the tools beneath the counter, taking an awl from the array of implements there, as he did so, and dropping it into the pocket of his leather apron. With his hand in his pocket, he came around the counter to confront Sir Andrew.

He kept talking, as he stalked his quarry, to distract Sir Andrew from his intent. "It's my livelihood I would gain—an honest livelihood. I ask nothing of these people that they are not bound by the laws of the settlement to pay. Indeed, Mistress Vendeley has shown great patience in awaiting the return on her enterprise. She, too, has suffered her share from the reverses of fortune." He was now within inches of his prey.

But Sir Andrew had witnessed—and quelled—too many fights among his men to be taken by surprise. He saw the way Simeon moved, placing his weight on his front foot to balance himself for the blow, and the slight movement of his arm the moment before he struck. He turned aside as Simeon stabbed at him, and thrust his shoulder into Simeon's chest, deflecting his aim and knocking him backward. Simeon was thrown off balance just enough so that the awl missed Sir Andrew's throat, instead slicing obliquely across his chest, ripping his jacket, and gouging him just below the neck.

Hardly aware of the pain, Sir Andrew seized Simeon's wrist and twisted his arm back sharply, forcing him to drop the awl, then thrust him back against the counter so hard that it shuddered, and jars and bottles flew from the shelves and broke against the floor. Fearing for his life, Simeon flailed wildly and caught hold of one of the stools by the counter. He swung it with all his strength, striking Sir Andrew squarely in the knee. At the sudden shock of pain, Sir Andrew loosed his grip for a moment, and Simeon dove for the floor, clutching the awl again. As he sprang to strike, Sir Andrew caught him in the stomach with his boot, and he doubled over, retching.

Sir Andrew dragged him to his feet, pulled the awl from his hand, and hurled it against the wall. Simeon stood panting and glaring at him, as if defeated, but then suddenly he grabbed a mallet from the counter and came at Sir Andrew with all the swiftness of desperation. It was very much the sort of move Sir Andrew had expected. Blocking the blow with his left arm, he struck Simeon's jaw with his right fist, and Simeon fell back, banging his head against the counter. When he staggered to his feet, Sir Andrew snatched up a harness strap and slashed at him with it, driving him back against the counter and raining blow after blow on him, until at last his long pent-up rage had been satisfied.

Simeon sank to the floor, and Sir Andrew only

glanced down at him, as if he were a loathsome insect, then turned away. Suddenly he was aware of the throbbing pain where the awl had struck him. Without looking back, he said, "If you give any more trouble, next time I'll break your worthless neck."

* * *

Though it was late, the door to Rolande's shop still stood open, and Katin hurried in, remembering that the cook had bidden her fetch a cone of sugar when she was next in town. She found the counter unattended, and was about to call out, when a much better idea occurred to her. Simeon was no doubt lounging about somewhere, avoiding his duties while Rolande was out, and this was too good an opportunity to neglect, of looking about the premises unobserved.

She knew that Rolande had continually tried to thwart Sir Andrew's efforts to arrange the colony's defense, and that Simeon had incited the farmers to begin burning the forest again. Lady Celia had even suggested that the Chamber was behind it. Since their mission to the Yerren, Sir Andrew had seemed to think better of Rolande, but Katin mistrusted her as much as ever. Now, here was her chance to do some spying of her own, and perhaps uncover proof that she could present to Sir Andrew.

But she'd just started toward the stairway at the back of the shop when she heard footsteps approaching the door. She had just time to slip inside a tall cupboard before Rolande strode into the shop. Glancing around to make certain that the place was empty, Rolande slammed the door, then stormed into the back room and bellowed for Simeon to come up from the cellar.

Even from where she hid, Katin could hear her shouting, "Where the devil have you been these three days past?" Then, as Simeon climbed the stairs, she gave a whistle and said, "God's blood! What happened to you? Did one of your wenches take a stick to you?"

While he explained, with as little detail as possible, about his encounter with Sir Andrew, Katin crept closer, keeping below the level of the counter. She heard him say, "I've been about our business along the coast. They've begun building the watchtowers."

"We'll come to that. First, I've another bone to pick with you, you mangy cur!"

Katin listened intently, barely breathing.

Simeon, however, was not listening to Rolande's tirade. Taking a fresh cloth from a bowl of water, he pressed it to his swollen face, as her voice hammered at him furiously. Only plans of vengeance filled his thoughts. He would see Sir Andrew paid for the humiliation of that beating.

Rolande picked up a tap hammer from the plank worktable and smacked it against the side of the cask Simeon was leaning against, causing him to jump.

"Please," he said, rubbing his temples. His head felt as if a cannonball had hit it.

"Don't you whine to me. I want to know what you thought you were about." Seeing that he didn't have the faintest notion what she was talking about, Rolande tossed the hammer onto the floor, barely missing his foot. "If that stiff-necked guinea cock hadn't been beforehand about it, I'd beat you to splinters myself!"

"I've done nothing!" Simeon protested, wishing he'd slipped out before Rolande's arrival to get a mug of rum to dull his pain.

"Nothing? I don't call it nothing to set a pack of bandits upon us!"

Simeon had been working on an explanation of the purpose for which he'd sent the bandits, ever since word had reached him that the attempt had failed. Indeed, he'd been avoiding Rolande for just that reason. But the pounding in his head seemed to keep any information from reaching his tongue.

Rolande grabbed him by the shirt, wrenching his sore shoulder. "Explain yourself, damn you!"

"It was a misunderstanding," he said, wincing. "I just wanted the girl."

"For what purpose?"

He gave her a deliberately lascivious look. "For what purpose do you think, Mistress?"

"Don't try your lies on me—you'd not have hired that lot to catch one coney."

"That was the misunderstanding." Now his tone turned cajoling. "When I found she had left to follow you, I bade Lorin snatch her, that's all. Of course, I assumed that he'd find her long before she reached your camp. It should have been that easy! It never occurred to me that she'd evade them, or that they'd be fool enough to attack the whole party."

Rolande looked at him narrowly, uncertain whether to believe him or not. "Even you aren't lecher enough for that. Why would that one be worth gold to you?"

Simeon shrugged painfully. "The little minx taunts me, with her airs and her wild ways. It galls me to be always thinking about her, and she holding herself off—why should she smile at Sir Andrew's stableboy, and sneer at me? She does it apurpose, and I've had my fill of it!"

Enough of this was the truth to make it convincing. Confident that Rolande had no idea of the girl's true station, Simeon said boldly, "Besides, why *else* should I want her?"

Having no answer, Rolande abandoned the question for now. "Forget her," she advised. "You'll never have that one. She has too much sense and too much spirit, for a worm like you to get the better of her."

Katin's eyes widened in astonishment. Was Vendeley actually *praising* her?

"It was not my intent that you should come to harm," he said defensively, "but I can't speak for the bandits. Perhaps Lorin had ideas of his own, and meant to take more than the girl." He rose, setting the cloth down, and came closer to her. "I will see that he suffers for the liberties he took."

"I'll deal with Lorin myself," Rolande said firmly. "He's worth two of you." The bandit could be made to understand that it was against his best interests to cross her—but she had her doubts about Simeon. "Very well, then, what have you learned of the fortification of the coast?"

Glad to leave the subject of the bandit attack, Simeon leaned back against a crate of crockery and detailed what had been accomplished to date, ending by saying, "But the crabs have been at work along the shore, gnawing holes where holes will do the most good. The 'accidents' should set them back some weeks."

Rolande frowned. "Not by my order! You've been doing too much, fool, and accomplishing too little. If our people interfere with the work now, it's bound to draw attention to their presence. We need our own watch points in place, well hidden and supplied. When the fleet is in sight, then it will be time to act, to stop word from reaching the colony. You've done nothing useful, and time is growing shorter!"

"I've had but myself to arrange all these things in your absence," Simeon said sullenly. "I have matters in hand, never fear."

But Rolande's fear was that Simeon had taken matters too much into his own hands. It was time that she reasserted control over their activities—and saw to it that those who did their bidding understood who was in charge. "I have arranged to meet with the watchers tonight at Crescent Cove," she said, "and you are not to make a move without my orders—is that clear?"

Katin had heard enough. She quickly crawled back to the cupboard, and she soon heard someone leave the storeroom and go up the stairs. Could she sneak out before either of them came back into the shop? She opened the door a crack, then stopped, frozen, as Rolande came down the stairs and hurried out of the shop. But she left the door open behind her.

Katin had almost reached it, when Simeon came out of the storeroom and saw her. "What are you doing there?" he demanded, coming around the counter after her.

Katin resisted the urge to run for the door. Instead, she turned to face him and said coolly, "Oh, so there you are," as if she had just looked in and, seeing no one, turned to go. "I want a cone of sugar, fellow, and be quick about it."

Simeon watched her go, thinking, *Soon, my proud maid.* And soon Vendeley would see what the other side of the whip looked like, as well. But at least he was rid of her for tonight. That would leave him free to make the preparations for his revenge on Sir Andrew. His plan would not only make His Lordship suffer but would further the Chamber's cause by removing the mainstay of the colony's defenses. And by the same stroke, he would remove the girl's protector as well.

Katin galloped back to Silverbourne, only to find that Sir Andrew had left at mid-morning to review the state of the fortifications. She dared not send a messenger after him, not for a matter of this import. From Rolande's and Simeon's discussion, she'd gathered that they had subverted any number of colonists to their cause, and the same was no doubt true of the soldiers at the stockade. She had no concerns about Captain Jamison's loyalty, but now she remembered incidents involving militiamen whose families were in Rolande's debt. There was no way of knowing for certain who was trustworthy and who was a traitor. She would have to ride after Sir Andrew herself.

As she entered the warm, straw-scented barn, Jerl looked up from oiling a saddle, and immediately asked, "What's wrong?"

Katin hesitated only for a moment. Jerl couldn't possibly be Vendeley's spy, and he would know the way to the new fortifications, for he'd been working on the construction of the watchtowers since their return from the forest. She herself, she realized, had no idea how to find Sir Andrew, and she couldn't ride up and down the coast in the hope of encountering him.

After taking care to see that no one else was about, she dropped down onto a bale of hay and related what she had overheard at Rolande's shop. "I must inform Sir Andrew of Vendeley's treachery," she concluded. "Do you know where to find him? Will you show me the way?"

"He'll be at Hag's Head Point, I should think," said Jerl. "I was there early today, and heard that he meant to go there. It's not far." Jerl was not at all averse to being alone with Katin on a twilight ride through the woods, but he added dutifully, "There's no need for you to go—I can carry the message for you."

Katin was taken aback. He was perfectly right, but it had never occurred to her to send him alone. And now she found that, as usual, she couldn't resist being in the thick of things. "No, I'll come with you," she said. "And we'd best not waste time—we must find Sir Andrew before Vendeley reaches Crescent Cove."

Jerl did not try very hard to dissuade her.

Simeon was watching from the woods when Katin and Jerl led two horses out of the stable and rode off quickly, passing not far from where he hid. He had no doubt what they were up to, and the thought spurred his jealousy as never before. So Her Highness was no better than a common slattern, sneaking off to the woods to lie with a farmhand! How dare she treat him like a mongrel—he, who was a presentable and prosperous householder—and then give her favors to the likes of Smit? Outraged, he decided not to wait to carry out his purpose. He had planned only to scout the area and note the routines of the household, then return at a time when Katin was safely away. But seeing her ride off with Jerl, he changed his mind. Tonight would do very well indeed. He would only wait until full dark.

From the shadow of the drying shed he watched patiently to see if anyone else would appear. When sufficient time had passed for him to be certain that he could cross the kitchen yard without being seen, he hurried to the well and hauled up the dripping bucket. From beneath his cloak, he withdrew a pouch of dried leaves of devil's trump—so the sailor who sold it to him had said—a poison as deadly as the plague. Unlike the madwort, which had certain rare and particular properties, poison was readily available from those who dealt in illicit wares.

He had to restrain himself from whistling as he crumbled the leaves and smeared them over the inside of the empty bucket. He was meticulous at his task, covering the whole surface, and rubbing the powdery leaves hard against the staves of the bucket, to be sure that the poison was absorbed into the damp wood. When he had finished, he left the bucket raised to dry, then stole away as silently as he had come.

Chapter 11

The outposts along the coast were meant to consist of tall wooden watchtowers. Near each was to be a barracks, to house the small number of soldiers stationed at the tower, and a small powder magazine for the storage of a limited quantity of arms. Sir Andrew knew better than to store all the army's ordnance in one place that might be destroyed by the enemy. Further, should fighting take place along the coast, the militia would be able to resupply itself from these storehouses.

But the actual construction of the fortifications was taking far longer than Sir Andrew had anticipated. Mortar used in constructing the stone walls of the storehouses had turned out to be faulty, and walls crumbled; the cross posts supporting two watchtowers cracked and gave way; workers suffered accidents felling trees; urgently awaited supplies never arrived . . . the list went on—a list too long to be laid to mere mischance.

At Crescent Cove, there was nothing to be seen in the way of completed workmanship. A mass of posts and planking, suitable for constructing a watchtower, lay on the shore, with a great mound of stones nearby that was to have been used for the construction of the storehouse. But there was no sign of any of the militia who worked here during the day. They had been called away to assist at another site, for it was urgent to see that some of the fortifications were completed, as time grew ever shorter.

This was the third stop made by Katin and Jerl in their search for Sir Andrew. When they'd arrived at Hag's Head Point, they'd been told that he had changed his plans, and no one knew his present whereabouts. At Gullwing Cove, word had been received that His Lordship meant to reverse the order of his review, beginning with the fortifications at the most distant point north of the colony and working back along the coast, because of a calamity that had occurred at Ringmaron Bay that very day. But by the time Katin and Jerl had learned that, it was too late in the evening for them to reach that location in time to warn Sir Andrew of Rolande's plans. She and her fellow conspirators would be long gone before he could send anyone to deal with them.

They dismounted on the hill above the shore, leaving their horses to graze on the tough grass. Jerl looked down at the waves along the moonlit shore. Standing there with Katin, he didn't, for a moment, care what happened. She had insisted that they must go to spy on Rolande themselves—that they could trust no one to take their place, or even to accompany them. He'd been reluctant to agree, knowing that Sir Andrew would never allow her to do something that could be so dangerous, but she'd made it clear that she intended to go with or without him, and he couldn't very well let her go alone.

But the cove was peaceful and silent, with only the wind and the waves to be heard, and the fortifications were abandoned. He didn't expect any trouble. Perhaps they'd missed Vendeley and her band, and even if she came here, they needed only to watch and listen. The idea of lying in wait, with Katin next to him, caressed by the warm, pine-scented air—perhaps all night—was too delicious and dangerous to think about for long. . . .

Katin broke into his reverie, saying, "Come on, let's go down to the shore. Perhaps we can tell if they've been here." She grabbed his arm and started down the hill, leaving him to keep his balance as best he could.

As they approached the site of the watchtower, it became apparent that work had actually begun, but had suffered some disaster, for what at first appeared to be building materials proved, at close quarters, to be the tumbled down posts and walls of the tower itself. Remembering something he'd heard at the stockade, Jerl clambered over the fallen cross posts and found a piece of wood that he held out to Katin, so that she could touch the end. "Feel this."

"It's sharp," she said as she drew her hand back with a splinter in it.

"The edge is cut clear across. And you can feel slashes here on the side."

"It looks to be true. They weakened those beams deliberately, to slow the progress of the fortifications." *Does Sir Andrew know?* Katin wondered, adding this information to the many other things she had to tell him.

"This is coward's work," Jerl said angrily. "No one—" But Katin suddenly gestured to him to be silent.

"Someone's coming," she whispered, "listen!" the sound of horses heading their way could now be heard above the pulse of the waves. They scrambled a short way back up the hill overlooking the beach and hid in a small copse of trees. A few moments later a cloaked rider cantered up to the remains of the watchtower.

The rider swung down from her bay horse,

threw back her forest green cloak, and stood waiting expectantly. "Vendeley," Katin said.

Rolande suddenly glanced around like a wolf catching the scent of prey on the wind, but then her attention was caught by the arrival of a group of men and women who joined her by the fallen watchtower. As Katin and Jerl continued watching, several newcomers appeared. They were a rough lot, dressed mostly in furs and leather, although one or two sported shirts of homespun cloth. Last to arrive was an enormous, shaggy-haired man in a sheepskin vest and torn leather breeches, who swaggered up and took a place by the small fire the earlier arrivals had lit at the base of the watchtower.

No sooner had he settled down than Rolande, silhouetted by the firelight as she stood on one of the fallen crossbeams, announced, "There's to be no more of these damn fool accidents! Your job is to keep watch on these outposts, not to destroy them, and see that you don't forget it again!"

"So you want us to protect the towers now?" the shaggy-haired man said sullenly. "Don't you know your own mind, woman?" He was clearly the worse for drink.

"We were just doing as we were bid," someone protested.

"You'll continue to do as you're bid—without question," Rolande said, looking at the drunken man as she spoke. "One tower might fall accidentally, but not all of them. Chop them all down, and Lord Edenbyrne and his officers will know there's sabotage afoot and come searching after you all. Don't take the man for a fool. The success of our course lies in secrecy."

The big man snorted at this and Rolande glared at him. "You have something to say, Jacom?"

He looked Rolande over as if she were a tasty morsel he might consider consuming, then said, "Let them come. I'm not afraid of lords and officers."

"Good. Your mangy carcass will make a fine example for the rest, hung from a gibbet." She turned away from him as if dismissing him as of no importance, and addressed the others. "I trust that the rest of you, unlike this sot, can understand that our task is not to warn the enemy of our intentions! We are to prepare the way for the successful campaign of the Chamber's forces—"

The man she had insulted snarled and rose from beside the fire to move toward her, his gait deliberate and threatening. Rolande broke off in mid-sentence and faced him again. "Sit down," she ordered.

"Go to the devil." He moved a step closer. "I say you're a fancy bit who's only fit to fight with words in some meeting hall full of fat townsfolk." He spat, then advanced still closer. "But you don't know a turd's worth about real soldier's work. I was in the field in Albin when we whipped the nobles like mongrel dogs—them and their *officers.* And I say if you hit them hard enough, they roll over and beg for mercy." He looked around the circle of conspirators as if daring anyone to challenge his words. "Maybe the Chamber'd do better to deal with one like me, who has experience of blood work. If Mistress Vendeley were out of the way, I wonder what they'd do, eh?"

The man was standing only a few feet from Rolande now, but the figures around the campfire were watching her, waiting to see what she would do. If she backed down now, she would lose all her power over them. "Sit down and shut your fool mouth," she said, so quietly that Katin and Jerl could barely hear her. "I'm warning you, oaf, and I'll not warn you twice."

The man drew himself up to his full, menacing height and threw out his massive chest. Rolande was tall, but he loomed over her. "You're warning me? I can break you like a twig!" He glanced with a broad smirk at the others watching from around the fire as Rolande pulled the pistol from her belt and shot him in the chest. He gasped once, then clutched at the wound and fell back onto the sand.

Rolande unhurriedly reloaded the pistol. "Now are there any others," she asked, "who think they know better than I how our work should be conducted?"

They glanced pointedly away from Rolande's gaze, denying any such presumption.

"Very well." Rolande restored her weapon to its place and said, "Take that carrion down to the shore and leave it for the fish. Then I will explain how we shall go about accomplishing our ends."

Katin clamped her hand over her mouth, forcing herself to choke down the bile that rose in her throat. She had seen people wounded and killed before, in the heat of battle, but the very *calmness* of Rolande's manner sickened and terrified her. She suddenly remembered Rolande standing over Jerl in the forest, her pistol cocked. How many people had she killed, how many more would she kill? Sir Andrew didn't realize how dangerous an enemy she was, and would Katin live to warn him? Without thinking, she moved closer to Jerl, and he put his arm around her to comfort her. He would not have dared such a gesture, nor she accepted it, only a few minutes before. But the scene they had just witnessed had given their closeness an intimacy that mere moonlight and the mild summer air could not have created for a peasant and a princess.

When the conspirators had returned from their grisly task, they gathered in a tight circle around the fire. Rolande was now sitting on a crossbeam at the edge of the fire, and her words did not carry to Katin and Jerl, as she began to explain what she expected her minions to accomplish. Katin, feeling ashamed of her weakness, drew away from Jerl and whispered, "We must get near enough to hear!"

The only way to do this, without exposing themselves, was to move back into the woods and circle around behind the fallen watchtower from the other side, where they could secrete themselves behind the pile of building stones. "It might be done," Jerl said doubtfully, when they reached the higher part of the hill. "But if they spot us that close, we'll have no chance of getting away."

"I'm not afraid."

I am, Jerl thought, *but not for myself.* Helplessly, he followed her down the hill on the far side of the tower. The descent was steeper than they had anticipated, however, and they made the last few yards scrabbling and sliding as small stones rolled down the hill before them. Near the bottom, they froze as Rolande looked for a moment in their direction, but then she turned back to her lackeys and continued speaking, as if satisfied that nothing was amiss.

"Katin, come away," Jerl whispered uneasily.

"You go if you like. I have to hear her plans, and tell Sir Andrew." If she noticed that Jerl had addressed her by her given name, she gave no sign of it.

"You can't tell him anything if she shoots us!" Jerl insisted.

Katin wanted to say, *Nothing will happen to us.* They'd come unscathed through so much danger already, that she half believed it was true. But the information they had was too important to risk. "You're right," she agreed. "You'd better go back and tell him what we've learned so far, and I'll see if I can learn any more. I'm small—there's a good chance they won't see me."

Before Jerl could protest, she crawled the rest of the

way down the hill, stopping behind the sheltering pile of rock. Jerl, of course, crept after her. He had just reached the rock pile when Rolande turned, pulling her pistol from her belt, and strode in their direction. A sick shiver ran through Katin as she realized that Rolande had been aware of their presence all along. She had been waiting for them to come closer. . . . Katin heard her cock the weapon—it seemed the only sound in the still night—and Jerl pulled her to the ground, trying to shield her. The retort of a shot echoed.

More shots followed the first, but the volley was somewhere off in the woods. Rolande shouted at the already running conspirators, "Scatter, or they'll catch you!" then ran to her horse and was galloping down the beach before the next round was fired.

The plotters dispersed like windblown leaves, those with mounts riding away as if demons were at their back, the rest scrambling up the hill and disappearing into the woods.

Jerl and Katin rose to their feet and looked at each other in astonishment, scarcely able to believe that they were still alive. "By the Good God, it's a miracle she didn't kill us!" Jerl said reverently.

"Miracle or no, we'd best get out of here. I only hope our horses are still to be found."

But as they came from their hiding place onto the beach, a voice from the hillside called, "Stop right there, you two. We shot some of your comrades in the woods, and you'll be next if you take another step!"

"Don't shoot, we're unarmed!" Jerl shouted, and a tall man came down the hill toward them, carrying a musket. Several others were visible behind him, crouched on the hillside, their muskets trained on Jerl and Katin.

The man strode up to them, but then stopped and

lowered his musket. "Jerl Smit? What the devil?" He signaled for the other militiamen to approach. "Who's that with you, Smit?"

"Katin Ander, Sergeant. She belongs to Sir Andrew."

"Oho, the little herb-girl. So you two have been hunting night-sprouting mushrooms, have you?"

Jerl blushed.

"We're here for the same reason you are," Katin snapped. "Hunting the Chamber's agents."

"How do they know about that?" a skinny soldier asked suspiciously. "Unless they're part of the conspiracy? Just because they serve Sir Andrew doesn't mean they're so innocent. Where better to put a spy?"

The sergeant rubbed his chin. "Suppose you tell me how you *did* come to be here, then."

"We're no spies!" Jerl began, "it's—"

But Katin interrupted him, saying, "I had reason to believe that the conspirators would be meeting here tonight. We tried to warn Sir Andrew, but we couldn't find him—they'll tell you at Hag's Head Point and Gullwing that we were looking for him. So at last we came here to spy on *them* and try to find out their plans—which we might have done if you hadn't scared them away!"

Jerl was surprised by this version of events, but he wisely held his tongue. Surely she realized that Rolande had already discovered their presence by the time the militiamen appeared. If not for the shots the soldiers had fired, they would probably be food for fish by now. He thought it strange, too, that Katin had not mentioned Rolande's part in the conspiracy.

"You said you shot some of them in the woods," Katin continued.

"I shot at a lookout stationed at the hilltop," the skinny soldier boasted.

"Did you hit him?"

He shrugged. "Well, we've not had time to look. We came straight on through here."

"It was a curious thing to do, was it not?" she asked.

The sergeant looked at her sharply. "Why so?"

"If you plan to take people by surprise, it seems odd to announce your presence with musket fire, before you're close enough to catch them. A scout could have been avoided easily enough, in these wide woods, without shooting. It seems to me that this soldier gave a warning to the ones you were seeking—else they'd not have gotten away."

The sergeant glanced around the empty space surrounding the tower, where a short time before the conspirators had been clustered, then turned to the skinny soldier. "What say you to that, Bander?"

He shuffled his feet uneasily. "It's not so, Sergeant! I came on him unawares and had to shoot at him or be shot myself."

"And did anyone else see him?" Katin persisted.

"Not I," said one of the others. "I was behind Bander all the way. He suddenly spun about and shot at the top of the hill, yelling that he saw a man there. But even if there was someone, we could have cleared the lower hill without his being the wiser."

At this, Bander dropped his musket and bolted for the woods, knocking aside the other man as he passed. The sergeant sent two soldiers after him, then turned back to Katin. "Damn it all, the maggots are everywhere these days. I hardly know who my own friends are."

"That's why I would tell what little I know to Sir Andrew alone," said Katin. "Can you take us to him?"

It was just before dawn when they arrived at Ringmaron Bay. Sir Andrew was rousted out from the makeshift cabin that the soldiers had erected to provide them with a barracks while they went about the construction of the watchtower, and he arrived alert, like any soldier who is used to waking at a moment's notice, but still none too pleased about it. He was even less pleased to find Katin seated on a tree stump near the half-finished tower, with Jerl sitting cross-legged on the ground beside her. They rose hastily as Sir Andrew stalked up to them.

"I suppose I shouldn't be surprised," he said grimly. "You have, I trust, a satisfactory explanation for this escapade. If you haven't, I strongly suggest that you think of one quickly."

Meeting the commander's stony gaze, Jerl felt sure that no explanation he could offer would prove at all satisfactory. It had occurred to him, though not to Katin, how His Lordship was likely to react, upon finding his ward in company with a young recruit, far from home, in the dead of the night. He wondered glumly whether Sir Andrew would beat him to death or just shoot him.

"Jerl and I have come on most urgent business," Katin began. "We've been spying on the conspirators responsible for the sabotage at the watchtowers—"

"*Spying on . . . !*" Sir Andrew shouted. "Have you taken leave of your senses? You know how dangerous these people are! You're determined to get yourself killed in spite of me!"

Thinking of how close they had come to dying at Rolande's hands, Jerl cursed himself for ever having agreed to take Katin to the watch posts. He'd deserve whatever Sir Andrew did to him, even if it was for the wrong reason.

Katin, taken aback at Sir Andrew's vehemence, said quickly, "But we didn't *set out* to spy on anyone, My

Lord. We only meant to go as far as Hag's Head Point, to find you."

"Well, you have found me—now explain yourself!"

Katin first told him of the conversation she had overheard at Rolande's store—glossing over, as well as she could, the fact that she had been spying then. Indeed, when she thought how cold-bloodedly Rolande had shot the man who'd challenged her, she was appalled to remember her own recklessness. But when she had described the meeting at Crescent Cove, Sir Andrew wasted no more time on recriminations. He informed the sergeant that they must ride back to the colony with all possible haste, then finished dressing and called for their horses. He couldn't be certain that Rolande hadn't already taken to her heels, knowing that someone might be able to identify her. But if they moved fast enough—or if she returned to Thornfeld, planning to bluff it out—then they might catch her, and gain critical information about the Chamber's plans. He did not think that she would divulge this information easily, but in the end they would have it.

It was not without a touch of satisfaction that he pictured Rolande locked away, yet he was aware of a certain disappointment as well. Despite himself, he'd been impressed by her prowess, during their journey to Creshgahar. If he could have made an ally of her, she'd have been worth a battalion to him. And if he failed to apprehend her now, she would make a formidable enemy.

He kept the others to a furious pace. He knew that Katin must be exhausted, but there was no time to be lost, and he didn't intend to let her out of his sight. What was done was done, and it was pointless to worry over what might have befallen her, but he resolved to see that she didn't repeat such an adventure in the future. Just how he would prevent it, without keeping the girl in fetters, was a question for another time. As for her wandering around alone with . . . well, he'd deal with young Smit himself, and leave Celia to explain matters to Her Highness.

Though it was mid-morning when they arrived at Silverbourne, there was not a soul visible in the yard or the garden. No groom came to take Sir Andrew's horse, and the stables, too, were deserted. Only Carl's old mare stood tethered near the front of the house.

That, too, was unusual, for Carl rarely came to the manor house, and when he did, he walked. It had amused Katin, at first, to find that Sir Andrew always went himself to consult Carl, instead of sending for him, but this had since come to seem altogether natural to her. If Lady Celia had sent for him now, and he had troubled himself to hurry, then something most unusual was brewing. Katin leaped from her horse and tied it to the post in the yard, in a matter of moments. She was running for the door by the time Sir Andrew had dismounted and given his reins to Jerl.

Inside the house, there was bustle everywhere. Field hands and dairymaids rushed by, carrying buckets and bowls and cloths, but the only house servant to be seen was a young housemaid who stopped halfway down the stairs when she saw Katin, and wailed, "Oh, thank the Good God you're here at last, miss! Goodman Schellring wants you at once, and is the master with you?"

"Yes—but—what is it?" Katin stammered, dumbfounded.

"What is this?" Sir Andrew echoed, as he came through the door and took in the scene of disarray. "What's happened here?"

"I hardly know, sir," the girl said tearfully. "When I came from my mother's house this morning, all your people were laid low with a grievous sickness—all who were in the house this night—"

"A sickness?" Katin asked. "What sickness moves so fast? No one was ill when I left in the afternoon."

Sir Andrew didn't wait to hear the answer. If everyone in the house had been taken ill, then *Celia*— He forgot about catching Rolande, about the imminent invasion, about the Yerren and the danger of dragons. The maid had barely time to get out of his way as he raced up the stairs to Lady Celia's bedchamber.

An older woman, one of the farmhands, answered Katin, "To be sure, 'tis no natural malady." She raised her hand, palm outward, in the Deprivant gesture of renunciation. "'Tis as the Ministra says, divine retribution for unrighteousness!" The sonorous words clearly gave her great satisfaction.

"Nothing of the sort!" Katin said impatiently. "It is not the Good God who inflicts evil upon the world." She had no strong religious feeling herself, but she detested on principle the Dep doctrine of a vengeful, punishing God. "Hold your prating, and get about your work!" Katin had no real authority to give orders to Sir Andrew's people, but she was obeyed nevertheless. The woman merely sniffed in disapproval and marched off with her armload of blankets. "Where is Carl Schellring?" Katin asked the housemaid.

"He's with the mistress now—oh, it's pitiful to see her!" the girl sobbed. "She's taken so bad, she doesn't know who's there, or where she is herself. And Mistress Wicken's nigh dead, they say, and Deke's been crying all the morning that he's lost in the woods!"

Katin comforted the girl as best she could, and sent her about the tasks that Carl had set her. Thinking about Sir Andrew finding his wife delirious, Katin was reluctant to intrude just yet. She decided to see if there was anything she could do for her friend Mistress Wicken, the cook, and then go look for Carl.

She lay against the goose down pillows, her eyes closed, her face as pale as one of the white feathers. When Sir Andrew took her hand, murmuring her name, she did not seem aware of his presence, but only moaned, "Ah—drive them away! The fields will burn—" Her hand was hot and dry, her breathing shallow. Suddenly she cried out and twisted violently away from him, tearing her hand from his. He tried to stroke her face, to calm her, but she struck out wildly with her hands, as if battling some beast only she could see.

Carl sat at her bedside, mixing something in a pewter bowl. "In God's name, what ails her?" Sir Andrew asked him.

Carl continued to grind the mixture in the bowl on his lap, and added water from a pitcher. "I believe it is devil's trump, M'lord. The entire household has been stricken."

At this moment, Sir Andrew didn't care a fig for the entire household, or the fate of the entire colony, for that matter. "What manner of malady is this devil's trump?" he demanded.

"No malady, M'lord. A poison."

Sir Andrew could only look from him to Lady Celia in disbelief, as Carl continued, "I have, I think, identified the cause, if not the source. For everyone was taken ill at the same time, and the only thing all had shared in was the water drawn from the well by the cook's lad. The coachman fetched me, and we summoned all others who'd not drunk from that well to attend to those who had—but I fear that some are past any help we can give them."

"Not Celia?" Sir Andrew begged. "You can save her?"

Carl gave him a pitying look. "Her Ladyship's heart beats strong still. I have hope for her, but I cannot promise a cure. I am preparing an infusion that may serve as a purgative against devil's trump, and if I am correct about the cause, the cure will follow." He added another herb to his mixture, and began to heat it over a candle. "I am reasonably certain of my facts. When I examined the well in the kitchen yard, I found in the bucket a dried residue which had the distinctive scent of devil's trump, and near the brink of the well there was a dried leaf, dark green above and lighter below, with the toothed edges characteristic of this plant. There is every reason to believe that this alterant will have the desired effect, but chance plays its part in every cure."

He poured the steaming decoction into a wooden bowl, and brought it to Lady Celia's bedside. "She must have all this, M'lord, over the next twelve hours, every quarter hour, a swallow at a time. You will give it to her, that I may tend to others?"

Sir Andrew took it from him at once. "Go. I shall stay with her until she recovers." *Or she dies,* both thought, but neither man said the words. As gently as he could, Sir Andrew lifted her head and made her swallow a mouthful of the liquid. *Dear God, make his physic work!* he prayed.

Katin stole into the room, cast a glance toward Lady Celia and Sir Andrew, and said softly to Carl, "What am I to do?"

"Fireweed and thistle," Carl told her.

It sounded like a nursery rhyme to Sir Andrew, but it evidently made sense to Katin, for she nodded and said, "Steeped in water?"

"Come, I shall show you how it is prepared. The kitchen will be best—we must brew a great supply.

And I've had barrels of untainted water brought here." He began to gather up his materials.

After a sleepless night and a hard ride, Katin wished above all for rest, but she said only, "I've quantities of thistle leaf. I'll fetch it."

Hearing her, Sir Andrew was recalled to his own duties. "Katin," he said, without looking away from Lady Celia, "send Smit to Captain Jamison at once, to apprise him of Vendeley's treachery. He is charged to apprehend her, on my order."

Katin, too, had forgotten their urgent business. "I shall meet you directly," she said to Carl, and clattered off down the stairs on her errand.

Carl withdrew, taking with him his mortar and bundles of herbs, but Sir Andrew did not seem to notice their departure. "You can't leave me now," he whispered to Lady Celia, as if he could will her to live, but this was no enemy he could fight.

He had asked for an enemy he could see, and instead he was cursed with more deadly subterfuge, with invisible foes who struck in the darkness. Not content with undoing his work, now they threatened the very reason for all that he had done or tried to do. Without Celia, this new world would be as empty for him as the old.

Helpless to protect her, he could only watch and wait and hope for some improvement. His fists clenched and opened, over and over, as he paced the chamber, trying to pray, aching to fight for her life somehow. If Carl was right, if someone had deliberately poisoned his household, then that someone would die for it.

"He has dark eyes," Lady Celia said suddenly.

"Who has?" Sir Andrew asked, startled. Was she speaking of the poisoner? He bent over her anxiously. "Celia . . .?"

But she was not talking to him. "Oh, I know well

enough my duty, Mother," she said faintly. "But his eyes are shadowed with indifference, and he cannot see me. What is it he does see, I wonder?"

He knew it was the Baron she meant—a man so absorbed in his own affairs that he had left his young wife at Wildmoore for months on end, while he pursued peace abroad, in the King's service. The dowry Lady Celia had brought him allowed him to spend much of his time in the lowlands, dealing with diplomats and their futile alliances. Only late in the rebellion, when every man was needed, had the Baron taken to the field and fallen at Breicenshire, unlamented by his young widow.

His blindness had suited Sir Andrew well enough, for it left Celia free to spend her time with him. "I would willingly accompany him," she had once told Sir Andrew, "but he never even thinks of such a thing, and I am too proud to suggest it. If he will not ask, I shall not offer."

Now she opened her eyes, staring straight at him, and said, "The shadows cover everything. Andrew, are you there?"

He reached for her hand, thinking that she was rallying at last. "I'm here, my darling. Can't you see me?"

Her eyes opened wide in terror. "They will rend us like pomegranates. Andrew! You must save the young ones."

Sir Andrew's heart sank. Had her senses been addled by the poison? She clung desperately to his hand, then fell back upon the pillow, so still that for a moment he was frozen with fear. But then he saw the gentle rising and falling of her breast and realized that she had merely fallen into a deep sleep. He glanced toward the bowl on the table, but there were only dregs in it. There was nothing else he could do.

"Wings . . ." Lady Celia murmured.

* * *

Wings curveting and gliding across the pale sky, flocks of wings of all colors and shapes, so beautiful and graceful that she laughed with pleasure to see them. "Catch some for me, Andrew!" she teased. "Those green ones—to match my eyes. You must have a pair, too, and we'll fly away together."

She turned to him, laughing, but found the Baron beside her, instead of her lover. "Why, you should have sent me word of your coming, Philip," she said politely. "Your rooms are not in readiness." At first, she had kept his apartments aired and warm at all times, but she had long since let the fires die and the dust gather. It only made extra work for the servants, to no purpose.

"It is no matter," he assured her. "I shan't be staying."

She wondered if he remembered her name. She was tempted to ask, but that would be childish. "Then you have come in good time to see this charming spectacle," she said, gesturing at the fluttering, swooping wings. Didn't he see Andrew waiting on the terrace below? Didn't he see the *wings?*

He looked where she pointed, but as he did, the wings began to cluster into a great cloud, more and more of them, coming from all directions and massing together till they covered the sky as far as she could see. They merged into one great creature, then broke apart again, combining and separating, shifting and melding, finally forming a horde of monsters whose vast wings cast the countryside in shadow.

But the darkness gave no relief from the overpowering heat. Blinded by shadows, scorched by the fiery breath of dragons, she did not know where to run for shelter, where to seek for protection. Where was Andrew? Was the Princess safe? She tried to call out for help but, absurdly, she could only cry, "Wings . . . !"

Carl looked in from time to time, to listen to her heartbeat, and observe her color. He seemed satisfied, and bade Sir Andrew send for him if he found any change in her. Katin, he said, was doing the work of three, and no more had died. Sir Andrew supposed that he must have been told who had died, but he didn't remember hearing it. Someone brought him a tray of food, which he left untouched.

For the hundredth time, he laid his palm to Celia's brow, as Carl had instructed him, and for the first time, he thought her skin a shade cooler than before. At his touch, she stirred and her eyes opened.

"Andrew . . . ?"

He waited, not daring to hope after so many disappointments that this time she'd truly returned to her senses.

"You've come back," she said weakly.

"And have you come back?" he asked, taking her hand and kissing it.

She half smiled, but then said worriedly, "Is Oriana here? I couldn't find her."

"She's busy dosing all the household with Carl's medicine, though I daresay she's ready to faint with fatigue herself. She has fought with death for her people this day, like a true monarch. The illness fled before her." He did not tell her of the risks Katin had run, or of Carl's suspicions about the well water, thinking to spare her further shocks until she was stronger.

But she shook her head feebly. "Not illness, but poison. Like Holistowe. Meant for you, my dear."

"Hush," he said, "we'll speak of it later. Rest now. I'll send for Carl."

And on Carl's heels came the exhausted housemaid,

with word that Captain Jamison awaited below. Reluctantly, he left Celia to Carl's able ministrations. As Carl plied her with black snakeroot to complete the cure and make her rest easier, Sir Andrew followed the girl downstairs.

In the salon he found not only Captain Jamison but Katin, who was collapsed on the hearth fast asleep, with a long wooden spoon still clutched in her hand. No doubt she had lain down for a moment's rest and succumbed to sleep at once. The soarhound, curled beside her, watched Sir Andrew and the captain suspiciously.

"Is Vendeley taken?" Sir Andrew asked in a low voice. Katin didn't stir.

Captain Jamison wiped the dust from his face with the back of his hand. "I regret she escaped us, My Lord. We've searched leagues in each direction, but we could be a long time combing the forest before we find her hiding place—if we find it. Shall we continue the pursuit?"

Sir Andrew shook his head, cursing himself for the delay in sending word to the stockade. "It will take too many away from other tasks. I've no doubt that she has hiding holes in plenty, and they'll not be easy to find." He peered out the window as if searching for signs of where she might be hidden. "Have scouts search for traces of where she's gone to ground," he said, turning back to the captain, "but for the rest, we need every man to be on duty."

"Very good, sir."

"My review of the coastal fortifications was cut short by this matter. I'll have to go back almost at once." *If Celia is out of danger,* he thought. *And I'll damned well double the household guard before I go.* "I had thought to deal with the cannon emplacements on my return, but there's been too much delay already." From a locked court cupboard he took a crude map marked with a series of X's, and gave it to the captain. "Have earthworks built at these sites, and see that Murdock instructs the regiment how to load and fire the cannon. I've arranged with the smith to mold us two dozen large cannon, and some smaller ones, which can be moved. It's not much, but it should help block the advance of the Chamber's troops when they land. We haven't much time left to prepare."

And the Chamber's agents are still at large. Then why did he feel a trace of regret that he would have to hunt Vendeley down?

Chapter 12

From Crescent Cove, Rolande rode straight for Holistowe, where she took refuge with her confederates in the Chamber's employ—those who had poisoned the colony's Scrutinor leaders, while tending to the sick during the great pestilence.

The Chamber's chief agents in the various settlements had worked together to ensure that those colonies that stood close enough to aid one another against the invasion would be in no position to do so. Holistowe was but two day's ride from Thornfeld, but Holistowe had been reduced to a remnant of the original colony, and it no longer possessed a militia. This solution had satisfied Rolande, who intended to be Governor of a thriving, prosperous settlement when the Chamber seized power. Why sacrifice Thornfeld, when a poor, hardscrabble place like Holistowe would be so much easier to destroy?

But Rolande had maintained good relations with the Chamber's agents at Holistowe, and now they proved most valuable to her. Their spies learned from hers about the aftermath of the meeting at Crescent Cove and reported all to her. Three of the conspirators who'd fled on foot had been shot and killed by the militia, and she herself had been identified by Katin and Jerl as the ringleader. For another few days, Rolande lay low and waited for more information. When her people brought word that one of those shot was Meg Dwyer—a woman nearly as tall as herself—she laughed and said, "Capital!" And when she heard that Sir Andrew had left once more for the coast, she immediately sent a messenger to Headman Farnham with a letter saying that she had just heard of the outrageous calumnies being directed at her, and that she was coming at once to answer all charges against her and clear her good name. She was willing, she wrote, nay, indeed, she was determined to defend herself to the Wardership before her accusers, and she would appear at any time of their choosing to do so. She was by no means in hiding, but merely conducting her usual business in Holistowe, and she would return immediately.

Far from being dragged back to Thornfeld a prisoner, Rolande rode into town freely, only seven days after her flight, in company with her confederates from Holistowe, and graciously allowed Captain Jamison and Sergeant Merton to escort her directly to a meeting with the Headman.

She listened patiently as Katin and Jerl told their story, then, when invited to speak, she shook her head regretfully and said, "Much as I'd like to take credit for shooting one of the vermin, I'm afraid I can't claim the ability to be in two places at once. Goodman Warren and Mistress Clark of Holistowe can vouchsafe that I was making my regular monthly delivery of goods to their community on the evening when these fanciful youngsters claim to have seen me at Crescent Cove." She sounded as if she found the whole proceedings rather amusing. "But it needs no great penetration to solve this mystery, as it seems to me," she went on. "Surely the discovery that the woman Meg Dwyer was present, as I am informed, is satisfactory to explain the business?"

Katin and Jerl protested that they were well able to tell Rolande from other folk, having lived at close quarters with her throughout the expedition to the Yerren. But Rolande merely shrugged and spread her hands, with a smile at Farnham, as if to say, *Headstrong creatures, aren't they?*

"Very well, then, I confess," she said flippantly. "I was really at a gathering of rogues on the coast, and I shot—who was it I shot? Well, no matter. Neither I *nor* my carter was at Holistowe, and these good people are simply deluded. Will that answer?"

Faced with the choice of accepting the word of a 'prentice lass and an unschooled laborer, or that of a fellow Warder and mainstay of the community, as well as two respectable citizens of Holistowe, Headman Farnham had no difficulty in deciding.

"Sir Andrew believed us!" Katin protested. "Else he'd not have ordered her arrest!"

"Lord Edenbyrne was, of course, duty-bound to act upon such an accusation," Headman Farnham said pompously, "just as I am bound as Warder and Magistrate to examine the evidence and judge whether the charge is warranted. Sir Andrew had no way of knowing, as we do now, that Mistress Vendeley was in Holistowe at the time."

Lady Celia had wished to come and bear witness as to the youngsters' veracity, but she was still weak from the effects of the poison, and Carl had forbidden it. Her written testimony to that effect was duly noted, but Lady Celia's persuasiveness depended much upon her presence.

Captain Jamison was uncertain whether to believe them or not. He'd heard from his sergeant of the girl's quickness to discover Bander's treachery, and that sat well with him, but he remembered her glib story at the stockade, about the reasons for the Yerren's escape. She could tell a brazen lie when she chose. Smit he considered honest, by nature, but where the girl was concerned, young Smit would probably swear to anything. He suspected that they might be right about Vendeley, as they'd been right about the Yerren, but that didn't mean they were telling the truth. If he'd been at Crescent Cove himself that night, maybe he'd know what to make of their story. But with all the unrest in the colony—folk in a frenzy over the damned dragons—and Sir Andrew away, he'd not dared to leave his post to investigate a mere rumor.

But the testimony of the sergeant, who had been present, was no help to them either, for the conspirators had scattered by the time he arrived. And he was bound to admit that the youngsters had said nothing to him about Mistress Vendeley at the time.

"Of course not," Katin cried. "How could I, when I suspected you had a traitor in your midst—and maybe more than one—who'd have given her warning!"

"And very sensible, too," Rolande agreed. "We can't be careful enough in these times."

Her mockery came close to making Katin lose her temper—just what Rolande wanted her to do, no doubt. Instead, she comported herself with all the dignity she could muster, but how could she convince the Headman that her word was worth more than Rolande's, unless she revealed her true rank to him? She didn't trust Farnham that far, but even if she did, she couldn't say anything in front of Rolande, whom she knew to be the Chamber's agent. She seethed, unable to defend herself, as the Headman remonstrated with her and Jerl.

"It's a serious matter bringing such imputations against an upstanding citizen," he said. "We've discord enough, God knows, in this unlucky community, without your stirring up further enmities! Do you think you can go about making malicious and unfounded accusations with impunity? You're answerable for the mischief you've wrought." He, too, remembered that Katin and Jerl had been responsible for the escape of the Yerren prisoner from the stockade. A pair of troublemakers if he'd ever seen any.

"Oh, let us not be too hard on them," Rolande said tolerantly. "It was night, the Dwyer woman's near my height, and one cloak looks much like another in the dark. 'Twas an honest mistake—I'm certain these young folk bear me no malice." She smiled at them benignly. "No doubt they thought they were acting in the interests of the colony. And think how plucky it was of them to be spying on the conspirators."

"*If* that's what they were really doing," Headman Farnham said with disapproval. "I'd not be surprised if they were about more carnal pursuits than that—and invented this tale when they were discovered."

Rolande gave a wolfish grin. "Youth . . ." she said.

"How dare you—" Katin began, but before she could give vent to her indignation, the door was thrown open and a boy in worn breeches and a leather apron burst into the hall. "Master Farnham, there's great uproar at the Common, and Elliott Cavendish bids you come at once!"

Captain Jamison turned to the sergeant. "Ride to the stockade at once and bring troops to the Common, in case of need." The sergeant took to his heels, and Captain Jamison bowed to the company and left for the Common at a run.

Headman Farnham glared at Katin and Jerl. "If there's any further trouble from the two of you, you'll not get off so lightly next time!" He rose and strode to the door with Rolande close behind him. But in the doorway she turned and winked at Katin before following him out.

Jerl looked at Katin as they stood alone in the deserted assembly hall. "It *was* her, wasn't it?"

"Of course it was! You saw her as well as I."

"I know, but . . . then why did she defend us? Why didn't she lodge a complaint against us?" The penalties for bearing false witness against a neighbor were severe and painful. If Rolande wanted to take cruel revenge upon them, she had only to lay a complaint before the Wardership.

"I suppose it's in her interest to have the matter forgotten," Katin ventured, unwilling to attribute any higher motive to Rolande's benevolence. "And then, it made her seem reasonable and moderate—and that in turn made us look all the more ridiculous and spiteful."

Unwillingly, Katin had to admit a certain grudging admiration for Rolande's self-assurance and her skill at artifice. What a courtier the woman would have made!

Captain Jamison arrived to find a crowd gathered at the Common, a mixture of farmers and townsfolk, including a large number of Scrutinors in their unmistakable gray. At the center of the throng, Reverend Hrabanus stood on an upturned crate, and Captain Jamison pushed forward to hear the speech he was making.

"The calamities that threaten us are not the work of our God, to punish us for our sins—no, nor the work of the Devil's sworn minions, as some would have it." He addressed this challenge to the Ministra Cirana, who was standing at the center of a group of Deprivants in the crowd.

One of them shouted, "And what are dragons but creatures of Hell?"

"What indeed, brother?" the Reverend responded.

"For we have not so much as seen the beasts in the flesh. Then surely it is too soon to say what they are. We have encountered strange and unknown beings enough on these shores, that none can say what is beyond the bounds of nature. Are the Chamber's forces demons sent to chastise us? The greed and ambition of our enemies are responsible, not the will of our most gracious God! I tell you, it is by the way in which we meet these challenges that we show ourselves to be the children of God, or pawns of the Devil!" He looked around the restless, muttering crowd, and admonished them, "I have seen neighbors fighting neighbors over the way to deal with these threats, and one thing is certain, harming each other serves none of our good. This strife must cease—we must work together!"

Captain Jamison thought it a pleasure to hear someone trying to infuse sanity and common sense into the situation. But the Reverend didn't seem to have many supporters in the crowd.

"Liar!" a harsh voice from the mob shouted. "You would blind us to the evil which brought these horrors upon us."

"I tell you this colony is accursed," cried another.

"Superstition!" objected a third. "We must be prepared to fight these things with muskets, not with incantations."

Captain Jamison, worried about the tenor of the crowd, looked around for the arrival of the militia, whom he could use to disperse the mob if things turned ugly. It wouldn't be the first time. The people were at each other's throats these days—those who believed that the dragons would come and destroy them all—those who believed it was all nonsense—those who feared the invasion, and would hoard everything they could against future need—those who believed it was a ploy to keep them under the thumb of the military—those who believed it was a judgment of God, and those who believed it would never come to pass. . . .

The Reverend, exasperated, raised his hands for silence, but as he did, a voice shouted, "Thus fall the ungodly!" and a musket shot exploded from his right. Someone screamed, and the Reverend clasped his hands to his side and fell to the ground in a heap.

Captain Jamison tried to force his way through the panicked people, who were now running wildly in all directions. He moved not toward the Reverend—his followers would see to him—but toward a stand of trees from which a wisp of smoke was still rising. No further shots were fired, but the throng of people around him blocked his progress, and outraged members of the Church of Albin and the Scrutinors had begun hurling blows at each other, to cries of "Murderers!" and "Blasphemers!"

Captain Jamison deflected a blow from a wild-eyed man, disarmed him of a hunting knife, and shoved him out of the way. He despaired of being able to bring any type of order to the mob, but at last he managed to extricate himself in time to see Sergeant Merton arrive with a mounted troop from the stockade. "Separate these people!" Captain Jamison ordered, in a tone that implied he'd far rather give orders to shoot them all. The cavalry rode slowly forward into the crowd, forcing the combatants to disperse.

The captain was finally able to make his way to the spot from which he suspected the shot had been fired. The villain, of course, was long gone, leaving only a musket lying on the twigs and grass. He picked it up, but there was nothing to distinguish it from any of the dozens of others sold at Rolande's shop.

With the gun tucked under his arm, he returned to the fallen Reverend. The Common had now been cleared of all except a few folk who sat on the grass nursing minor wounds and bruises. Captain Jamison laid down the musket and knelt beside Headman Farnham, who told him, "He's dead, no doubt of that."

"That will give us all the more work, keeping order," said Sergeant Merton. Captain Jamison looked up to find the sergeant standing by his shoulder, holding the reins of his horse.

The captain nodded, his face grim. The Reverend's people would certainly blame the Scrutinors, and in this they might be correct, but might not this murder be another plot on the part of the Chamber's agents, to increase the disruption in the colony? It could well have been a Scrutinor zealot who'd shouted those words—or someone who wanted to sound like one, to incite a war between the various religious factions, when all should be preparing for the invasion.

We're about to lose another war through no fault of our own, he thought, *and this time I probably won't live to regret it.* For the canker had spread to the militia, too. Some of the recruits believed the Scrutinors' prattle, and some hated all Deps and blamed them for everything. There were many who were reluctant to follow an officer of the other sect, and that could undo all their training. Impossible to make folk fight side by side, when they wanted to be fighting each other.

"Curse the Scrutinors!" the sergeant snarled. "Can't the fools see they're setting themselves up for slaughter, carrying on as they are?"

"They believe their destiny is in the hands of the Good God, who will unfailingly save the righteous," Captain Jamison said heavily. That answer was inescapable, and it damned the colony. He turned to watch the cavalry still mustered on the Common to assure against further outbreaks of violence. "We must keep discipline among the soldiery, no matter what else befalls," he told the sergeant. The only hope, he thought, was that most of the militia still felt loyalty for Sir Andrew, even those who mistrusted one another. That might hold them together. Chaos among their own troops would be a worse enemy than the invading army.

* * *

"There can be no doubt that the horrors we now face were brought about by your excursion to the mountains," Ministra Cirana said firmly. She leaned across the table in the back room of Rolande's shop, her eyes lit with a dangerous gleam in the candlelight. For the moment, she held the strongest sway over the people in the colony, and now, before any could interfere with her, she planned to use that power to see that the colonists were saved from the forces of the Evil One.

" 'Tis so," Minister Arhan affirmed. "We warned you what would come of dealings with such as the winged folk."

So now they're folk even to you, Rolande thought. After their experiences among the Yerren, it was impossible to doubt the Yerren's nature, but the Scrutinors had merely decided that the Yerren were demonic beings, instead of demonic creatures. Created by the Evil One, as people had been created by the Good God, they were therefore destined to be humanity's enemies. Such a belief would be useful in assuring the downfall of the colony, and Rolande once more found herself, against her own inclinations, on the same side as the Scrutinor Ministers. Besides, it would hardly do for them to think her a friend of the ill-omened Yerren.

It was just such a point that the Ministra was making. "All of us are in grave danger, and the Good God will only intercede to remove the curse that lies over us if we punish those who are allies of the Evil One."

The Ministra sounded as if she were making a public speech. No doubt, Rolande thought, it was just such a tone that she used to stir up her disciples to the point where they would do violence to any that she labeled as their enemy. Rolande had not missed the lesson of Reverend Hrabanus's death. Despite the strength of her own following, she could still suffer at the hands of an enraged mob. And well she knew that the couple sitting across from her despised her as a sinner who flaunted her debaucheries. *Not that I've time for much in the way of debauchery,* she thought, trying not to smile. But that was the way they saw her, and had seen her from the first, even before the ill-fated visit to the Yerren. Now it would only be worse.

"The expedition to the mountains was not my idea, and was undertaken against my advice, as you well know," she said cautiously. "You will recall that I only accompanied Sir Andrew as the Wardership's agent, to see that he did not overstep his authority."

"True," the Ministra said. "Nonetheless, in consorting with the demons you have erred." *Even an evil thing may be put to good use in the hands of the righteous,* she reminded herself. Vendeley could not be counted among the godly, but she commanded much support among the Warders and the community.

"That journey was most certainly a mistake," Rolande said brusquely, "and I was fortunate to return with my life. But what has this to do with you and your plans?"

The Ministra smiled. "We were hoping you would see the error of your ways, and desire to redeem yourself. You may now be of assistance to us in our holy work."

Rolande sat back in her chair. If it were only her cooperation the Ministra desired, then perhaps she could not only protect herself from these fanatics, but also turn the situation to her own advantage. She decided to hear the Scrutinor leaders out. "How? What's your price?"

The Ministra looked disapproving at her choice of words. "There is no cost, but your salvation."

"What does that require?" Rolande snapped. They needed something from her, evidently, and she felt back on solid footing. But, by God, when she made the law here, she would see every damn Scrutinor stoned from her borders! When she'd worked for the Deps in Albin, she'd found them to be ruthless, but they were lambs compared to this lot.

"All we need is your testimony."

"Regarding what?" Rolande asked, puzzled.

The Ministra said impatiently, "You're to bear witness as to the dealings that the other members of your party had with the demons."

"The other members . . ." Rolande gave a snort of laughter. "*All* of them?"

"Not at present. We have tried to lay hands on the hermit, but he's nowhere to be found. But then he's mad and perhaps not answerable for his actions. Sir Andrew is away from the colony, and so beyond our reach for the time, but the other two are ready to hand, and we mean to have them arrested at once."

Before Sir Andrew gets back and stops you, Rolande thought, *you sly bitch.*

"There's little doubt the boy's in league with the Enemy," the Ministra continued, "possessed by evil spirits, from all folk say. And there's no dearth of evidence against the girl, but in order to punish them, we must first prove their guilt and declare that we as a people condemn their actions." It was not lightly that the Ministra undertook to arrest a member of Sir Andrew's household, but she knew that if she could challenge his authority and triumph by obtaining Katin's condemnation as well as Jerl's, it would strengthen her position in the community even more.

"I see," Rolande said, thinking of the effect on Sir Andrew of returning to find that his retainers had been taken without his consent and imprisoned, or pilloried, in his absence. One more thing to harry him while he tried to set the colony's defense in order.

She could have accomplished this by swearing a complaint against the youngsters herself, of course, but that would only have called more attention to their story, and convinced Sir Andrew of her guilt. She knew that her magnanimity had given her an air of innocence that no amount of outraged denial could have evoked. How amusing it had been to be gracious about the accusation, to have the brats in her power and then let them go, like a cat who toys with her prey but isn't hungry enough to kill it. She bore them no particular grudge, for that matter. She would certainly have done the same, in their place, although she would have done it right. She rather liked their daring, but they oughtn't to go a-spying if they couldn't do a better job of it.

Then, too, Rolande approved of the spirited way the girl stood up to Sir Andrew, and the courage she'd shown during their sojourn in the forest. It was almost a pity to let her be denounced on these idiotic charges, but the opportunity to placate the Scrutinors *and* thwart Sir Andrew was too good to lose. Besides, the high-handed little chit thought too well of herself—a public humiliation wouldn't do that one any harm.

And the cream of it was, Rolande thought, that she herself had not instigated a thing. If her testimony were circumspect enough, Sir Andrew could not blame her in the least. The Scrutinor Ministers would be the villains in his eyes.

"We must act at once," the Ministra was saying, "for

our situation worsens daily. Will you act with us or not?"

Rolande sighed. "You leave me little choice," she said humbly.

* * *

Havoc and disaster—and no end in sight, Lady Celia thought wearily. Sir Andrew's steward had only one crisis after another to report nowadays. In the panic over the impending threat from the dragons, laborers were leaving the fields to participate in the Scrutinor rabble-rousing, crops were being destroyed by townspeople charging through the fields on wild forays to search for imagined enemies . . . when God knew there were enough real ones they needed to prepare to meet. Fights between factions had become common in farm and town alike, and it was ill-advised to venture forth without armed guards. It was all too familiar.

And even with an escort, one could not be sure of safety, Lady Celia knew. How long could they be depended upon, before their heads were turned by one group or another? She had thought that these dangers, at least, had been left in Albin, but here she was more than ever at the mercy of strangers. With the exception of those who had journeyed from Albin with her or Sir Andrew, their people were not loyal retainers who had served their families for years. They were unknown quantities, and where their loyalties lay was impossible to be certain of from day to day. If only it were not necessary for Andrew to be away so much of the time. . . .

Oh, this is cowardice, she told herself impatiently. *This is weakness. Look at the child—she's not afraid.* Katin and her dog were playing tug-of-war with an old stocking that Lucifer had stolen from the workbasket and worried into shreds. Before leaving for the coast, Sir Andrew had exacted from Katin a promise to stay at Silverbourne, and Lady Celia kept her on a short rein. Katin did not complain, but did what she could to help Lady Celia with the increasing difficulties of managing the estate. She could see for herself that Lady Celia was not yet fully recovered from the effects of the poisoning, and she would have been ashamed to add to her worries.

They were closeted in the salon, where Lady Celia was distractedly reviewing the weekly tradesmen's bills and household accounts. Katin had been lying before the hearth, absorbed in a treatise on bone-setting, until Lucifer dropped from the rafters and landed on the book, with the tattered stocking in his mouth.

Katin heard Lady Celia sigh, and looked up to see her sitting back in her chair, her eyes closed, her hands lying listlessly in her lap. "Let me fetch you a tisane," Katin offered. "Wild thyme and rose hips work well to restore vitality to the blood." Lady Celia smiled at her and nodded, and Katin jumped up and ran off with the soarhound at her heels, still dragging the stocking after him.

Really, Lady Celia thought, the girl was turning out very well. She had kept the discipline and duty of her royal upbringing, but her years in the wilderness had allowed her to slough off much of the arrogance and callousness of the court. She combined the best of the old world and the new. She was the Queen Albin needed.

But Katin had not been gone for a minute before she burst into the room again, followed by two of the household guard, both out of breath, as if they'd come at a run. *What new catastrophe?* Lady Celia wondered, starting to her feet.

"They say there's a mob on its way here!" Katin cried.

"Crossing the south field now, My Lady," said one of the watchmen. "And they've taken the Smit lad prisoner."

"Jerl?" Katin gasped. "Why? He's done nothing."

The man shook his head. "I didn't stop to ask. They were spouting Scrutinor cant, but there were militia-men among them."

Another guard appeared in the doorway. "The Ministra's with them, My Lady, and they claim to be acting under the authority of the Wardership."

"Impossible! The Wardership does not act by mob," Lady Celia said. *But who knows who rules the colony now?* She shook her head and ordered, "Summon your fellows and have them stand ready."

"I doubt, M'lady, there are enough of us to fend them off," the first man said, as one of the others ran off to obey. "And if they've really the warrant of the Wardership . . ." His voice trailed off uncertainly.

What could they want here—unless—had they somehow learned of the Princess's identity? Glancing at Katin, Lady Celia knew that she was thinking the same thing, but to the guard she said only, "Tell me, if I leave immediately, can I get off the estate before they stop me?"

He looked doubtful. "They've not far to come. They could stop the carriage, but perhaps on horseback—"

"Good, let us waste no time." She peered out of the window, but there was as yet no sign of the mob. "Hold them off from entering the house as long as you can, so that they'll think we're still here. I shall ride for the coast myself and find Sir Andrew." Gesturing toward Katin, she said. "Come, girl. You've been to the fortifications. You shall show me the way."

Lady Celia led her through the kitchen, noticing as

they passed that none of the servants usually busy cleaning and cooking was to be seen. Had they gone to ground for fear of the mob—or had they gone to join it?

Katin ran ahead to the stables, and had Lady Celia's horse out of the stall and saddled by the time Lady Celia entered. Katin threw open the door to the stall where she kept her own horse, and found herself facing one of the grooms, who advanced on her, holding a pistol. Then another stableman rose up from behind a tall stack of hay bales, brandishing a pitchfork in a way that left no doubt that he was not there to defend them.

"What is the meaning of this?" Lady Celia demanded.

"Orders of Their Honors, the Warders of Thornfeld." The groom gestured to the doorway with his weapon. "This way, if you please, M'lady."

The man's calm increased Lady Celia's alarm. He appeared to know that he could act with impunity, which meant that this was more than a spontaneous outbreak of violence. She remembered well the ravages wrought by the uprisings in Albin. Could the same thing be occurring here—with the sanction of the Wardership? It seemed impossible. The aristocracy were well represented among the Warders.

"You lie!" she said boldly. "You dare not interfere with me—"

"Not with yourself, no, M'lady," the first man agreed. "'Tis the lass there that's wanted."

"The Good God wills it so!" the other added triumphantly. To his cohort he said, "Do you hold her here, and I'll direct the others to this place."

Lady Celia felt faint. She couldn't let Oriana be taken, but how could she prevent it? "You will answer to Sir Andrew when he returns," she warned the remaining groom, whose pistol was still leveled at Katin.

"He'll see you suffer for this outrage, no matter who put you up to it!"

"Those who do God's work need fear no man's reprisal," he recited, with maddening conviction. "The Good God protects the righteous."

Useless to threaten someone who believed that. Would greed serve? Lady Celia offered a bribe, and thought she saw a hesitant temptation in the man's face, but then he shook his head stubbornly and declared, "It is for the Good God to reward—"

"Enough!" Katin exclaimed. Turning on her captor, she demanded, "You say you've no authority to hold Her Ladyship? She is free to go?"

The groom frowned, as if trying to remember his exact instructions. "Only the girl," he agreed.

"Very well." To Lady Celia, Katin said, "You are not well, My Lady. Pray return to the house and rest yourself."

Lady Celia could scarcely believe that the man did nothing to stop her as she made her way to the door. "You are quite right, my dear," she said vaguely, and hurried off to find the watchmen she had left to defend the house.

But by the time she returned to the barn with half a dozen armed guards, it was too late to make an escape. The groom had led Katin into the stableyard, and already they could hear the sound of voices and tramping feet approaching. The guards had only time to disarm the groom and surround Lady Celia and Katin before the mob poured into the yard, led by the Ministra Cirana. She was clearly in charge, for the others stopped as she raised her hands. In the midst of the throng was a mule-drawn cart, and in it Jerl stood with his hands bound.

Lady Celia stepped forward to face the Ministra.

"Explain yourself, woman! How dare you set this rabble on my household?"

For a moment, the Ministra merely regarded her scornfully, as if from a height of moral and spiritual superiority, then, with an air of calm authority, she announced, "I have been duly empowered by the Wardership to arrest Jerl Smit and Katin Ander on the charge of engaging in witchcraft and consorting with demons, to the detriment of the well-being of this colony and all its God-fearing inhabitants."

At a gesture from the Ministra, several militiamen came forward, most looking as if they dearly wished they were somewhere else. Sergeant Merton handed Lady Celia the Warders' orders, signed and sealed. "The warrant is in order, My Lady," he said heavily. "We've no choice."

Lady Celia nodded, speechless. Among the household guard were those who would resist, on her order, but they were too few to prevent Katin's arrest. The rest were themselves members of the militia, who could not be expected to defy the lawful instructions of the Wardership. "This is madness," she said weakly. But at least her worst fears had not been realized—they had come for Katin, not for the Princess.

Katin, for her part, had dissolved in laughter. "Witchcraft!" she cried. "How silly! I wonder you're not mortified to make such a fool of yourself." She was giddy with relief, and not at all afraid. Her secret was safe after all, and this was such arrant nonsense—! Still laughing, she allowed the reluctant soldiers to bind her hands and lead her to the cart. "Don't be afraid," she said to them cheerfully. "I shan't change you into anything nasty." In fact, these were Sir Andrew's men, chosen by Captain Jamison, when he'd received the order for her arrest, to see that she came to no harm. Katin was bound so loosely that she could have slipped her hands free in a trice.

Lady Celia watched helplessly as the cart passed, unable even to think of reassuring words to call to Katin. But the girl needed reassurance less than she herself did. *I must get word to Andrew at once.* The Princess could not be left in the hands of these fanatics. Spent and ashen-pale, she waited, surrounded by the armed watchmen, till the yard was cleared of the Ministra's victorious followers, and she could make her way to the house without interference.

Sergeant Merton had remained behind. "A word with you, My Lady . . . ?" he said, drawing her aside. "The captain sent messengers to find His Lordship as soon as the warrant was delivered to him. And he delayed the whole business, to give them a few hours' start. Sir Andrew will know all about it ere long."

So that was done. Lady Celia felt tears of gratitude rise to her eyes, and she said unsteadily, "Pray convey my thanks to Captain Jamison. Your arm, sir, if you would be so kind? I've not been well of late." Leaning on the sergeant's arm, she directed all her efforts to reaching the house before she could succumb to exhaustion and fall into a faint. Carl had warned her that she must rest a great deal, lest she suffer a decline. And, unlike Katin, she suspected that the affair was very far from a joke.

* * *

The Ministers had seen that the tribunal took place the day after Jerl's and Katin's arrest, arguing that the longer the Warders delayed in acting, the more the colony would suffer from the unchecked demonic influences. It was held behind closed doors, attendance being restricted to the Warders and certain witnesses hastily summoned by writ.

Katin, having been made perfectly comfortable at the stockade, was still in good cheer when she was brought before the court, but her first flush of intoxicating relief was past. She was no longer amused, and as the morning wore on, she began to take the proceedings very seriously indeed. It had not occurred to her that the Scrutinors could make such a convincing case for Jerl's guilt, and she soon felt distinctly uneasy for him.

As the questioning commenced, soldiers from the fort were called on to bear witness that the Yerren who had been brought there half-dead, as a prisoner, had somehow escaped while Jerl was on duty. Reluctantly, one admitted that Jerl had seemed to fall into a sort of fit when a watchman had fired at the creature, and another recounted that the boy had been muttering strange words as they carried him into the stockade.

And then Rolande gave her testimony.

"You saw the Yerren engage in magic," the Ministra stated.

"True," said Rolande. She was seated at the front of the assembly hall facing the Warders who were acting as judges in the case. "They carried on a great ritual, with an image of some monstrous winged beast at its center—no doubt meant to be one of their dragons."

"A ceremony designed to bring down dragons upon us?" the Minister demanded.

"I had no way of knowing its purpose," Rolande pointed out.

The Ministra gave her a cold look, finding her statement insufficiently incriminating. "You did see your companions conspiring with the Yerren, did you not?" Her tone gave a clear warning that she would not tolerate equivocation.

"Sir Andrew and the hermit conferred with them repeatedly," Rolande said, with perfect truth.

But this did not satisfy the Ministra, since Sir Andrew and the hermit were not—as yet—on trial. "What of the communion between the accused and the Yerren?"

"Well, the boy does seem to have an ability to sense their thoughts—or they his. And on one occasion he was clearly possessed by them. He ranted wildly in their language. And he came at me with an ax."

This was much more to the Ministra's taste. "An irrefutable instance of demonic possession," she said triumphantly.

Jerl stole a look at Katin where she stood beside him at one side of the hall that had been cordoned off, under guard, to separate them from the Warders. How could he have let this happen to her? Why had he ever let anyone know about his affinity with the Yerren? Maybe he *was* a witch of some sort—but she wasn't. If he were to confess, could he take all the blame upon himself and get them to free Katin? But the Minister's next question to Rolande put paid to that idea.

"And what of the girl? Did she consort with these Yerren as well?"

"Not in the same way, but she did speak to them. One morning we found her sleeping curled up with one of the small ones, and that dog of hers."

"You mean her familiar?" the Ministra said quickly.

That idiot animal, a demonic familiar? How credulous could people be? "As to that, I couldn't say. It's a pesky enough creature. I kicked it out of our prison once, but it came back."

Rolande resented being forced to sacrifice the harmless youngsters to the Scrutinors, and she refused to perjure herself to please the Ministra. Every word of her testimony would be the plain, unvarnished truth.

But she'd realized by now that the Scrutinors were out for blood, and it wasn't going to be her blood if she could help it. "I tried to strangle the little Yerren the girl befriended, but the others stopped me," she added, in case the Ministra had any ideas of trying to imply that she was tainted as well.

But the Ministra was not to be put off the track by Rolande's evasions. Coming a step closer, she asked, "Has Katin Ander's familiar a name?"

There was no help for it. "Yes—she calls it Lucifer."

There was a collective gasp from those listening, and the Ministra smiled complacently, knowing that she had won.

Others, fearful of the Scrutinors, came forth to bear witness to Katin's uncanny healing abilities, and the soldiers were called upon to repeat that the Yerren prisoner had been more dead than alive before she had somehow revived it. But Rolande's testimony had already turned the tide. Katin felt no surprise when the men and women sitting in judgment upon them declared them guilty—but she was still unprepared for the sentence. In the end they were condemned to be hanged as soon as a gibbet could be constructed.

Chapter 13

We'll escape from the stockade, Katin thought. The soldiers who had been so reluctant to arrest them would no doubt arrange an opportunity for them to get away—doors accidentally left unlocked, sentries who looked askance as they slipped past. . . . And as a last resort, if all else failed, she *could* reveal her secret to Captain Jamison. She knew that he was loyal to the Crown. If he knew who she was, he would see to it that she escaped—and she would see to it that Jerl did. There was, she told herself, no real danger that they would be hanged.

But then her attention was abruptly drawn back to the hall, as the Ministra began to speak again. The Scrutinors were well aware of the loyalty the militia had to Sir Andrew. This devotion to their commander might be very well in war, the Ministra allowed, but would be misplaced where civil justice was concerned. They might—mistakenly—feel it their duty to protect members of Sir Andrew's household, despite the lawful condemnation of the community, even despite the dictates of conscience and the Holy Will, manifested in the judgment of a tribunal convened in the service of the just and beneficent God. She asked for and was granted permission to secure the prisoners in one of the outbuildings on the grounds of the Scrutinor church.

Katin was pierced with a blinding panic and despair. Had she escaped her enemies and myriad dangers, only to suffer such an ignoble death at the hands of fools? Jerl stood clenching his fists in hopeless frustration, trying to think of any way he could protect Katin, but he was powerless to resist as they were seized roughly by the Ministers' followers and dragged off to be locked up.

Ordinarily, Simeon would have been pleased by any ill that befell Sir Andrew, but when he heard from Rolande of the outcome of the trial, he saw his dreams of reward drifting away like smoke in the wind. With the Princess dead, he had nothing to offer the Chamber. This was not to be countenanced. He'd suffered enough in this godforsaken country, and he wasn't about to allow the Scrutinors' mania to destroy his one chance at real power.

But he needed help to get Katin away from the Scrutinors. He soon discovered that the shed was well-guarded by Dep devotees, who relied on arms as well as the protection of the Good God to see to the security of the prisoners. He had no lack of henchmen he could call upon, but those who answered to Rolande could not be trusted for this job. . . . The bandits' secrecy could be bought—but there was the difficulty. He customarily paid for their services with money provided to Rolande by the Chamber, and he couldn't very well ask her for funds to secure Katin's release—not without telling her the truth, and letting her claim the glory. By God, he'd let the girl hang before he'd let Vendeley have her. As for his own funds, he had exhausted those in the last abortive attempt to have the bandits snatch Katin. Damn it all, why couldn't Sir Andrew be at hand when he was needed, and rescue his beloved sovereign himself?

And that gave Simeon an idea. There was someone else who might pay handsomely to save the girl's life. It would be an irksome interview, he did not doubt, but the reward would be worth the groveling. He rode for Silverbourne without delay.

Lady Celia was still far from well, and the news of the tribunal's sentence only made matters worse. She had no respite from her desperate worries. There was no telling how soon the militiamen would be able to locate Sir Andrew, or whether he would get back to the colony in time to save the Princess. Worse, since the execution was lawful, it was unlikely that Sir Andrew could force the Warders to reverse their decision, even if he arrived in time.

No, he would have to resort to an armed attack, she was certain, and the result could only be a civil war in the colony, between the soldiers loyal to him and those loyal to the Scrutinors. She had no doubt that his people would prevail, with their greater numbers, but such an engagement would make it impossible to muster a unified defense against the Chamber's invading forces. And then, suppose he *didn't* get back before the gibbet was constructed . . . ?

Like Katin, Lady Celia had considered the possibility of going to Captain Jamison for help. He would bring the militia to Katin's defense, if he knew that she was in reality the Princess Oriana. But would the soldiers follow him without question, as they would Sir Andrew? He would have to give them a good reason to defy the Wardership, and soon the secret would be known throughout the whole community. How long, then, before it was known to the Chamber as well? Lady Celia saw disaster every way she turned.

When Simeon Pryce was announced, her immediate response was fury that he should have the gall to present himself at Silverbourne. She was tempted to have him turned from the door, but the note he sent up by her serving maid said that he had the means to free Katin, and she dared not refuse him entrance. He was the last person she would have chosen to trust with such a task, but any choice she made would be drastic and fraught with danger. If there was any chance at all that his claim was true, she must deal with him, despite her disgust.

She had her suspicions that it might be he who had poisoned their well. Not only did he have a grudge against them both, but it was in the Chamber's interests to eliminate Sir Andrew. Lady Celia believed Katin's evidence against Rolande and Simeon, whether or not it could be proven before a magistrate. Had they been responsible for the poisoning of Holistowe as well . . . ?

But if he had some practical plan to offer, she must give him a hearing. Summoning what strength she could, she rose and told the servant she would see Simeon in the salon.

"You claim to possess a way to help Katin Ander?" she asked, dropping wearily onto the settle opposite where he stood.

He smiled and bowed. But then, angry that she did not invite him to sit, he snarled, "I have—and it's more than you can accomplish, with all your airs and graces."

"Dogs can do many things better than their masters, yet I would not be a dog," Lady Celia said evenly. "Tell me what you have come to say, or leave me."

Simeon swallowed his pride and said reproachfully, "You do wrong to treat me thus, when I have come in a spirit of reconciliation, to offer my services."

Lady Celia impatiently threw down his note at his feet. "Can you do what you say there, and if so, how?"

Simeon cut to the heart of the matter. "I have many men and women to do my bidding. Some are schooled in use of arms—enough to wrest the girl from the Scrutinors who hold her."

Lady Celia nodded. She knew well what mischief Simeon had worked over the past months, and he certainly hadn't done it alone. If he had the resources to free Katin, then she might be able to use him. Better that he and his minions take any musket balls that flew than that Andrew did. "What do you want in return?" she demanded.

"Such a mission will come dear, Your Ladyship. There are many risks involved—"

Lady Celia waved away his explanations. "Money, then. Very well, you shall have it." She rang for a servant. "Tell me how much you require."

Simeon smiled again, confident now that he would succeed, not only in this, but in his ultimate goal. It was meant to be—why else should fortune keep placing opportunities in his way? And when he held the reins of power, he would revenge himself on Silverbourne at last. But for now—what delightful irony it was to have Lady Celia pay to deliver the girl into his hands.

* * *

Katin and Jerl hunkered down on the straw-covered floor of the storage shed where they were imprisoned. Katin had peeled away little bits of bark from around a chink in the rough wood through which she could see the back of one of the Scrutinor guards passing, his gray cloak silvered by moonlight. *How long does it take to build a gibbet?* she wondered, but to Jerl she said only, "Oh, dear, there's Lucifer. He must have tracked me here. Go home, fool of a dog, before the guards see you!" But the pup merely looked up toward the hole and whimpered longingly. "Curse it, if they find you, they'll probably want to hang you, too!" There were several Scrutinors guarding them, she knew. She could hear their footsteps and their voices discussing the fate of the blasphemers—Jerl and herself—with more relish than was warranted by religious devotion.

"There must be half a dozen of them," she said in disgust, "just for show, to make us seem dangerous. Do folk suppose that we can make doors unbar themselves, or pass through solid wood? If we could do that, surely our demonic powers could overcome the guards, too."

Jerl shook his head. "They're not worried about keeping us in, but about keeping someone from sneaking up in the night to let us out." He had hoped that some of Sir Andrew's people might attempt to free Katin, until he'd realized how many guards the Scrutinors had posted. The Ministra had thought of everything. He looked at Katin forlornly and said, "I'm sorry you're to suffer for this. It's all my fault."

"Why? Are you any more guilty of engaging in witchcraft than I am?" Katin asked scornfully.

"Maybe I am. It's not natural, the way I felt what the Yerren did—"

"Nonsense! Carl says only idiots think things can happen contrary to natural law. It only seems that way because we don't yet understand all the laws of nature. Unfortunately," she added, "the Scrutinors are idiots, and we're both suffering for their idiocy. But I tell you, Sir Andrew won't let us hang. I'm sure Lady Celia has sent for him." Rather than surrender to despair, Katin clung to the chance that her benefactor would return in time to save her, or failing that, that Lady Celia would think of something.

Jerl wanted to believe her—and he also wanted to know what made her so certain that her welfare was paramount to Sir Andrew. "Do you think he can make the Warders pardon us?" he asked cautiously. He himself didn't think it likely.

Katin considered. "I doubt it," she admitted. "Folk want a scapegoat, to take away the curse of the dragons. They won't listen to reason. But don't worry, Sir Andrew will marshal the militia to the rescue, if he must. We'll not hang, I promise you."

So she did believe that her patron would turn the militia against the citizenry to save her. And Sir Andrew could do it if he chose, Jerl realized. As a militiaman himself, he knew that he would obey the commander, even in defiance of the Wardership, and he suspected that most of the troops felt the same. Sir Andrew could do it, yes, but why would he?

"Katin—who are you really?" he asked abruptly.

Katin started. Jerl was no fool. She should have spoken more carefully. But then, if Sir Andrew—or Captain Jamison, for that matter—did rescue her by force of arms, everyone would soon be asking that question. And Jerl deserved an answer.

Katin wanted to tell him the truth, but she knew that she shouldn't. She felt sure she could trust Jerl, but the more people who knew her secret the greater the risk . . . and then, suppose Jerl should hate her if he knew who she was? He had no love for the monarchy.

"I can't tell you that," she said at last. "I'm sorry."

"Not even when we're about to be hanged? What difference can it make now?"

"We *won't* hang," Katin insisted, but she could see that Jerl was hurt by her mistrust. It wasn't right. And suppose they *were* executed soon . . . ? "You see," she began, "I'm—connected to the royal family—and I know you don't hold with the Crown."

"Well, maybe if *you* were Queen, I'd be a royalist," Jerl said gallantly. It was just his luck, he thought, that the one time he finally managed to say what he felt was on the eve of his execution.

Even Katin was speechless at that. Then she smiled almost shyly and said, "To be sure, you do have intuition. But I—"

At that moment Lucifer commenced a loud barking, and footsteps approached the shed.

"Grab him!" a voice yelled.

"Not I—that's the devil-dog does the witch's bidding—"

"The grace of the Good God is our shield. I'll catch the creature."

Katin was on her feet and at the peephole, fearing for Lucifer, but she could see nothing. Putting her ear to the hole instead, she heard the sound of running feet, then a squeal from the soarhound as one of the guards grabbed it, followed by a most ungodly curse as Lucifer's teeth found purchase. Suddenly a shot rang out, and Katin gave a cry of dismay. How could they shoot a harmless little dog? Pounding on the wall of the shed, she shouted, "You inhuman butchers! I wish I *were* a witch—I'd change you to worms! I'd—" More shots exploded, and a great tumult erupted in the yard outside.

Katin and Jerl dropped to the floor, but no musket balls pierced the walls of their prison. They could smell musket smoke and hear yelling and cursing as the Deprivant guards fired wildly, facing a far more vicious mass assault than they were prepared for. "Godless vermin—" one unseen Scrutinor shouted, only to have his impending diatribe cut off with a choking sound in mid-sentence.

"I told you Sir Andrew would come for us!" Katin said excitedly. It seemed strange that he should cold-bloodedly shoot down his fellow colonists—even Deprivant fanatics—without first offering them terms, but there must be some explanation. Besides, who else could it be? She was entirely unprepared, as the bolt was drawn back and the door thrown open, to look up and see Lorin, the bandit chieftain who had tried to capture her in the wilderness.

As she scrambled to her feet, Lorin and several of his followers crowded into the shed, and before she could ask a single question, he had grabbed her arm in an unbreakable grip and started dragging her toward the door.

Jerl threw himself at the bearded bandit, only to be stopped by two of Lorin's henchmen, who held him fast. "What about this one?" one of them asked.

Lorin looked back at Jerl uncertainly. "Him again! I'm cursed if I know—we've no orders about him. Best bring him along, we can't let him go now. Let the one paying the price decide if he wants him. Come on. Do you want to stay here and be hung?" he added to Katin, pushing her out the door and into the arms of one of his confederates.

It was a reasonable question, Katin thought, as one of the mounted bandits pulled her up in front of him. Wherever the bandits took them, it had to be safer than the Scrutinor prison. "Did Sir Andrew send you?" she gasped, remembering that he'd enlisted the bandits to help fight the Dep invaders, when the time came. But no one answered her. The bandits were busy swarming over the muddy ground, stripping anything worth taking from the bodies of the fallen Scrutinors.

Lorin took the reins of a chestnut stallion from a boy who was holding a string of horses. "Now!" he ordered. "Before the ones who got away come back with reinforcements." Jerl was thrown onto a roan gelding ridden by another bandit, and the rest grabbed their reins from the boy and leaped astride, one of them pulling the boy up after him.

They covered about a league, the horses' hooves spraying loose soil as they pounded at full gallop. Then, as the sun was rising, they turned toward the coast, having arranged to meet Simeon at Bogner's Pond, where he would take possession of Katin. But suddenly the bandits riding in front of her drew up sharply, and a few began firing. A string of militiamen rode toward them, and as they closed the distance between the two parties, she could see Sir Andrew riding near their head. He *had* sent Lorin and his crew after her, then. But why the shooting? Hadn't the bandits recognized him?

"Hold your fire, you fools!" she cried.

It took Lorin less than a minute to see how badly outnumbered his small band was and to calculate their dismal chances of surviving the encounter. Could they outrun the soldiers? He had opened his mouth to order flight, when he saw Sir Andrew, and a much better plan suggested itself to him. "Aye, hold up your fire," he ordered, laughing. "The lass is right!"

"What—we'll be slaughtered!" the man riding with Katin protested. "If they don't shoot us now, we'll be hung for taking these two!"

Lorin just turned to look at him, and the man subsided. The others, knowing that look, put up their guns as well. "Bring the young'uns forward where they can see them," Lorin ordered. "They'll not risk hitting them." He urged his horse forward. "Now follow along, keep your weapons ready, but don't shoot. This is going to fall out very well indeed—for us." With Lorin at their head, they rode toward the cavalry.

The militia, being better disciplined than the bandits,

had not yet returned their fire. It was a brigand's trick to shoot while still out of range, just to throw a scare into the prey, and to the well-trained soldiers it was nothing but a waste of good powder and shot. They were well within range now, though, and waiting for Sir Andrew's order to open fire.

But the bandits had ceased their fire, and Sir Andrew—as Lorin intended—had spied Katin. When they were within earshot, Lorin hailed Sir Andrew and called a halt. He let the bandit with Katin draw up beside his own horse, then ordered his people to dismount, as a sign to Sir Andrew that they were not about to bolt with their captives. Sir Andrew halted and told his men to hold their weapons ready, then waved Lorin forward, and rode to meet him. Lorin knew that he was safe while the youngsters were vulnerable, and Sir Andrew knew that the bandits wouldn't dare fire on him, outnumbered and dismounted as they were.

"Greetings, Your Lordship," Lorin said, smiling with mock gentility as he brought his horse to a stop beside Sir Andrew's. "We've rescued your pet for you." He gestured back toward Katin. "You were so set on retrieving her from us in the woods, I was sure you'd not want to lose her again—so I took the liberty of snatching her from the gray folk, before they could hang her. Did I do right?"

"So it would seem," Sir Andrew said tersely, not wanting to show how desperately relieved he was to see the girl alive and safe. Gesturing to the soldiers to follow, he trotted to Katin, Lorin still at his side.

"Well done, My Lord!" she cried, as he rode up. Sir Andrew dismounted to see that she was unhurt, then handed her up onto his own horse.

"You'll take this one off our hands as well?" asked Lorin, with a jerk of his thumb toward Jerl.

"I suppose I must." Sir Andrew gave Jerl a long look, remembering that he'd been meaning to have a talk with him about Katin. It had better not be too late for that talk. "How is it, Smit, that every time there's trouble, you're in the thick of it? Never mind—ride with Mallory."

He turned to mount his mare, behind Katin, but just then the boy who had earlier been holding the bandits' horses suddenly pushed forward, trying to reach Sir Andrew. A soldier leaned down to shove him away.

"No," the boy said desperately to Sir Andrew. "Please!"

"Leave him," Sir Andrew said. "What is it?" he asked the boy.

"I was captured, too. Take me with you," he pleaded, looking around apprehensively lest someone—brigand or soldier—drag him off against his will.

Sir Andrew frowned. "What manner of tale is this?"

"It's true," the boy insisted. "I didn't join them—I was forced to serve them. Me and others."

Sir Andrew turned to Lorin. "Well? Did you abduct this child?"

Lorin glanced at the soldiers around him and shook his shaggy head. "Not I."

"Good," Sir Andrew said dryly, "because such an act would be considered a hanging offense." He let the words weigh upon Lorin for a moment before he went on, "And how did you come by him, then?"

"I tell you," Lorin said quickly, "it was not I who snatched those children. They were given me for use, and—"

"Given?" said Sir Andrew.

Lorin shrugged. "All right, I bought them—but the price was damned cheap. And what else could I do with them but keep them? They say they come from

Oxwold, but the place no longer stands. We couldn't well walk into some other colony with them, could we now?" he asked in an aggrieved tone. "We'd only be accused of killing their parents or kidnapping them, or some other hanging offense. What were we to do—leave them to starve in the woods?"

Sir Andrew imagined that the boy's usage at the brigands' hands had been anything but easy. But that was not a matter to be pursued now. It was the mention of Oxwold that interested him at present. He leaned down to the boy and asked, "How came you to this man?"

The boy swallowed and bit his lip, as if reluctant to give voice to his memories, but at last he said, "We were in the church, at our lessons, when a great swarm of villains overran us and drove us from the school. They killed Ministra Leann when she tried to stop them—and others, too, I think." Tears welled up in his eyes. "They made us walk a great way into the woods—I thought they would kill us. But a man came with carts, and we were taken off in different ways."

Sir Andrew was listening attentively. "These villains who attacked you, they were people, not Yerren?"

The boy only looked at him, puzzled.

"The featherfolk, he means," Katin said gently.

"Oh, no, they were men and women, not feather'uns."

"Yet Paeter Cellric of Oxwold has told us that feathers were found throughout the schoolroom and the churchyard there."

"There *were* feathers," the boy remembered. "I saw them scatter some from pouches—I don't know why."

I do, Sir Andrew thought. Suppose those who'd stolen the children were not mere bandits, but agents of the Chamber, sent to start a war between the colonists of Oxwold and the local clan of Yerren? And those visitors who'd sought shelter later at the garrison houses and opened them to the enraged Yerren were no doubt more of the same. "What of the man who came for you in the woods?" he asked. "Can you say what he was like?"

The boy shook his head. "No, sir. He wore a great black cloak and a big hat. I could not see his face for it. But I could hear what he said. He told the others to sell us to the bandits—but not to any too near Oxwold."

"How many of you are with Lorin's band?"

"Five in all. Will you take me with you?" he begged. "I swear I'm not a bandit!"

"You'll come with us," Sir Andrew promised. To Lorin he said, "You will release the rest as well."

"Not all want to be released, despite what this ungrateful brat says."

"You will release them nonetheless," Sir Andrew said firmly. "Those who wish to return to you will be allowed to do so."

Lorin shrugged again. "Fair enough. I'll send the lot to you." He had no intention of leading the authorities to his camp. Grinning at Sir Andrew, he nodded toward Katin and said, "Didn't I save your lass for you? She's whole and hale, which she would not be, if I'd left her in Dep hands. Do you grant that we've done you a service?"

"You have," Sir Andrew was forced to admit. Lorin's actions had not only freed Katin, but spared him the necessity of taking arms against his fellow colonists. The bandit had proved very useful indeed.

"Well, then, M'lord, you remember we struck a bargain in the forest—I believe you owe me payment for my services."

As they approached the crossroads on the outskirts of the colony, Lucifer came bounding up, panting and barking, having followed Katin's trail by scent. He frisked around the horse's feet, trying to jump up to her, until Sir Andrew was forced to call a halt.

"You can go no farther than the crossroads at any rate," he said to Katin. "You're still under condemnation, and I've no doubt the Deps are mounting a search even now for their stray sacrificial lambs. What's to be done with the two of you I don't know. Silverbourne's not secure, that much is clear." He sent the company of soldiers on to the stockade, keeping back two of the horses for Katin and Jerl.

Katin jumped down from Sir Andrew's mare and nearly tripped over the eager soarhound before she mounted the cavalry horse. "Aren't you the clever dog, then, to find me!" she cooed, laughing. Having escaped yet another peril—with no idea of how close she'd come to falling into Simeon's hands—she could not but feel lighthearted and hopeful, though she knew, in truth, that the danger was far from over. "Perhaps we could go stay with the Yerren for a time," she suggested. "I should like that, and we'd be safe enough there."

Sir Andrew shook his head. "Safe from the Scrutinors, perhaps, but not from the shraik." *Where, then?* he asked himself. Now that he had returned, he could demand that the Warders reconsider their decision, but that would take time, and might very well be unsuccessful. He must keep her away from the town for now, where she would be in danger not only from the Scrutinors, but from the ever increasing violence. He himself had enemies on so many fronts—the Chamber's spies, the Scrutinor fanatics, the Warders who opposed him—any of whom could be a threat to the Princess as well.

But there was one person with no ties to the colony, who lived far enough from Thornfeld to offer a haven, perhaps. Her Highness would be safer hidden in the woods than anywhere in the settlement. "Come along now," he said, turning his mare, "we'll see if Frend Pierson will bear with you for a time."

The hermit raised no objection to sheltering Katin till she could safely return to Silverbourne. "The Scrutinors came hunting for me and didn't find me," he assured Sir Andrew, "and if they come back, they'll not find the girl either. But what of young Smit, then?"

Sir Andrew had been considering the question of what to do with Jerl. He couldn't very well abandon the boy to the vengeance of the Scrutinors, but neither did he incline to the idea of leaving him alone with Katin, with only the preoccupied old man as guardian. "Yes, as for you, Smit," he said, "you're to ride by way of the forest to Ringmaron Bay. I doubt the Scrutinors will send so far north in search of you, but if they do, you'll be able to see them coming, and disappear into the wilderness before they reach the watchtower. Take word to the garrison there that I plan to return to the coast within two days. You're to stay at Ringmaron and make yourself useful, until I send for you." *Which will not be any time soon,* Sir Andrew promised himself. *Quite possibly not for months.*

After taking his leave from Katin, Sir Andrew rode back through the woods with Jerl, planning to accompany him until the point where their paths would part, and then impart to him a few well-chosen words on the subject of Katin. But as they approached the edge of the forest, Sir Andrew had gotten no further than, "See here, Smit—" when suddenly, carried on the wind, they heard the sound of distant church bells tolling the alarm.

Chapter 14

As they crossed the open fields, they could see huge bat-winged forms gliding and darting through the sky. Too large to be birds, or even Yerren, unfamiliar and terrifying in form, they could only be the dreaded shraik. The tolling bells continued to ring in ceaseless ominous warning. Without a word, Sir Andrew and Jerl made for the road and galloped toward town at a frantic pace. If the settlement was under attack by such monsters, no one would spare a thought for Jerl's supposed crime, and every person who could shoot would be desperately needed.

The colony was in chaos. The streets were filled with people who'd been caught out of doors, and were now running madly in all directions, seeking shelter. No matter which way they fled, they remained exposed to the great leather-winged beasts that swooped from the sky and tore at their unprotected prey with talons and sharp-toothed beaks.

Sir Andrew took in the scene and flung himself down from his horse, pulling Jerl after him into the doorway of the clothier's shop. The luckier folk who had been abroad at the time of the attack had reached the refuge of the buildings along the street, and now the shutters were closed and the doors barred.

Other townspeople and members of the militia were firing from the shelter of the buildings, and Sir Andrew lost no time in taking aim on an ugly mud-colored shraik as it dove in low over the main street, claws extended to grasp a youth who was trying to reach the livery stable. Sir Andrew opened fire, along with the others within range, and blood spouted as musket balls penetrated the beast's hide. The shraik screeched with a piercing, unearthly sound and crashed to the ground. Sir Andrew reloaded his weapon, and a moment later was firing again on an even larger beast.

Gradually, he worked his way around to the block of stores where the bulk of the militiamen were located. He reorganized the defense, sending some up to the rooftops. They would be more exposed there, but they would have a less obstructed view and a better chance of shooting the vicious beasts before they reached low enough to strike. As he worked feverishly, he tried not to think of Celia and what might be happening at Silverbourne. There were sufficient guards and ammunition at the house to protect her, he told himself. He was needed here. Then, at the height of the chaos, the Ministra emerged from the door of the church. Sir Andrew shouted for her to go back, but she ignored the warning, striding into the center of the market square. Raising her arms, she exhorted the shraik, "In the name of our Good God, protector of the righteous, I command you to depart this place, creatures of darkness! In the name of the gracious God who is our shield against evil, flee from us." One of the smaller shraik soaring overhead spotted the figure standing upright and exposed, and dove straight toward her.

"In the name of God who is our fortress and defender against all foes natural and unnatural be gone—"

"Hraaak!" the shraik cried, as its claws sank into her flesh.

It was a long and bloody attack that left carnage on all sides. Children were snatched from yards in the outlying farms before their parents could reach them, men and women were killed in the hopeless defense of their families, and soldiers on patrol, caught in the open, were slaughtered. The beasts were large enough to destroy fences and break windows in buildings as they flung themselves against all barriers, to get at their prey.

The soldiers deployed by Sir Andrew made a valiant defense, and dead and dying shraik soon crashed to the streets, but their own losses were heavy as well. For it was only when the shraik swooped low enough to inflict damage that they came within musket range—a mere hundred feet—and by then it was often too late. Before long, Jerl was able to seize a musket dropped by a fallen comrade and join in the desperate defense.

By dark, the shraik had finally flown off to roost for the night, leaving bloody bodies and lamenting throughout the colony. *I asked for an enemy I could see,* Sir Andrew thought bitterly.

"Our losses will be devastating, unless we can shoot them before they descend to strike," Sir Andrew insisted. He stood in the candlelit assembly hall where an evening meeting of the Wardership had been called to discuss this new calamity. "We need armed defenders high in the trees—defenders who can move swiftly from one height to another, following the shraik's flight. We need the Yerren. They can reach greater heights and travel at greater speeds than we can. They have the skill, and the desire—they want nothing more than to destroy shraik. They lack only weapons powerful enough to pierce the creatures' hides, without coming dangerously close to them. Armed with muskets, they could shoot the damned things out of the sky in prodigious numbers."

The other Warders, chastened by the losses of the day, were quick to acquiesce to what he proposed—that they at last send muskets to the Yerren in return for their help in eradicating the shraik.

"Eliminating the beasts would be to their advantage as well as ours," Sir Andrew told the Warders. "But to be certain of them, we shall send only a cartload of muskets now, as a sign of our good faith. More would be difficult to get through the forest in any event. The rest will be provided when they join us here."

Faced with the immediate, deadly threat of the shraik, the Warders put aside their differences and left Sir Andrew with a free hand to undertake to win the Yerren to their cause. Even Rolande concurred. True, if the Yerren joined forces with the colonists now, the Chamber's troops might have to face a formidable alliance later, but that was a problem for another day. If something wasn't done about the shraik now, there'd be nothing left of Thornfeld for her to claim as reward for her part in the Chamber's conquest. If the Yerren could destroy the dragons, let them—and if the dragons should destroy a great many of the Yerren, so much the better.

Rolande's head was bandaged from a dangerous gash aslant her forehead, the result of a dispute with a shraik as to which side of her shop windows it ought to be on. She had finally succeeded in killing the thing, but only after a considerable loss of glass—and blood. She had then gone on to kill more of them, out of sheer rage, but there seemed to be no end to the monsters. Before the day was out, she had emptied her shop of musketry, handing out flintlocks and ammunition to all who could use them against the horde of bloodthirsty beasts. Sir Andrew, knowing full well that she was a spy and a traitor, nonetheless found himself grateful for her help once more.

"By all means, bring on the Yerren," Rolande advised the Warders. "I've had to double board my shopwindows—those damned dragons are bad for business."

Others agreed. Without the Ministra there to protest that the Yerren were soulless spawn of the Evil One, they seemed harmless and benign compared to the horrifying shraik.

"It is God's will," Headman Farnham declared piously.

"As to that," said Sir Andrew, "we will now discuss the matter of this absurd charge of witchcraft. . . ."

As soon as the meeting was completed, Sir Andrew was at last free to ride for Silverbourne and satisfy himself that Lady Celia had come to no harm. He had sent Jerl ahead of him, when the last of the shraik had taken flight, to reassure her as to Katin's safety, and to bring him back word at once if anything should be amiss at the house. But the boy had not returned, which meant, he told himself, that all was well . . . or that something had happened to Jerl.

But Jerl had been sent to get some sleep, and Sir Andrew found Lady Celia waiting for him with a hot meal. She looked rather better than when he'd seen her last. Jerl's message that Katin had been rescued from the Scrutinors, and that Sir Andrew had not been eaten by a shraik, did more to renew her spirits and vitality than all Carl's tonics and restoratives.

"We saw only a few of the dragons here," she told him cheerfully. "One carried off a calf, and another harried some of the field hands, but Hannah Franesh was nearby, and she shot it down most handily." Hannah had taken to visiting Silverbourne often, to bring Lady Celia news, and sell Mistress Wicken game for the kitchen. "I bade her stay till the danger should be past, and she and some others dragged the creature to the barnyard and skinned it! Carl took copious notes concerning its anatomy."

She had heard from Jerl about the bandits and the dragons, and now she heard from Sir Andrew about the Warders and the Yerren. "You don't think of returning to the Yerren yourself?" she asked anxiously.

"Impossible. I can't be spared now, and no more can Jamison. No, I shall send a pair of soldiers as escort, but Pierson and Smit must carry the message. I don't know that I should be of any use to them. In truth, I was more hindrance than help on our last mission! Only Pierson can explain our intentions, and only Smit has the rapport with the Yerren that will persuade them of our good faith."

"You do know, I trust, that Her Highness will insist on accompanying them?"

"All too well. And I've half a mind to allow it, what's more. She'd be safer in those dense woods than here, at present. The shraik prefer open ground, it would seem. There can't be more of them at Creshgahar than here, and at least there are no Scrutinors there. The greatest danger in the scheme is letting her traipse about the woods in company with young Smit. . . . You may laugh, Celia, but the boy's clearly infatuated with her."

"So much the better, my dear. He'll protect her from dragons."

"And who'll protect her from him?"

"Our young lady is *perfectly* capable of defending her own virtue, never fear." Lady Celia brushed away tears of laughter. "But with all our lives at risk, at every moment, how *can* you distress yourself over what a boy and girl may do in the forest?"

Deeply delighted to see her laugh again, Sir Andrew could only shake his head in mock reproof. "Put in those terms, it sounds harmless enough," he said, smiling, "but you know very well what I—"

"And such sentiments do you credit, my love, but what do you suppose you can do about it? Indeed, I'm not altogether sure that it's our place to interfere. If Oriana lives through this dreadful summer, you will have done all that could be expected of you."

There really was nothing he could do about the Princess's behavior, but he vowed to find a few minutes in the morning to put the fear of God into Jerl, before he sent him on his way. "All the same," he said, "I shall expect *you* to have a talk with her, when she comes back."

"And am *I* a fitting model of propriety for a young girl?" Lady Celia mocked. "Oh, of course, just as you like, Andrew, but why not ask Hannah Franesh to go along with the party, if it will set your mind at rest? She knows the woods as well as anyone, she seems quite capable of dealing with dragons, *and* she can keep an eye on the girl, better than you could if you were there yourself."

"A splendid idea—you'll speak to her? I would as soon have Her Highness away from town, for the time, as well as the boy, until the Wardership can declare an official revocation of their odious condemnation."

"Will they do so, then?"

"They'll go through their paces first, for form's sake, and call a special session, and make sworn statements, and draw up documents, to make all lawful according to statute—and all that can hardly be accomplished while the colony's under siege by dragons. But they'll do it in time, make no mistake. I was prepared to threaten them with most drastic measures if they refused, but there was no necessity, in the event. I found them particularly compliant. Vendeley, of all people, took my part at once—called the sentence a disgrace—and others will follow her lead. To say the truth, though, I think most were glad to be quit of the business."

Lady Celia nodded. "'Twas the Ministra's madness drove them on."

"Did Smit tell you . . . ?"

Lady Celia was a civilized woman, and she tried not to smile at the thought of the Scrutinor leader's fearful demise. "God grant her peace," she said primly.

The party set off with the muskets at first light, making their way through a woods that seemed more forbidding than on their earlier trip. Animals and birds that had been noisily active before were now scarce, having fled the new predators in their territory, and the woods were eerily silent. Now and again a flight of shraik came into view over the trees, winging toward the colonies or the mountains, and the party took cover, but the shraik were after more easily accessible prey. With their immense wingspans, they could not easily dart down among the dense trees, and it was not until the party reached the clearer land near the Yerren city that the hunting shraik took much interest in them. When they reached stretches of open land, they were forced to wait in the forest by day and cross them after dark, when the shraik roosted for the night.

But the farther north they traveled, the fewer of the beasts they saw, and the heavily-armed party could easily defend themselves from attack by a single shraik. "They've all gone to Thornfeld," one of the soldiers said grimly.

Game, too, was rare, and their supplies were growing low. Even Hannah's snares often remained empty, and they depended more and more on the edible plants the hermit found for them. When Lucifer darted into the brush on the track of a promising scent, Katin nocked an arrow at once, hoping that he'd flush out a pheasant, or at least some quail—but instead, a moment later, they heard him give a howl of terror.

Before Katin could object, Jerl said, "I'll get him," and charged into the thick growth in search of the soarhound. Sir Andrew had made clear to him, in no uncertain terms, exactly what would happen to him if he made any advances to Katin, but, after all, the commander hadn't forbidden him to chase after her dog. Now that Jerl knew Katin was somehow connected to the highest nobility, he hadn't much hope of winning her, but Sir Andrew wasn't there, and there was nothing to keep him from trying to please her.

He fiercely forced his way through the underbrush, pushing back branches with his musket, until he broke into a small clearing, where he found himself facing a large wounded shraik, hunched over a fallen tree. Lucifer was cowering in a hole in the log, just out of reach of the beast's long toothed beak. Seeing Jerl, the shraik decided that he would make a much more satisfying meal than the smaller animal it had been trying to capture, and it reared itself upright, its wounded wing hanging askew. Jerl backed away, sure that if he turned to run it would strike him before he could get away. As he tried to untangle his musket from the branches and bring it into position to fire, the shraik dragged itself after him and swiped at him with its claws, sending him leaping backward. He nearly collided with Katin, who had followed close behind him.

"Katin—go back—there's a shraik!" Jerl cried in warning, and tried again to brace his gun for a clear shot as the shraik lurched toward him, its mouth gaping open. Katin stepped clear, raised her bow and let fly, all in one smooth, seamless motion. The arrow struck the shraik through the mouth, piercing its throat, and it fell to the ground sideways, scrabbling at the air with its claws.

"Jerl? Are you hurt?" she asked with concern.

"No," Jerl said curtly, disgusted with the poor display he'd made.

Lucifer crawled from his hiding place and ran to Katin, who lifted him up and said absently, "You are a very, very bad dog." She was still staring at the thrashing, hissing shraik. "In God's name, why doesn't it die?" she whispered.

Jerl picked up his musket and shot the beast in the head.

Their destination was Creshgahar, but they made for the treetop city first, in hopes of finding Civornos there. "For he is an able diplomat," Katin said. "And there's sure to be ill will over the losses they might have been spared, had we given them the weapons to begin with."

Remembering with force the anger and pain that had stricken him on their last visit to Creshgahar, Jerl suspected that she was right. He told himself that he would be prepared for it this time, that he would not let the Yerren's responses overwhelm him, but it took some courage for him to keep going, as they moved into Yerren territory.

But they were not challenged as they approached the city, and even when they stood at the foot of the giant trees that formed its foundation, there was no sign of a Yerren sentry, or any of the inhabitants flying overhead. The ladders were fastened up, and there was no way for the party to reach the platforms overhead to search for the Yerren.

Katin turned to Jerl. "Are they here, can you tell?" She found herself whispering.

Jerl shook his head. "Either they're gone, or I can no longer sense them." If only he *could* lose his unwanted ability, what a relief it would be.

But no Yerren appeared, though they waited a good while. *Can the shraik have killed them all?* each of them wondered. But when they searched the forest near the city, they found only the remains of a few Yerren hunters who must have been caught in the open. There was nothing to suggest that a large-scale massacre had taken place. The Yerren were simply gone.

All they could do was press on to Creshgahar. No one said what everyone was thinking. What would they do if the Yerren were gone from the mountain stronghold as well?

They brought the mule-drawn cart up to the base of the mountain, but saw that it would be impossible—and perhaps pointless—to take the muskets up with them. They had seen no sign of the Yerren on the way, and even here none of them were circling the dark peaks of Creshgahar. Nonetheless, leaving the others to guard the cart, Jerl, Katin, and the hermit made their way once more up the steep path.

No Yerren appeared as they climbed, and by the time they reached the ridge that marked the boundary of Creshgahar, they were discouraged, exhausted, and half-starved. Their supplies were all but gone, and Lucifer was starting to look decidedly edible. The soarhound was the first at the entrance to the main cave. This time there were no angry guards to frighten him off, and he pounced hungrily on a long green lizard he found sunning itself on a rock in front of one of the brightly painted walls. Katin had not been able to feed him much, as they worked their way north, and he'd been living on an unappetizing diet of grubs, bugs, and lizards. When Katin called to him, he looked back at her with the lizard's tail hanging out of his mouth, then returned to sniffing around the entrance to the cave.

The absence of guards seemed to confirm their fears, and Katin asked Jerl anxiously, "Do you feel them here?"

"No," he said sadly. "They're not nearby."

They searched the cavern anyway, using a lantern to light the way in the otherwise total darkness. In the main chamber, they found the candles still in place on their long poles, and lit them, suffusing the stones around them with a soft glow. But they searched in vain for any sign of what had become of the Yerren.

"There's nothing for it, we'll have to go back," Katin said heavily. "Shall we leave the muskets, do you think, in case the Yerren return? They don't know how to fire them."

"But they'll know we left them," Jerl offered. "They'll come to us to ask how it's done."

The hermit nodded. "It may be the best we can do. And if we must slaughter the mule for food, we shall have to leave the muskets behind whether we will or no."

"We may as well go, then," Katin sighed. "We haven't enough food to wait here for them. I hope Hannah's managed to snare something. Lucifer!" she called. "Where are you, fool dog? Come here!"

They went out to the ridge and looked around, but the soarhound was nowhere to be seen. Katin called again, and a faint bark answered her from one of the smaller caves.

"Come out of there!" she ordered, but Lucifer neither answered nor appeared. She shrugged. "He'll follow."

The hermit hesitated. "That animal's hungry. He may be on the track of some game."

Katin and Jerl looked at each other. "Maybe," said Jerl. "The cave's too small for a shraik, I'd say."

"It's worth a look," Katin agreed. "I don't think even Lucifer's idiot enough to go after another dragon."

The cave narrowed to a passage that sloped downward and led them deep into the heart of the mountain. The lamplight showed them nothing ahead but more of the long, descending tunnel.

When they had been walking for some time, Katin asked, "What sort of game lives so far underground?"

Her question hung on the air for a moment, till Jerl said excitedly, "It's not that—he's found the Yerren."

They soon came to a branch in the passage, and when Katin hesitated, uncertain which way Lucifer had taken, Jerl confidently pointed to the left. It was the hermit, coming behind them, who took a rock and scratched a crosshatch on the wall, indicating the way back.

At the end of the passage, they drew to an awkward stop as they found themselves facing a large natural chamber where a number of Yerren were huddled in small groups around makeshift campfires. Jerl felt their astonishment, but the feeling was not overwhelming. They were not frightened of the Ysnathi. There was a far greater threat on their minds.

Lucifer had already found his quarry, and was frisking around the little Yerren who had fed him in the treetop city. "Snimmer!" the child squealed, and swept him into her arms.

The High Lord sent scouts to verify that the cart of muskets was indeed where they claimed, and assured by Jerl, in painstakingly memorized phrases, that they would indeed receive more in the colony, he agreed to send warriors to fight alongside the colonists.

To the Yerren, being confined underground was a living death, but when they made forays against the shraik, or sent out hunting parties, their losses were heavy. The fighters were eager to engage the monsters with the powerful new weaponry promised by the colonists, and Civornos took charge. He had the party demonstrate the use of the muskets, and directed Yerren craftsmen to fashion slings that would allow the warriors to carry muskets while flying, although they would have to land to fire them.

The party returned to Thornfeld on foot, while the Yerren flew ahead and reached the colony well in advance of them. But Jerl and the hermit had explained Sir Andrew's strategy of attack to Civornos, and even without interpreters, they were able to put it into effect. By the time the party reached the outskirts of town, there were dead everywhere—colonists, Yerren, and the great bodies of fallen shraik. Nonetheless, it appeared that Sir Andrew's tactics were working, and with the return of the party, he and Civornos were able to refine the defense.

Yerren scouts in trees around the perimeter of the colony spotted flights of shraik approaching, and instantly the wordless warning spread among all the Yerren, who converged in great numbers at the point of attack. Perching in the branches near the very tops of the trees, they sent storms of musket balls against the monsters as they swept across the sky. Any shraik that were not killed outright, the colonists attacked and slaughtered on the ground.

In a matter of days, the great flights of shraik had been all but annihilated. Once the last few stragglers were driven off, the Yerren departed in triumph, taking with them a great quantity of musketry, and the colonists gathered at the town Common for a celebration. But their festivities were tinged with sadness, for victory had come at a price, and there were many dead yet to be buried.

Before Civornos returned to the forest, Sir Andrew met with him, to try again to convince him that the Chamber's army would wreak devastation on the Yerren far in excess of anything the shraik had done. Once again, he pressed the issue of an alliance. This time, Civornos was more inclined to listen.

* * *

The attack of the shraik had interrupted all the work of the colony, including the casting of the cannons Sir Andrew had ordered. The blacksmith had joined the battle, leaving his apprentices to carry on with such of the work as they could. But when the shraik had been routed, and the community gathered on the Common, the 'prentice smiths, too, went to take part in the celebration—all except one, who stayed behind, so he said, to watch and pray.

In fact, he did both, but he did a good deal else besides. First, he added a large quantity of extra tin to the bronze mixture simmering in the smelting pot. This would make the metal softer and less able to stand up to the stress of firing repeatedly in battle. Then he turned his attention to the cannons that had recently been poured, which had cooled enough so that they'd begun to solidify, but had not yet hardened completely. With a metal rod, he made holes here and there, then dripped water from the tempering vat into each. When he smoothed metal over them, pockets were left in the molten bronze, flaws that could later cause the barrels of the guns to crack. Finally, satisfied with his work, he took up a musket and went to meet Simeon in the woods near the smithy. Simeon had warned him not to go about unarmed. *The enemy is everywhere,* he'd said.

When the 'prentice had reported his doings, Simeon smiled and said, "Well done! When I inform the Chamber of your services, you'll receive a pardon for sheep stealing, and sail on the first ship home. You'll have a hero's welcome."

"'Tis God's will," said the youth, his eyes shining.

Simeon smiled. "So it is, brother. What are we but the instruments of Heaven?" He took a final look around, to be sure they were not observed, and said, "Go now, before you're missed." Then as the youth turned back toward the smithy, Simeon slipped a knife from his belt, pulled the 'prentice back by the hair, and swiftly slit his throat. He pitched the body over his horse, and before long he threw it down beside a newly-killed shraik, leaving the musket by the lad's hand. No one would question that he had come upon a stray or wounded dragon, tried to shoot it, and been killed in the attempt. One more body would excite no curiosity in the colony just now.

* * *

It was no more than two months after the last of the shraik fell that a militiaman stationed on the watch-tower at Hag's Head Point spotted the needle points of tall masts piercing the sky, as the triangular shapes of ships' bows came into view between the rocky out-croppings at the curve of the bay. He raised a brass spyglass to his eye, and the shapes of double-masted brigantines and smaller sloops sharpened in his sight.

The Chamber's forces had chosen to land as close to the colony as they could without sailing directly into the harbor itself, which Sir Andrew had fortified with redoubts and some of his precious cannon. As the Chamber's men and supplies were limited and could not be replaced without a long delay, their commander, General Hough, did not mean to waste them unnecessarily. He had a good idea of the lay of the land, from the reports sent by Rolande, and his plan was to come ashore within striking distance, so as to attack and subdue the colony without resorting to a long march.

The soldier in the watchtower immediately gave the alarm, and a messenger prepared to set out for the stockade to alert the militia. But the watcher assigned to the outpost by Rolande was already prepared.

As the soldier approached the picket where the horses were tethered, Rolande's minion slipped up behind him and slid a garrote around his neck. The wire bit deep into his throat, and the militiaman flailed wildly, silently, to no avail. A few moments later, the watcher dragged his lifeless body into the woods, where another of Rolande's people waited by an open pit. Working in silence, they buried the soldier and concealed the grave in a matter of minutes. Then they parted, still without a word, one to take warning to Rolande that the ships had arrived, the other returning to his post, in case the militiamen should send forth another messenger to follow the first.

Thirty-six ships sailed around the tip of the rocky cove, into Hag's Head Point, unseen by any human being save the soldiers remaining in the watchtower. The invasion was about to begin without the colonists' knowledge.

Chapter 15

Sir Andrew had not forgotten the sabotage that had occurred during the construction of the coastal fortifications. With the conspirators still at large, he dared not rely on a single source of warning, and he had arranged with Civornos for Yerren scouts to patrol the coast, searching for signs of ships. No one else, not even the Warders, had been informed of this particular scheme.

Thus as the Chamber's fleet sailed toward Hag's Head Point, the lookouts of the troop ships saw a strange, large, dark green bird flying high above them, seeming to follow them. It circled the ships several times, then went winging swiftly shoreward and disappeared over the forest. To some, it seemed an ill omen.

During the weeks just past, a system of communication had been established with the Yerren, by means of a series of simple codes for locations along the coast, and sets of basic words necessary for military purposes. When the Yerren scout arrived at the stockade, Sir Andrew was at least able to ascertain that the Chamber's ships had been spotted and where.

When he had grasped the purport of the message, he at once sent a soldier to fetch Jerl. Both Jerl and Katin had continued their lessons in the Yerren tongue with the hermit, at Sir Andrew's orders. Jerl's grasp of the Yerren's language was halting at best, but it was just sufficient for him to interpret the scout's report that "nine hands of vessels" were on their way. "That would be three dozen, sir," he explained. Carl had pointed out, to anyone who'd listen, that the Yerren merely *appeared* to have four-fingered hands, the fifth finger taking the form of the long bone that gave shape to their membranous wings—but it was clear that the Yerren themselves thought otherwise.

Sir Andrew posed a few more questions to the scout, trying to gather some idea of the makeup of the fleet, then he made sure that the news would be brought to Civornos. If the Chamber's army proceeded as he expected, the Yerren were going to play a crucial role in his plan for the defense.

The Chamber's fleet had been hastily outfitted for the expedition. The best armed vessel carried thirty guns. Many of the ships bore only a few cannon, and fully a third none at all, being mere transports. All in all, some three thousand soldiers had embarked, this being the opening strike in the Chamber's conquest. Should this attack succeed, more ships would be sent to reinforce the army, so that it might subdue the other colonies.

As the first boats rowed ashore at Hag's Head Point, carrying the Chamber's soldiers, the militiamen in the watchtower fired upon them steadily, to harass them, but with no real hope of driving them back. The small band of defenders could not hold the outpost, and they retreated into the forest, following the orders they'd been given. Before they slipped away, however, the soldiers ignited the powder magazine, to keep the weapons and ammunition stored there from falling into the hands of the enemy.

General Hough stroked his neatly trimmed brown beard in consternation as he stood on the bow of the flagship, watching the conflagration. An erect, stern-visaged man of mature years, he wore the uniform of a Deprivant officer, its somber gray relieved only by the silver buttons on his coat and the silver fringes of the epaulets. He had served the Dep cause from the first, with distinction, and with success, which manifested the Good God's favor, in the view of the Church. That he had been chosen by the Chamber to lead this campaign to subdue, and so bring to salvation, the souls of the unrighteous, was further evidence of that favor, and Hough confidently expected to be made a member of the Chamber himself when he returned to Albin victorious.

But he had been taken aback by the explosion of the powder stores, fearing that the smoke from the explosion would be observed by the main body of colonial soldiers, revealing that the Chamber's forces were on the coast. He turned abruptly to order his officers to hurry the pace at which the soldiers were disembarking. Still, he assured himself, the colony could no doubt be taken in short order, forewarned or no, for it was of no great size, and its resources were severely limited, as he knew from the reports of the Chamber's spies.

Thornfeld had been chosen as the first to fall, because it was known that Sir Andrew had charge of the militia there. If anyone could present an effective defense, it would be the Lord Marshal, and once his forces were overthrown, the rest would stand no chance. The Chamber's informants assured them that the scattered colonies could not join forces against them, but it would be as well to have Sir Andrew out of the way from the start.

After perusing a map of the area, which had been

sent him by Rolande, he had decided to lead his troops from Hag's Head Point to Thornfeld along the path of the Destiny River. Such soldiers as could be carried in the longboats would sail down the river, and the rest would march or ride along the banks, thus avoiding an arduous trek through the dense forest. This would bring them within striking distance of the colony, along the edge of the outlying farmlands irrigated by the river. From there, Hough planned to sweep across the cultivated fields toward the town, cutting the inhabitants off from their source of food and making it more difficult for them to form a coordinated defense. After that, he thought, it should be a small matter to bring the colonists to their knees.

He was surprised that they met no further resistance as they made their way along the marshy banks of the river, but it did not worry him. His estimate of the colonists' defensive capabilities was confirmed. He knew from Rolande the limited number of the provincial militia, and he assumed that they had set up their main defense around the town itself. Not even the Lord Marshal could be expected to mount a serious campaign under such conditions. The general felt a certain sympathy for him, as a fellow officer, though, of course, the man was a despicable heretic. His own troops were also raw and half-trained, peasants and conscripts for the most part, but at least he had enough of them for his purposes.

Wild blueberries and blackberries covered the slope leading to the riverbank as the forest thinned. Relying on the last report he had received and without bothering to make a careful reconnaissance, General Hough directed his forces toward the one spot where the water was shallow enough to ford. The first troops surged across the river and found themselves facing a crude but solid earthwall, spanning a league along the opposite shore. A line of militiamen manned the length of this bulwark, maintaining a steady rain of musket fire as well as volleys of small ball and grapeshot from the widely spaced cannon.

The Chamber's soldiers had been penned up on board ship for better than two months, with little opportunity for disciplined drill. Under the force of the colonists' barrage, the inexperienced recruits fell back in disarray. General Hough thundered at his officers to marshal the men into lines, and had his own cannons brought up, with the intent of destroying the defenders' artillery. This proved a more difficult task than he anticipated, however, for the colonists' small cannon had been mounted on large wagon wheels, which allowed the guns to be fired, then rolled down the sloping earth behind the barricade, out of sight. There the militiamen could sponge their barrels, pack them with powder and load them, then roll them back up the incline, fire them, and roll them down again, frustrating the enemy's attempt to fire upon them.

Sir Andrew rode the length of the earthworks, encouraging the men—and some women—who were firing furiously, with the intense concentration he'd worked so hard to instill in them. He observed Hough's troops on the opposite bank with considerable satisfaction, for he'd constructed this barrier on the assumption that the Chamber would send Hough, and that Hough would choose this way to come. He'd faced the Deprivant General in one of the last battles he'd fought in his homeland, and he knew him by reputation as well. He was not without courage, certainly, but he was decidedly without imagination. He was prone to take the simplest course toward any goal, an approach that had a better chance of succeeding when his regiment was one of several deployed from different points.

Even then, Sir Andrew thought, he probably lost more men than necessary, in brutal direct assaults. In Albin, where the peasants had been innumerable, Hough had had his share of victories, but Sir Andrew had defeated him when they'd met on the field, and he had every intention of doing so again.

Under the assault from Hough's artillery, the colonists' cannons fell silent one by one, disappearing from their portals in the wall. Heartened by the failing defense, Hough directed his troops forward, and they rushed the earthwork in line after line, fired by his confidence. The defenders at first continued shooting steadily at the oncoming wall of soldiers, and dozens of the enemy fell, but as the first ranks broke through the colonial lines, the militia began a headlong retreat toward the woods to the west. General Hough ordered an all-out pursuit, determined that a single definitive blow now could batter the colonial forces to the point of surrender. Taking Thornfeld in such an impressively short span of time would undoubtedly win him the Chamber's commendation.

But as the troops flowed into the dense woods in pursuit of the fleeing colonials, hundreds of arrows and musket balls rained down upon them from the massed Yerren, invisible in the trees. Too late, General Hough realized that he'd been led into a deadly trap.

Yerren let out piercing calls and flew from tree to tree, wherever the press was thickest. Many of the Chamber's soldiers were stricken instantly with terror at their first sight of their inhuman foe. Wild stories of the New World monsters had reached Albin, to be half believed, half scoffed at, but nothing had prepared the invaders for this intense, coordinated attack from nightmare creatures wielding muskets. The superstitious as well as the religious among them believed themselves to be at the mercy of soulless demonspawn.

Many made no attempt to fire upon the Yerren, certain that mere gunpowder could not kill such horrors. Shot and shell flew from overhead, and as the battle raged around them, a number threw down their weapons, and raced back to the farmland beyond the forest, as their officers tried in vain to stop the rout.

Most of the regular troops were more disciplined, yet they could not stand against the onslaught from above. With the ranks of his troops cruelly reduced, Hough was forced to retreat through the colonial forces, who picked off his men from behind trees and boulders as they passed. As the Chamber's soldiers crossed the fields, they now faced the gauntlet of the cannon, which had earlier been pulled back from the wall and concealed in the woods, leaving the impression that they had been struck and disabled. Now they were brought back from their hiding places and used to shower the enemy with iron nails, which made vicious missiles. The movement of hours earlier was reversed, and the militia pursued the Chamber's soldiers across the trampled farmland until they cleared the now battered earthworks and retreated to the far side of the river.

By now it was growing dark, and the fighting of necessity came to a halt, for both adversaries knew that night attacks on enemy lines invariably ended in disaster. Most of the colonists were confident that the invaders, having been driven off at such high cost, would soon be forced to retreat to their ships and return to Albin. This might require another battle or two, but almost all felt, in the flush of victory, that they could repeat their success, and continue to whittle down the enemy's size until victory was inevitable.

The militia settled themselves into camp for the night, leaving picket guards along their fortifications. They buried their dead, tended the wounded and set to cooking their dinners around small campfires. It took no time at all for word of the victory to spread to town, and before long a stream of townspeople had begun to trickle into the fields, bringing with them baskets full of food. At the sight of these offerings, the soldiers turned from cooking their own provisions around the fires, and soon there was a great feast under way.

At first Sir Andrew tolerated this influx of the citizenry, his main concern being that everyone but the militiamen should be cleared from the field before first light, when fighting was likely to begin again. As time wore on, however, the colonists commenced playing flutes and bells, more fires were lit, and casks of ale had appeared from somewhere. The soldiery became rowdier, and here and there fights broke out. This wouldn't do. The defenders had done themselves proud that day, and deserved some respite from discipline, but if such revelry continued, they'd be in no condition to fight on the morrow.

Sir Andrew was too experienced to fall prey to overconfidence, and he was under no illusion that Hough would be easy to defeat. The colonists' euphoria was natural enough, after having bested the Chamber's army in their first encounter, but the invaders were a potentially deadly force that still outnumbered them. The soldiers would need to be well rested for the encounters yet to come.

He was about to summon members of the regular militia and set them about the task of clearing the townsfolk from the fields, when he spied Rolande deep in talk with Elliott Cavendish. She was leaning on the cart that held the casks of ale, and Sir Andrew realized that most likely it was she who had brought them from her shop. To get the militia drunk? But it would take more than a mug or two of ale apiece to do that. No, as usual she was cleverly courting the goodwill of those she meant to betray. And as usual there was nothing he could do about it. As he watched, Simeon Pryce drew two cups of ale from the cask, handing one to Goodman Cavendish and the other to Rolande. They drank a toast to victory.

Sir Andrew had no doubt whose victory Rolande had pledged, but he still had no proof of her perfidy to place before the Warders. He'd had her watched, but had never caught her out in any act that would stand as incontrovertible proof of her guilt. Now, concerned about her presence here, so close to enemy lines, he called over a trustworthy member of his cavalry unit and bade him stand ready to follow Vendeley when she left the gathering.

Sir Andrew's attention was next drawn to the center of the field, where Minister Arhan was standing atop an empty cask and addressing the revelers. He waved one hand toward the heavens drunkenly and proclaimed, "This is a most contemptible enemy we face. Godless and abandoned men who fall by our swords as wheat before the scythe." He wavered on his makeshift platform as if about to fall, but regained his balance and continued, "The Good God will keep our hands strong in these perilous times, and sanctify us all. . . ."

"Get that man down from there," Sir Andrew commanded the soldiers nearest him. True, no one seemed to be paying much heed to the Minister, but he didn't mean to risk having any of his militiamen convinced that they could rely on God's protection in battle instead of their own efforts. Then, gathering his officers, he ordered them to have the militia set about clearing the fields of townspeople. He missed having Captain Jamison to assist him, but the good captain had been left in charge of the troops garrisoning the stockade and the harbor, in order to protect the town lest any of the invading forces make an attempt on the settlement from the ocean side.

Many of the citizens resented being forced to move on, but the approaching soldiers made it clear that the festivities were at an end, and all those around the keg faded away.

Rolande took a final swig of her ale. "I want you to return to town and learn what you can of the plans of the soldiers there," she said to Simeon. "That captain's almost as dangerous as his master."

"Yes, Mistress," Simeon said subserviently, barely managing to suppress a grin of triumph. He'd done for her at last, and she had not the least idea of it. The decline of her star would come tonight—now he had only to assure the rise of his own.

Rolande handed Simeon her mug and mounted her horse. As she rode back across the fields in the direction of town, the rider Sir Andrew had charged to follow her detached himself from his cavalry unit and rode after her at a discreet distance.

Sir Andrew watched the townspeople trailing back to their homes, some still singing, arguing, laughing. *Have you forgotten the face of war so soon?* he wondered. Well, before this conflict was decided, they'd have reminders enough to refresh their memories. As the camp settled down for the night, he walked along the length of the earthworks, setting men to the task of repairing the damaged fortifications, and talking to the groups of soldiers gathered around their campfires. In wartime, it was more important than ever that he remain close to his troops, that he know their mood and their will—and they his. He made the rounds of the whole camp before he withdrew to his own tent. With a word, a question, a tired smile, he bound the regiment to him, and bound them together into a determined, confident body with a single will.

* * *

Rolande continued to ride toward town, never straying far from the earthworks along the riverbank, until the wall ended by the deepest part of the river. Here the Chamber's army could not pass without bridge or boats. Along the riverbank on both sides ran thick woodland, and now Rolande increased her speed, riding into the heavy brush at a gallop. Behind her, the cavalryman picked up his pace as well, but when he rode into the forest, he was forced to rein in his horse, uncertain of which way she had gone.

He examined the surrounding trees and ground closely in the dark to see where the foliage was broken and follow in that direction, determined not to lose track of his quarry. He was rewarded for his perseverance a short time later, when he spotted Rolande's horse tethered to a branch in a small clearing, but Rolande was nowhere in sight. He had barely time to withdraw under cover himself before he saw the familiar figure run from a patch of birches, leap astride her horse and ride off at breakneck speed, her green cloak billowing behind her. He'd have given much to know who'd been waiting for her there, and what information had changed hands, but his orders were plain, and he dared not lose sight of Rolande. And then, had she really had time to meet with a confederate? Possibly she'd only been concealing something, and he could return later and find it. Kicking his horse into a gallop, he rode after her toward the edge of the forest nearest the town.

Rolande, watching from her hiding place among the birches, burst into mocking laughter at the sight of the soldier pursuing her decoy with such dedication. She'd reasoned that Sir Andrew would have her followed, if he had half the brains she credited him with, and he had not disappointed her. It would have been amusing to lead the fellow a chase herself, but she dared not proceed on her mission this night without first being certain she was free of surveillance. It had been the work of a moment to throw her hat and cloak to her waiting minion, and hide herself as the woman took her place. It was an old trick, but there was use in it still, she thought, laughing to herself again. And this simple ploy was but a spark to the great explosion that would rock Sir Andrew's ragtag army and deliver Thornfeld into her hands!

But time was passing, and she must not be late at the river, where the soldier waited who would conduct her to General Hough. She made her way down the grassy bank, once or twice almost losing her footing. *Perhaps I've had too much ale,* she thought, as she grabbed a clump of bracken to steady herself. Why, after all, should she feel so elated at the success of her deception? The day's events boded ill for her plans and prospects. The militia's victory was her defeat—but only a temporary defeat, she assured herself. With all the provisions she had made to assure the colonists' failure, not even Hough's incompetence could stand in the way of her success now.

Suddenly she felt water slop over her boots, and realized that she'd reached the edge of the bank without noticing. What the devil ailed her tonight? Cursing, she waded out of the river, then knelt to splash some water on her face, to clear her head. When she looked up, a dinghy was being rowed to the shore, only a few yards from her. "Vendeley . . . ?" said the oarsman.

No, Jen Quick, thought Rolande, but she answered, "Who else would be waiting here with wet boots?"

The boat rocked precariously, and though the soldier reached up to assist her, she banged her knee against the side as she clambered into it. "God, the water's black as blood tonight," she complained. "It'll never wash off." That was not at all what she'd meant to say, but what did it matter? When the soldier turned to stare at her, she only snapped, "Row, man, and be quick about it!"

As the boat slipped through the dark, still water, she felt that the thoughts in her head were as unsteady as the shimmering ripples that danced in the oars' wake. Sooner than seemed possible, the boat hove up against the opposite shore, and she was escorted to General Hough's tent.

"This is intolerable!" General Hough bellowed at Rolande. He paced the confined space of the tent like a large tiger in a small cage. "I want to know why I am encamped on this side of the river!"

Rolande peered at him curiously. She knew he expected her to do something, but for the moment just what it was escaped her. She did know the answer to his question, though. "I expect you're here because the colonial forces whipped you," she said helpfully.

General Hough glared at her. "And that is a fault I lay at your door."

Rolande considered this with great seriousness. "I don't see how you make that out. It seems to me that Sir Andrew outmaneuvered you, plain and simple. He foresaw your every move—"

"Enough!" General Hough banged his fist on the small camp table between them. "If you'd done your job, the colonial defense wouldn't have stood up to our assault. If we'd had adequate warning, we would have—"

"If, if, if . . ." Rolande sneered. It seemed absurd that this blustering, stiff-necked Deprivant should think he was a match for Sir Andrew. Even she had been hard-pressed to stay a step ahead of that one. "I've seen His Lordship suffer serious reverses more than once," she remarked, "but I've never heard him offer excuses for his failure. You've only yourself to blame. You've been at sea for two months—how did you expect me to send you messages, eh? You should have scouted the land better before you marched into his trap." She walked her fingers across the table in imitation of marching feet.

"Don't you tell me how to mount a campaign, you overgrown guttersnipe!"

Rolande sighed. "Well, if someone doesn't tell you, we're liable to lose Thornfeld in spite of all our advantages."

Only the self-discipline instilled by Deprivant principles enabled Hough to keep his temper in check. Unfortunately, he needed Rolande, and she knew it. But the time would come when he wouldn't need her. . . . He leaned across the table, glowering. "So you set yourself up as a general now?"

"No, but I've eyes—I've been observing them for some time, remember. I'll wager Sir Andrew will make a fair challenge of this."

"If you'd seen that Lord Edenbyrne met with a fatal accident before now, we wouldn't be in this situation. Why didn't you?"

Why hadn't she? she wondered. The answer seemed somewhere very far away, lost inside the swirling fog that filled her head. She shrugged. "The man's not so easy to kill as all that. You must have noticed that yourself before now, no?" She didn't know of Hough's defeat by Sir Andrew during the final phase of the Uprising, but she saw from his face that her thrust had hit home. She started to laugh, and sang mockingly,

"You may have the means, you may have the will,
But Edenbyrne won't be so easy to kill—"

She was laughing too hard to go on.

Hough stared at her in disbelief. "You're drunk! You *dare* to come here—"

She shook her head vigorously, then stopped as the room started to spin. "Not I. I've had only a little—ale." She looked puzzled. "I do feel a bit giddy though," she admitted. "Perhaps I've taken a fever. What did I say? I beg your pardon, sir."

Spies were notoriously undependable, he thought. He'd heard from his contacts in the Chamber that Vendeley was supposed to be more reliable than most, but all that meant, as far as he was concerned, was a better class of mongrel. She was either drunk or crazy, and either way she might well be revealing her true sentiments. She had altogether too much regard for Sir Andrew to suit him. Was she to be trusted?

"We will triumph in the end, make no mistake," he said sternly. "We will win because the Good God wills it so. We were victorious in Albin, and we will conquer this nest of heretics because it is God's plan that the Deprivants bring righteousness to the ungodly, and to all of the earthly kingdom!"

Rolande had made use of Deprivant rhetoric in her time, to impress her superiors, and to control those of her underlings who believed such rot, but she was damned if she'd listen to it from the likes of Hough. "Spare me," she said. "I've heard enough Dep cant to last me a lifetime. Empty promises. Hypocrites, the lot of you! The poor of Albin are as poor as ever, from all that I hear."

"The Church is the guardian of the people. It is by following the will of God as manifest in the True Church that *all* shall flourish in this life and the next."

"Don't try that on me. Obedience in this life, and reward in the next! That suits your Church's purposes well indeed, and benefits the people not at all."

The expression on Hough's face darkened. *Had she turned traitor, then?* That she had questioned his fitness to command was inexcusable, but no more than he expected from trash of her sort. But to question the doctrine of the Church was another matter altogether. "Perhaps you've been in the New World too long, Mistress Vendeley," he said stonily. "It is all very well to understand the enemy, but it is not necessary to go to the extreme of adopting his point of view. But no doubt you'll welcome the opportunity to explain to the Chamber in person."

Anger, and her keen sense of self-preservation, sobered Rolande somewhat. "I've been as loyal to the Chamber as any agent who ever served the cause. I sent you detailed and accurate information. It was you who put it to ill use." With some difficulty she undid the pouch at her belt and withdrew a roll of parchment. "Here—I've brought you more, for all the good it will do. This map shows all the present fortifications and the deployment of the troops."

"At last something useful." Hough snatched the document from her hand.

"If you had waited and sent for me first, you would have fared better."

Hough dropped the parchment onto the table and turned to her in fury. "You overstep yourself. I am in control of the Chamber's forces here."

Rolande attempted to stare him down, but her vision kept blurring, and his form seemed to waver and shift before her. "Oh, aye, the ass always pulls the cart from the front," she said with a smile.

The general turned beet red. "Hold your tongue, sot! The Chamber may have indulged you in the past, but you answer to me until further orders, and don't forget it! Another word from you, and I'll have you thrown in irons. Is that understood?"

Rolande subsided, wondering vaguely what he was so angry about. She hadn't said anything untoward, had she? She didn't remember just what she had said, but she knew better than to offend the commander of the Chamber's forces. He must be touchy because he'd lost the day to Sir Andrew. Well, that wasn't *her* fault, she thought indignantly. She sulked in silence for some minutes, as he examined the document she'd given him. Wasn't there something she'd meant to tell him . . . ?

Hough, too, was silent, studying the detailed map and list. There was no doubt that they contained all the information Rolande claimed they did, but was it reliable? At that moment, Hough was tempted to have her thrown in chains and returned to Albin or better yet shot on the spot.

"He's fortified several small merchant vessels, too," Rolande said, suddenly remembering what she'd meant to impart. Hough looked up with interest. "We haven't many. Most trade comes the other way, from Albin—or Acquitania. But he's put some guns aboard the ships we do have, and anchored them in a cove south of the harbor. Should the harbor be attacked, they can come 'round from behind while the cannons on the redoubts fire from the front." She drew lines on the table with her finger, to illustrate the positions. "If you sail into the cove directly, they'll have the advantage, for the mouth of the inlet is narrow. They believe you can't take the town by sea, so long as they protect the harbor, but if you could draw them out in some manner, you should be able to destroy them, with your superior numbers and weapons. Their captains are traders, not naval officers."

Still silent, Hough considered the situation. This information, if it was trustworthy, would be crucial to his success, but was she trying to lure him into another trap? Was she only *pretending* to be drunk . . . ?

He resolved to have his own scouts verify the locations she had given for the colonial soldiers. If her word proved good—as it had in the past—then he was bound to use her further. Now that they were engaged in battle with the colonists, he couldn't afford to lose his primary source of intelligence. She could not be depended on by the Church, but he was worldly enough to know that agents who worked for gold could be as useful as those who toiled for love of ideals. Once their usefulness was done, however, they had to be dealt with very carefully.

At all events, it was far too late to insinuate another in her place. For the time being, he was constrained to deal with her, doing what he could to control her rebelliousness. Still he resolved, as soon as they had succeeded in securing Thornfeld, he would see that her insolence and her apostasy were punished as they deserved.

On the following day, while the commanders plotted their strategy, there was only sporadic firing between the two armies who faced each other across the river. The main reason for Hough's delay in renewing the attack was his implementation of a new plan, based on Rolande's information about the fortification of the harbor. He had ordered men back to the coast to sail on those ships adequately equipped with guns. Sir Andrew was content to wait for his next move. He could make good use of the delay to repair his earthworks and artillery.

On the next morning of this uneasy truce, Sir Andrew had already been awake for hours and was conferring with his officers, when the camp was jarred from sleep by a terrifying barrage of cannon fire. The calvary was up in minutes, but before they could reach their mounts, the horses, panicked by the artillery fire, broke free from the picket ropes and stampeded across the open fields. As the cavalrymen gave chase, Sir Andrew saw to the manning of the earthworks. As soon as he could spare a moment, he sent a sergeant to check the picket lines for signs of sabotage.

The man returned with one of the ropes and showed Sir Andrew where it had been partially cut through, so that the constant pressure from the motion of the horses would cause it to fray until it snapped. No enemy soldiers could have gotten through their lines to do it, but any of the townsfolk who'd flooded the field after the colonists' victory could have been responsible. As to those guarding the horses—why should they have been suspicious of someone they knew, perhaps offering them ale, distracting them long enough for another conspirator to commit villainy? He thought again of Rolande and her free libations for the troops that night. Most of her lackeys had never been identified. The enemy within was as great a danger as the one they faced across the river.

Luckily, the horses contented themselves with reaching the surrounding farmland and grazing on the young crops. Still, it took the cavalry most of the morning to capture them all, eliminating their usefulness in the defense.

The militia, firing zealously from the earthworks, hoped to repeat their previous success, but this time Hough had brought heavy cannon to the front of his line, and the enemy artillery gouged great gaps in the wall. On this morning, calamity continued to plague the colonists at every turn. Sir Andrew tried to slow the enemy's advance by having his artillery fire into the oncoming ranks of the Chamber's forces, hoping to keep them from getting through the entrenchments, but before long fully a third of the cannon were found to have cracks in their barrels, and had to be abandoned. The defenders fired the remainder continuously, but the reduced number of cannon and the patches of fallen earthwork offered clear openings that the Chamber's troops could penetrate.

The colonists resisted fiercely, determined to keep the invaders from reaching the outlying farms and the town beyond. By midday, large sections of the wall had been reduced to rubble by cannon fire and the fields churned to mud by the constant passage of men and horses. The cries of the wounded were lost in the thunder of cannon and the roar of musket fire.

The colonials were firing in two alternating lines, one of which would fire, then fall back to reload while the second rank came forward to shoot. In this way they had been keeping up a steady barrage. Sir Andrew rode ceaselessly along the lines, encouraging his people, and for some time the militia held out against the torrent of enemy soldiers rushing forward. Then across the field, guns began to fall silent.

Sir Andrew was close to the wall at the west end of the field when he heard Sergeant Merton shouting at the soldiers kneeling there, reloading their weapons. "What do you whoresons think you're about? Get back to the line!"

"We can't reload," one objected. "The shot's no good."

"What the devil—? Give me that!" The sergeant shoved the man aside and picked up his gun.

The soldier dropped a musket ball into the sergeant's outstretched hand. "Here, see for yourself, sir."

Dismounting, Sir Andrew strode over to the company. "What is it?"

The sergeant showed him the shot. "He's right—the damned thing's too big. I don't understand it. The ammunition we've been using has been right enough."

One more problem—and a critical one—was the last thing Sir Andrew needed, but he had to know the worst at once. "Take these men and examine the shot in all the barrels," he ordered. "Let me know immediately if it be good or bad." Sir Andrew remounted and made his way down the length of the entrenchment, attempting to ascertain how many men were still adequately supplied with ammunition and could be counted upon.

All too soon, the sergeant returned to report the news that Sir Andrew dreaded. "There's some good left mixed in. Like as not that was what we've been using—what was on top that's spread through the rest. But most of what's still there is too big to fit. I can't believe it's the smith's doing."

"Nor can I," Sir Andrew agreed grimly. The smith knew well the size of ball to make—indeed, they'd had a fair supply from him. But whether the misfit shot, like the horses stampeding, was the work of deliberate sabotage, or mere mistake, it was too late to undo the damage now. They would have to give ground. But if they could manage to retreat to safety with their supplies, they might be able to regroup and later dispel the invaders from whatever ground they might take. It was a desperate hope, but better than none. "We shall have to hammer the balls down to slugs that will fit. Get all those who aren't actively engaged and set them about it."

"We'll not be able to do enough to supply all the troops, sir."

"I know that! Do what you can. The longer we can hold out, the more of our ammunition we can salvage." Sir Andrew withdrew to write a message to Captain Jamison, alerting him to the situation and warning him to prepare for an attack on the town itself. This he sent with one of the Yerren scouts. They, at least, could not be suspected of working for the Chamber.

A thin line of soldiers kept on fighting against great odds, providing steady enough fire to prevent the defenses from being overrun while the main body of troops reached shelter in the woods. This company bore the brunt of the attack when the Chamber's army burst through the line, overrunning the field and cutting down everything in its path.

This time, General Hough did not attempt to pursue the retreating colonial forces into the woods. Another attack by those feathered fiends might lose them their hard-won advantage. Instead, he turned his army east, marching inexorably through the fields toward the town. Hough had been well supplied with recent information from Rolande on the disposition of the militia. Knowing that there was no great number of soldiers garrisoned in the stockade, he had initiated an assault on the harbor by sea, to coincide with the attack on the town from the landward side. He was certain that Jamison's forces would not be able to defend both fronts adequately. It would not be long before he accepted first the captain's surrender, then the commander's.

As Hough's troops marched toward town, they were fired upon from every copse and thicket by Yerren, who stung them from trees like angry wasps—but despite heavy losses, the invaders moved steadily onward. When the army cut through the open fields, destroying the ripening crops, the Yerren were forced to leave off their attack. Here they had no perching places from which to shoot, and they would not land in the fields where they were certain to be slaughtered. Though they could make short sprints at great speed, their legs were not made for running, and they could take flight only from a height. Most lived their lives in the air, the treetops, and the mountain peaks, rarely descending to the earth at all, and then only in densely wooded areas where they could quickly climb to a safe height again—never in a broad, open expanse of land.

But as the invaders crossed the fields, the Yerren followed, flying high above them, out of range of musket fire, and shrieking threats and curses that were unmistakable in any language. Having them circling overhead like monstrous birds of prey was enough to terrify many of the enemy, who regarded them as harbingers of death. Hough had to drive his troops hard to keep them on the march.

He was furious at the toll taken on his forces by the colonists' defense, which was far more coordinated and fierce than he had anticipated, and he was little inclined to mercy as he drove through the farmland! The invaders made short work of undefended farmhouses and mills, taking whatever livestock they found there, then burning the houses and barns.

No sooner had Sir Andrew seen his forces safe in the woods than he gathered all those who were able and still had ammunition, and led them at a furious pace through the southern forest. If the company could reach the outskirts of town in time to attack from the flank and join Captain Jamison, they might still have some chance of holding off the invaders.

Captain Jamison's troops had positioned themselves behind a stone wall that ran between the farmlands and the town, not far from Bogner's Pond. They fired steadily upon Hough's troops, briefly halting the advance.

In the harbor, a great uproar could be heard as the redoubts were assailed by the Chamber's ships. Hough had been of two minds about Rolande's information. It was possible that the colonists had as few ships as she said, and that they were keeping them hidden to prevent his scouts from finding out how limited their naval protection was. On the other hand, it could be a ruse. If Vendeley were lying, or misinformed, there might be a far greater number of ships secured elsewhere in the vicinity, waiting for his fleet to sail into a trap. Thus he had ordered his naval commander to proceed cautiously, sending only half of the armed ships into the harbor for the assault.

The soldiers manning the battery defended their ground stoutly, firing furiously until one of the cannon exploded, killing a great many and causing the collapse of part of the wooden dock. Now Sir Andrew's refitted merchant vessels came up from the cove, positioning themselves to the rear of the Chamber's ships. They fired all guns at once, disabling two of the smaller vessels.

Following General Hough's instructions, the commander of the Chamber's fleet had held half of the armed vessels in reserve, and these now sailed into the harbor. Foreseeing no difficulty in destroying the small merchant fleet, these ships simply turned on the beam and fired broadside at the colonial vessels.

The colonial ships concentrated their fire on the ships at the rear of the line, and they succeeded in damaging several, but they were hopelessly trapped between the two halves of the enemy fleet. In the end, the Chamber's ships sank or disabled all the defenders' vessels except one sloop that managed, by sheer speed, to slip past the damaged vessels at the rear of the enemy's line. The Chamber's vessels, blocked by their own disabled ships, could not get out of each other's way and offer pursuit in time to stop the colonial ship. Nonetheless, with the full force of their seaborne artillery nearly intact, the invaders were able to destroy the remaining harbor defenses easily. They could count the day a victory as they brought their ships up to the dock.

Some townspeople, seeing they were doomed, fled before the advancing troops. Many took nothing but what they wore, that they might travel faster, while others attempted to carry whatever possessions they held dear. Those swift enough to gain the fields beyond the edge of town headed for the outlying houses near the forest, which had been fortified as garrisons. Others tried to reach the safety of the stockade, only to find themselves intercepted by the Chamber's soldiers.

As the enemy marched through the town, those folk who had remained peered in terror from their doors and windows. They saw the armed, gray-clad strangers filling the square and the streets on every side. Those who tried to run were driven back by a hail of musketshot. Death was all around them, crueler and more malicious than the attacking dragons had been. The colonists were entrapped by the enemy, the town surrounded, and escape impossible.

By the time Sir Andrew and his company arrived at the outskirts of the settlement, the Chamber's seaborne forces were already well advanced in securing it. He joined Captain Jamison's brave troops as the battle by Bogner's Pond raged hotly, and the pond turned red with blood. But the Chamber's army gradually gained control of the entrenchment, and at last the outnumbered militiamen had no choice but to retreat with great losses. Sir Andrew hastily issued orders to Captain Jamison to take the troops to the fortifications at Ringmaron Bay, there to await further instructions. Sir Andrew would rejoin the main body of the army.

In the dusk, he rode past the edge of town, having sent all but a few of his company up the coast with Captain Jamison. Among those he'd kept was Jerl, for his value lay principally in his services as a translator, and communication with the Yerren would still be critical in the days to come.

The Chamber's soldiers were continuing to fire at the fleeing townspeople. The fields were scattered with the debris from panic-stricken victims, and the cries of the wounded and dying rent the night. Sir Andrew's heart was leaden, but he was very far from surrender. They would take back what was rightfully theirs. *I lost everything to these jackals once, but now they are on my ground.* The thought had come unbidden, and he frowned to himself, surprised at the tenor of his own idea. Had Albin not been his own ground, then? The answer that came to him was a strange one: that Silverbourne belonged to him as Stoneridge never had, because he himself had made the land his own, not inherited it as an accident of birth. It was a treasonous sentiment for a man of his station, but . . . was it not something of the sort that all the colonists felt?

Sir Andrew glanced thoughtfully at Jerl, remembering that the boy had once said, with uncharacteristic fervor, that they had claimed the land in God's name and their own. Jerl had fought valiantly this day, defending the earthworks against deadly odds—and so had countless others. Was it this same sense of being on *their own ground* that had made his host of raw recruits into a formidable fighting force? With such resolution, Sir Andrew thought, he and all his fellow colonists could not fail to drive the invaders from their land. Heartened by a sense of renewed hope and confidence, he turned back in the direction of the forest. As he did so, a cannonball burst open the ground in front of him, and he was struck senseless from his horse.

Chapter 16

The room was stifling, and Sir Andrew's head ached unbearably. He was vaguely aware that there was something he had to do, something important, but when he tried to remember this duty, the effort only made his head ache more fiercely. Perhaps if he lay absolutely still and didn't think, the pain would abate. . . .

But Lady Celia had seen him move his head, heard his low moan. Ever since Jerl had brought him to the garrison house, she had been keeping vigil, as he had done while she lay delirious with devil's trump poisoning. "Andrew?" she said tentatively.

Was Celia calling him? With some difficulty, he opened his eyes and found himself looking up at her worried face. The room gradually resolved itself into a recognizable form, bare wooden walls, a washstand, a small walnut bed in which he was lying. When he smiled at Celia, he saw relief ease her drawn features. "What . . . happened?" he said slowly, trying not to move his head. Cautiously, he reached out for her hand.

She knelt beside him and took his hand, raising it gently to her lips. "You were thrown from your horse when a cannon shot exploded, my love. Carl says you've suffered a 'concussive shock,' but that you'll mend well, with rest. Jerl put you on his horse and brought you here."

"Where—?"

"All those who escaped have taken shelter at the garrison houses," she explained. "This is Goodman Greele's."

At that, he remembered everything, and he knew there would be no time for rest, whatever Carl said. "What of Her Highness?" he asked, slowly raising himself to sit upright. The pain was worst just at first.

"She's here, assisting Carl to tend the wounded. There are a great many." There was no need to say more, for they were both well acquainted with the toll of war. "But she left this for you, and she said I was to make you drink *all* of it." She crossed to the hearth and returned with a large cup of Katin's unpleasant herbal remedy. "And that is a royal command."

Sir Andrew regarded the brew with distaste, but obeyed. "Bless the girl," he said, when he'd choked it down. "A cannonball's no match for that potion of hers." He threw back the coverlet and pulled himself around to sit on the edge of the bed. "I must have a report from my officers."

"I will have them sent for—such as may be reached. I fear things are not in very good order. There has been much confusion since the retreat." He knew how to interpret her words. Everything was in hopeless chaos. She gave him a brave smile and went to fetch a messenger.

Those who could report on the state of the militia met with him in the same small room in which he had woken, for the rest of the dwelling was being used to house the wounded. Even as their consultation went on, carts continued to draw up with fresh bodies removed from the fields. These houses, scattered throughout the outlying land between the river and the forest, had been specially constructed to provide a safe place for the colonists in the event of attack. Enormous two-story buildings with thick walls of brown timber, they were virtually impossible to shoot through, and stout wooden fences kept assailants at bay. Loopholes in the walls allowed the defenders to shoot out at the enemy, making attack costly. But Sir Andrew knew they could not drive off the invaders from inside the safety of their shelter.

The bulk of the able forces were billeted outside, he was told, in makeshift camps. *I still have the core of an army, then,* he thought. It would be enough—it would have to be. The future of every man and woman among them depended on his decisions over the next few days, and he could not afford to consider defeat. He rose stiffly, waited a moment for the pain to subside, then went to examine his remaining troops.

Throughout the campground, the soldiers, bleak and discouraged, brightened at the sight of Sir Andrew. "We heard you were well nigh dead, sir!" one lad with a bandaged hand told him.

"Why, 'twas no more than a bruise," Sir Andrew said cheerfully enough, but he frowned as he considered the boy's words. Many an army had been defeated by rumor. It was imperative that he bring his forces together into some form of order. He sent messengers immediately to the officers at all the garrisons, to Civornos, and then, finally, to the bandit leader, Lorin.

Rolande strolled about the town as if she owned it—as she soon would, she thought complacently, when that ass Hough finished the job and returned to his just reward in Albin, turning Thornfeld over to her. And now that Sir Andrew had obligingly tamed the Yerren for her, and discouraged the dragons, she'd be able to make a prosperous concern of the place. It would flourish under her hand as it never had with a pack of fools and cowards trying to govern, when they couldn't agree amongst themselves about the simplest thing, even for the good of the community! How easy they'd made it for her to bring about their downfall. Well, there'd be no more of that. She'd have a troop of municipal guard—the pick of the Chamber's invasion force—to enforce her authority, and she would answer to no one.

Except, of course, the Chamber. That was a taint of gall in her sweet draught of contentment, but after all, the ocean lay between her and her masters—how much of a nuisance could they be? She suspected that as long as they received their due tribute of goods and taxes, they'd not interfere overmuch with her direction of the colony's affairs.

When her tour of inspection brought her to the harbor, she noticed with approval that repairs were being carried out on the docks and the redoubts—*her* docks, *her* redoubts—by townspeople conscripted by the invaders for the purpose. She watched for a time, with a proprietary air, thinking of how far she'd come from the wharves of Avenford.

Then, curious, she stopped beside one of the soldiers overseeing the repairing of the dock, where it had been damaged by the exploding cannon. "Tell me, why are they rebuilding the battery now?" she asked. "I heard that the colonial fleet was destroyed."

The soldier looked up, wiping the sweat from his face, for the noonday sun was hot. "I couldn't say, Mistress. They give me orders, not reasons." He spoke respectfully enough. He had not been told officially who Rolande was, but most of the occupying forces realized that she was the Chamber's agent—and some had already heard of her reputation. He leaned toward her conspiratorially and added, "They say one of the colonial ships got away somehow, and no one knows where it's got to, or if there's more. The general's not one to take chances."

Acorn Cove, Rolande thought. Near the town, yet screened from easy view on the ocean side by Heirios Point. No one would know the inlet was there at all, unless they also knew how to sail between the rocks at the end of the point. She'd suggest to the general to search there when she made her next report.

"But my task's just to see the dock's finished ere it's needed," the soldier was saying, as he looked over his work crew.

"You have supply ships coming in?"

"Aye, so we're told." He shrugged.

"You doubt it? Surely they'd not leave you without adequate provisions."

"I'd not be surprised to hear that they expect us to live off the land. It's hard to say if they've enough for themselves in Albin these days."

His words confirmed other reports Rolande had received of conditions in her homeland. "Do you say so?" she said encouragingly. "Do the folk not work the land with a will, now that it is their own?"

Was she making sport of him, the soldier wondered, or did she truly believe that the Deps had carried out their promises to the peasantry? Was she trying to trap him into talking heresy? Warily, he answered, "I don't know the whys and wherefores of it, to be sure. But most of those who would be plowing are now in the army fighting here, or against the Acquitanians, and many others have sought the promise of work in towns. I only know there are shortages of everything since the Uprising."

"Well, we will soon remedy that," Rolande said confidently.

The man looked at her dubiously for a moment, then said, "I suppose that's what they sent us over here for. But I don't see heaps of foodstuffs and riches waiting for us."

Rolande laughed. "Then stay over here and you will, my friend. This land holds riches enough for all." *Aye, even you,* she thought, meeting the glares of some of the conscripted laborers, who now knew her for a spy and a traitor. She smiled down at them benevolently, then turned her steps toward her shop.

Simeon hastily pushed aside the document he was writing, as Rolande threw open the door and strode in. *Luck's with me again,* he thought, for she gave him no more than a passing glance, assuming that he was making out a bill or some such correspondence related to her business. Had she taken a closer look, she would have been surprised to see that it was actually a sheet of vellum attached with candle wax to an older letter.

But Rolande had other matters on her mind. "Have you loaded the supplies for the garrisons?" she asked.

Simeon started. "For the *garrisons?* You mean—?"

"Yes," Rolande said impatiently. "Are they ready or not?"

"The cart's loaded, but . . ." He had assumed the supplies were for Hough's troops or her own outposts. "We're provisioning the enemy?"

"How else to get close enough to spy out their preparations?"

"'Tis madness!" Simeon protested. "They know we're working for the Chamber!"

Rolande shook her head, smiling. "Those here in town know. Those in the field may suspect, but they've no proof. They'll not turn away a cartload of goods and medicaments."

"But they'll want to know why it was permitted to leave here."

"No doubt. And they'll be told it was in readiness for the attack and laid by, in Holistowe. They'll be ready to believe anything, I should think, for some fresh supplies."

Simeon wanted no part of it. He had just put the finishing touch to his plan for Rolande's undoing, and his own rise to prominence in the Chamber's graces. He was too close to success to risk all for such a rash enterprise. "It's too dangerous," he objected. "If you think I'll go riding right into the enemy stronghold, just to—"

"You? By no means," Rolande laughed. "As if I'd trust you with a task that requires some skill and subtlety! I shall go myself, of course. The general expects an accurate report—a full report on the state of the colonial forces."

Soon, Simeon told himself. Soon, she would pay for these slights and insults. He said only, "A full report? That will take some time."

"No more than two days at most."

So she would meet with Hough again in two days' time. That was all that Simeon needed to know. He was well pleased with the arrangement, but kept up a pretense of arguing, knowing that nothing he said would change her mind. "I see no necessity for such a risk," he said sullenly. "Sir Andrew's troops have been soundly beaten—they must be on the brink of surrender."

"If you think that, you're as big a fool as Hough." Rolande's tone and manner grew altogether serious. "The greatest risk is in underestimating the man. I know Sir Andrew. As long as that one has soldiers, he'll go on fighting."

* * *

"Will we allow our land to be taken from us?" Sir Andrew demanded of his assembled troops. "Have we toiled and bled to fill the pockets of the Chamber of Statesmen?"

The colonial forces were discouraged by their losses, by the continual calamities that had plagued their efforts, but they rallied at Sir Andrew's words nevertheless. Enrich the Chamber? Not bloody likely!

"We are on our own ground!" Sir Andrew continued. "If we've given ground, 'twas at the price of betrayal, and that price is paid in full. Henceforth it will be the enemy who bears the cost! Not only will we defend our homes, but exact vengeance for our losses. Not only will we regain our ground, we will drive the Chamber's soldiers into the sea like the vermin they are! I know this general of theirs. I have led troops against him before and defeated him, and I tell you we can do so again, if we have but the resolution. We shall never bow to the will of usurpers. They shall not take this land as they took Albin!"

There was no more disarray, or talk of defeat. If Sir Andrew said they could still be victorious, then it must be so. The officers of the militia made haste to restore order, the troops were drilled, weapons repaired, and food foraged for. The smith oversaw the reworking of the faulty ammunition, assisted by more hands than were needed for the job. But there was work for all, repairing weapons, running reconnaissance, making bandages, mending clothing. Everyone not otherwise employed was busy training to load and aim muskets with dispatch.

If it were only a matter of courageous and determined soldiers, Sir Andrew thought, victory would be certain. But he needed more than that. Not merely provisions, ammunition, supplies, and transport. He needed information.

In the small room at the top of the garrison, Sir Andrew was conferring with Lorin. Before him on the table lay a map drawn up from information gathered by Yerren scouts who flew continuously over the town. It provided a broad outline of the deployment of the enemy forces, but for details Sir Andrew had to rely on the bandits, who could penetrate the settlement itself. Lorin's people were more skilled than any land-scout in the militia, at sneaking past sentries, evading patrols, and slipping through the streets unseen.

"The troops are employed in making entrenchments around the town to protect themselves from attack," Lorin reported. "And those unlucky folk who remain are impressed into service, doing much of the labor."

Impatiently, Sir Andrew tapped his fingers on the table. "I could have told you that, without going near the town. If you think I'll pay for information like that, you can think again. Or is Hough paying you better?"

Lorin grinned confidently at him. "I don't trust the Deps," he said. "And I don't suppose they'd trust me. But maybe this information will be more to your taste. They've brought ashore much ammunition and ordnance, and converted the largest of the storehouses near the harbor for use as their powder magazine. The place is so heavily guarded any dolt could guess what's kept there."

This was indeed of interest to Sir Andrew. "What more?" he said.

"I know little more than that, now. Their general has set up headquarters in the assembly hall, and he uses Headman Farnham's dwelling nearby to house himself and the highest ranking of his officers. They've folk from the town 'pressed into service to cook and clean for them, but they're too scared to talk."

Sir Andrew nodded distractedly, not really listening. "You've done well," he said, thinking, *We've no more than days.* The bandit could be playing him false, of course, but what he reported made all too much sense. He paid Lorin and dismissed him, with orders to relay anything more he learned, and all the while he was considering Hough's position, and what his next move would be.

No doubt as soon as the fortification of the town was complete, Hough planned to advance on the colonial forces in the forest, seeking to force them into surrender. That he had delayed even a few days, Sir Andrew attributed to the presence of the Yerren. Before venturing into the woods again, Hough required time to prepare a means of combating them. This time, though, the delay was less of an advantage for the defenders. It gave them time to recoup, but also to run short of provisions, while Hough's troops established a secure stronghold in Thornfeld.

Sir Andrew knew that his people couldn't maintain this defensive position indefinitely. They had to leave the protection of the forest and attack if they were to regain what was rightfully theirs—before it was too late. Taking back the town would not be simple, but if they were to attack unexpectedly, with surprise on their side, they'd stand a chance. *And we've a better chance with their fortifications half-completed than wholly done.* But was the militia, with its ill-equipped soldiers and half-trained volunteers, capable of such a maneuver?

When Lady Celia came in, to bring him a meal, he looked up vaguely and said, more to himself than to her, "But even if I had someone posted inside the town, supposing he could somehow evade discovery, how would he get word out, when the time came?"

"I've no idea," said Lady Celia, laying a platter

down firmly on top of his maps and charts. "When what time came?"

"What I really need is notice of when they plan to attack, when they're prepared to make their move," he explained, looking down at the stewed venison as if he couldn't imagine how it had come to be there. Lady Celia had found that it was no use to send someone else to bring him food, when he was engrossed in strategy and tactics. No one else had the authority to make him eat it instead of putting it to one side and forgetting about it.

"I see," she said, taking away his quill and putting a spoon in his hand. "Someone to sound the alarm. But why not the Yerren? You have them flying over the town night and day—couldn't one of them bring word when Hough's troops are massing for the attack?"

"That would be cutting it too close, I'm afraid, but I may have to risk it. The ideal moment—"

He was interrupted by a messenger who came running up the stairs to announce, "The patrol's brought in a prisoner—accused of supplying provisions to the enemy."

"That was good work," said Sir Andrew. Someone who'd been providing for the troops occupying Thornfeld might be well informed about the state of their preparations. "I'll come at once."

The soldier hesitated. "As you say, sir," he said, awkwardly, "but the sergeant sent me to fetch Her Ladyship."

As they hurried down the stairs, they could already hear shouting coming from outside, and in the yard behind the house they found Sergeant Merton and another militiaman attempting to drag Hannah Franesh toward the makeshift stockade where prisoners were secured. Hannah was apparently a match for them, however. "Let go of me, you misgotten mongrels!" she yelled. "I demand to speak with Lady Celia!"

"Damn it, woman," Sergeant Merton said, exasperated. "We can't have you going about providing food to the enemy." She was someone known to him, and he was not about to shoot her out of hand, as she knew very well.

"Where is Lady Celia?" she demanded.

"Here," Lady Celia said firmly, stepping into the yard and placing herself in the path of the two soldiers. "Let us have less shouting, if you please. We've wounded here who need their rest. Now, what in the Good God's name is this about?"

"This woman's been trapping game in the woods and delivering it to the troops in town. It's rank treason, I tell you."

"You astonish me," Lady Celia said calmly, and turned to Hannah. "Can this be so? You, who so value the freedom of the forests?"

" 'Tis true enough," said Hannah, her voice grim, "but the stinking hounds hold my sister there, and force her to act as servant to the officers. If I do not do their bidding, they threaten her life."

"They threaten all our lives," Sir Andrew said sternly. "If protecting your kin means meat for the enemy, it cannot be permitted. We're at war."

"Sara's no soldier!" Hannah protested. "I'll not let her be sacrificed—"

"The survival of the community is at stake, and that includes your sister." Sir Andrew could see that his words held little weight with Hannah. He gestured for the soldiers to take her away.

"My Lady!" she appealed. "You'll not let them keep me here? What will become of my Sara?"

"Andrew," Lady Celia said thoughtfully, "perhaps

you could have Mistress Franesh released to my custody? I believe I can answer for her behavior."

Sir Andrew was equally reluctant to refuse her suggestion or to accede to it. On the one hand, Lady Celia would not make such a request without good reason. On the other hand, she could not be expected to prevent the prisoner from escaping, and he had no intention of allowing food to be brought into the occupied settlement, however much Celia might sympathize with Hannah's plight. He had the greatest respect for his wife's good sense, but the necessities of war were something he understood far better than she.

Lady Celia knew very well what doubts were in his mind. To his silent, questioning look, she replied, "After all, we are surrounded by your soldiers here. Mistress Franesh is not so foolish as to attempt an escape, when I can summon a dozen militiamen at a word. No deliveries of game will be made to Thornfeld without your sanction, trust me for that." He could read her look as well as she his, and her look said, *Leave this to me.*

"Very well." He dismissed the soldiers, who withdrew with relief.

"And you trust me, Hannah, do you not?"

As far as she trusted anyone, Hannah trusted Lady Celia. Most people did. "I daresay I do, My Lady, but—"

"No harm will come to your sister," Lady Celia assured her, "if my plan bears fruit. Tell me, what work does she do for the enemy officers?"

"Cleaning and washing mostly, M'lady."

"Ah, very good. And can you speak to her?"

Hannah looked at her sharply, wondering what Her Ladyship had in mind. She'd not agree to anything that would put her young sister in danger. "Aye," she said cautiously. "When I make my deliveries to the Provisioner there, I am allowed to stay with her."

"Better and better," said Lady Celia. "Come, we must talk of this further. And you, Andrew, come along as well—you've still not eaten a thing."

* * *

Rolande arrived early for her meeting with General Hough, for the abrupt tenor of the summons, which bade her return before the time scheduled, had made her uneasy. With natural caution, she approached the rear door of the house silently, planning to get the lay of the land before she was expected. The soldier there drew himself to attention and peered at her face in the lamplight, to be certain of her identity. His tone was too elaborately casual as he said, "Follow me. I'll escort you to the general." When he turned to the door, Rolande made up her mind and dealt him a swift, stunning blow to the back of the head with the butt of her pistol.

She left him in the bushes in the back garden, then slipped through the door, determined to find out if her suspicions were correct. No one accosted her as she made her way up the servants' stairs to Hough's quarters. He had not yet returned for their meeting, and she let herself in, shutting the door softly behind her. By the light of a low hearth fire, she found the stretchered table that served the general as a writing desk, and the locked writing box upon it, some two feet in length and half-again as deep. Ornately carved leaves and tendrils curled around the keyhole on its front panel. Rolande lit a candle from the fire and studied the box for a few moments, then used her narrow-bladed knife to pick open the lock.

Lifting the lid on its wrought iron hinges, she found

several documents within, but the first she examined were no more than routine correspondence regarding the conduct of the war. One read, "We have the satisfaction to acquaint you with the success of our mission in taking the town of Thornfeld. The bravery of our officers and soldiers is not to be equaled in the attack . . ." *I've seen it equaled,* Rolande thought, *and bettered, too. Without my help, you'd never have taken the town from His Lordship.* She quickly scanned the rest of the letter, but found no mention of her own part in Hough's victory. That boded no good for her. Rolande next turned her attention to a half-finished piece of correspondence lying beneath the first, and this she found of greater interest. "It is my understanding," she read, "that the powder brig carrying ammunition and much warlike stores was sent three weeks behind us and should be due by now, yet no sight of her has been seen. I have heard that there have been recent storms at sea and hope she has not fallen afoul of gales and that she is large enough to survive such weather if she encounters it. I recall past instances when ships sent to us carrying provisions such as pickled cabbage and rum had full thirty guns and a large number of men, while ordnance was sent on boats of four guns and merely a dozen hands. It is something which should be looked to, meaning no reproach, but recommending that which is best for the success of our cause. Meanwhile we shall stand watch for the powder brig, which we shall expect any day."

Setting this, too, back in the box, she picked up two sheets folded together, laid them flat, then stared in amazement at what she saw, for the topmost page read, "I have herein enclosed proof of the treachery of one you lay misplaced trust in. As further proof of my loyalty I beg to inform you that the Princess Oriana never died in Albin as was claimed but lives yet—here in this colony—with an assumed name and guise. Her whereabouts are known only to me and I shall secure her in a safe place and provide her to you for transportation to the Chamber if it be your will to meet with me, that we may agree on suitable terms."

The note was signed "Simeon Pryce." This was an unlooked for piece of news, and Rolande's mind raced at the implications. If Oriana were indeed alive, her very presence would be a rallying point for those opposed to the Chamber. How had Simeon found her? Who was she? Why hadn't he told her?

But the answer to the last question became all too clear as she searched the second sheet for further information. It dealt not with the subject of the Princess, however, but with the disposition and activities of the Chamber's forces in the town—and it was signed with her signature. Yet she had never written it.

That it was a forgery was clear enough to her, but might not be so evident to others. She glanced at it again; the handwriting was close enough to hers to stand comparison. Not only had Simeon betrayed her, but he had done a fair job of it. This was the proof he referred to in the note. She had underestimated his ambition and his daring. Was the general really gullible enough to believe this brazen imposture, she wondered, or was it rather that he disliked her enough to welcome any excuse to condemn her, however fraudulent? Either way, she knew that every minute she tarried in the house set her at greater risk.

Closing the box, she stood still and listened intently for a long moment, then moved to the door and slipped silently into the hall. But as she crept toward the stairs, she heard someone climbing up from below, with a heavy tread. Drawing her knife, she opened the door to Hough's room again, and hid herself behind it, waiting. She hoped that it was Hough or one of his officers coming upstairs, and not some menial, because whoever it was had only minutes to live.

But then the sound of voices came to her, and she realized that there were at least two men approaching. Damn and blast! She did not doubt that she could kill them both, but it would be impossible to do it silently. Desperate, she dashed to the opposite end of the hall, where a narrow flight of stairs led to the walkway on the roof.

She threw open the hatchway and emerged into the night, hunkering down so as not to be seen from the ground. Flat on her belly, she dragged herself to the edge of the roof, where she grasped the ledge and let herself down far enough to catch hold of the trellis. She knew she would be seen, and a moment later, she was. As she dropped to the ground, a shot ricocheted off the stone wall beside her, and she heard the clatter of heavy boots behind her as she raced for the row of horses tethered by the fence. The first of the soldiers fired at her, and she threw herself down and rolled, pulling her pistol from her belt. She fired back and hit the foremost man in the chest, knocking him backward into his companion, who went tumbling down into a patch of blackberry bushes. The noise immediately brought more soldiers running, but Rolande was already on her feet and making for the horses. She could hear shouts and cursing in the yard as the soldiers shoved their comrades out of the way and came after her.

She slit the rope holding the nearest horse, leaped onto its back, and cleared the fence. Shots echoed behind her, but in the darkness she made an elusive target. It took the soldiers only minutes, however, to free their own mounts and come in pursuit. Rolande rode at full gallop through the town. As long as she was ahead of them, and they were faced with the difficulty of shooting from horseback in the dark, her chances of remaining unscathed were good, but if they caught her, she was as good as dead.

Without thinking, Rolande headed for the harbor, where she had always fled as a child—her own territory, where she knew every den and hiding hole and avenue of escape. Her horse galloped onto the slick wooden surface of the dock right past the soldiers manning the batteries at the harborside. They were thrown into confusion by the tumult of the soldiers pounding onto the dock, with no sign of an enemy attack. One of the guards from General Hough's headquarters shouted demands for assistance, which only increased the chaos. Rolande by now had abandoned her mount and gained the wharfside. As the soldiers converged on her, readying their weapons and certain that they had her cornered at last, she made a flying leap into the black water below the pier and disappeared from sight.

The soldiers ran to the edge of the dock, peering down into the inky darkness, but they could not have seen her even if she were directly below them. When a lantern was brought by one of the batterymen, the light revealed no sign of their quarry, either beneath the pier or in the water as far out as they could see. "She's either swum away or drowned, more likely," someone muttered.

No one offered to go in after her, for few of the soldiers could swim, and none was willing to risk the treacherous ocean currents.

"Say she's done for, then, and leave it," the batteryman with the lantern suggested.

"Well, there's nought more we can do tonight," said the head of the guardsmen. "It's no use searching further till morning, by any means. But she's done for, right enough, even if she survives the water. Let her show her face anywhere around the countryside, and we'll do for her, no question."

* * *

Katin was assisting Carl in cleaning the instruments they'd used in treating the soldiers, when a boy of some twelve years was admitted to the house with a note addressed to Carl. "It is from Captain Fogarty," Carl said, scanning the contents briskly. Captain Fogarty had charge of the farthest garrison house, beyond Lechton's Marsh. "He says he has a most worrisome outbreak of breakbone fever among his troops, and begs me to come at once. He fears it will lay low half his people if it can't be checked." Carl nodded knowingly. "*That* was only to be expected. I've said time and again, that marsh ought to be drained and filled. The miasma—"

"Will you go?" Katin interrupted. "There's nought more to do for these souls here, but keep them comfortable, and I can see to that."

"There's plenty others can see to that, just as well—you'd best come with me. You can be of more use there."

That was what Katin had been hoping for. She jumped up eagerly. "I'll go tell Sergeant Merton." Sir Andrew had left that morning to deploy his troops in strategic positions around the town, in anticipation of the coming attack. In his absence, Sergeant Merton was in charge of the garrison.

He sent two soldiers with them as escort, though he anticipated no trouble. The enemy had not been seen in the area near the garrisons, according to the militia's patrols. But when the party had reached the wall separating Lechton's Marsh from the farmland beyond, shots rang out from the woods to the west and both the militiamen fell, one killed outright, the other with a shattered hip. Before Katin and Carl could flee, a dozen rough men and women rode out from the trees and surrounded them, then forced them into the forest at gunpoint.

"What do you want with us?" Carl demanded, searching for a way out of the circle. "We've nothing worth stealing."

"You've one thing we want." One of the men rode close to Katin's horse and laid his hands on her reins. "Give me your pistol," he ordered her.

Carl wheeled his horse around, crying, "Let the girl be!" but he was unarmed, and his protest was unheeded.

Katin drew her pistol and aimed it at the man holding her horse. "Go to the devil," she suggested.

He grinned at her. "You can shoot me, lass, but the rest will get you before you can reload, you know. Now if you hand over that gun nicely, we'll let the old man go. Give us any trouble, and we'll kill him." The rider nearest Carl laid her musket against his ribs.

"Don't listen to him," Carl insisted, but this time Katin obeyed. The woman who held Carl at gunpoint flipped her weapon around and struck him in the chest with the stock of the gun, knocking him from the saddle. He lay where he fell, gasping for breath, and Katin tried to dismount and go to him, but two other riders now flanked her, and a third aimed his musket directly upon her. Her arms were swiftly tied behind her and she was gagged, then the man still holding her reins led her horse deeper into the woods, followed by the others. Beyond a dense thicket, they drew up in a small clearing and turned their prisoner over to the rider who waited there.

Katin could only stare in outrage as Simeon paid his

henchmen for her. "You can keep her horse as well as the others," he told them. "Give her to me."

As the leader of her captors tried to hand her from her horse to Simeon's, she kicked out and caught Simeon's horse with her heel, making the beast rear dangerously. Simeon barely managed to maintain his seat, but he brought the horse under control at last and trotted back to her. The others held her fast as he struck her hard across the face with the back of his hand. "I said I would have you, in good time," he said, smiling. "And I prefer to have you alive, but I've no objection to hurting you, none at all." He drew his pistol and held it against her shoulder.

Katin had not the slightest doubt that he meant what he said. She gave up the useless struggle, and the others trussed her legs securely, so that she could give no further trouble. Simeon threw her across his horse and rode back toward the town.

Rolande arrived at the bandits' camp wet, shivering, and with a pistol too damp to fire, and demanded dry clothes, food, and shelter without so much as a by your leave.

"So you're wanted on all fronts now?" Lorin asked, as he passed her a piece of roast hare from his side of the campfire. "What do you think the Dep general would pay for you?"

Rolande took another bite of meat, not seeming in the least disturbed by the bandit's question. When she'd swallowed and wiped her mouth on her sleeve, she said, "What do I think? I think he'd thank you kindly for finding me, and then have you hanged for a bandit. That's the payment you'd get from him."

Lorin laughed. "That's what I think, too," he admitted. "All the same, Vendeley, you owe me a favor."

"Agreed."

"What will you do now?"

Rolande stretched. "Well, first I'll have a bit of a rest. But then I must be on my way, with due thanks for your hospitality. I mean to sneak back into town."

"Have you lost your wits, woman? Why would you walk back into the very place you just escaped from?" Lorin protested. "You're safe enough with us. We'll not give you away. You know my word's good."

"So I do," Rolande said seriously. "But there are two things I want now, and I can't get either of them here in the woods. I want revenge on that weasel Pryce, first of all. And I want to salvage some gain out of this affair. I refuse to lose everything I've worked for. I'll come out of this game ahead, you mark me!"

Lorin nodded, thinking, *I'll wager you will, too.* "Still, it's a great risk," he said. "If you're seen, you're sure to be recognized."

"I won't be seen." She studied him thoughtfully for a moment. "Give me your jacket."

Like many of the other bandits in the camp, Lorin was wearing a gray army jacket, snatched from a dead Deprivant soldier. Resignedly, he shrugged it off and handed it over to her, watching as she slipped it on.

Rolande wore a linen shirt and breeches culled from one of Lorin's band. Now she stood and buttoned the jacket. "Well, what do you think? Could I pass as a soldier?"

Lorin grunted, then plucked a soldier's cap from the head of one of the bandits sitting nearby and tossed it to her. He gave her a critical gaze. "I suppose you might, with a musket and all, if no one looks close."

"Good enough," Rolande said. "When I return, I'll repay you in gold for this favor." She hefted one of the muskets Lorin had left leaning against an oak tree. "Come, then, let me have a horse. I'll leave it tethered by the crossroads, for you to find. I'll attract less notice if I go into town on foot."

Lorin rested his hand on Rolande's saddle as she readied herself to depart. "You're stark, raving mad, Vendeley, but good luck to you," he said.

She grinned down at him. "You know, you just might be worth looking at, if you shaved off that mop and had a bath."

He stared after her openmouthed as she rode away.

* * *

Simeon had tied Katin to one of the support posts in the cellar, "for safekeeping," he'd said smugly, "till I can come back and attend to you properly. You'll have to wait. My work's not done tonight." The room was dark and dank, with the only light coming from a lantern he'd set upon a stack of wooden crates that sat on the hard-packed earthen floor. The lamp illuminated only a small part of the stone wall and Simeon's leering face.

He sat down on another crate and regarded her helpless form with satisfaction. "Though I've accomplished a good bit already," he went on. "I've seen to my erstwhile mistress—by now I daresay Hough's had her shot." Still gagged as she was, Katin could not question him, but Simeon replied as if she had, "Yes. She lorded it over me just as you and your protector did, but I proved a match for all of you in the end, you see. I spiced her ale with madwort, on the night of the victory celebration, and sent her off to meet with Hough as tipsy as a gull in a gale. I thought that would be the end of her, but the general showed far more forbearance than I would have expected from a man of his high moral standing. I was most disappointed in him. It seems no one's to be relied upon in these unprincipled times."

Simeon was clearly enjoying himself, and Katin hoped he'd keep talking. The longer he contented himself with boasting and gloating, the better for her. "Still," he said, "the general was far from pleased with her behavior, and I heard from the soldiers that one false step would finish her—so I tripped her up." He laughed at his own wit. "I forged a letter in her name to Sir Andrew, and sent it to Hough with my compliments. Now he's convinced of her treachery, and she's gone off tonight to report to him. She won't be back, you may be sure. This place is mine now."

Triumphant, Simeon jumped up and strutted back and forth as he spoke, his voice rapid and tense with excitement. "Now there is no bar to my receiving the governorship of the colony, which would have gone to her," he said, and suddenly stopped in front of Katin. "For, having you, *Your Highness,* I can name any price I choose." Her eyes widened in fear and astonishment, and Simeon smiled at her. "Oh, yes, I know what you are. No one knows but me! And in return for turning you over to the Chamber I expect to profit well. Did you think I went to such lengths to abduct you, just to have my pleasure of you? You're not so pretty as all that, my girl." He looked her over with a lascivious eye. "Pretty enough though, perhaps, to tarry with tonight. I've not decided. I'm not sure I want any part of a slut who gives her favors to Sir Andrew's hirelings—and half the militia, for all that I know to the contrary." He shook his head in reproof. "That a Princess of the Realm should be such a little whore—it's shocking. Still . . . we can discuss that later. I've yet one more task to do. I've paid Vendeley out for insulting me, and you too will soon have the reward for your disdain, my royal wanton. But I still owe Lord Edenbyrne repayment for the humiliation he has worked on me. That won't take long." Simeon patted her hip, then picked up the lantern and turned toward the stairway, laughing. At the top step, he paused to call back, "Don't fret yourself, I shall be with you before you know it." He went out, locking the door behind him, and left her in absolute darkness.

Having observed the shop long enough to see Simeon ride away, Rolande let herself in, feeling oddly like an intruder in her own property as she mounted the stairs to the second floor. Simeon's quarters could have done with more order. The top of the trestle table and low pine chest overflowed with papers, bits of clothing, riding gear, and other impedimenta, but she controlled her desire to hasten her search, determined not to miss any clue.

She had not told Lorin that her reason for returning to town was to seek out information among Simeon's belongings that would lead her to the Princess—for the Princess's existence was a secret she meant to keep to herself for now. With such a prize she could not only recoup her losses, but attain new heights of wealth and influence. But first she had to find the wretched girl.

She painstakingly examined every scrap of paper she found, but to no avail. Only one document had any bearing on the matter at all and that was little help. This was a note from the general, which Rolande found lying beneath an empty pewter plate on the table. Hough thanked Simeon for the information he had conveyed and agreed to meet with him to discuss the matter, should he present himself at headquarters. *That's probably where the worm was off to just now,* Rolande thought, tossing the note down in disgust. Was there no evidence as to the Princess's whereabouts?

Turning to the pine chest, she pried loose the lock

with her knife and sifted through the contents, but found little there except clean clothes, a small pouch of silver coins, and another pouch tucked far at the bottom of the chest. When she opened this, however, she found that it was filled with dried purple and yellow flowers. What the devil—?

At first she just stared at them, thinking hard, then she retrieved the first pouch, spilled the coins into her own purse, and poured a quantity of the flowers into the empty money-pouch. The pouch with the rest of the flowers she returned to its place at the bottom of the chest. If Simeon had already gone to Hough, she reflected, then the secret was out, and it was too late for her to find the Princess herself. But she could see to it that Simeon never enjoyed the reward for capturing Her Highness.

But perhaps Hough would take care of that for her? Once he had the Princess, what was to keep him from disposing of Simeon and claiming the credit for himself? Would his vaunted Dep principles be stronger than his greed for glory? In Simeon's place, Rolande wouldn't have trusted Hough with the secret, but it was best to take no chances, she decided. The man might well be honest—or stupid—enough to let such an opportunity slip. And besides, her plan would allow her to avenge herself on him as well as Pryce. A very tidy result all 'round.

Very well, what was the best way to go about it? She thought for a moment, and smiled to herself. Yes . . . she'd need one of the bandits' boys to help her, but it would work. . . . Pausing only to snatch up the note from the general, she hurried down the stairs. From a secret panel behind the tall cupboard, a hiding place unknown even to Simeon, she removed two pouches of gold. Then, she slipped out the back way, the better to remain unseen.

She'd just started across the rutted yard, when a scrabbling noise behind her made her freeze, her heart racing. She threw herself down behind an old cart and peered around it, immediately cursing herself for a fool—for the noise came from nothing but Katin Ander's soarhound pup, scratching at the back door to the cellar. But what did the creature want there . . . ?

Holy God, thank you! Rolande thought. In a trice she had dashed back inside the shop, lit a lantern, and seized the key to the cellar from a brass pot beneath the counter. Young Ander, of course, Sir Andrew's mysterious minion, with her haughty air and her rebellious ways! Her identity seemed so obvious now that Rolande could scarcely believe she had been so blind. What she would do with this knowledge she hadn't yet decided, and it would be best to keep her own counsel for now. She would not let on that she knew a thing.

Katin raised her head as the light pierced the gloom of her prison. She had been struggling so hard against her bonds that her wrists were rubbed raw and bleeding, but she had not been able to loosen the ropes. Now she stared in disbelief as Rolande set the lantern down and regarded her with seeming astonishment.

"Well, well, Mistress Ander! So Simeon got his hands on you at last, did he?" Rolande removed her gag, and began to cut her loose. "How often must I get you out of trouble, eh?"

"You!" Katin gasped, then broke into a fit of coughing. When she recovered, she said, "Pryce said he'd set the general against you—that you were dead."

"He did, did he? Well, he was mistaken, as you see, and he's made one mistake too many, this time. He's going to pay dearly for it." She looked thoughtfully at the disheveled, bruised Katin. "And God knows what he's done to you. You can help me bring him down if you like—indeed, you're just the one I need. Come, how would you like to have your vengeance on him, and strike a blow for the colonial cause at the same time?"

Katin collapsed onto a crate, weary and bewildered, trying to make sense out of the shifting allegiances. "Why?" she asked weakly. "Why would you help the colony? What side are you on?"

"There's only one side, girl—mine. If you know what Pryce did, then you know the Chamber will be after my head now. It will suit my purpose best for the invasion to fail, and it will fail if you assist me. Look here—what are these?" She took out the pouch and shook some of the dried flowers out on the crate, being careful not to touch them.

Katin drew back. "That's false mendersleaf. It's a deadly poison."

"So I thought, but I wanted to be sure." Taking the general's note from her pocket, Rolande used it to sweep the blossoms back into the leather bag, then went to the winerack and removed three stoneware bottles. "And here's what I came down here for," she lied glibly. "How fortunate I found an herbalist as well. Now I know how to proceed."

Katin swallowed painfully, her mouth still sore from the gag. "You—you're going to poison someone?"

"No," said Rolande. "You are."

Chapter 17

"They said nothing to suggest where they might have taken her?" Lady Celia asked Carl.

"Not a word," he said abjectly. The patrol that had found him and his escort had taken them to the nearest garrison house—where Captain Fogarty had assured Carl that there was no outbreak of fever among his people. It had been no chance encounter, then. Someone had deliberately lured them out, in order to seize Katin. But *why?* Carl wondered.

Who? Lady Celia worried. "Could the Scrutinors be behind it, do you think? Some of the Ministra's followers, who blame Katin's witchcraft for her death—or even for the invasion?"

Carl considered. "Our attackers hadn't the appearance or manner of Deprivants, though I suppose they could have been in the employ of the Scrutinors."

"Still, that takes us no further," Lady Celia sighed. "Even if we knew who had her, we've no way of knowing where to start looking for her." Lady Celia tried to think of some action to take, but she was forced to admit there was nothing that she could do at the moment. Perhaps the bandits that Sir Andrew had enlisted in their service might find out something, but even for that slim chance she must wait for their leader to appear with a report. She knew of no way to send for him.

And this time, she could not send for Andrew either. Even if he knew of the peril to the Princess, he could not delay the decisive battle in order to search the countryside for her. "Sir Andrew is in the field," she said to Carl, "and unlikely to return before the battle is decided. But should he come back, tell him nothing of this." There was nothing to be gained by worrying Andrew. He would be helpless to act.

Lady Celia stood abruptly and said, "There are still plenty here who need help, however, and that is a matter we can do something about. Let us be about our work." Work was the only possible comfort. If she kept herself occupied, perhaps she would not dwell every moment on the danger to the Princess, and on the dreadful likelihood that Andrew would never return from this battle.

The streets around the assembly hall were filled with soldiers, for the buildings nearby had been turned into mess stations and headquarters for the quartermaster and other officers. Everyone was aware that the final battle would be soon. The talk in the street was of nothing else, and General Hough was even now meeting with senior officers in the assembly hall, which was Katin's destination.

Rolande could not possibly gain access to the meeting hall, where she had so often sat as one of the Warders, for the doors were heavily guarded, and she dared not let herself be seen clearly, lest she be recognized. But Hough's men would not know Katin from any other youngster. Rolande stood in the shadows just inside the livery stables, intending to duck into one of the stalls if anyone entered, and pretend to be a soldier tending to the horses. But for the moment she watched Katin moving toward the rear yard of the assembly hall with her basketful of wine bottles, a servant on an errand, unheeded amid the flowing mass of an army preparing for battle.

In the yard there were a great many carts arriving, carrying clothing, small arms, and other goods from the abandoned homes of the townsfolk who had fled. Other carts held fresh-killed game or sacks of oats and corn taken from the town stores and brought to provision the troops. Joining the throngs of soldiers going about their business, Katin drifted to the large back door to the kitchen, which stood open to allow the cool fall air to penetrate. Inside, servants waiting on the officers in the assembly hall scurried to and fro. *This, too, is war,* Katin told herself. Surrounded by the enemy, who would slay her on the instant if they knew her true identity or her true errand, she was engaged in a battle as surely as the militiamen in the field, as surely as her ancestress, The Warrior Queen.

"What have you got there, girl?" demanded a man in a greasy apron, as he brandished a carving knife over a trussed goose on the carving block. Katin smiled uncertainly, like any shy serving lass. "Well, speak up, girl, what is it?"

With a nervousness not altogether feigned, Katin asked, "The general's meeting is here, isn't it, sir?"

"Aye, what then?"

"I've some wine, sir. Sent by Simeon Pryce—for the general."

"Where do you want this?" demanded a man with a pig on his shoulder.

"Over there." The cook turned away to direct the victualer, leaving Katin standing inside the doorway. When he looked back he seemed surprised to see her still waiting there. "What are you lolling about for? If that's spirits you've got, put them on the sideboard with the rest." He turned back to the goose, slicing it with a sweeping motion of the knife. Katin looked around in confusion for the sideboard.

"Here, this way with that wine, girl," a weary-looking woman said, taking pity on Katin, and leading her into the alcove at the back of the hall. "When they're done talking, they'll retire here for a drink to wash down their words."

"These are a special gift from Simeon Pryce," Katin repeated dutifully, as if following orders. She meant to make certain that someone remembered this.

"Oh, aye," the woman said indifferently. "They all want to curry favor." She took a small cake from the sideboard and gave it to Katin, saying, "Run along, now, or you'll be 'pressed to fetch and carry."

"Yes, Mistress, thank you." Katin bowed awkwardly and scampered off, relieved that the woman had not offered to give her back the basket. Tucked into the straw that cushioned the bottles was a scrap of paper that read "For the Officers' Mess." If anyone should turn it over, it would immediately be apparent that it had been torn from the general's note to Simeon.

It looked at first as if sneaking out of the town would prove more difficult than sneaking in had been. The invaders did not intend to let word get out to the enemy that the mobilization was underway, and all ways out of the settlement were under constant guard. From the window of an abandoned and looted house, Rolande watched the main roadway for over an hour, then woke Katin, who was asleep on the floor, and told her, "We're going back to the shop."

"Oh, good, I can fetch Lucifer then," Katin mumbled. She'd had to shut the soarhound inside, to keep him from following her to the assembly hall. "Then can we go home?"

Rolande overcame the urge to slap her. From the swollen bruise across her cheekbone, it looked as if someone had already done that. Instead, she dragged her to her feet and shook her, ordering, "Wake up and look lively, my fair-haired dreamer. If the general's men have had their wine, the whole regiment will be looking for you. We'll need all our wits about us to get out of here alive."

"I'm awake," said Katin, startled. "Was I asleep?" How could she possibly have slept in the midst of this danger and uncertainty? "Why are we going to your shop? What if Pryce has come back?"

"If he's there, we'll kill him, of course," Rolande said, "and make it look as if he cut his own throat, to 'scape punishment for the murders. A noble self-sacrifice for the colonial cause. Now come along, we have to fetch the cart."

But Simeon had not yet returned. Katin harnessed the cart while Rolande loaded it with shovels and picks from the shop's wares. Together, they added rope and staves and some large empty crates.

"That's for you," said Rolande, pointing to one of the crates. "Get in, and I'll nail it shut. And if you want to take that fool dog of yours, see you keep him quiet."

Katin made no move to obey. She wasn't sure she trusted Rolande at all, and she certainly didn't trust her enough for that. Who knew what this unpredictable woman would do with her, once she had her trapped in a box? "No," she said hoarsely. "I won't be nailed in."

"Then you can find your own way out of here, and good luck to you, for you'll need it. I'm not going to wait for you to come to your senses. In an eyeblink, half the regiment will be swarming over this place looking for Pryce—and for you. If I try to smuggle you out of town in an open crate, and someone takes it into his head to have a look inside, I'll hang with you. The whole business is risky, and I'll not make it more so, just to humor you."

Katin, pale and still as a statue of marble, seemed paralyzed by indecision. When Lucifer pawed at her knee and whimpered, she picked him up and clutched him to her, but stayed where she was, unmoving. Rolande shrugged and climbed onto the seat of the cart, taking up the reins. She couldn't afford to waste any more time, but she didn't care to let the Princess slip through her hands either. "I ought to just club you and throw you in—for your own good," she said. "Do you think I couldn't?"

"Oh, no," Katin whispered. "I think you could."

"Well, then, do as I say! Use your sense—why should I want to take you prisoner? And if I did, why should I trouble to trick you? I already *had* you prisoner, when I found you in the cellar! Right now you're nothing to me but an extra risk, but I got you into this danger, so I suppose I should try to get you out. Now are you coming with me or staying?"

There was sense in Rolande's argument, Katin told herself. Rolande could force her to go, if she chose, so perhaps her only choice was to go with or without being hit again. But Rolande didn't seem to be threatening her, and indeed, why should she? Simeon had said that no one else knew her for the Princess. He certainly wouldn't have told Rolande. And if she stayed here. . . .

In the end, Katin crept into the crate, holding Lucifer, and Rolande brazenly drove the cart out of Thornfeld along the main road, at the tail of a convoy of other wagons carrying supplies for the coming battle. Observing those ahead of her, she called out, "Tools for entrenchments and pickets," as she passed by the guards.

* * *

Simeon was impatient as he laid the last of the powder against the front door of Silverbourne Manor. With all the household guard gone with Sir Andrew, there was no one to question his activities. The Chamber's forces were massing for the final attempt to subdue the colonials, and Silverbourne, too far from town to be of use to them, had been left unoccupied.

He resented the sheer size of the house. It had taken him far longer than he had anticipated to place the wood and powder all around it. At last, he lit the strips of tar-soaked cloth he'd laid as fuses, then ran back to his cart and watched with elation as the powder exploded and the flames caught.

He had decided that Rolande was right—it wouldn't do to underestimate Sir Andrew. He would make certain that even if His Lordship survived the Chamber's attack, he would return to nothing. *You and your lady wife have humiliated me for the last time. Soon I shall be in ascendancy over the colony—I whom you despised—and you shall be destitute, if you still live. It is I who have destroyed your home. I who have put ruin to your plans for the Queen of Albin!* Simeon could hear the crackling of the flames for some distance as he drove the cart back to town. The sound filled him with immense satisfaction, and he was still whistling cheerfully as he approached the shop. He would have a drink to celebrate work well done, and then pay a visit to the cellar. . . .

He smiled at the sight of several horses, in military tackle, tethered in front of the store. Hough must have sent an escort for him. That was the way he should be treated. He hadn't meant to present himself at headquarters just yet, but it was no matter. He could come to terms with the general now, and deliver the girl to him in the morning. No doubt he was impatient to have such an important matter settled.

But—suppose the soldiers had searched the cellar and found the Princess already? There was no reason they should, he assured himself, and the door was locked, but still the idea was alarming. Straightening his clothes, he hurried into the shop.

"Simeon Pryce?" The officer who asked the question wore the uniform of a captain. He was standing squarely in front of the stairs to the upper floor, and several other soldiers stood on either side of the door.

Simon bowed. "At your service," he said, smiling easily at the man. To his great relief, there was no sign of the Princess.

The captain moved closer. "We have been sent by General Hough."

"And you are most welcome," Simeon said graciously.

But the captain appeared unmoved by his welcome. He held out the small pouch from the chest upstairs. "Does this belong to you?"

"What is it?" Simeon asked, puzzled. He took it and looked inside. "Oh, yes—these are just herbs of some sort, given me by a mad old hermit. What does it matter?"

The captain clapped his hand on Simeon's arm. "I am empowered by General Hough, who holds the authority for order within this town, to charge you with the foul murder of six officers, as well as the attempted murder of the general himself—"

Simeon indignantly pulled his arm free. "What the devil? Are you crazed, man?"

The captain ignored the interruption. "—on this day," he continued, "by means of poison most treacherously introduced into bottles of wine sent by you from this place. And by the same authority, I am further empowered to carry out sentence upon you therefore."

"I sent no wine!"

"There is nothing to be gained by denial. We found bottles of like vintage here in your store, and this pouch, discovered among your possessions, holds flowers like those found in the dregs of the poisoned wine. What you have done is treason, in the sight of our God, and the punishment is death."

Panic surged through Simeon. Foolishly, he made to run, but the soldiers by the door seized him firmly.

"Take him outside, where his fellow heretics may witness his fate and take example," the captain ordered.

"Wait, listen to me!" Simeon cried, as the soldiers dragged him toward the door. "You cannot kill me—only I know where the Princess Oriana is hidden!"

"The Princess Oriana was executed in Albin at the end of the war. The market square will do," the captain added to his men.

"No, another was hanged in her place," Simeon insisted. "The true Princess is here!" Suddenly he understood the general's game. Hough meant to cheat him—to force him to deliver the Princess, and give him nothing in return but a pardon for a crime he hadn't committed. It was monstrous, but he had no choice save to accept those terms or be executed. "I have Oriana, and I will trade her to the general for my life, though I've done no murders!"

The captain looked at him in disgust. "This is one tale I've not heard before. You do not expect me to believe it, surely?"

"It's the truth, in God's name. I can prove it."

The captain hesitated. He didn't really believe Simeon's words. The man was a traitor and, faced with death, likely to claim anything to try to save his skin. Still, if there were any chance that what he said was true, and the captain did not investigate, he could be held responsible later for the oversight. "Very well," he said at last. "If you have the Princess, take me to her."

Light-headed with relief at this reprieve, Simeon said, "We've not far to go. She's here in the cellar." With shaking hands he lit a lantern, then fetched the key and led the way downstairs.

"Well?" said the captain. "Are we to have no audience with Her Highness?"

Simeon stared around the empty cellar in disbelief. Not only was Katin gone, but there was no sign that she had ever been there. Even the ropes he'd used to bind her were hanging neatly coiled from a peg in the wall. "She has to be here, I tell you!" Simeon cried. "She must have gotten loose and hidden herself. She couldn't get out—the doors were locked. Search, you fools, she's here somewhere!" He began frantically overturning barrels and crates, hunting into every space in the cellar that might conceal so much as a small child.

"Enough!" the captain commanded. "I care not if the man's mad as well as traitorous. We've a war to fight and no more time to waste on the likes of him." He gestured the soldiers nearest Simeon to take hold of him again, then lifted down one of the coiled ropes and tossed it to another man, who bound Simeon's hands behind him.

Folk scattered to get out of range as the soldiers dragged the sobbing, protesting Simeon to the stocks in the market square and tied him there. The captain read out the order of execution, and commanded his men to ready their muskets. Some folk watched and some turned away, as the blast of musket fire thundered through the square.

* * *

Like any poacher, Sara Franesh was accustomed to evading the authorities and taking risks, but she was accustomed to doing so in the cover of the deep woods, where she could disappear among the trees or vanish into a thicket in an instant. She felt trapped in the narrow dormer room at the top of Headman Farnham's house, with dozens of enemy soldiers on the floors below. Hannah had said she needn't do this unless she chose, but Sara knew that her sister wanted to help defend the settlement, and she, too, wished to do her part. The invaders were the same lot of bastards who'd banished them from Albin, after all. *If they take power here, too, where will they send us next?* she asked herself. Suppose she were separated from Hannah again? Resolutely, she unlatched the shutters and pushed them wide, then dragged the bright blue rug over the sill and hung it out the window. The wind caught the fringe at the bottom and tousled it merrily.

Behind Sara the door flew open and a young soldier stepped into the room, his musket leveled at her. "What are you doing there, woman?" he demanded.

Sara's tongue felt like lead. "Just airing this rug, please, sir," she quavered, certain that death was staring her in the face.

The soldier was almost as uneasy as Sara. Having heard a suspicious noise in a room that should have been empty, he'd bravely bolted in, only to find a scared girl doing her housework. He strode to the window and looked down at what she held there, which was, indeed a rug. "Here, that looks heavy," he said, embarrassed. "I'll help you with it." Grasping the rug firmly, he shook it back and forth against the windowsill, releasing clouds of dust, and Sara watched wide-eyed as he gave the signal to his enemies.

One of the Yerren scouts gliding over Thornfeld

spotted the flash of blue in the dormer window and flew off at once to alert Sir Andrew. His Lordship in turn sent word to Civornos, and the Chamber's soldiers had barely begun their march when two dozen armed Yerren landed on the roofs of the storehouses near the harbor. The soldiers there began firing at once, but the Yerren refused to abandon their perches. As some returned the soldiers' musket fire, others fitted their bows with pitch-dipped arrows, which they lit with flints. When the archers had fired these flaming missiles into the rafters of the adjacent building, all the Yerren suddenly threw themselves from the roofs and flew off, winging high above the town as the powder magazine caught fire and erupted in a massive explosion.

It was Katin who suggested that they seek the hospitality of the hermit, and Rolande, like Sir Andrew before her, thought it as safe a place as any to leave the Princess for the time being. It might be as well not to take her to the bandits' camp until she could decide what to do with her, Rolande reflected. Lorin would ask questions, and feel that he had a right to answers. It was all very well to owe him a favor, and she meant to repay it, but sharing the secret of Oriana would be payment far beyond what she owed.

Simeon had been a fool to think he could turn the Princess over to Hough and not end up dead in a ditch somewhere, she thought. The only way to assure a bargain with the Chamber would be to present her there directly. At the moment, Rolande's chances of reaching the members of the Chamber in safety were not good, and if Hough passed on Simeon's damning document to them, they'd never fully trust her again. Still, she was reluctant to let the girl go until she had thought things through more thoroughly.

The hermit, upon their arrival, had merely given Rolande a long look and asked, "So you've turned on your confederates now?"

"They've turned on me," Rolande snarled, "and they'll regret it before I'm through. Don't worry yourself—I don't mean to sully your hearth with my presence. Just keep the girl. She's half perished."

"I think you'd both better stay for now," the hermit said. "It's going to storm soon. Come, I'll give you a meal."

Katin had eaten nothing but the piece of cake since she'd left the garrison house with Carl, and she was faint with hunger and exhaustion when they arrived. But a large bowl of rabbit stew did much to revive her. "Where do you mean to go?" she asked Rolande, fishing a stew bone out of the pot for Lucifer.

Rolande could see no reason to lie. "To the bandit camp. They may be able to do something to inconvenience the Chamber's people."

"You know how to find them?" Katin asked doubtfully. Even Sir Andrew didn't know that.

"Of course."

"I shall go with you, then." Now that she was no longer weak and famished, she felt she must be in the thick of things again.

"Crossing through the fields will be most difficult, now that the battle is underway," the hermit pointed out.

His guests turned to him eagerly. "Who made the first attack?" Rolande demanded.

"Sir Andrew. A party of Yerren passed by here not long before you, and told me that they'd destroyed the powder store in town, by setting the building ablaze with flaming arrows."

Rolande laughed. "Ah, that must have been a fine explosion! I'm sorry I missed it! But we've not been idle either—the regiment will be short some officers, unless our stroke missed its mark."

"But there must be something more we can do," Katin insisted. "We'll not just wait here till all's over, will we? We have to help Sir Andrew somehow!"

"Patience," said Rolande, with a grin at the hermit. "I'm thinking on it."

Rebuffed, Katin left Rolande to her thoughts, and turned to the array of rare simples and medicaments lining the shelves of the hermit's hut. These had always fascinated her. "Coltsfoot . . . isn't that good for breakbone fever?" she asked the hermit. "But I'll wager there never was an outbreak of breakbone fever at the garrisons," she added before he could reply.

"There's been a good bit of it around," the hermit told her, smiling to himself, "but one thing to remember is that it doesn't cause a cough."

Rolande, lost in her pondering, paid no heed to this exchange. What course should she take now? she asked herself. She could, of course, return to Lorin's camp and lie low until the smoke cleared, but that would achieve nothing. If the general won, then she was doomed to face capture and execution by the Chamber, unless she was willing to spend her days in hiding. If the colonials won, at worst she would have to head for another settlement before they recovered from the confusion Thornfeld was in. Unlike the Chamber they did not have the resources to hunt her down. Indeed, she doubted they'd even bother to try. If she helped them win, she would still have a place in the community.

As matters stood she still had a chance to play both ends against the middle. Her bargaining card was Oriana. If, having rescued her, she returned her safe to Sir Andrew, he would owe her a debt he would be honor-bound to pay. Her position would be better if Sir

Andrew's forces were victorious, since one of Hough's first acts, if he won, would be to order her arrest. In that case, her only hope would be to get the Princess to the Chamber, but the forces ranged against her would be formidable, and she would be without resources. She knew she could trust Sir Andrew in any bargain they made. Had that ever been true of the Deps? But even if she aided Sir Andrew's cause, there was no guarantee he would win, and until she was certain, she would keep Oriana against future need. The idea of turning her over to the Chamber was distasteful, but if it came down to a choice between her own life or the girl's, she would do it.

Therefore, she would do what she could to aid the colonists' cause. But was there anything more she could do to weigh the scales against the Chamber, even with the bandits' help?

From the doorway, the hermit said, "The storm's coming in. Blowing from the east—storm's coming off the sea."

"Then there have been gales out on the ocean recently?" Rolande asked him thoughtfully.

"I would say so. It seems that every ship that comes to harbor runs afoul of them."

"There is a supply ship overdue, which carries weapons and ammunition for the Chamber's men," Rolande said, as if to herself. "If it has been delayed by storms, it might still be coming this way. Now that the powder store in town has been destroyed, those supplies will be crucial to Hough's efforts. If we could intercept it, it might well make the difference."

Katin looked up from feeding Lucifer a piece of rabbit. "How?" she asked eagerly. "Could the Yerren explode it, too, do you think?"

Rolande thought this over. "Possibly . . . but what a waste of good powder. I'll wager Sir Andrew's supplies must be running low, too. I'd rather capture the brig than destroy it."

Still studying the sky, the hermit said, "Powder brigs are generally reluctant to fight unless they are so well-equipped with weaponry that they can destroy an attacker before it has a chance to fire."

"Well, I doubt that's the case with this one," Rolande told him. "I saw correspondence concerning her, and Hough thinks she's only four guns and about a dozen crew."

The hermit turned to face her, and spoke with unusual directness. "Then with a warship you may take her. They'd no doubt surrender rather than be fired upon, for if you can strike her, she'll go up like a torch. Few men relish being burned to death."

Rolande remembered his claim to have sailed on the first ship to arrive in the New World. He seemed to know whereof he spoke. "There is at least one ship still afloat. I heard that one of the merchant ships that Sir Andrew outfitted escaped destruction at the harbor," she said.

"But we've no idea where it is," Katin objected.

"Oh, I've an idea."

"Have you hands enough to run her?" the hermit asked.

"Lorin has. And if she's not at Acorn Cove, they can search the coast nearby for her."

The hermit nodded. "That's where I'd leave my ship if I wanted her not far off, and undiscovered."

Rolande pushed her bowl aside and rose. "Much thanks for the stew, and the advice," she said, then, turning to Katin, added, "I'll have to take you after all, worse luck. If I'm to have dealings with Sir Andrew, you can smooth the way. Come along. You're fed and rested, now we've work to do."

Katin couldn't be bothered to take offense at Rolande's peremptory tone. She rose obediently, only asking, "But do you know how to sail a ship?"

Rolande had worked the smuggling ships since she was strong enough to haul a rope. "I know enough. And plenty of Lorin's people are deserters from the navy. Are you with me or not?"

Katin dragged Lucifer out from under the table, where he was trying to catch a cricket. "Very well," she said. "Can I take my dog?"

Chapter 18

Taking advantage of the confusion created by the explosion of the powder store, Sir Andrew had ordered the militia to attack. The defensive breastworks thrown up by the Chamber's forces were well planned and constructed, but the batteries contained mostly small artillery pieces. Since the ordnance brig had been delayed, the invaders were short of heavy cannon.

The colonials advanced in small rushes, staying as much as possible within protective cover. The fighting continued all day. A light rain began to fall, making footing uncertain. It seemed as if any time they made headway, managed to clear part of the enemy's fortification and gain a foothold, still more of the Chamber's soldiers surged up from the lines. Sir Andrew encouraged his troops ceaselessly, but there was no way to deny the truth. Their initial advances had been due to the disarray following the explosion of the magazine, and now, as Hough restored order, they lost that advantage. Again and again, Sir Andrew searched the sky for signs of a Yerren messenger. At any moment, he expected word that Captain Jamison had arrived from the coast and was in position to lead an attack from the flank with the companies he'd take north.

But no respite came. Sir Andrew watched the troops

suffering under repeated barrages from the Chamber's batteries, saw that they could not take the breastworks, and ordered them to fall back. But still they kept on fighting, taking cover behind trees, logs, and stumps, anything that offered protection from the relentless fire of the enemy.

Night fell, but still the fighting continued sporadically. Some of the wood in the old forest was still dry enough for campfires, but they yielded little warmth and less cheer. The fields were full of dead and wounded. Further bad news was received from Captain Jamison, who sent word that although the forces he led were on the move from the coast, they'd been delayed by the storm, which had struck hard there.

Sir Andrew rode from point to point, searching for any sign of weakness among the Chamber's forces that might be turned to the colonials' advantage. By the light of the sputtering campfires, he watched militiamen wearily struggling to load and fire. A musket ball struck a tree within a handbreadth of him. *I'm very likely to die tonight,* he thought, glancing back at the tree without much interest. *And so are many more. But it would be of no use to call for surrender. That's the one order they wouldn't accept from me. They'd go on fighting despite me.* Sir Andrew was accustomed to an army made up largely of professional soldiers, hired substitutes, glory seekers, and reluctant conscripts, who had no real idea of whom they were fighting or why. Never had he commanded a force that fought with such heartfelt resolve and will. With such an army, one should be able to overcome larger numbers and desperate odds.

It began to rain harder, but still the fight went on. Throughout the night, the invaders kept up a steady fire designed to wear the defenders out. The two armies were close enough now to yell to each other across the lines.

"Where is your commander?" one of the Chamber's soldiers called. "Tell him to pray for his soul, if he has one still. We shall have his head before morning."

And that, Sir Andrew thought, was fair advice. But he prayed instead for a miracle.

The brig drew too deep a draft to sail down the river, so Rolande and her crew packed guns, shells, balls, flints, and powder into longboats and rowed them inland, as close as possible to where the embattled colonists were encamped. Lorin and the other bandits had covered the crates and sacks with layers of canvas to protect them from the rain, but Rolande and the rest were soaked to the skin. They dragged the captured supplies ashore, covering them with the overturned boats to keep them dry. Lorin, looking dismally across the expanse of muddy fields that separated them from Sir Andrew's forces, wondered how Rolande had talked him into this escapade. True, he had no wish to see the Chamber seize power in New Albin, but he hadn't planned to take such an active role in the defense. "Well, what now?" he asked Rolande.

"You stay here and guard the supplies. The girl and I will go to the camp for carts to transport the weaponry." Rolande turned to Katin. "Now you can make yourself useful. Sir Andrew may not be inclined to accept my word."

Katin had already made herself useful, as Rolande very well knew, by climbing far higher into the rigging than any of the others could do, and sighting the powder brig when it was still at a great distance. But she contented herself with replying, "You can hardly blame Sir Andrew for that," as she started off across the fields after Rolande.

They slogged wearily through the swampy ground, which had been a dry field not long before. In no time Rolande's boots were soaked and mud-caked. "If I survive this campaign, I shall expect His Lordship to stand me a new pair of shraik-skin boots, mind you," she muttered.

Katin pushed her streaming hair out of her face. "If I survive, I'll see to it," she said grimly.

The roar of guns grew louder, the air became smoky, and several times they were forced to take cover. Before long they found themselves challenged by soldiers, and having explained their mission, they were escorted to Sir Andrew. The noise now grew deafening, and the air bitter to breathe. The long fight in the harsh weather had worn the colonial troops down, but they were determined they should not surrender while there was yet shot to load a gun. Sir Andrew was standing beneath an oak tree, having his hand bandaged.

Katin, seeing him wounded, ran to him. "You're injured! Let me see—" But he grasped her with his other hand and pushed her back against the tree, where she'd be better covered. "Have you completely lost your senses? However you got here, get away again—now!"

"But I was kidnapped—" Katin began.

Catching sight of Rolande, Sir Andrew demanded, "By her?"

"No, no, by Simeon Pryce. She rescued me."

"Why?" Sir Andrew asked suspiciously. What was Vendeley's game this time? "And why bring the girl into the brunt of the battle, in God's name? To distract me from the defense?"

Rolande jumped as a cannonball crashed through a tree nearby. "We've brought arms and ammunition," she shouted over the din. "It's due west by the riverbank, but we need carts to transport it."

It had to be a lie, it was impossible. "There's no ordnance to be had this side of the ocean!"

"Ask the girl, then—that's what I brought her for!"

"It's true, My Lord," Katin insisted. "We captured an enemy vessel, an arsenal ship—I was there—and we've brought you the cargo."

"Why?" Sir Andrew demanded of Rolande again. "I know the Chamber is your master."

"No one is my master." The moment Rolande had spoken the words, she realized that they were true, and she knew exactly what she meant to do. To deliver the Princess to the Chamber would only be to put herself under their patronage again. She might be in favor once more, she might regain all her lost ground, but she would be their creature forever—and that would be intolerable. Above all else, she must be her own master. "If you want the ammunition, give me the carts," she said to Sir Andrew. "I'm not about to tarry here."

Gazing at the embattled soldiers in the field, Sir Andrew was forced to admit that it mattered little whether or not she was telling the truth. They were short on guns and ammunition, and Hough's forces must also be running low, now that the powder store had been destroyed. If Vendeley had really kept the enemy from receiving the ordnance they needed, and the colonials had those supplies, it just might turn the tide. And if it were a fatal trick, so be it, for they had nothing to lose now. He turned to one of the soldiers nearby and sent him to fetch men and carts to accompany Rolande.

"I'll take the girl back with me, shall I?" said Rolande. Though she meant to let the Princess go, still it wouldn't do to leave her in the midst of the battlefield. As long as she lived, the secret of her identity would be valuable. There were other ways to profit from it besides dealing with the Chamber.

"Yes, that's best," Sir Andrew agreed. Wherever

Vendeley took the Princess now, it would be safer than this. *And if I perish here, I'll know she lives.*

"I can stay and fight!" Katin protested. "I know how to handle a musket!"

Sir Andrew almost smiled. "Drag her if you must," he said to Rolande. "Just get her away from here."

But Katin made no further objection. Even to herself her words had sounded childish. She was an Obelen, not a soldier, and her duty lay elsewhere.

As Captain Jamison's troops crossed the last of the lowlands between Hag's Head Point and the town, the storm that had obstructed their march from the coast now sheltered them from the enemy's view. The rain and gloom masked their approach through the trees until they were almost at the edge of town.

At dawn the next day, Sir Andrew received a Yerren scout who brought word that the captain had arrived at last. Sir Andrew sent him back orders by the Yerren, praying that the action he had now initiated did not come too late. Calling for Jerl, he bade him render a message for another Yerren scout, and sent his final orders to Civornos as well.

Soon, Yerren filled the trees in the forest south of town. From their number, companies armed with muskets and bows flew around the stockade, landing on the roofs of buildings and firing at the soldiers guarding the approach to the settlement. No sooner had the first Yerren landed, however, than the soldiers fired a great catapult from the yard below, releasing a deadly spray of nails and grapeshot. Hough had ordered a number of such catapults built to protect his men from the winged enemy, but the Yerren, enraged, only responded in greater force, shrieking their eerie, high-pitched war call. The soldiers reloaded and fired again, and this time the Yerren sent a flight of flaming arrows down onto the catapult. It failed to catch fire, but the soldiers manning it were driven back and forced to take cover. One by one the Yerren shot the guards from the watch posts and occupied them as the watchmen fell from the platforms.

The troop who'd been left to hold the stockade were more than ever convinced that the attacking monsters were possessed of unnatural powers. They held out until half their number were dead, then they fled to rejoin the main body of the army, leaving the fort to the fiends. They had come to fight other folk like themselves, not murderous feathered demonspawn.

Not long afterward, Sir Andrew gathered his soldiers for a decisive assault. "We will take the redoubts. Captain Jamison has brought fresh troops from the coast, who will attack from the flank, and we will trap Hough's men between us," he told them. When he gave the signal, they made a rush for the breastworks, yelling like demons. Spurred on by Sir Andrew, they boldly ascended the hill, jumped into the ditch Hough's men had dug and climbed the breastworks. The forces at the wall were running low on powder and shot, but the colonials were now well supplied, and it was futile for the Chamber's officers to order their men to stand firm. They fired briskly for a few minutes, but as the colonials set fire to the supports of the redoubts, they retreated in haste. Sir Andrew's troops pressed on with renewed hope and confidence. Even though they were inferior in numbers, they had succeeded in driving the invaders from their fortifications. From their newly gained foothold they kept up firing throughout the morning, harrying the Chamber's forces from the rear, moving ever closer to the town.

General Hough ordered his troops to regroup to the north of town, thinking to escape that way. Townsfolk who had seized weapons from their fallen enemies hid in holes, cellars, and wells, picking off the Chamber's soldiers as they passed by. Dangerously low on ammunition by now, the invaders dared not waste it by firing at this unseen enemy. Then, as the troops attempted to push through to the north, they came upon the wall of Captain Jamison's soldiers, who were armed from the stores Sir Andrew had stocked along the coast. The captain's forces charged, driving the invaders back. Sir Andrew's militiamen held the western side of the town. The Yerren were massed in vast numbers in the woods to the south, blocking any hope of retreat through the forest, and there was only the sea to the east. Finding his troops surrounded and his ammunition all but depleted, Hough had no choice but to surrender.

In the cold gray morning light, Sir Andrew accepted the sword from General Hough. The rain had stopped at last, but the day promised to be chill and damp still. The triumph of his victory should have warmed him, but looking down the hill toward the battered town, Sir Andrew felt only dull anger and weariness. He listened impatiently as Hough acknowledged defeat in formal terms, and recited his acceptance of the surrender in a leaden tone.

Having dealt with the exchange of prisoners, Sir Andrew turned to the final business to be addressed. "Now we come to the matter of the disposition of your troops."

Now that Hough was forced to admit himself beaten, he wanted nothing more than to remove his men from the colony as soon as possible. "We beg permission to embark on our vessels and return to Albin." Hough grimaced as if the words tasted bitter to him. He would report to the Chamber that he could not lead mere men against fiends and monsters, that the colonists had so far abandoned the Good God and allied themselves with the Evil One that inhuman, hellish creatures fought at their side, that demons did their bidding and gave their paltry forces the might of an immense army. It was no more than the truth, after all.

Sir Andrew considered this request thoughtfully. He'd ordered the defeated soldiers to leave their weapons, which had been collected by the colonials, and the remains of Hough's army were now under watch outside the town. But the colony could not possibly absorb the prisoners—merely to feed them for any length of time would be too great a burden for their already scant resources. And it was unthinkable to execute the lot, of course. Better to send them back, then. "Very well. I will accede to this—after my men have seen to it that all remaining guns are removed from your vessels. But when you report to the Chamber, warn them that another time we shall not be inclined to be so lenient."

This contemptuous threat was more than General Hough could bear with. "Your victory was won at the price of your souls, I doubt not. Were you not defended by your demon allies, it would be you now suing me for peace!"

Sir Andrew smiled. "You know and I know, sir, that the rules of war forbid me to visit vengeance on you, once you have surrendered. But my people are not experienced soldiers, and the rules of war mean little to them. They know only that they have suffered irreparable and unprovoked losses at your hands. Only I stand between you and their desire for justice, and I have not the authority over these free people that you may think. You would be well advised to hope and pray that we still possess souls capable of human mercy."

Hough realized that he could not afford to anger Sir Andrew, who held his very life in his damned aristocratic hands, and the humiliation of his position burned like bile. "You will allow us to leave this cursed shore unmolested?" he said stiffly.

"We shall indeed rejoice to see the last of you. My men will see to the ships today. Have your officers ready your troops to board them on the morrow—all those, that is, who wish to return to Albin. Those who wish to remain—and I gather there have been numerous deserters—we are willing to accommodate." Sir Andrew gestured to the soldiers guarding the general to see him removed, then bowed and turned away. Hough cast a look of pure hatred after him before allowing the militiamen to lead him off. He had come sweeping into New Albin with full expectation of easy victory. Instead he'd experienced the most crushing defeat of his career—to be bested by a force not only smaller than his own, but one that by all rights should have been ill-equipped and poorly trained. It could only have been accomplished by means of satanic powers, he told himself . . . but it was a defeat he would never forgive Sir Andrew.

This I shall never forgive him, Sir Andrew vowed, staring in rage at the smoldering ruins of Silverbourne. He thought little enough of Hough, but he would not have expected this sort of villiany of him. The general had every right to try to kill the enemy commander in the field, but to send men to put his home to the torch, while he was engaged in battle, was a dishonorable act unworthy of an officer. The man was unfit to command!

I could have him horsewhipped. I could have him hanged. Yet he knew he would do neither. All his training, his principles, made it impossible. Hough was his prisoner; he could not so much as challenge him to a duel. He would have to be content with handing him a defeat that he would not soon live down. But should they ever meet in honest warfare again, the General would answer for this outrage, he promised himself. To leave him homeless again—to destroy the home he had built for Ceila—that was indeed unforgivable.

In a heartbeat's time, Sir Andrew passed from fury to fear. *Where was Celia?* He had sent a messenger to the garrison house, bidding her to join him at Silverbourne, assuming that she had remained at her duties there while he was gone. *She would not have returned to Silverbourne before, would she? She could not have been here when this conflagration occurred?*

Suddenly panic-stricken, as he had never been in the midst of battle, Sir Andrew leaped from the saddle and ran to the house, frantically calling her name. He passed through a gaping hole in the blackened wall into what had been the salon, looking around wildly and taking in the devastation without attending to it.

"Andrew?"

He turned, feverish with relief, as Celia stepped carefully across a fallen beam to reach his side, then threw herself into his arms. "You've come home at last! But what a homecoming for you, my dear!"

He had no idea what she meant. "Thank God you're safe!"

"I? Why should I not be safe? I had far more reason to fear for you than you for me!" she reminded him.

When Sir Andrew had at last released her, they looked about them, surveying the destruction, and a measure of his frustrated wrath returned. There was not so much as a place to sit. The settle and chairs were all burned through, the table charred, and the cabinet where he kept his papers locked had burst to pieces. "Have you seen the rest of the house?" he asked.

"It is much the same." Resting her hand upon his

arm, she added gently, "Andrew . . . we'll rebuild it together."

It was useless to attempt to conceal his anguish from her. "How?" he said bitterly. "I expended the last of my money in mounting the expedition that brought me to this land, and in establishing my household here. All that remained was some valuable plate and such among the furnishings, and, God knows, whatever there was of worth that survived the blaze has probably been looted." He picked a silver inkwell from a pile of ash and dusted it off. "Whatever I can salvage here and the land I've cleared is all that is left to me."

Lady Celia shook her head, smiling. "You forget the dowry I brought you. A fortune in jewels, still hidden safe where I buried them, against the coming of the enemy. I feared they would take possession of the estate and confiscate your property, if the invasion succeeded. But even if we hadn't a penny between us, Silverbourne would soon stand again. Don't you realize, my dear, that you are a hero? All of Thornfeld hails you as their deliverer, first from the dragons, and now from the Chamber! Folk are so grateful, they'd do far more for you than put up a house."

"Do you think so, in truth?" Sir Andrew asked, brightening somewhat. He had long since ceased to expect gratitude from his fellow colonists.

"You are the only person in town who is not sure of it." Seeing him take heart at her words, Lady Celia steeled herself to wound him again. "But Andrew . . . I must burden you with a worse disaster than this, I fear. It's the Princess—she was abducted days ago, at gunpoint, and nothing more heard of her. I blame myself—I ought not to have let her out of my sight! But the sergeant sent an escort with them, and—"

"Celia, don't—I've seen her, I tell you, two days ago. I believe she's safe." Taking her in his arms again, he told her of Rolande's and Katin's mysterious appearance in the midst of a desperate battle. "Till the last moment, I suspected a trick, but the shipment of arms Vendeley brought us was genuine—and without it, we might well have fallen to Hough. For some reason she's thrown over her allegiance to the Chamber, and that one does not do things by halves."

Lady Celia considered this extraordinary tale in silence for a time, but with all her insight, even she could make nothing of it. At last she shook her head helplessly and said, "There's more to Mistress Vendeley than we believed. I must come to know her better, should chance offer."

The area around the dock was packed with folk, as everyone in the colony turned out to watch the embarking of the Chamber's troops for their return to Albin. The militia was out in force at the dockside, as much to keep order among the townsfolk, who had suffered so heavily at the enemy's hands, as to assure the compliance of the Chamber's troops. The fire from the explosion of the powder magazine had spread through much of the town, and artillery damage was everywhere. Buildings left standing had been pillaged by the Chamber's troops to supplement the meager pay provided by the Deprivants, who declared that the opportunity to do God's work was its own reward.

Under the direction of their officers, the enemy soldiers boarded their ships in surprisingly good order. There were catcalls from the townspeople, but the Chamber's men, unarmed, were too subdued by their defeat—and by the flocks of curious Yerren swooping overhead—to respond. Seeing that there was likely to be no trouble about the embarkation, Sir Andrew left charge of the wharf to Captain Jamison, who had turned out with his arm in a sling rather than miss the event.

Sir Andrew was determined to go in search of Rolande and find out what had become of the Princess. Within six yards, however, he was accosted by Headman Farnham, who strode across the wharf to intercept him, accompanied by Elliott Cavendish and several other Warders. "Excellent work, most excellent—ingenious strategy," Headman Farnham said proudly, as if he'd personally engineered the colonists' victory.

"Indeed, we all congratulate you, sir," Elliott Cavendish seconded.

The Warders continued their declarations, but Sir Andrew heard little, his mind still occupied with locating Rolande. She was not among the Warders. Sir Andrew knew it unlikely she'd dare to claim her previous position now that her double-dealing was known, yet the woman might have gall enough even for that. She'd made an admirable effort in helping the colonial cause, after all . . . but who knew where her loyalties truly lay? It was imperative that he find the Princess. Perhaps the first place he should try was Mistress Vendeley's store. She might have returned to gather her belongings while everyone else was at the wharf.

With more haste than courtesy, he excused himself from the Warders and started away, only to be hailed by Frend Pierson, who had made one of his rare visits to town for the occasion. He was accompanied by Civornos, who wanted assurances that the colonists still intended to teach the Yerren how to make powder and shot for the muskets, as had been promised.

"Tell him we will honor our bargain," Sir Andrew said, but their discussion was soon interrupted by the arrival of Minister Arhan, accompanied by a group of Scrutinors. Taking up a station by one of the mooring posts, the Minister started to declaim, his strident voice rising above the general tumult of the wharf. "It is by the grace of the Good God that we have been granted victory over our enemies. He has called down his wrath upon the unrighteous, the degenerate church which corrupts our homeland. . . ."

For the first time, grumbling was heard among the Chamber's soldiers. Fearing that the Minister's words would enflame them to retaliation and start a brawl, Sir Andrew ordered the nearest soldiers to remove the Minister. The Scrutinors surrounded their leader as if to protect him, but he ceased speaking abruptly at the sight of the militiamen and contented himself with glaring at the passing enemy troops.

Sir Andrew was finally about to make his way to Rolande's shop, when a small urchin came hurrying up to him and insisted that Lady Celia wanted to speak to him. He followed the child to the viewing platform overlooking the harbor, where Lady Celia was surrounded by a cluster of people who seemed to represent every segment of the community. There were farmers, shopkeepers, artisans, and laborers. Sir Andrew recognized among them Hannah Franesh and Sergeant Merton, who was leaning heavily on a crutch.

"Have you seen any sign of . . . Katin?" Lady Celia asked in an undertone, as soon as she caught sight of him.

"No—I'm on my way to look for her." Sir Andrew glanced at the people surrounding Lady Celia. "Is something wrong?"

"These people have a proposition for you, my dear. They plan to follow the coast west and seek a suitable spot to found a new colony, where one may live according to one's own lights, without interference from Scrutinor fanatics. They would like you to lead the party."

Sir Andrew stopped scanning the harbor for any sign

of the ship commandeered by Rolande, and turned to stare at Lady Celia as if wondering whether he'd heard aright. "They want me to lead this expedition?"

"Well, sir, we thought you might take the post of Governor," Sergeant Merton said hesitantly. "Once there's a settlement to govern."

"You intend to be part of this group?" Sir Andrew asked him.

"If you agree to go—and Captain Jamison says the same."

"I see. Are many of the militia considering this step?"

"A fair number, sir. The destruction is so heavy that many of us feel it would be equal effort to rebuild here or to start anew in a place of our own choosing. It's been said that there are vast veins of silver to the west."

"There are always stories of that sort."

"They also say that the land there is fertile and less forested than here," Lady Celia said. "We would have an easier time building an estate there."

Sir Andrew glanced at her questioningly. "Then this is something you think I should do?"

"As Governor, you wouldn't be answerable to the dictates of the Warders and their ilk."

"It is a point," he said, beginning to entertain the idea. "Well, I am willing to discuss the matter further, when I can give it my undivided attention." He drew Lady Celia aside. "I must go and search for Katin."

But Lady Celia suddenly darted past him and seized the grimy, disheveled Katin, who was trying to push her way through the spectators crowding the steps to the platform. "There you are, girl! We didn't know what had become of you."

Katin dropped Lucifer and gave Lady Celia a kiss.

"I'm quite safe, Your Ladyship. I had a glorious time—I helped capture a powder brig!"

'If we could tell folk you were with us, Your Lordship," Hannah put in, "many more would join us, without question."

Sir Andrew scrutinized Katin for any sign of ill-usage, but she seemed unharmed. It occurred to him that she might be safer away from Thornfeld, away from the Scrutinors and whoever had been behind the attempts to abduct her. Simeon Pryce was dead, but if he'd known Oriana's secret, he might have told others. "These people mean to start a new colony down the coast to the west," he told her. "They desire me to be their Governor."

"What a splendid idea," Katin said enthusiastically. "Carl *will* be pleased—he says travelers have reported giant lizards in the marshes there. We shall go, shan't we?"

"I think the idea has merit," Lady Celia agreed.

"Celia, if I were to go, it would mean years of hardship before I could establish an estate such as I had in Albin—or even here. Until then, living in the wilderness would be primitive. Would you come with me—or would you wish to wait somewhere more civilized until such time as I can provide for you?" He tried not to sound apprehensive, but in fact he was determined not to be parted from her again.

"I shouldn't dream of staying behind. If you go, of course I shall. I think I'd find most beneficial employment in establishing such a place."

Peering at the harbor, Sir Andrew said, "The passage would be easier by ship than overland." He turned to Katin. "Where is the vessel Mistress Vendeley used to capture the powder brig?"

"It sank! We came upon the brig in the gale and lashed the ships together, so we could board her, but the lines came loose and the ships collided. It made a great hole in our hull, so we had to cut her free and she capsized—"

"Then where is the ship that was seized?" Sir Andrew interrupted. "As captured enemy property, by rights it belongs to the colony."

"Oh, I doubt you'll see sign of that brig again. Mistress Vendeley had me rowed to shore by longboat, then she put out to sea. She said that I was of no use to her, but the ship was. She sailed off to the south with that bandit leader and a crew of his people." She sounded as if she wished she could have gone with them.

"There's no cure for it then. We'll have to go by land," Hannah said.

"But we will make the journey, won't we?" Katin asked anxiously.

A glance passed between Sir Andrew and Lady Celia. "There's nothing left for us here, I suppose," he said. "We may as well see what lies on the other side of the coast."

"Oh, good," Katin exclaimed, dancing with excitement. "I'll go tell Jerl." She raced off before Sir Andrew could protest.

"You don't suppose there's any way we could see that the boy stays behind?" Sir Andrew said wistfully to Lady Celia.

"Short of killing him, I can't think of one."

Sir Andrew sighed. "At least I shall be quit of the Warders, the Scrutinors, and that lunatic Vendeley."

"The Warders and the Scrutinors, perhaps," Lady Celia agreed, "but I wouldn't be too certain that we've seen the last of Vendeley."

Jennifer Roberson

THE NOVELS OF TIGER AND DEL

Tiger and Del, he a Sword-Dancer of the South, she of the North, each a master of secret sword-magic. Together, they would challenge wizards' spells and other deadly traps on a perilous quest of honor.

☐ SWORD-DANCER UE2376—$4.99
☐ SWORD-SINGER UE2295—$4.99
☐ SWORD-MAKER UE2379—$5.99
☐ SWORD-BREAKER UE2476—$5.99

CHRONICLES OF THE CHEYSULI

This superb fantasy series about a race of warriors gifted with the ability to assume animal shapes at will presents the Cheysuli, fated to answer the call of magic in their blood, fulfilling an ancient prophecy which could spell salvation or ruin.

☐ SHAPECHANGERS: Book 1 UE2140—$3.99
☐ THE SONG OF HOMANA: Book 2 UE2317—$4.99
☐ LEGACY OF THE SWORD: Book 3 UE2316—$4.99
☐ TRACK OF THE WHITE WOLF: Book 4 UE2193—$4.99
☐ A PRIDE OF PRINCES: Book 5 UE2261—$5.99
☐ DAUGHTER OF THE LION: Book 6 UE2324—$4.99
☐ FLIGHT OF THE RAVEN: Book 7 UE2422—$4.99
☐ A TAPESTRY OF LIONS: Book 8 UE2524—$5.99
